T0116985

RANGER WINDS

RIDE ON

E. RICHARD WOMACK

IUNIVERSE, INC.
NEW YORK   BLOOMINGTON

Ranger Winds
Ride On

iUniverse books may be ordered through booksellers or by contacting:

iUniverse
1663 Liberty Drive
Bloomington, IN 47403
www.iuniverse.com
1-800-Authors (1-800-288-4677)

ISBN: 978-1-4502-3632-4 (sc)
ISBN: 978-1-4502-3634-8 (dj)
ISBN: 978-1-4502-3633-1 (ebk)

Printed in the United States of America

iUniverse rev. date: 6/30/2010

ACKNOWLEDGEMENTS

It is with grateful acknowledgement that I express my gratitude to the following contributors who made this book possible.

To Jeannette Ryno: For her helpful and dedicated encouragement. She kept me going anytime I lost confidence in myself. She always offered helpful hints, suggestions, and constructive criticism.

To Sylvia Hernandez: For her "deciphering" my handwritten manuscript. She was also an excellent "sounding board" for ideas, feedback and honest critiques.

To Richard "Dick" Guidry: For his untiring hours of dedication to the editing process.

Also for his recommendations on story structure, characters and timelines. He was instrumental in suggestions on maintaining continuity and historical data.

Without these credits the completion of this novel would not have been possible.

I am forever indebted.

E. Richard Womack

CHAPTER 1

Five years had passed since the death of J.J. Fox. Boots and Jerry Jack were both twenty-three while JoJo had turned twenty-six. They had become inseparable since Glen Ray and Jim retired. The threesome was headed for Laredo; the horses were in a boxcar while they rode in one of the passenger cars.

Boots was thinking about how the times were changing. Five years ago this trip from Uvalde would have been on horseback and taken several days. He could see changes coming for the Rangers also; with the railroads ending many of the cattle drives, drovers were out of work. Then, coupled with the ending of the Civil War and the advent of railroads, many men, who were left either homeless or un-employed, turned to a life of crime.

At one time the Rangers were viewed much like the army. Their job was to protect settlers from the Indians. Now, they were required to be lawmen protecting towns and ranches; primarily dealing with outlaws and ruffians.

The three Rangers, at the request of Herman Fox, brother of Sheriff Oral Fox of Uvalde, had been sent to Laredo to put down a range war. Herman's ranch had water and his fencing it off is what was fueling the war.

The train came to a halt; they unloaded and went directly to the boxcar holding the horses. The horses, saddled with a loose cinch, were led out of the car and down the street to the jail. There they tied the horses to the hitching rail and entered.

"Hello Rangers, how you boys doing?" asked the sheriff, Luke Starrett, "How's your Captain Laughlin these days, still in Uvalde raising horses?" The Rangers nodded as Luke continued, "Have a seat, set down; Boots, I remember when I located you and your brother over in Atlanta."

"Yes sir," said Boots, "that really changed our lives. I'm a Ranger now and my brother, Sterling, is a lawyer over in Austin."

With an approving nod, Luke queried, "How's your Pa'.....still a Ranger carrying that sawed-off double?"

"Yes sir," replied Boots, "he's helping Oral over in Uvalde and goes out on Ranger Patrols when needed."

"Here, let me pour you boys some coffee," spouted Luke as he set cups down and started pouring. Then, with a stern look on his face, he snorted, "Boys, we got some problems brewing out at Herman's ranch." He paused, took a sip of coffee, then continued, "He's fencing and Ben Kingston, owner of the Circle K, isn't taking kindly to it. He's tearing them down as fast as Herman puts them up." Luke's face hardened as he growled, "Hell, there's already been a couple of men killed; both off Fox's ranch, the Lonesome Chaparral. Kingston wants to buy the place but Herman won't sell; so Ben's tearing down the fences and driving off cattle."

Luke took off his hat, scratched his head, replaced his hat, looked at the Rangers and said, "You see, Fox's grandson, Ronald, who Kingston hates, married his granddaughter. When she died during child birth, Kingston blamed the Fox family. Now he's hired about thirty outlaws and professional gunslingers like, Curlee Johnson, Cherokee Jack and Lefty McCauliff, among others that you can find on wanted posters; all working for him."

With a somewhat defeated look on his face, Luke added, "Herman's no match for 'em, and I ain't either. I got no deputies; they've all been scared off by those hired guns of Kingston's. Matter of fact, Curlee and some of his boys are over in the saloon right now."

Boots thought about going to the saloon and confronting Curlee and his men, then decided against it and said, "We're gonna take our horses to the livery stable then get some supper and a room. Tomorrow we'll ride out to Herman's place and see what needs to be done."

The Rangers took their horses to the livery stable, removed their saddle-bags and rifles before heading toward the hotel. As they passed the saloon, six men came out and mounted up. They rode up behind the Rangers who were still walking down the street. As they stopped their horses, the rangers turned to face them when the fellow on the lead horse said, "Hold up boys, we need to talk a while."

He was medium in build and height; had curly hair with his hat cocked back and the brim turned up in front. He was fairly nice looking with half grinning but daring eyes. There was a 44 pistol on his right side with pearl handles. It was in a cutaway quick draw holster with tie downs.

Boots said, while looking straight into the man's eyes, "What can we do for you?"

"Well boys," said the stranger, "Laredo's not too friendly of a town; don't take to strangers real good."

Boots, who hadn't taken his eyes off the man, growled, "You must be Curlee!"

Curlee, with a cocky smile, shot back, "Yea, that's right....Who are you?"

Boots answered, "I'm a Ranger; we're all Rangers, and we'll be staying a while."

Curlee leaned over and spat on the ground, looked up and barked, "You know Rangers, me and my men don't cotton to no lawmen, especially Rangers. I'll tell you again, Laredo ain't friendly. If I were you boys, I would go play lawman somewhere else." Curlee paused, looked defiantly at Boots and warned, "Don't get in our way or in our business; bad things could happen to ya." He paused, then with a final stare said, "Let's go boys, we got work to do."

As they rode off at a gallop, Jerry Jack looked at Boots and said, "Friendly fella ain't he."

Boots looked serious when he said, "Maybe he'll be friendlier after he gets to know us." Then he laughed and uttered, "Let's go eat, my stomach thinks my throat's been cut."

The next day Starrett and the Rangers rode out to the Chaparral. The ranch was located in an area once referred to as Apache Flats. Herman and his two brothers came to Texas when they were young men. While his oldest and middle brother became Rangers, Herman stayed and built his cattle ranch. In his younger days he had fought Indians and Mexicans as well as serving his time in the Civil War before returning to his ranch.

He was a rough and rugged individual living in an area where only the strong survived. Although he was a decent and fair man, it was said he would kill anyone who harmed a kid. Now in his sixties, he was still a slender man with a full head of hair that at one time was dark brown, but now was mixed with gray. His face was weather beaten from spending most of his life in the saddle.

The Chaparral was a cattle ranch and was reported to be about sixty thousand acres. A close observation of the ranch house revealed the original one room structure and then the many additions built around it through the years. From this, one could tell the history of the ranch.

When Starrett and the Rangers arrived there, Herman was at his blacksmith shop shoeing a horse. He finished what he was doing, waved his hand and said, "Hello Luke, this must be the Rangers you told me were coming." He put down his tools, took off his apron, turned the horse out and continued, "Get down and come to the bunkhouse; I'll get us some coffee."

They entered the bunkhouse, sat down and introduced themselves; Herman got cups and poured coffee all around. As Herman sat down he said to Boots, "Boots, I knew your Pa while he was Luke's deputy here in Laredo. Heard lots of good things about him, heard they call him 'shotgun'."

Boots laughed and said, "Yea, him and his shotgun; I suppose he's a good Ranger, matter of fact, you know he works over in Uvalde with your brother, Oral. They probably play a lot of dominoes in that jail."

They all had a good laugh, then, got serious as Herman said, "Here's what's going on." He sipped his coffee, settled back in his chair and began, "Ben Kingston, owner of the Circle K ranch, is trying to build an empire. He wants my ranch but it's not for sale. He needs my water and resents my fence building. Hell, he tears 'em down quicker than I can build 'em and, if that's not bad enough, he shoots my ranch hands."

Herman shook his head, sipped coffee and continued, "But the main problem is, he don't like me or my family. When my grandson, Ronald, married his granddaughter, April, Ben wanted them on his ranch but she came to live with us. He always said we were the reason she lived here with us instead of with him. It wasn't true, she loved us and we loved her. Besides I built this house large enough for several families; then, after my wife died about ten years ago, I had plenty of room."

He paused for a moment, took a deep breath, and continued, "In fact, my boy, Billy and his wife JoAnn also live with me here on the ranch, so Ronald and April decided to stay here. Now Ben never liked Ronald, didn't want April to marry him; then, when she and the baby, her and Ronald's first, died during birth, Ben went crazy. Hell, he tried to kill Ronald."

Once again Herman paused. He was a little teary eyed as he went on, "Ronald couldn't bear to stay in the 'big house' once April passed on, so he took to sleeping in the bunkhouse with the hands."

Herman sipped his warm coffee, lowered his voice and said, "You know, Ben and I were real friends.....we helped settle Apache Flats, fought side by side. Then after all this happened, Ben turned mean. That's when I had to start fencing between my place and Bens'. Hells bells, he wouldn't allow us to come on his place at roundup time to get our strays. Curlee, his henchman, has killed two of my men at the saloon. He threatens 'em, forces 'em to draw....same as murder. My men aren't gunslingers, just ranch hands. Curlee says he'll kill any of my men he catches in town."

With a resigned look on his face, Herman finished his cold coffee and looked up at the Rangers. He was a rugged old man but Ben was an old friend. Herman was truly at a loss and needed the Ranger's help.

Jerry Jack and JoJo looked over at Boots. The trio had been riding together for five years and they always let Boots take the lead; they back him up. This time was no different; whatever Boots decided they would honor, they respected Boots.

Boots looked at Herman then at Jerry Jack and JoJo, knowing whatever he said was okay by them. Then he pushed his hat back on his head and said, "Boy's, tomorrow we'll ride out and pay Ben Kingston a visit. Herman, you stay here. I'd like to meet Billy and Ronald when we get back."

Early the next day, Sheriff Starrett and the three Rangers headed for the Circle K. It would take them half a day to reach the main gate to the ranch. When they arrived, they proceeded to the main ranch house. They were met at the hitching post by Mr. Kingston and three men; Curlee, Cherokee Jack the half-breed and one other rider wearing his gun on the left side, Lefty McCauliff.

Boots looked at Ben; a robust man with gray hair sticking out from under his hat. He had a large white mustache and bushy white eyebrows on a face that reflected anger and hate.

In a gruff voice, reflecting excessive use of booze, Ben said, "Don't bother to get down, y'all won't be staying. Say what you got to say and then be gone."

Boots looked at Kingston and responded, "We're Texas Rangers; we've been sent here by the Governor to investigate what's been going on." He paused to let his statement sink in, then continued, "We have orders to restore law and order and that is exactly what we are gonna do."

"Don't know why you're over here talking to us," said Kingston, "We ain't done nothing." Hell, any drover that gets hung up in that wire will tear it down, it's not us."

Curlee chimed in, "I told you boys in town that you won't like it around here; be best if you moved on while you can." Feeling confident the Rangers were out-gunned, he went on, "People around here don't care much for Rangers, especially me and the boys."

Boots, whose eyes were no longer carefree and relaxed but rather like penetrating daggers, ignored Curlee and looked hard at Kingston, and barked, "Sir, its spring roundup time and Mr. Fox will be gathering his herd. When he comes over to get his strays, I strongly suggest you let 'em ride in and cut 'em out."

Boots paused for effect before continuing, "Any more fences torn up, or gunplay, and we'll be back. Don't make us come back; if we do, we'll be angry and it won't be pretty, comprende?"

Kingston, showing his whiskey courage, shouted back, "Y'all don't scare me; I'm gonna make Fox pay for killing my granddaughter." Encouraged, and mistaken, by the Rangers calmness, he continued, "when I get my sights on that varmint, he's dead and my boy's here will bury you Rangers out there on Apache Flats." Then, sarcastically, he pulled his shoulders back and grumbled, "comprende?"

Without taking their eyes off Kingston and his three gunmen, the Rangers backed their horses, wheeled around and rode off at a walk.

They hadn't gone far when Jerry Jack said, "Did you see all those men outside the bunkhouse?" They weren't ranch hands, they were hired guns."

JoJo responded, "I counted sixteen; plus Kingston and his three prime guns, that makes twenty.

Boots chuckled and chirped, "Three of us, twenty of them.....that makes it just right for a good fight." His smile got bigger as he added, "Cut off the snake's head and the body dies with it." He spurred War Paint and they galloped back towards the Lonesome Chaparral.

When they were about a quarter mile from the ranch, the horses slowed to a walk as Boots said to Luke, "Sheriff, tell me about Billy and Ronald."

Without hesitating, Luke said, "Bill is in his mid-forties; he's a strong man with dark hair and piercing eyes. He's stubborn at times and can be a hand full if riled. He's well known as the best rifle shot in the county, hell, maybe the entire state. He can be real forceful with his fists and quite effective with a rifle if need be." Luke paused for a moment, then continued, "On the other hand, Ronald is a young, good-looking boy who's afraid of nothing. He's a damn good horseman and probably Ranger material." Then, as though an after-thought, Luke said, "Since all the trouble started, so far Herman's been able to keep both of 'em under control; how much longer, I don't know."

When they arrived back at the Fox ranch, they entered the house, met Billy, Ronald, and Herman's daughter, Donnie Rae. She came to live at the Chaparral when she lost her husband five years ago in an Indian raid on their spread. She had two true loves in her life; her husband, Harold, and her daddy, Herman.

Donnie Rae had prepared supper; as they ate and talked; Boots relayed his instructions to Ben Kingston about roundup time and added, "When you go, we'll go with you. Carry on as usual; should there be any trouble, we'll handle it. Starrett needed to get back to Laredo, so they all rode out that night.

The next day, Saturday, Boots wondered how long before something would happen. At nine o'clock that night, it was time for Luke to make his rounds.

7

The four of them had been playing dominoes when JoJo offered to accompany him on his nightly walk around.

Luke had a sawed off double in his hands; he handed it to JoJo and got another one from the gun rack. They walked out of the jail and Luke said, "See y'all in about thirty minutes."

About ten minutes had passed when Boots and Jerry Jack heard two pistol shots coming from the direction of the saloon. They looked at each other, jumped up and ran out the door toward the sound. As they rushed out the door, they met JoJo and Luke running towards the shots.

Boots said, "Y'all have the scatter guns, go in the back way. Jerry Jack and I will go thru the front door."

Boots went to the side of the swinging doors and looked in. He saw two cowboys lying in a pool of blood. Curlee was standing over them with a smoking pistol in his hand and a big grin on his face. Behind him was 'Cherokee' Jack and 'Lefty'. Boots and Jerry Jack entered the saloon and said, simultaneously, "Put your gun away, you're under arrest."

Curlee laughed and mocked, "Hear that boys, the Ranger says I'm under arrest. My gun's in my hand but he thinks I'm under arrest. Well come on Ranger, arrest me."

Suddenly, the distinct sound of hammers being cocked on scatterguns filled the room. JoJo had is shotgun on Curlee and Luke had his on the other two.

Then, with cold determination, JoJo said, "Curlee, the Ranger says you're under arrest, now drop your gun or this scattergun's gonna drop you.

Curlee stared at the Rangers and shouted angrily, "It was self defense, ask anyone in here; it was self defense; they drew first"

JoJo swung the barrel over toward the table where Curlee was standing, pulled a trigger on his double and blew off a table leg. Before the sound of the blast could die down JoJo said, "The next shot's gonna cut you in half.....get rid of that damn gun, NOW!"

Curlee dropped his gun, and then, with a cold hard stare, said defiantly, "You're gonna pay pretty boy, I'll get you."

The Rangers took all three men to jail. Of course, Cherokee Jack and Lefty, as well as other men in the saloon, swore it was self defense. It was evident they were lying but feared for their lives.

After taking their statements, Luke released Cherokee Jack and Lefty but held Curlee until the next day. When he was released, he looked at the Rangers and said, cocky as ever, "You'll pay fer this, nobody throws me in jail and gets away with it." Then he pointed directly at Boots and continued, "The boys and me will be coming back to town."

Boots reached down and tapped the handle on his 44 and barked, "Be best if you boys leave your guns. Cause if you bring 'em into town, troubles waiting." Curlee didn't respond; he just slowly strolled out the door.

After Curlee left, Luke said, "The two men that Curlee shot were Herman's ranch hands. As usual, Curlee pushed them hard, forcing them to draw.

Ranch hands against a gunslinger; they had no chance.....same as murder."

Boots thought momentarily then answered, "We'll tell Herman to keep his men at the ranch; no one is to come to town."

Monday, Luke and the Rangers rode out to the Chaparral. They met Billy Fox about a mile from the ranch. "Hello Billy," said Boots, "you're riding hard, any problems?"

"Yea," said Billy with excitement in his voice, "I was riding out to get ya'll." He hesitated to gather his thoughts, and continued, "About twenty masked men attacked our fence building crew. They killed a couple of our Mexican vaqueros. Drug one of them to death; then they tore down a good stretch of fence and ran off about a hundred head of cattle." He took a deep breath, wiped his brow, and blurted out, "Ronald's been missing since early this morning; it's not like him to disappear with all the trouble that's been going on. I'm worried sick about it."

What Billy didn't know was that Ronald had ridden up to the Circle K earlier that day. When he got there, Kingston, who had ridden into town, was not at the ranch. Ronald was met by Curlee and his boys.

As Ronald rode up he said to Curlee, "I've come to talk with Mr. Kingston about this range war. I'm here to ask him to call a halt to all this killing; April wouldn't have wanted this to happen."

Curlee, in his usual contemptuous manner, responded with, "Well sonny boy, he ain't here and you shouldn't be out riding around by yourself. I guess we'll just have to teach you not to go where you're not wanted."

About that time, one of the men on horseback hit Ronald with the butt of his rifle, knocking him to the ground. Curlee walked over, picked him up by the collar and said to no one in particular, "Come on boys, let's play 'bull ring' with him."

The men formed a circle around Ronald and then Curlee hit him in the face knocking him across the circle. He was picked up and hit again sending him back across the ring. This went on perhaps ten or more times. Finally, when one of the men picked him up to hit him again, he said, "Hey Curlee, he don't want to play no more, he's dead."

Curlee didn't give it a second thought, he just had the boys tie Ronald to his horse with barbed wire and turn it loose; he knew the horse would go straight back to the Chaparral.

When the Rangers, along with Starrett and Billy, got to Herman's ranch, Ronald still had not been found. No one knew where he was. They all sat down on the front porch with Fox when Boots said, "Herman, we have no proof as to who killed the men that were building your fence or, who took it down."

They all knew Kingston's men had done it but it couldn't be proven. Boots told Herman that he and the Rangers were going to stake out the fence crew for the next couple of days in an attempt to catch Curlee and his men in the act.

JoJo was turned toward the main gate when he looked up and said, "Horse coming in."

Billy looked over and shouted, "That's Ronald's horse; oh my God, there's someone tied over the saddle."

They all mounted up and rode out to the horse, which had stopped as soon as it entered the main gate. As soon as Billy saw it was Ronald, he broke down and cried. Mr. Fox's face turned to stone; expressionless as if he was in a trance.

There was a note pinned to Ronald's shirt, it read; 'Rangers, we've got some of this for you."

Herman, who was now holding his grandson in his arms, looked up at Billy and said, "Take 'im to the house, after we bury him, we ride."

Kingston, having returned from his trip to town, was met by a drunken Curlee who mumbled, "Boss, me and the boys did real good while you were out; we beat that Fox boy, Ronald, to death and sent him home tied to his horse with barbed wire."

Almost in disbelief, Kingston barked, "You did what? You killed him!"

"Yep," said Curlee, rather proudly, "he came over here to beg you to stop the fighting, said April wouldn't want it." He staggered a little, then, slurring his words, stammered, "I sent him home with a note telling the Rangers they were going to get the same treatment."

"You fool," growled Kingston, "You drunken fool, they can have fifty Rangers here in a matter of days. Not only that, you idiot, old man Fox and all his men will be here by morning with lots of guns." Kingston took off his hat, slammed it against his leg, let out a big sigh and ordered, "Have all the men on the ranch gather at the bunkhouse in the morning with guns ready and plenty of cartridges."

The next morning, after placing the last shovel of dirt over Ronald's grave, Mr. Fox told Billy to round up all the men, they were going to the Circle K.

Boots, JoJo, Jerry Jack and Luke, rode over to the Chaparral bunkhouse where Herman and all his men were gathered; ready to ride. He had about thirty-five riders. They had formed a column and were preparing to ride toward the Circle K.

As the Rangers rode up, Boots said, with authority in his voice, "Herman, I don't want you and all your men going with us, just the sheriff." Herman opened his mouth to voice his objection but was cut-off by Boots who continued, "I'm trying to avoid as much bloodshed as possible; we'll eliminate the three main guns. Remember, the body dies with the head.

Herman could hold back no longer as he blurted out, "You won't have a chance, Hell; he'll have his hired guns and forty or more riders waiting on you."

"Yea," said Boots, "you're right, but we're just gonna deal with four of 'em." Then Boots looked directly into Herman's eyes and ordered, "You stay here with your men; if we don't come back, you can go after them."

"Alright," said Herman, "I'll hold the men back, but I'm telling you, me and Billy are going with you."

Boots thought for a minute then, knowing it was useless to argue any further with Herman, grudgingly nodded his approval as the six of them rode off toward the Circle K.

As they neared the ranch, Curlee saw the horses coming. He opened the door to the ranch house and hollered, "They're coming, ain't but six of 'em!"

Kingston stepped outside and said, as he stared at the approaching riders, "Only six of 'em? Wonder what they're up to." Then he barked orders to Curlee, "Get the men, line them up next to the fence at the main gate. Let's go, I want to meet 'em there."

When they reached the gate Kingston had Curlee on his right, Cherokee Jack and Lefty on his left and forty or more men equally divided to his right and left mounted in a line along the fence.

Boots and his men were about a hundred yards away when Boots said, "Let me do the talking. If I pull leather, y'all do the same. I'm going after the head of the snake, Curlee."

The group rode up facing Kingston and his three gunfighters. They were all face to face when Boots said, "Gentlemen, you four men are under arrest for the murder of Ronald Fox. Drop your guns to the ground or be prepared to die."

Kingston and his three henchmen had all been drinking heavily. Kingston wiped his shirt sleeve across his mouth and snorted, "That boy got what he deserved; he killed my granddaughter. I wish I had put a hole in his head before we sent him home."

Curlee said, with whiskey courage, "You Ranger boys just don't understand, we make the laws out here, not y'all. Look at all these guns, this is the law."

Then he continued, "Yea, we killed that boy; beat him to death and now we'll kill y'all and anybody else that comes on this ranch."

Boots had heard enough. He hollered out to his left and then to his right, addressing Kingston's men lined up at the fence, "That boy came here to ask for an end to all this and he was beaten to death for his efforts! Now you men have a chance to get out of this." He paused, giving them a little time to think, then continued, "Ride, no questions asked. We're gonna take these four men in alive or stretched over their saddles. This is not your fight. Ride while you've got the opportunity."

You could hear mumbling as one horse turned and started to ride away. Then another and another until all the men had ridden off leaving Kingston, Curlee, Cherokee Jack and Lefty to face the Rangers.

Boots looked at Ben and said, "Mr. Kingston, be aware, you and your men are under arrest. Drop your guns to the ground or die in your saddles."

Jerry Jack, the preaching Ranger as he was called, said, "God forgive these men of their sins as they are about to die."

Kingston shouted, "Kill 'em boys, kill 'em all."

CHAPTER 2

Curlee had barely cleared leather when Boot's shot hit him in the chest dropping him dead. Cherokee Jack didn't clear leather before Jerry Jack ended his life and Lefty's gunslinger days were ended by a single shot through the heart from Billy.

Herman Fox rode up beside Boots, looked at Ben, who had never drawn his piece, and said, "Ben, you murdered my grandson, now I'm going to kill you."

Kingston had an unseen shoulder holster under his coat; when he reached for it, Herman drew from the hip, pointed his big 44 at Ben's head and fired. The slug struck Kingston in the forehead rolling him backwards off his horse. He was dead before he hit the ground.

The Rangers helped tie the four bodies on their horses as they rode back to town. Herman and Billy rode back toward the Chaparral; tonight it would truly be lonesome.

Boots, Jerry Jack and JoJo delivered the four bodies to the undertaker in Laredo. All the bodies, except Kingston's, were put on display in the street for pictures and public viewing. Kingston's body remained in the funeral home awaiting burial. Herman had requested that Ben not be displayed like the other three. It was evident that his feelings for his old friend ran deep even after all the trouble and heartache Ben had caused.

After dropping off the bodies, Boots sent a wire to Captain McFarland in Uvalde with high lights of the shootings. Laughlin wired back with instructions for them to hang around for a week then, if everything was calm, take the train back to Uvalde for reassignment.

A few days had passed and it was quiet in Laredo. Herman and Billy were grieving the loss of Ronald, but everything else was back to normal.

The three Rangers were at the restaurant having supper and engaging in conversation about the shootout when JoJo said, "Boots, I've seen you draw and shoot before, but when you outdrew Curlee, that was the fastest draw I've ever seen you make.

Boots responded, "Ranger Weaver once said, "Killing a man is easy, getting over it is the hard part. He said, you must be very careful when you kill, be certain that it's justified; if you ever have doubts, it will slow you down; then you're dead! Boots let that sink in then went on, "I suppose you're right, I am fast and fast lets me survive; but, just like Laughlin taught your Pa', I practice my draw one hundred times a day while looking at my eyes in the mirror. You must practice; your life depends on it."

The three men continued eating their meal when, without looking up from his plate, Boots continued, "The Circle K shootout ended because I knew Curlee had to be eliminated. I also figured I was faster than he was."

"Hell," said JoJo, "you put three bullets in him before he could get off one shot."

Boots replied, "JoJo, he was a saloon fighter, shooting drunks and drovers. We're in the gun business facing all kinds of 'guns'. Our lives depend on how fast, and smart, we are." Boots took a bite, sipped his drink and offered, "Look, Curlee thought we would high tail it out of town; we didn't, so he tried to bluff us with more guns. When they left, all the fight was gone out of Curlee; it was the whiskey that made him pull on me. By the way, you two boys ain't slow, and I want you to know; I'm confident anytime you two are backing me."

They finished their meals and drinks when Boots asked, "What do y'all think of Old Herman. I bet he was a handful when he was young. As a matter of fact, all those Fox brothers are a special cut above average."

Being rhetorical, the question went unanswered as Jerry Jack said, "JoJo, it's your turn to pay; Boots, what say, we have some apple pie for desert."

Boots nodded his approval as JoJo shook his head and reached deep in his pocket, knowing he had been had.

The remainder of the week went without incident as once again the Rangers were on the train back to Uvalde when Jerry Jack said, "Can't wait to get back and see Cindy. Then I'll go to church and talk with Brother Morgan.

Boots wondered, "Does Brother Morgan know they call you the Preachin' Ranger?"

Jerry Jack responded, "Naw, and don't you be telling him either." Then, as if to change the subject, queried "How are you and Audrey getting along?"

Boots responded, "We're alright; she wants to get married, not me. She may get tired of waiting on me; if she does, I'll have you and JoJo arrest her new boyfriend." Then, to pick at Jerry Jack, he looked at JoJo and asked, "JoJo, what do you think, should we start calling old Jerry Jack, Preacher?'

"Yea," said JoJo, "them outlaws won't shoot a preacher......let's call him Preacher, absolutely. You know he does say a prayer for them just before he shoots 'em."

They had a good laugh, at Jerry Jack's expense of course, then Boots, being sure to spread some of the ribbing around, said, "JoJo, when we get back to Uvalde, we've got to get you a new horse, yours is limping. Tell you what, we'll go see Laughlin; maybe we can get you a nice tame one like War Paint," then he chuckled and added, "get 'Preacher' to tell you that story."

Jerry Jack couldn't stand it, so he chimed in, "A new horse and a girlfriend for JoJo; gotta hurry back and work on that."

JoJo fired back with, "Boys, I'm capable of finding my own girl."

"Yeah, right," said Boots, "But you ain't got one now and every cowboy should have a girl. I tell you what, I'm gonna have a reward poster made and post it in every town we go to." Then Boots drew a square in the air with his hands and added, "Your picture on it reading: Wanted, Dead or Alive, Girlfriend for this homely looking Ranger." Knowing when to stop, Boots chided, "I'm sorry JoJo, I'm gonna leave you alone now; never know when another gunfight might come along and I'll need my buddy." Boots really respected his two companions but couldn't resist his love for poking fun at them occasionally.

Meanwhile, up in Austin, Sterling opened a letter he received from his brother, Boots. It had been sent from Laredo and read, 'I miss you brother; I am so proud of you and tell everybody about my brother the attorney. Tell Emily hello; if there are ever any bad boys in Austin, maybe Laughlin will send me and I can meet the future Mrs. Sterling Law. Love; your Brother.

P.S. Pa is doing real good. His reputation is growing daily and nobody calls him Nathan, it's 'Shotgun'.

Sterling's thoughts flashed back to when he and Boots were on the battlefield in Georgia. Boots was ten and he was twelve. He recalled how his mother died from pneumonia; how he found out his Pa' was alive; his meeting Ranger McFarland; his attorney friend Stewart and most of all, Mr. Fox. He wished Fox was still alive, he had promised him he would become a State Senator some day and was presently half way there.

Then he fondly remembered his chance meeting with Emily on his first day in Austin as well as their initial dating and attending school together. Now she is teaching and he's received his law degree. He thought of Stewart Coffee, the man who offered him a partnership back in Abilene and how he had decided to remain in Austin and continue his efforts to become a State Senator. Emily's Father, Attorney Lloyd Henderson, a very influential man in the political field and a close personal friend of the Governor, had agreed to help his future son-in-law pursue a seat in the State Senate; he was having him attend all the political functions. I am becoming well known, thought Sterling, and I'm well liked by the Governor. Life is good, he pondered.

When the train with the Rangers arrived back in Uvalde, it was a lovely day and they hoped it would be a while before they were sent back out on patrol.

They retrieved their horses from the boxcar and rode over to Sheriff Oral Fox's office to fill him in on the events at his brother Herman's ranch.

Oral and Nathan were playing dominoes when they entered the office and Boots said, "Hello Oral, hi pa'. How y'all doing, who's winning?"

"Aw," answered Oral, "your Pa', old Shotgun is. He likes to beat up on an old man like me." Nathan and Boots laughed as Oral offered them a cup of coffee and then asked about Laredo.

Before anyone had time to comment, Nathan walked over to Boots, shook his hand and said, "I heard you put a man down, a gunslinger; was he fast?"

As if on cue, 'Preacher' chimed in, "He was fast, but not as fast as your boy; he barely cleared leather when Boots had three slugs in him." Nathan pumped Boot's hand a little harder as 'Preacher' continued, "He's close to Laughlin and Laughlin's gun is legend."

Boots, being a little embarrassed by all the whoop-la, said, "Oral, your brother's a good man; all you Foxes are a special breed." Then, like a sly old devil, he casually inquired, "How is your granddaughter, and my girlfriend, Audrey?"

Oral threw his hands up in the air and blurted out, "She'll really be glad to know you're back in town, for Pete's sake, she drives me crazy asking about you every day when you're gone."

Boots grinned that boyish grin only he has and said, "I'll see her in church tomorrow and tell her," pointing at JoJo, "we're trying to find this old homely boy a girlfriend. Except for JoJo, who was not amused, everyone had a good laugh. After going over the details of the events on the Lonesome Chaparral, the men had supper and spent the night in town knowing they would see Laughlin in church and would report to him after the services.

Sunday morning the trio went to church early; Boots and 'Preacher' were anxious to see the girls and give their report to Laughlin. 'Preacher' taught the youth Sunday school class while Boots and JoJo sat in. They learned a lot as 'Preacher' read from the Bible and discussed the scriptures. 'Preacher' loved David and talked about how he became a great warrior; fought and killed Goliath then later became King. He said that God was with David and made these things possible. Boots enjoyed the stories about David even though he had heard them from 'Preacher' in the bunkhouse at night. He enjoyed the stories more each time he heard them.

When church started they sat with Laughlin, Melissa and their son, little Sam. Boots referred to little Sam as the 'Littlest Ranger'; he was four years old.

Brother Morgan preached about Moses and the Promised Land. He said that Texas could be compared to the Promised Land and that all of us needed to work hard and enjoy what has been provided.

After church they had the usual covered dish lunch, mixing, mingling and engaging in conversation. Preacher was with Cindy, Boots was with Audrey and JoJo.....was by himself. During their conversations, Brother Morgan told Boots that he prayed for all the Rangers; asked God to keep them safe and was glad to see him back in church.

Afterwards, Boots and Audrey walked outside and strolled around the church grounds. Boots, who was holding her hand as they walked, stopped, looked in her eyes and said, "Audrey, you're beautiful. I think about you all the time I'm away and I worry you might find someone else." He looked directly into her eyes and softly said, "I care for you deeply but I'm just not ready for commitments." Audrey could sense he was having difficulty explaining himself as he continued, "I enjoy riding the Ranger Winds; it's an exciting life and it's imbedded in my blood. I'm a Ranger."

They walked on silently for a few more yards before Boots stopped again and said, "Audrey, until I became a Ranger, I didn't understand what it's like; but, once a Ranger, always a Ranger. As Brother Morgan said, 'Texas is a Promised Land' and the Rangers play a large part in its development. My brother, Sterling, will be enforcing the law with books and knowledge; I will do it with my six gun. Both are necessary for the development of Texas."

Audrey had been listening intently with her head down; Boots gently raised her chin and looked into her eyes as he spoke lovingly, "I know you are thinking of marriage, children and starting a family. Sweetheart, I'm just not ready yet and it's not fair to ask you to wait for me. Audrey, we are experiencing the same thing that Laughlin and Mellissa went through."

Boots cleared his throat, choked back tears and quietly whispered, "I guess what I'm trying to say is this; if you want to see other people, you can."

Audrey, without speaking a word, lowered her head as tears began to run down her cheeks. Boots, wondering if he had done the right thing, put his arm around Audrey, squeezed her closer and slowly continued their walk.

Later on the Rangers all rode out to the former 'Rocking Horse' Ranch. Since it was being used as a District Headquarters, Laughlin had fittingly renamed it the 'Big Iron'.

After giving Laughlin a detailed report of the Laredo episode and receiving a "well done", Laughlin asked them who was that new man they referred to.

Boots responded, "Oh, that's Preacher. He's a preaching Ranger." Boots chuckled and laughingly said, "Kinda favors ole Jerry Jack."

Laughlin had a good laugh with the boys over their antics and said, "I'm real proud of you boys, y'all are all good Rangers."

"Well," said Boots, "one of your 'good Rangers' needs a horse, his is lame. Do you reckon we could swap one out for lonely ole JoJo?"

"Sure," said Laughlin, "pick one out and let lonesome break 'im. There's a big Sorrel down there that I really like; looks a lot like Fred's horse, Whiskey." He gave thought for a moment then spouted, "By the way, you boys will be going to Abilene. The town's filling up with gunslingers and horse thieves. Saloon shootings are getting out of control. It's getting so bad; Glen Ray and Fred have to post guards around their horse corral every night. Speaking of their horses, you should see that colt Three Paws run; gives his paw Whiskey a helluva good race. Fred ran 'im over at Stephenville and embarrassed the other horses; finished eighteen lengths ahead in the mile race."

You could see Laughlin was reminiscent as he said, "Since J.J. died and left them the ranch, they're doing real good. Hell, they're ahead of me; my horses aren't as good as theirs." "That Whiskey is a great stud and making them some big money," he added.

"Come on boys," said Boots, "let's go get that sorrel."

They rode out to the pasture with their ropes looking for him when JoJo said, "Look over there, on top of that ridge, that's the biggest horse I've ever seen. If that ain't him, I don't care, that's the one I want; let's go check 'im out."

It was a beautiful sorrel with golden mane and tail; a big tall well-defined horse. Boots took a good look at him and said, "Preacher, let's go get him; see if War Paint and Pistol can catch him."

They didn't try to rope him, they wanted him to run and run he did. Head, body and tail stretched straight out, he was flying. They raced with him for about a half-mile then pulled up and stopped.

"He's fast," said Preacher, "he can run with our horses anytime, let's put a rope on 'im. I'm anxious to see a rodeo and just how good a cowboy JoJo really is."

As they eased up, Preacher put a rope around his neck. He balked at the rope, stood on his hind legs and fought all the way back to the corral. He was so strong, Boots had to put a second rope on him and use both his and Preacher's horses to get him in the corral. By the time they got him there, the sorrel had settled down somewhat but was still a bit skittish.

They carefully put a saddle on him while he stood their stiff legged and wide-eyed with both nostrils flared. Boots said, "You lucky son of a gun JoJo; you gonna get to rodeo."

JoJo, looking just a bit apprehensive, put a foot in the stirrup and swung his leg over; the rodeo was on. JoJo wasn't quite ready and at the first jump, he was thrown over the big sorrel's head landing belly first in some 'horse puddin'; JoJo was a mess! Back up he went; with puddin' all over his shirt.

Every time Preacher let the sorrel's head loose, he would explode.

Seven jumps and JoJo was on the ground again. The horse was so strong; he was pitching JoJo ten feet in the air. Boots helped pick JoJo up and mused, "You want me to ride 'im for you?"

"Hell no," shouted JoJo, "I'll ride 'im if it kills me."

Boots laughed and snorted, "I don't blame I'm, I'd buck you off too; I wouldn't want something as smelly as you on my back either."

"Hold 'im Preacher, let me back on 'im," said JoJo, then added defiantly, "watch this Boots."

Six jumps and JoJo went flying again. Laughlin came down from the ranch house to watch the fun. When he got there he said, "JoJo, haven't they told you to keep his head up?"

JoJo replied, "Hell, I've tried; he's too strong." Then he remounted the sorrel and growled, "One more time boys, the Captain's here, can't let him down."

Explosion time again as the sorrel bucked hard. Once he fell to the ground and JoJo stayed on while he got back up. Around the corral they went, dirt flying from his feet, slobber from his mouth, and that was just JoJo; you should've seen the horse. Finally the big sorrel slowed to a walk, it was over. JoJo had himself a horse.

As he walked him around the corral Preacher hollered, "Hey JoJo, whatcha gonna name 'im?"

"Well," answered JoJo, "the first time I ever got on 'im, he threw me into a pile of horse puddin', so I guess I'll call him 'Puddin'.'"

Laughlin was laughing, he had enjoyed the show. He told the boys, "Meet me at the bunkhouse, Flap Jack should be about ready to ring the supper bell."

They were sitting at the table eating when Laughlin said, "JoJo, you don't talk much; tell us about yourself."

"Well Captain," said JoJo "ain't much to tell. I was born up in Ft. Worth; my Mom was a saloon girl in 'Hell's Half Acre'. She wasn't married when she got pregnant with me. Never did know my Pa'; guess that makes me a bastard. She knew who he was but she wouldn't tell me. All I know is he left and went to Kansas." He thought for a moment, then continued, "She did tell me he made a living with a gun and cards, which pretty well meant he was no law man."

"Where's your Ma now?" asked Boots.

"Dead," said JoJo, "drank herself to death; died when I was only six. After her death, I went to live with my Aunt Hattie and Uncle Arch. It was while I was living with them that I learned my Pa' was a gambler, gunfighter and ladies man. They thought he was probably living in Abilene, Kansas."

"Did you ever try to find 'im or get in touch with 'im" wondered Boots.

"Naw," answered JoJo, "Ma' said he never would claim me, he'd say I wasn't his."

Laughlin, having listened to the story, chimed in, "JoJo, if you want me to, I'll see what I can do to find him."

JoJo answered, "Hell, if he won't claim me, it don't make any difference to me." Then he thought for a minute and said, rather bitterly, "Can't be much of a man anyway!"

Laughlin, figuring it was better not to press the issue any further said, "All right boys, let's call it a night and I'll see you in the morning. I need to give you the route to Abilene, Ole Cletus needs some help; he's got a saloon full of gunfighters."

It was Saturday night back in Abilene when Sheriff Cletus Meeks was making his nightly rounds. It was a bad night with rain, thunder, lightening and a saloon full of drunks. In the last month there had been three men killed in gunfights, all by the same man, Jack Wilson. Wilson was an ex-lawman who had turned into a gambler, hired gun and bounty hunter.

Cletus was carrying his sawed off shotgun hidden under his duster while his other hand was free to draw his pistol if need be. When he walked into the smoke filled saloon, you could smell the stale smoke and whiskey. Above the din of usual saloon sounds, you could hear the drunks swearing loudly.

At a poker table in the corner sat Jack Wilson. He was your typical gambler and gunfighter. He was wearing a coat, high collar shirt and black hat. Behind his thick moustache and cheap cigar, was a pair of puffy bloodshot, whiskey and smoke filled eyes. He was playing five card stud and had a rather large stack of chips in front of him. Cletus walked over to the bar and ordered a shot of whiskey; he turned it up, set the glass down and stood silently at the bar.

The bartender was an old-timer named Jim Raines. He had poured many a shot and had a feel for what was going on as well as what was likely to happen. He had a full head of brown hair, parted down the middle and a handle bar moustache. He wore a vest over a long sleeve blousy shirt, carried no gun but had a double barrel under the bar that he very well knew how to use.

When Raines came over to see if Meeks wanted another drink, Cletus waved him off but asked, "Jim, anything happening?"

With his years of barroom wisdom, Jim responded, "No, but it's going to; see that drifter playing cards with Wilson, he's drinking too much and losing his wages. It's just a matter of time before he causes trouble."

With this information, Cletus walked over to the table, tapped the cowboy on the shoulder and said, "Young man, take a break, maybe it will change your luck, I'd like your chair." The young man, seeing the sheriff's badge, got up and went to the bar. Cletus sat down and, addressing the table, said, "Howdy boys, how are the cards treating you?"

Jack, having been angered at losing his pigeon, said "The cards were good; but I don't particularly like you horning in and runnin' off the players."

Cletus, knowing that Wilson was responsible for the three "so called" self defense killings, said, "Just a little warning, Jack, keep that pistol in it's' holster, there'll be no more killings in my town."

Jack, who was already irritated, shot back, "Sheriff, don't be telling me what to do. I ain't broke no laws." As if waiting to see what Cletus would do, he hesitated, then continued. "I'm an honest poker player just trying to make a living. The men I shot were sore losers. They drew on me so I had to defend myself." Having said this Wilson smiled defiantly at Cletus.

Not to be intimidated, Cletus barked, "I'll tell you what you are......you're a two-bit card shark taking drover's wages and killin' drunk cowboys that have never pulled a shooter before." Cletus stared at Wilson and continued, "I'm looking for any reason to put you in my hotel and I'm hoping you might be fool enough to draw on me; please do."

Having taken some of the starch out, Jack said, "Why sheriff, you're down right unfriendly; I've got three brothers on their way here to visit with me. They're good ole boys; you'll like 'em." Then having regained his contempt, he growled, "Hell fire, I'll introduce them to you. Or maybe even better, I'll introduce you to their lightning fast 44's."

With the speed and smoothness gained by experience, Cletus pulled the scattergun from under his duster, cocked both hammers, stuck the barrels in Wilson's face, and said with cold deliberation, "And I'll introduce them to this. Be sure and tell them how slow I am."

Having made his point with Wilson, Cletus looked at the other players and said, "You boys have a good night." Then he turned and slowly walked out of the saloon.

Having completed his rounds, he went to the restaurant for a cup of coffee. When he sat down at a table, he was joined by retired Ranger Jim Weaver.

As Jim sat down he asked, "How's it going? Gossip has it there's some trouble brewing."

"Yea," said Cletus, "got a little thing going that I'm watching. That dude in the saloon, Jack Wilson, says his brothers are on their way to Abilene and there'll be hell to pay."

"You been able to hire any deputies," asked Jim.

"Naw," answered Cletus, "everybody's scared; it seems a new gun rides into town everyday. Cletus took a sip of his coffee then reflected, "It was easier chasing Indians." After a moment he said, "You did your share of that as a Ranger eh Jim........ You miss it?"

Jim thought for a second and responded, "Yea, I miss it; you don't ever get Rangerin' out of your blood"

"Yea, but you were smart," said Cletus, "you married Linda; y'all have the saloon and restaurant, hell you don't have to make a living with your gun anymore, I'd say that's smart."

Jim replied, "Yea, I guess you're right, but remember, when you need some help, I'm always here."

"I appreciate that," said Cletus as he turned his cup up, drank the last of his coffee and continued, "Got to get going, tell Linda I said hello." He got up, and went back to the jail where he laid down on a cot in one of the cells and tried to get some sleep.

As promised, back in Uvalde Laughlin was meeting with Boots, Preacher and JoJo. They were in the bunkhouse; it was early morning when Laughlin spoke, "Boys, I want you to go from town to town on your way to Abilene.

From here in Uvalde, head to Junction, Menard, Ballinger, Buffalo Gap and then on to Abilene. With that much exposure it will be known that the Rangers are on patrol." He picked at the breakfast Flap Jack had just served then said, "When you get to Abilene, cool it down for Cletus; he's got more than he can handle and, I'm told, there's more on the way. There's gonna be another street dance and celebration. That'll bring in lots of money to town because of the cattle sales."

He paused, took a bite of eggs, sipped his coffee and cautioned, "One other thing, be on the alert for Iron Eagle and his raiding party;

25

I'm told he's in the area. Word has it he burned out a family of five out in Buffalo Gap. There are too many troopers from the Fort looking for them; slows 'em down. Now, two or three men, like yourselves, can find 'em and catch 'em."

Laughlin ate a piece of smoked bacon, looked up and, with the serious manner that only he had, instructed, "If you make contact with Iron Eagle's band, go after 'em, dead or alive, makes no difference; they must be stopped."

The trio of Rangers made ready for their trip; filled their saddlebags and decided to take along a packhorse. It being early April they new it would still be chilly at night with good riding during the day. When they had gathered all their provisions, they mounted up and headed for Junction.

As they rode, Boots recalled the first time he had heard the name, Iron Eagle. It was shortly after coming to Laughlin's ranch; they were delivering horses to Ft. Davis. Back then there were large Indian uprisings sometimes involving complete tribes. Now it was only small raiding parties of ten to twelve braves trying to kill 'white eyes'. Boots had always heard people say, 'the only good Indian is a dead Indian'. He chuckled to himself and thought; I bet the Indians are saying 'the only good white man is a dead one.'

The Rangers knew that out on the trail, you couldn't be too careful so, periodically, they rode to vantage points and surveyed the terrain ahead. When they reached Junction, they saw the stage loading and unloading cargo and passengers. As they neared the stage, Boots recognized his old friend, Bob Bell, the stage driver. As they nodded in recognition of each other, Boots said, with a grin, "Hello Bob, seen any Indians or outlaws?"

Bob replied, "None, but I heered Iron Eagle's on the move again. Reckon he's hidin' out in the Davis Mountains. Nobody knows where he camps or how many he's got with him, just figger he's up 'ere."

Boots nodded his understanding and queried, "Bob, you hauling any money?"

"Nope," answered Bob, "Just a strong-box full of mail and the purtiest young lady you boys ever laid eyes on." The three Rangers all looked around as Bob continued, "She's inside the depot trying to get some of the trail dust off; when she comes back all you boys will be hankerin' to board my stage and ride with 'er." She's sho nuff purty," he added.

Without being asked, Bob ranted on, "Not married now either; going out to live with her sister in Abilene. Understand she's from somewhere 'round Weatherford; husband ran off to Tombstone. Got hisself kilt by some feller named Holliday; shot 'im in a saloon."

Just then a lady about twenty-five came walking toward the stage. She had long blonde hair, bright blue eyes, a very beautiful smile, was well built and seemed to be bursting with energy. When she reached the stage and saw the stars on the three Rangers, she said, in a coy manner, "My, My, am I under arrest." Then she giggled.

With a red face, Boots, who doesn't blush very easily, responded, "Howdy Ma'am; I can see you already know we're Rangers, so allow me to introduce ourselves." She continued that beautiful smile as Boots introduced them. "I'm Boots, this is Preacher and that one over there, is JoJo."

Her smile grew even larger, if that's possible, and she replied, "My name is Patti McKenzie; I'm proud to meet y'all." Then she got that 'little girl' look on her face and crooned, "First time I ever met me a Ranger." As she was talking, she frequently turned her eyes to JoJo, who incidentally, hadn't once taken his eyes off her.

Not having missed a thing, Boots said, "Bob, since Iron Eagle is on the prowl and you don't have a guard, we'll send JoJo along with you. We're going on to Abilene so we'll meet up with him there."

"Sho nuff," said Bob gratefully, "that'll be fine; need a guard with a pretty lady like Miss Patti." Knowingly, Boots looked at JoJo, grinned and winked.

The stage loaded up and rolled out. JoJo was on top beside Bob Bell, riding shotgun. It was a sure bet at some point he would be riding inside with Patti.

JoJo asked Bob if he thought they might run into Iron Eagle. Bob told him Iron Eagle could be anywhere; said he had a hideaway somewhere in the Davis Mountains, rumored to be in the area where the river made a big bend.

That area was extremely rugged and nearly impassable. For several years he had holed up in the safety of these mountains, venturing out on raids then returning. The word was, anyone following him into his sanctuary, white man or soldier, never came back. A wise man travelling through this area would always save a bullet for himself, Iron Eagle loves to torture. He's usually seen somewhere between Del Rio and Ft. Davis. His party consists of twenty-five or more well armed braves. They generally strike settlers around the Rio Grande. The Army believes his hideout is near Presidio across the river into Mexico and the heart of the Davis range. But Bob said he fears hold-up men more than the Indians; said there had been a lot of hold-ups lately.

They rode on to a location called Paint Rock where the stage took a rest stop. After stretching and walking around, they all re-boarded the stage; next stop, Ballinger. As expected, this time JoJo joined Patti inside the coach.

She was a pleasant girl and asked a lot of questions about the life of a Ranger. JoJo, quite obviously taken by her good looks and charm, was not a talkative person, but soon found himself talking freely. During their conversation, JoJo learned that Patti was a singer and was going to live in Abilene to start a new life. She was hoping to seek a career other than singing. JoJo and Patti continued their small talk as the stage rolled on.

Suddenly, about ten miles south of Ballinger, two men started chasing the stage and firing their pistols from horseback. JoJo hollered out the window to Bob, "Pull up, Pull up, don't take a chance on catching a bullet."

Obligingly, Bob stopped the team of horses. The two masked men rode up and one of them pointed his pistol at Bob and said, "Throw down that strong-box or taste lead, your choice."

"Ain't got no money, just carrying mail and passengers," growled Bob.

The one with his gun out barked back, "Throw down the box like I said or I'll put a big hole clean thru you."

As requested, Bob threw down the box; they shot off the lock, opened it and, just as Bob had told them, there wasn't any money, just mail. JoJo knew things would probably escalate but decided not to make a play for fear a stray shot, into the stage, might hit Patti. Just as he suspected, the outlaws told him and Patti to get out of the stage.

JoJo had pinned his badge on his shirt and hidden it under his coat. He told Patti to stay in the coach, not to get out. When he stepped off the stage, he walked away to prevent wild gunfire from hitting Patti.

As he walked, the outlaws said, "Hold it right there, stop where you are and unbuckle that gun belt."

They were standing about seven yards away facing JoJo, who slid his coat back and, in a calm but deliberate voice, said, "I'm a Texas Ranger; you're under arrest. Drop your gun belts now." One of the men was tall and lanky, the other one was drunk. JoJo knew to take the sober one first, then the drunk.

The lanky one said, "Ranger, you're all by yourself and I have my gun in my hand, how you gonna arrest us." Then he gestured to the drunk and blurted out, "Hear that Otis, you want to kill 'im or you want me to."

CHAPTER 3

JoJo didn't flinch, he just stood his ground and advised them, "One or both of you is gonna die. It's certain I will kill one of you, question is, which one? Will it be you slim, or Otis? Tell you the truth, I don't know until I draw, but I'm faster than y'all so drop 'em to the ground or get ready to die."

The lanky one snorted, mistakenly, "You ain't that fast, no one is; you're a dead man Ranger."

Before Slim could raise his gun and squeeze the trigger, JoJo sent a 44 slug into his chest. Otis, the drunk, hadn't cleared leather when JoJo swung his pistol toward him and ordered, "Drop your belt to the ground, hands behind your back." Then he motioned to Bob and said, "Bob, come down here and tie his hands."

Once he was tied, he was told to stay where he was while Bob and JoJo tied Slim over his saddle and then tied his horse to the back of the stagecoach. Otis, who was still mounted, was secured to the stirrups. His horse was then tethered at the side of the stage where he could be seen from inside the coach. Bob released the brake on the stage and resumed their trek to Abilene.

When they arrived in town, a crowd followed the stage to the sheriffs' office and waited around in hopes of gaining information on what had happened.

Otis was locked up and questioned.

One member of the crowd was Jack Wilson; he walked up to the jail and asked, "Cletus, who killed that man?"

"If you must know, Jack, this Ranger here shot him," answered Cletus.

Jack responded, sarcastically, "That's surprising, he ain't back shot; that's where the Rangers like to shoot 'em."

JoJo heard the remark, walked over, looked Wilson in the eyes and barked, "Mister, I heard that remark." Then he pointed at the corps and barked, "Don't let your mouth put you on display with him over at the undertakers!"

Jack mumbled something inaudible as he walked off. Then he stopped, turned around looking back at JoJo and quipped, "Your times a coming Ranger; me and my brothers will be talking with you, your times a coming."

Fred and Glen Ray, of the old JJ Fox ranch, were in town getting supplies and overheard the ruckus. They walked over to the jail and introduced themselves to JoJo. When Cletus saw who they were, he said to JoJo, "Fred here and Glen Ray, a retired Ranger, are purely ranchers now but they help me out on occasion."

"That's right amigo," said Fred, "were here to help, kinda enjoy a little fight every now and again."

"I don't know what's going on yet;" said JoJo, "just know I need to get this pretty lady over to the hotel."

Fred chimed in, "Come on, I'll go with y'all and introduce you and this nice lady to Jim and Linda, owners of the hotel, saloon, and restaurant. Just so happens, Jim is also a retired Ranger."

After their introductions, and a little small talk, Linda learned that Patti would be staying and seeking employment; so she told her she needed help at the restaurant, if she was interested. Patti thanked her for the offer and said she would probably be in touch once she got settled in. Having said their pleasantries, Jim and Linda helped Patti with her baggage and escorted her to the boarding house.

After seeing to it that Patti was situated, JoJo returned to Cletus Meeks' office where he filled out his report then sat and talked with Cletus. He advised Cletus that Boots and Preacher should be arriving late the next day along with his new horse, 'Puddin'. JoJo told Cletus that Laughlin wanted the three of them to hang around Abilene for a while, so word would get out that Rangers were in town.

"By the way," asked JoJo, "Who's this smart mouthed fella you called Jack?"

"That's Jack Wilson and he's trouble," said Cletus, "two bit hired gun, thief, card shark, you know the type. He's waiting on his three brothers to get here. When they arrive, we'll have trouble alright. For now they're just trouble makers; could be when the brothers get here, they'll try the bank." JoJo had listened intently; thought that the jump from just trouble makers to bank robbers may be a quantum leap; but he figured Cletus knew what he was talking about.

When he realized there had been a long silent pause, JoJo said, "Cletus, when do you make your evening rounds?"

"I could do it now," said Cletus.

"Good," responded JoJo, "let's drop by the saloon, pay Jack a visit; whatcha think."

Cletus chuckled and said, "Could be interesting." Then, as they left the jail, he picked up his sawed off shotgun and walked towards the saloon.

It was almost sundown and the saloon was crowded as they pushed the swinging doors open and stepped inside. There was Jack; playing poker with a half empty fifth of whiskey on the table. JoJo and Cletus casually sauntered over to the bar and ordered a shot of whiskey. Cletus turned his up; JoJo only took a sip before turning to Cletus and saying "Cletus, stay here; cover me with that scattergun." Then he walked over to Jack's table.

Jack, sitting at the table holding his cards, stared up at JoJo. The mood of the saloon changed from a loud roar to a deafening silence. The crowd sensed there was trouble brewing. Men moved out from around the table and out of the way of gunfire, fully anticipating a shootout.

JoJo stepped up to about six feet from the table, stared into Jacks' eyes and said, "Hello Jack, still waiting' on your brothers?"

"Yea," answered Jack, "what business is it of yours?"

"No business," said JoJo, "just want to meet 'em when they arrive."

Jack didn't see any humor in JoJo's remarks, but he smiled and said, "Look Ranger, you better be worrying about getting out of town before they get here. My oldest brother, Bronco, don't like lawmen, especially

Rangers. Beryl and Big Boy feel the same way. They're the law when they ride in."

JoJo, who wasn't one to cow down to anyone, remarked, "Well, I sure hope there's no trouble, but if there is, I've got a nice place for 'em to stay; we'll put 'em up over in Cletus Meeks' hotel."

Jack chuckled then snorted, "That's a laugh; you won't be putting them, me, or anybody else in no jail; they'll have you out on the sidewalk in a coffin."

He continued to chuckle, then, with a smirk on his face, blurted out, "How the hell did you happen to shoot that feller holding up the stage? He paused for a moment, then with a side glance at the other players, said, "I went over and looked at him, he ain't back shot; must not have been one of you Ranger boys' that got 'em, from what I understand, y'all shoot 'em in the back."

"Is that so," inquired JoJo, "well I'm right here in front of you with my pistol in its holster." Then he stared real hard into Jack's eyes and said, "Why don't you stand up and try me; I'll show you how I put a hole in that fellers chest." JoJo was getting angrier by the minute as he barked, "Come on Jack, let's see if you can back up all your big talk or is that just the whiskey talking for you." When Jack just sat there in silence, JoJo prodded him some more. "Come on Jack, get up, make your play, here's your chance to get rid of a Ranger."

Finally Jack, knowing he had to respond or be laughed out of the saloon, shot back, "Naw, I ain't no fool; hell, if I get you, the sheriff will lay into me with that scattergun."

Realizing this was going nowhere, JoJo said, "Jack, I'm placing you under arrest for threatening a Texas Ranger. Drop your gun to the floor with your left hand, and do it now. All the talking is over; if there's anymore to be said, I'll do it with my shooter. Got it? When Jack didn't move fast enough for JoJo, he said, "Drop the hardware and I mean now, or the choice is yours, go to jail or dye where you sit."

Trying to save as much face as possible, Jack said, "Well as long as Cletus has that scattergun on me, I guess you're calling the shots." He dropped his gun and then, with a grin of defiance on his face, said, "I suppose I can use a good night's rest, especially when it's paid for by the good folks of Abilene. Hell, I suppose I should thank you." Then he said, mockingly, "Much obliged Ranger."

JoJo thought to himself, 'One of these days I'll have to shut that smart mouth of his', then he picked up Jack's holstered gun and lead him off to jail. When they got there, he put Jack in the cell next to Otis, the drunk that tried to rob the stage. After a few minutes, JoJo heard Otis telling Jack he was lucky he didn't try to pull leather. He said, "That Rangers fast, my partner never had a chance; had his gun out of the holster and that Ranger beat 'im. I'm telling you he's fast."

As JoJo and Cletus walked outside the jail, Cletus said, "Good job, now we only have the three brothers to deal with when they get here."

JoJo looked at Cletus and said, "Boots and Preacher will be here tomorrow; they're both top notch Rangers and they're fast. Matter of fact, Boots is second only to Laughlin; hell, he might even be faster." He paused; then added, "We'll be alright."

Cletus nodded his understanding and remarked, "Hey, what did you think about that gal on the stage?" Cletus paused for a moment. When JoJo didn't respond Cletus said, "She's a looker, is she your woman?"

"Not yet, but she's gonna be," answered JoJo with a big grin on his face.

The next day, late in the afternoon, Boots and Preacher rode into town. They were trail weary but went to the sheriffs' office looking for JoJo. He welcomed them; then he told them about the attempted stage robbery and the arrest of Jack Wilson. They were made aware that trouble was probably on the way; Jack's brothers were coming to Abilene.

JoJo said he drummed up a reason to lock up Jack; if there was going to be a shootout, that eliminated one gun.

Boots took that all in then decided to have a little fun; he asked if the girl passenger had been impressed with the Ranger saving the stage.

Without a second's hesitation, JoJo said, "Yes sir, she was most impressed, said I was brave and handsome; wondered if you two boys would be able to find your way here without me."

Boots, knowing he had been bested, made no response. After a little exchange of Ranger chatter, Cletus and the Rangers went to the restaurant, had supper and retired early; Boots and Preacher were saddle weary.

It was evening of the next day; the Rangers and Cletus were sitting on the jail porch when three men on horse back came riding down Main Street.

They weren't drovers and their appearance reflected they had been riding hard for quite a ways. They pulled up in front of the saloon, dismounted, hitched their horses and went inside.

Boots said, "You can bet these guys are no good, their horses are spent and they didn't take them to the livery stable. They're more concerned about themselves; don't like 'em already."

The Rangers, including Sheriff Meeks went to the saloon. All three riders were standing at the bar pouring whiskey down. They all wore their guns gunslinger style and were a rowdy looking bunch.

Cletus, to appear friendly but more in an attempt to gain information, walked over and said, "Hello boys, what brings you to Abilene?"

A large man dressed in chaps, jacket, bandana, tall crown hat and gloves tucked in his belt, turned and looked at Cletus. He was dark skinned, had dark long hair, a moustache, white teeth and dark blue intelligent looking eyes.

He looked up as he turned towards Cletus and replied, "Just passing through."

The man was in his thirties and it was evident he was the leader of the group. Realizing this Cletus asked, "What's your name mister?"

"Hell, I'll answer to anything," said the man." Then he asked "What're all these Rangers doing here?"

"We're waiting on some visitors to arrive," said Cletus, "figured y'all might be the ones we're waitin' on; your name Bronco?"

"Yea that's right, I'm Bronco," he said with a smile. Then he thought quizzically and asked, "How'd y'all know, my picture ain't on no posters."

Your brother Jack told us his brothers were coming," said Cletus, "figured you might be them."

"Yea," said Bronco, then he gestured towards the other too and continued, "that's Beryl and Big Boy."

Beryl favored Bronco, it was evident they were brothers. It was easy to see where Big Boy got his name; he was huge. Stood at least six foot five, two-hundred ninety pounds, narrow hips, broad shoulders, wide forehead, head full of dark long hair to his shoulders, no facial hair, large hands and big forearms. In a fistfight you would not want Big Boy to get his hands on you.

Cletus asked again, "What's your business in Abilene?"

Somewhat irritated by Cletus' persistence, Bronco barked, "Like I said sheriff, we're just riding thru, ain't got no business. Looking for my brother, figured he'd be over here playing cards and enjoying the ladies."

Cletus said, "Normally he would be, but, right now he's in my jail."

"In jail! What fer" asked Bronco?

"Oh, he made a few threats toward me and the Rangers" said Cletus, "he seems to let the whiskey talk fer 'em, so we thought we'd let him sober up and cool down a little." Cletus let that sink in then asked, "You boys wouldn't be here in Abilene to visit our little bank now would ya?"

"No sir sheriff, "said Bronco rather adamantly, "As I said, just passing thru."

Boots, JoJo and Preacher had been standing back several feet listening to the conversation. All of them walked up, stood beside Cletus and faced the men when Boots said, "Fellers, we've been sent out here to give Sheriff Meeks a hand. We're here to clean up this town and that's what we intend to do." He paused momentarily to see if there would be any response. When none was forthcoming, he continued, "Now you boys don't look like drovers and rest assured we'll have our eyes on y'all; but, if you keep your guns in their holster, we won't have any problems and we'll get along fine.

Still there was no response, either physically or orally, so Boots pressed his point, "Give us problems, resist us and we'll bury you. Abilene is full of saddle tramps, outlaws and ruffians but not for long. If you boys decide you want to see your brother over in the jail, make it one at a time and leave your guns behind. Wear your guns, and we'll throw you in jail."

All this time, Bronco and his two brothers had listened intently but showed no outward reaction; they were a cool bunch.

Boots ended their little confrontation with, "I'm glad we've had this friendly conversation; when we decide to let Jack out of jail, it'd be best if you all loaded up and moved on," he hesitated then added, "don't make us move you."

The Rangers and Cletus walked out of the saloon and toward the jail. JoJo told 'em to go ahead and have their supper; he'd watch the jail. They agreed and JoJo continued on to the jail, went in, locked the door and sat down at the table.

Jack asked if they had seen his brothers. When JoJo said they in fact had just talked with them, he started asking questions about their conversation. As JoJo related the jest of their meeting, Jack became belligerent and started cursing; saying they would break him out.

JoJo said, "Set down and shut up." When Jack complied, JoJo got up and poured himself a cup of coffee. He looked at the two men in the cells and thought, 'what the hell' so he filled two more cups and gave them to Jack and his cellmate. After a couple of weak 'thanks' from his jailbirds, JoJo sat back down, sipped some coffee and thought about Patti.

Suddenly there was a knock on the door; he got up, opened the sliding window, looked out, saw Bronco and said, "What do you want?"

"I want to see my brother Jack," answered Bronco, "ain't got no gun on me."

JoJo told Bronco to step into the street. When he did JoJo opened the door and let him come in. Cletus had painted a line on the floor several feet in front of the cells, far enough away that the cell couldn't be reached if you stayed behind the line. JoJo told Bronco not to cross the line; then he sat down at the table with his pistol in hand.

After speaking with Jack, Bronco walked over to the table where JoJo was sitting and asked, "How much is his bail?"

"Don't know," replied JoJo, "the circuit judge will set it when he comes to town."

Bronco was acting peaceably so JoJo invited him to sit a spell. When he did, JoJo poured Bronco a cup of coffee and sat back down.

With a little surprise in his voice, Bronco said, "Well, this is a first, me having coffee with a Ranger." Then suspiciously, he asked, "What's going on?"

"I want to ask you some questions," said JoJo, "You seem to be a smart fella, even likeable. What made you turn to this kind of life, challenging the law, one pistol shot away from death?"

Bronco wondered why this Ranger had an interest in his personal life but for some reason he answered, "My Pa' and Ma' had a cattle ranch; grew up on it; my brothers and me. I loved to break horses and I was good at it, that's where I got my nickname." Surprisingly enough, Bronco was becoming comfortable with JoJo as he continued, "War came along and everything was lost. When my brothers and me came back home we killed several carpetbaggers while trying to take back what was ours. We've been running ever since; working as drovers or paid guns; anything just so we could eat."

JoJo kinda liked Bronco and asked, "Bronco, why don't you get out of it before you catch a 44 slug or dangle at the end of a rope,"

"It's too late now," said Bronco, "every time we find work, someone shows up that knows us; no more work. Hell fire, you're the only lawman that's ever been nice to me; all of them ain't like you."

"Bronco," said JoJo, "I was on the same trail you're on now. One day I got drunk, took my shooter and made a feller with one leg dance. I didn't know he was a Ranger and I didn't count my shots, but he did. Next thing you know, I'm looking at the barrels of his scattergun. He could have killed me; instead he put me on a Ranger's ranch and made me go to work; best thing that ever happened to me. My life changed; change yours or you'll be dead in a year or less."

JoJo let Bronco absorb what he had said, then went on, "That Ranger Boots, the one who did all the talking in the saloon, I met him while working on that ranch. Rode with 'em a while and now I'm a Ranger; we're 'Ranger Brothers'. Bronco, we know you boys are here to hit the bank. It ain't gonna work; you'll die in the street, ride away." JoJo paused then said, "No more sermons but I do need to ask you a question. When you were in Abilene, Kansas, did you happen to know a man from Ft Worth, a gambler?"

"Yea, I knew one," said Bronco, "played some poker with him. If I recall, his name was Emmet Ryker"

JoJo asked, "What do you know about him. I'm not wanting to arrest 'im, its personal business."

"Well," said Bronco, "he's smart, doesn't work except at cards. Good looking guy, big tipper."

"Which side of the law is he on?" queried JoJo

Bronco said he was probably on the fence. Said he walked down the middle but on occasion staggers to either side. Bronco considered him fast with his pistol, which was a vest gun. Said he killed several men but it was always in self defense.

"Why you looking for him" Bronco asked?

Rather confusingly, JoJo answered, "Oh, I'm not really looking for 'im, just wondered if you had ever heard or seen anyone like that."

"Hell boy, I'm no fool," said Bronco, "sounds to me like you're looking for your Pa'. In fact, when I saw you I thought of Emmett, you're his spittin' image."

"No, he's not my Pa'," said JoJo, "at least he doesn't claim me; I've never seen me."

"Hell boy, mount up, go see him," said Bronco, "Talk to him."

"Yea, may do that," said JoJo, "you ready for me to let you out?"

"Yea but remember, you're still a Ranger and I'm still an outlaw. Hopefully we won't have to face each other" said Bronco.

"Yea, me to," said JoJo, "it would give me no thrill to kill you." In a strange sort of way, JoJo was beginning to like Bronco.

A short time later, the three Rangers returned from supper and gave JoJo a message that Patti was at the restaurant and wanted to have dinner with him. He hurriedly washed his face combed his long hair and left the jail heading for the restaurant. It was almost dark; JoJo was walking down the boardwalk at a fast pace when a rifle shot rang out. The bullet struck one of the porch posts; head high. It splintered the wood, throwing pieces toward JoJo with some of the splinters striking him in the face. The shot had come from across the street, between the buildings. Whoever it was took his shot and then ran between the buildings and down the alley.

Having heard the shot, Boots and Preacher joined JoJo and the Rangers made a thorough search. The Wilson brothers, who were in the saloon, all had alibis. Not knowing who or what the deal was, the Rangers decided to stay in pairs so Preacher went with JoJo to meet Patti for supper.

He told Patti what happened and she said to JoJo, "Maybe it's a friend or relative of the man you shot during the stage holdup." Choosing not to discuss it any further, they ate their dinner and indulged themselves in casual conversation. It was very evident that Patti was interested in JoJo. During their conversation she mentioned an interview at the bank and said she was very excited about the prospect. Linda had continued to help her get situated and was going to loan her the money to pay the boarding house in advance. Also, Linda told her she could work part time at the restaurant as a waitress.

Finally it was time to turn in for the evening. JoJo was tired so he went to his room, laid down and started thinking about his conversation with Bronco. He thought, 'when we get this mess cleaned up here in Abilene, maybe I'll just ride up to Kansas'. He was a little scared; he had never had a Pa', what if Emmett is his dad.'

The next day Cletus and the Rangers set up a schedule for patrolling the streets. They wanted word to get out that Abilene was crawling with Rangers. Cattle sales had increased tremendously and large sums of cash were being deposited in the Abilene Bank which would be drawing outlaws like bees to honey.

Boots and Preacher had been paired for patrols and, just to be safe, had decided to stay close to each other for a while. After their mid-morning patrol, they went to the office of Stewart Coffee – Attorney. When they walked into Stewart's office, there was a beautiful young lady talking with Stewart. She was very well built, around twenty-three years old, had curly, honey blonde hair hanging to her hips, beautiful green eyes, big full lips, dimples, and a beautiful smile. She was maybe five foot two and when she talked she expressed herself with hand and eye movement. Boots felt weak in the knees; she was the most beautiful woman he had ever seen.

Stewart stopped his conversation with her and said, "Jane Wyatt, I want you to meet a couple of Rangers. This is Ranger Boots Law and Ranger Jerry Jack Tenneson." He turned his attention to the Rangers and continued, "Jane is the daughter of Bill Wyatt, owner and editor of the Abilene Press. She's a writer and she also sells ads; I'm just about to renew my ad with her now," then kiddingly, he added, "Only because she's beautiful."

Boots and Preacher had their hats in their hands and shuffling their feet, when finally Boots said, with his best manners, "It's our pleasure to meet you Ma'am and Stewarts correct, you are beautiful." He felt like he was tongue tied but managed to say, "Just call me Boots and this is Preacher, we re-named him, he's gonna marry the daughter of our preacher back home."

They had just been looking at each other for several moments when Stewart said, "Jane, you could write some stories about these Rangers for your newspaper. One day they are in the streets of Laredo in a gun fight, the next

day they're chasing down Indians and now they've been sent here to do some housekeeping and get rid of all the ruffians in Abilene."

Jane said, "That would be fun." Then realizing her meaning may not be clear," she added, "what I mean is I would love to do an article about the Rangers, maybe we could have dinner some evening and discuss it."

"Yes, yes," said Boots rather anxiously, "that's a great idea,"

She waved bye as she left Stewarts' office and both Rangers ran to the window to watch her cross the street.

Afterwards, Boots and Stewart talked about his brother, Sterling, in Austin. Stewart brought Boots up to date; said Sterling was engaged to Emily and her father, the Governor, loved him.

Stewart said, "Boots, very soon your brother will be a State Senator and, maybe in the years to come, the Governor of Texas."

Having exchanged their pleasantries, Boots and Preacher were walking back to the jail when Preacher said, "How come you had to tell Jane I was gonna be a preacher and was engaged?" Boots laughed and said, "Remember Preacher, a good Ranger always keeps the odds in his favor." and then he burst out in a big smile and gave Preacher a friendly slap on the back.

It was still a mystery who had taken the shot at JoJo; perhaps it was associated with the stage robbery and the death of the outlaw. Boots said they needed to question the dead outlaw's partner, Otis, about Slim and his kinfolk. The body had yet to be claimed and was still at the funeral home. Mr. Presswood, the undertaker, told Boots that relatives were coming to take the body to Buffalo Gap for burial.

Boots advised JoJo they would make the trip with the body and relatives to the burial in Buffalo Gap, which was about thirty miles from Abilene. This way, they could ask questions and see who might be bitter toward the Rangers. He told Preacher to stay in Abilene, Cletus may need help as long as Bronco and his brothers were hanging around town and everyone is certain they'll hit the bank when Jack gets out of jail. Cletus had hired a deputy and armed him with a sawed off shotgun. His job was to be at the bank when it opened and stay there until it closed.

As late afternoon rolled around, it was time for the evening patrol. It was only yesterday when someone fired at JoJo from between the buildings. Boots told JoJo to walk the sidewalks with him while Preacher got mounted and rode the alleys.

They started their walk down the west side of Main Street toward the saloon, which was located at the end of the street. About a hundred yards from the saloon, they saw a body come flying out thru the swinging doors landing face down in the street. Before the dust had settled, another body came flying out and landed beside the first one. Boots and JoJo started walking faster toward the saloon when out stepped Big Boy; then Bronco and Beryl.

Boots and JoJo stepped between Big Boy and the two men sprawled in the street as Boots said, "Hold up boys, the party's over, hold up. What's the problem?"

Big Boy answered, "Ranger Boots, they call Big Boy big and dumb; me not dumb; nobody call me dumb."

CHAPTER 4

The two men in the street were in the process of getting up, brushing themselves off and making threats as they walked away saying, "You ain't seen the last of the Davis boys, we'll be back and settle up with the dummy; his brothers too, if they want some of it. We'll be back."

Boots said, "You boys ride out of town now, if you come back, check your guns in at the sheriffs' office; don't let me ketcha wearin' 'em."

JoJo looked at Big Boy and said, "I appreciate there was no gun play, thanks for holding it down Bronco." It was easy to see that Bronco was the leader of the brothers.

Bronco said to JoJo, "Did you ever find out who took that shot at you?"

JoJo laughed and said, "I figured it was you."

Bronco said with a grin, "You know me and the boys were in the saloon, besides, I wouldn't have missed."

With a smile JoJo said, "Be nice, I'm trying to like you."

Boots and JoJo completed their rounds; they were uneventful. Evidently the person who shot at JoJo was lying low, but who knows what their motive was or when they might try again.

The second Monday of each month in Abilene, four days away, is trade days with horse racing, chicken fights and a street dance. It could be a fun time and, it could be a busy time for Cletus and the Rangers. There would be lots of drinking, gambling, horse racing, fistfights, and possibly gunfights. Boots and JoJo, who were looking forward to dancing with Jane and Patti, told Preacher he would have to help Cletus; after all he was engaged.

Boots said to JoJo, "Why don't you invite Patti to dinner Friday night and I'll invite Jane, that way we can all get acquainted."

"Ok," said JoJo, "but I don't know if she even likes me."

"Sure she does," remarked Boots, "after all, you're a Ranger."

"Yea, big mouth," said JoJo, "what if Jane turns you down? It could happen ya know; she may have someone. Maybe she doesn't think you're as handsome as you think."

"I don't know, but ole Boots will find out," said Boots, with his usual smile.

Early the next morning, when the newspaper office opened, Boots was the first customer. When he went in, a balding, rapid moving man wearing reading glasses and wiping ink from his hands, introduced himself as Bill Wyatt, owner of the newspaper. He said, "I know who you are, you're the Ranger Boots that made quite an impression on my daughter, right?"

"Yes sir I'm Boots," he answered, "is she in?"

"No, be here any minute though, can I help you?" offered Wyatt.

"Well sir," said Boots, "if she's not spoken for I would like to take her to dinner tonight."

Wyatt scratched his chin, and spouted, "She mentioned she wanted to do some articles on you Rangers."

"Well," said Boots, hat in hand, "I was kinda hoping we could have dinner, more of a personal meeting and then an interview later with me and the boys. I think your daughter is very beautiful and I really want to get to know her. Do I have your permission to ask her out?"

"You surely do, I like you and I like the Rangers" answered Wyatt. You Rangers are making Texas a better place, we need more of ya."

The door opened, it was Jane, "Hello Boots, so nice to see you, Pa' have you met the handsome Ranger, Boots?" she asked.

"Yes, we've met," he said.

"Don't you just love his name, Boots, that's so different," queried Jane.

She was full of energy, smiling and talking; the room completely changed when she entered; it lit up and was filled with happiness. Boots was again overwhelmed; she was more beautiful today than when he met her.

After the introductions and small talk Jane asked, with a teasing smile, "Boots are you here for your interview? Now tell me all about what you boys do."

"No Ma'am, I'm not here for the interview" he said while shuffling his feet and playing with his hat.

She said, "Boots, I do believe you're blushing, what's the matter."

"Well Ma'am, Boots said kind of sheepishly, "I came over here to ask you to go with me for dinner Saturday night."

She walked over close to him, took each side of his unbuttoned coat in her hands and said, "Yes, I will go with you but only if you stop calling me Ma'am."

Mr. Wyatt looked at Jane and thought how proud he was of his daughter; she was strong in mind and in control of every situation, he smiled and said to himself, just like her mother. It would take a strong man, such as a Ranger to be in her life. Boots informed JoJo that Jane had accepted his offer. Patti had accepted JoJo's invitation and the date was set for Saturday night. They were excited; the girls were beautiful and they knew they would have fun.

Almost a week had passed since the attempted stage robbery, when a wagon, pulled by two oxen, came to town and stopped in front of the funeral home. It was driven by a young woman dressed in old faded worn out clothes; her hair was pulled back and tied in a knot. Her face reflected hard times and she looked tired and appeared older than she probably was. There was a young boy, approximately eight years old, with her. He was wearing bib overalls a faded shirt and worn out leather boots that looked four sizes too large; they were probably hand me downs. The wagon, the skinny oxen along with the boy and the woman, painted a picture of extreme poverty.

Preacher was in the jail with Cletus while Boots and JoJo were making their mid-day rounds. Boots said, "They're probably here to get the body, let's go over there and find out who they are."

By the time they walked to the funeral home, the woman and boy were inside. When the Rangers walked in they heard the woman saying, "I don't have no money to pay you fer taking care of my man."

45

Boots and JoJo walked over to her and Boots said, "Ma'am, the Rangers will pay the expenses for your husband. I'm Ranger Law and this is Ranger White, we're here to help you."

She turned toward the Rangers and, with a forlorn look on her face said, "My name is Estelle Cartwright and this is my boy Zeke. That's my husband Newt lying over there on the slab. We ain't got no money fer a pine box; gonna wrap 'im up in that blanket and bury 'im in it."

"Ma'am," said JoJo, "is this all there is of your family?"

"Yea," she answered, "there were three of us, now it's just me and Zeke."

JoJo said, "Ma'am, we're gonna ride with you out to your place and help bury your man. You and the boy come with us; we'll go over to the restaurant while Mr. Presswood loads your man in the wagon."

"Ranger," said the woman, "I don't got no money fer no restaurant vittles."

"That's alright, we're buying, even gonna get Zeke a piece of pie" assured JoJo.

They all went over to the restaurant. When they got there Boots told Linda, "Heap on the food, we've got two travelers here that are hungry." They both ate like they hadn't eaten for days.

Cletus and Preacher came in while they were both still eating. Boots pulled Preacher aside and whispered "Go over to the General Store and get some supplies, lots of 'em, charge it to the Rangers and put 'em in that wagon in front of the funeral home.

After eating their meal, Boots asked Estelle about her husband and Otis. She said Otis was a cousin; he had come to live with them and help work the farm. Said her husband was a good man; he had never been in trouble and was a good father. He couldn't find work and they were about to starve to death. She overheard Newt and Otis making plans to hold up the stage and begged them not to. Newt said the bank was going to take the farm and he wasn't gonna let his wife and son starve to death so they rode out to rob the stage and never came back. She said she drove the wagon in today just to see if she could find their whereabouts. That's when she found out Newt was dead and Otis was in jail.

After the meal, they prepared to ride out to the Cartwright place. Boots tied War Paint to the wagon; JoJo was riding behind on Pistol and Boots drove the wagon. The young boy sat next to his Pa's body; it had been wrapped in blankets. Estelle sat up on the wagon seat next to Boots.

It was late evening when they reached the farmhouse. It reflected hard times: broken down porch with rusted out old worn farm tools laying in the yard. The barn was missing pieces of the roof. There was a run down corral with a skinny jersey milk cow; a sow with piglets was running around in the yard.

Estelle directed Boots and JoJo to take Newts body in the house and lay him in the bed. She put a clean shirt and trousers on the body and then tucked him in. His eyes were still open; she told Zeke to get two nickels out of the jar in the kitchen cabinet. When he returned, she took her finger and closed one eyelid then placed a nickel on it. She repeated the process on the other eye, the weight of the nickel held the eyelids closed. She told Zeke to get a broom and a chair and sit beside the body to guard against rats. Otherwise, she said, rats would try to get on the bed and eat the earlobes and nostrils. If that happened, Zeke was to knock them off the bed. He was told to sit there until dark and then she would light a lantern and guard the body all night herself. After digging a grave, they would bury Newt the next day.

JoJo asked where she wanted to bury him and she said, "West of the house, about two hundred steps, there are two graves. His Ma' and Pa' are buried there. Bury him next to them."

Boots and JoJo dug the grave that evening so it would be ready the next morning. They returned to the house and Boots told Estelle he would sit with the body, she needed to get some sleep.

The next day at sunup Boots and JoJo carried the body to the gravesite. Boots said a prayer; they shoveled dirt in the grave until it was full, mounded over the top of it, drove a wood marker into the ground at the head, and piled some rocks around the marker.

Boots asked Estelle, "What will you do now?"

She said, "Me and Zeke will go to Abilene; maybe I can get some work and try to get him in school. God will provide."

Boots and JoJo mounted up, rode out the gate and onto the wagon trail where they turned and looked back. Estelle was lying across the grave and young Zeke was hugging her. Boots looked at JoJo and saw tears running down his cheeks. Boots said, rather sternly, "JoJo, when you shot Newt he was holding up a stage at gunpoint, he threatened to kill you; you asked him to surrender but he wouldn't. Mister, he had his pistol in his hand pointed at you. He was breaking the law and threatened your life; he was just another outlaw robbing the stage."

JoJo was taking it very hard so Boots pressed on, "You are a Texas Ranger upholding the law. You took an oath when you became a Ranger and that's what you did. Now that you know all the circumstances it's easy to say, 'I wish I had just wounded him'."

Realizing he hadn't quite gotten to JoJo yet, Boots voice changed to reflect his authority as he barked, "Ranger, hear me and hear me good; when you pull that shooter; you shoot to kill. Had you tried to wound him, he could be in Mexico and we could be readin' over you." This appeared to register in JoJo's mind as Boots continued, "Now, let's go to Abilene, we got dinner dates with the two prettiest girls in Texas."

Boots could see the mood softening so he joked, "I still don't know how you got Patti to go out with you, as homely lookin' as you are; as fer me, now I'm handsome. Just need to learn to sing a little better." Boots started stroking an imaginary guitar and tried to sing, 'Now git up old War Paint, git along to Abilene, got a pretty girl waiting on me, can't be late'. He laughed hard, spurred War Paint on and rode off toward Abilene town. He glanced back at JoJo and, seeing his expression returning to normal, knew he would be okay.

When they returned to the hotel in Abilene, Boots took a long soaking bath, trimmed his shoulder length hair and shined his boots. After putting on his fresh washed jeans, Sunday double breasted khaki shirt, red bandana tied around his neck and his black Stetson, he removed his pistol and all the cartridges before cleaning his gun belt and holster with saddle soap. Afterwards he cleaned and wiped down his pearl handled peacemaker. Now he was ready.

He looked in the mirror and said, "Look out Jane, here comes ole Heartthrob Ranger Boots." He laughed at himself, walked out of his room and down to the lobby.

JoJo was there waiting on him and said, "Boots what took you so long, we're gonna be late."

Boots said, "Aw, I went to sleep and didn't wake up in time to bathe or clean up."

JoJo said, "Yea, right." Boots punched him on the shoulder, laughed and they headed to the restaurant.

The dinner went really well. The girls seemed to like each other and both girls were extremely beautiful. Boots asked Jane if she would ask for donations to the Cartwrights' in the newspaper. He also asked if she would go with him to the local church and ask the preacher for help. She said she would be glad to do what she could on both counts.

Patti was happy that she had taken the job at the bank. After dinner, and a respectful amount of small talk, JoJo and Patti left.

After they left, Boots and Jane sat at the table, sipped wine and had talked for about an hour when Jane said, "Boots, I've got pretty high standards about the men I date. I just want you to know – I like what I have seen of you so far and I hope we can develop a relationship." Then she asked, "Will you dance with me tomorrow at the street dance?"

"Yes," said Boots, "and I will also dance with you tonight, in my dreams."

"Oh, that's so sweet," replied Jane, "we'd better say goodnight, its getting late."

Finally it was Saturday, the week long event was almost over and the Big day had come; there would be street dances, horse races and all sorts of gala events. Glen Ray and Fred had brought Three Paws, the son of Whiskey, in for the big race. When JJ Fox died, in honor of his memory, they changed the name of the ranch to the Double JJ and continued to raise Morgan horses and thoroughbreds.

By Midday, everyone was in Abilene; people were still swapping coon dogs, mules, oxen, pigs, chickens, etc. The women were helping to get the area ready for the finale, the street dance, which would start at six that evening.

Boots, Preacher and JoJo found Glen Ray and Fred in the horse race warm up area. They were rubbing down Three Paws and getting him ready. Jim and Linda had joined up and invited Patti to accompany them to the race when Jim said, "My, How times do change."

"How so," asked Preacher?

Jim replied, "I'm a retired Ranger, so is Glen Ray; Fred was too, part time."

He paused for a moment to gather his thoughts, then continued. "Look at you three boys; you're already experienced Rangers and doing a hell-of-a fine job. Preacher, I remember when you came riding up to me after the Indian attack."

"Yes sir," reflected Jerry Jack, "at that time I never dreamed I would someday be a Ranger, owe a lot to you and Laughlin."

Boots, trying to keep everyone's eye on the ball, said, "We've got to get back, need to stay close to the bank. With all the people in town, this would be a good day for a holdup."

Over in the saloon Bronco was playing cards while Beryl and Big Boy were at the billiard table when suddenly, those two Davis boys that Big Boy had thrown out of the saloon, stepped inside with pistols drawn. They saw Big Boy and Beryl at the billiard table and started firing; Big Boy was hit three times and Beryl was hit twice, killing them both instantly.

The two men turned and ran out the door of the saloon. Bronco got a shot off as they ran out; then they mounted up and rode down the street. Bronco followed out the door and into the street, held his pistol with both hands, aimed and fired at one of the riders' horse. They were about forty yards away and the horse dropped, throwing the rider over his head and onto the ground. The horseless rider then jumped up and ran for cover behind a wagon.

When this happened, Boots had been walking to the jail while Preacher and JoJo were still back at the restaurant. Boots ran out to the middle of the street facing the other on coming rider who drew his pistol and started firing. Boots, who by this time had his gun drawn, aimed, squeezed, and 'BOOM', the rider was rolled off the horse backwards. Then, suddenly, "BOOM', another pistol shot rang out; the wounded rider that Bronco shot earlier, was behind a wagon firing at Boots.

The wagon was in front of the newspaper office so Boots wouldn't fire towards it. He could see Bronco coming up the street toward them. Boots shouted out at the hidden shooter, "Give it up! You've got a man coming up behind you! Give it up or you'll die!"

"Hold your fire, I'm coming out!" came the answer from behind the wagon.

"Throw your gun out in the street," ordered Boots.

The gun went flying out and landed in the street. Bronco came up behind the man and hit him in the back of his neck with his fist, knocking him to his knees. The gunman reached for a belly gun as

Bronco drew his pistol, stuck it against the back of the man's skull and pulled the trigger. Blood and brains were blown out of a huge hole in the man's forehead where the bullet exited.

Jane had stepped out into the street and grabbed Boots. Boots put his pistol back in its holster, pushed her back inside, then turned and faced Bronco.

With a harsh tone in his voice, Boots, who hadn't seen the belly gun, said, "Bronco, you didn't have to do that, I had things well under control."

"They gunned down my brothers," barked Bronco, "they didn't have a chance, didn't give 'em a chance to pull, shot 'em down. You got one of 'em, I got the other."

Boots replied, "Yea, but taking him was my job, not yours; I've got to lock you up."

"What the hell," replied Bronco, "you don't gotta lock no body up; he got what he had coming."

JoJo, Preacher and Cletus, who had heard the shots, were now closing in on Boots. They didn't know what happened so they approached them with caution.

Boots repeated himself, "Bronco, you're under arrest, we're placing you in jail until I can find out what started this ruckus in the saloon. I need to conduct a full investigation."

Cletus and Preacher took a reluctant Bronco by the arm and headed for the jail. JoJo went to the man Bronco had just shot, rolled him over, pulled a belly gun out from under his shirt and said, " Boots, he was still armed when Bronco shot'im, probably would have gotten off a shot at one of us."

The four bodies, Big Boy, Beryl, and the Wilson brothers', were taken over to the undertakers. Boots went inside the newspaper office and tried to assure Jane that he was all right. Between her trembling and sobbing she managed to say, "Boots, I've read about things such as this, but I've never been a witness to a killing." Her sobbing continued as she cried, "That was the scariest thing I've ever seen," then she slid her arms around him and said, "hold me, I'm still frightened."

After a while she gathered her composure sat down in the office with Boots and her Pa' and said, "Boots, give me all the details." She had a pen in hand and wrote down all the happenings as Boots related them to her. When he finished she said, in a perfectly calm and business-like manner, "This story will go in next week's edition of the paper."

After the interview with Jane, Boots walked over to the jail and asked Cletus, Preacher and JoJo to join him for a walk. They knew he had something on his mind.

They walked for about a hundred yards; no words had been spoken when Boots said, "That feller that Bronco killed, he had just shot two of Broncos' brothers and had a belly gun hidden on 'im to use on one of us." He continued walking slowly then added, "JoJo, go over there, turn Bronco and his brother Jack loose but tell 'em not to ever come back to Abilene." Then Boots turned and asked, "You agree with what I say Cletus?"

"Yes sir," answered Cletus, "I sure do, just wish I had said it first."

Being reassured by Cletus, Boots said, "JoJo, about eight o'clock tonight take their horses to the jail, let Bronco and his brother go; tell them I said to get out of town and stay out."

At eight o'clock, just as Boots had instructed, JoJo tied two horses to the hitchin' post and went inside the jail.

Cletus said, "I'm gonna go get me a cup of restaurant coffee; see you in about an hour, then we'll make our rounds."

JoJo walked over to the cell, pulled up a chair, turned it around backwards and sat down with his arms draped over the back, pointed at Bronco and uttered, "Two years ago I was on my way to an early hanging party or a bullet in my heart; just like you coulda been. I was given a second chance by a Ranger, now I'm giving you a chance."

He looked at Bronco, who apparently had heard every word, and said, "I'm gonna let you out of this jail, no charges filed, all I ask is that you ride to Uvalde, talk to my Ranger Captain, Laughlin McFarland, and see if he'll consider making you a Ranger. I'll give you a written recommendation if you're willing. I can't vouch for your brother Jack, don't know enough about him." He got an understanding nod from Bronco as he continued,

"Hell, if you're gonna live by the gun, you may as well be on the right side of the law and get paid for it. Then JoJo stuck his hand out and said, "Do I have your word?"

Bronco, who hadn't uttered a sound the whole time, stuck his hand out through the cell bars, and said, "You have my word, and don't worry none 'bout Jack, he'll find his own way. Ain't cut out for no Rangerin' anyways."

JoJo opened the cell door, let both men out, then turned and went out in the street looking for Patti.

Glen Ray had brought Angel to the three-day event; Fred had come alone; he hadn't been with another girl since LaQuita died. After the day quieted down, they all gathered at the hotel for a late night dinner. Three Paws had won the horse race convincingly enough that three more orders were taken for stud service from Whiskey. Linda and Jim had also joined them for dinner; there was wine, conversation and lots of fun. Around two in the morning they retired to their rooms.

It being Saturday night; Preacher and Cletus were going to patrol till daybreak and would be relieved by Boots and JoJo. Bronco, and his brother Jack, had mounted up and headed towards Uvalde. The remainder of the night was peaceful and Sunday came early with the four Rangers meeting at the jail. Cletus went home; Preacher went to church; Boots and JoJo poured themselves a cup of last night's coffee and sat at the table.

They were sipping their coffee when Boots said, "JoJo, you alright partner?"

"Yea, I'm alright," answered JoJo, "just got something on my mind."

"Hey we're saddle pals," offered Boots, "you wanna share it with me?"

"No," muttered JoJo, "I gotta take care of it by myself. Need to be gone for a spell." I gotta ride up north before winter snows come, be back in the spring. Like to get on the way today if it's okay with you, "I'll send Captain a wire."

Knowing there was no use in pushing for more information, Boots nodded his approval. JoJo loaded up, saddlebags full of food, tied on his duster and made ready to hit the trail. He rode over to the bank where Patti was working. She looked beautiful; he knew he was going to miss her. When she saw him come through the door, she greeted him and they sat down on a sofa.

"JoJo, what's wrong?" she asked. She could tell he was bothered by something.

"Patti," he said, "I've got to leave town, be gone for a while, just wanted to say goodbye."

"JoJo what's wrong?" she asked again, almost pleading.

"Need to find some answers," he said mysteriously, "be back come spring."

He headed towards the door, turned back towards her and offered, "I'll be in Abilene, Kansas, gotta go."

She walked him out the door; he got on Puddin and rode down Main Street heading north. About a hundred yards from the bank he stopped Puddin, turned around and waved at Patti who was still standing in the doorway of the bank; then he rode away at a gallop.

The next day in the early evening, everyone that had a booth was loading their merchandise and heading home. Cletus was at the jail doing paperwork and reading his mail. Boots and Preacher were making the rounds through town. They entered the saloon; it was crowded. As usual, the smell of cigar smoke and tobacco was over powering the smell of whiskey. They went to the bar and asked the bartender, Jim Raines, for a couple of shots of whiskey.

He sat down two shot glasses and poured them full. Boots picked up his glass, turned to Preacher and said, "Here's to JoJo, may he have a good trip and solve his problem." They touched glasses, turned them up and downed the amber liquid.

Boots said to Jim, "Come over here and talk awhile; we need some information."

When Jim moved down the bar to where they were standing Boots said, "Jim, you know, we still don't know who it was that took a shot at JoJo. Got any idea, have you heard anything?"

Jim said, "See that young fella at the corner table over there." Boots looked at him; he looked like any young drover. Jim continued, "One of the girls, Marlene, spent some time with him, he's got money, doesn't stay in town, camps out on the east side of town. She said he's quiet and doesn't get drunk, but he hates badges."

This bit of info seemed to interest Boots and Preacher, so Jim went on, "He's been in and out of town for about a week now; always by himself."

"You say he's camped outside of town?" echoed Boots.

"Yep, according to Marlene, he's real hush mouthed; don't mix nor mingle, just sips whiskey and goes upstairs with her."

Boots and Preacher said thanks for the drink and the information and walked outside to the boardwalk.

Boots looked at Preacher and said, "What do you think?"

Preacher answered, "I think there are several people in that campsite and I think he comes into town then reports back the activities. I think there are more men in that camp and they're planning to rob the bank." He looked at Boots, who was nodding agreement, and mumbled, "You know six or seven men could have ridden in and held up that bank during the day while there was someone to unlock the safe. Now, when Cletus was by himself, they could have pulled that off. But now, with us in town, their plans have been upset." When Boots remained silent, Preacher said, "That sniper shot at JoJo was meant to reduce the guns in town when they ride in."

Boots broke silence and said, "I believe you're right, let's tell Cletus and then we need to find that camp."

It was midday, Bronco and Jack, riding toward Uvalde, had just reached the small town of Paint Rock where they stopped for a drink before riding on. Bronco had made a promise to JoJo and he was going to keep it; he would talk to Captain McFarland.

They were sitting in the saloon washing trail dust down when Jack started cursing the Rangers and anyone else that wore a badge. Bronco finished his drink, got up, walked outside and mounted up. Jack came out of the saloon and started for his horse.

Bronco said, "Don't bother to mount up, you ain't riding with me."

"What the hell you mean I ain't riding with you," shouted Jack; "we's brothers ain't we?"

"Oh, we're brothers alright," said Bronco, "but we don't think the same, you're already at the end of your rope. A lawman will shoot or hang you; you'll die soon. Stay away from me, that Ranger made a lot of sense to me. He said if you are going to live by the gun, you might as well be a lawman. I'm going to Uvalde and see about joining the Rangers."

"I'll be damned," said Jack, "I never woulda believed it. You, my brother, a gall-darned Ranger." Jack looked directly at his brother with contempt, and said "You ain't nothing but a low life, spineless, gutless excuse for a man. You ain't my brother."

Bronco, sitting on his horse said to Jack, "Disown me if you must, but I'll tell you this, you won't last a year; change your ways or you'll go to your grave and spend an eternity in hell." Without waiting for any further response from his brother, Bronco spun his horse around and rode away.

It was a week later when Bronco rode into Uvalde. His first stop was the sheriffs' office. Oral and Shotgun were playing dominoes when he opened the door and went inside.

As they looked up, he said, "My name is Bronco Wilson, I'm looking for Ranger Captain McFarland."

Nathan stood up and said, "I'm Nathan Law and this is Oral Fox. He's the sheriff, I'm a Ranger."

"You must be 'Shotgun'," said Bronco. "I kinda know your boy, Boots. Met 'im over in Abilene; but it was Ranger JoJo made me promise to come to Uvalde and talk with the Captain."

"Why did he send you here?" asked Nathan.

"Well, my three brothers and me couldn't seem to find no honest work so we went to Abilene to rob the bank. It never happened; two men shot two of my brothers down in cold blood. Your boy, Boots and me, got the two that killed my brothers." Seeing very little reaction from the Rangers, he continued, "JoJo made me promise to put my gun to work enforcing the law before I got my fool self killed."

Finally, the Rangers broke silence when Oral asked, "You got a place to stay tonight?"

"No," said Bronco, "I'll just sleep somewhere outside of town."

"No, take a cell here," offered Oral, "they're all empty. Tomorrow Nathan can take you out to the Big Iron ranch and you can meet Laughlin."

The next day, as Nathan had promised, he was riding with Bronco down the road to the Big Iron ranch, looking for Laughlin. When they arrived, Laughlin was at the barn brushing Sam and cleaning his hooves. As they rode up and stopped in front of Laughlin, Nathan said, "Hello Captain, this is Bronco, he rode all the way from Abilene to talk with you."

"Hello Nathan, Bronco," said Laughlin. "Y'all get down, let's go to the bunkhouse and get some coffee." Laughlin poured three cups, then as they sat at a table said, "Okay Bronco, let's talk."

"Well sir," said Bronco, "I don't know how to start. Met Boots in Abilene, I sure like him. Me and Boots were in a shootout with the two Davis boys who had murdered two of my brothers. Well, we me got 'em both then later on, JoJo made me promise to talk with you. Said if I was gonna live by the gun, I ought to be on the laws side."

When he paused, Laughlin asked, "Why weren't you on the laws side to begin with?"

"Well," said Bronco, "as you probably know, most of us southerners had our house and property taken over by carpetbaggers, so we had some problems with 'em and had to start running. Couldn't find work; always tried to stay on the side of the law." Bronco paused and thought about how to go on; then he said, "To be completely honest with you, we went to Abilene to rob the bank. Fortunately it didn't happen. Now you might laugh when I say this, but, contrary to what my brother's thought, I always admired the Rangers; actually wanted to be one; figured they never would have me."

Laughlin hadn't shown any emotion to Bronco's story but was seriously listening as Bronco went on; "Now I'm asking, will you consider me for the Rangers. I'd be willing to work here on your ranch; I'm a good cowboy, got my name because I can break wild horses."

When Bronco paused again, Laughlin encouraged him with "Go on, I'm listening."

Bronco said, "Sir, that's about it, you don't know me, but I want to be a Ranger; if I continue the way I'm going, I'm a dead man."

Laughlin looked directly into Bronco's eyes and said, "I'm going to ask you a few questions, if you lie, you're gone." Without waiting for a response Laughin asked, "You wanted for anything?"

"No sir," said Bronco.

"If you're telling me the truth, you can start today, working on the ranch. I'll talk to you again in ninety days. Being a Ranger is an honor, not everyone can meet the qualifications. It's up to you, show me what you're made of; everyone deserves a second chance in life." Laughlin looked at Nathan winked and said, "Now, how do I know you're not just a bagga wind and you're entire story isn't just a buncha sheep-dip"

Bronco, who took offense to the implication, said, "Mr. McFarland, I should've given you this note when I first got here, but I plainly forgot I had it." With that, he handed Laughlin the written recommendation from JoJo.

Laughlin read it, handed it to Nathan and told him to keep it on file. The three men shook hands. Nathan returned to town and Bronco remained on the Big Iron in anticipation of his ranch work and Ranger Training.

After the usual introductions to other ranch hands and Flap Jack, Bronco began working on the Big Iron. After a few weeks with Laughlin silently observing him, Bronco had shown his talents. He chased and roped horses, was an excellent rider and no man could break horses like he could. He had a good attitude and everybody liked him.

One day when Bronco was down at the bunkhouse washing up for supper, Laughlin walked up to him and said, "Go get your pistol."

"What's going on Captain, you've got your gun strapped on. I ain't done nothing, have I?"

Laughlin grinned and said, "Naw, just go get your gun and gun belt." He did. "Now strap it on," demanded Laughlin, "unload your pistol, mines unloaded. I want you to pull on me, let's see how fast you are."

Bronco backed off till they were about twenty feet apart, looked at Laughlin and started his draw; he had barely cleared leather when he heard the click of the hammer falling on Laughlin's pistol. Bronco stood speechless; live ammo and he would have been dead.

Laughlin looked at him and said, "A Ranger lives by his gun, he must be fast and accurate or he dies." He could see the anxiety in Bronco's eyes as he instructed, "Now I want you to do the same thing that all my boys have done. Relax, stand in front of a mirror, look into your eyes and draw one hundred times a day; a Ranger must be fast and accurate." Then Laughlin told Bronco, "As a matter of fact, without speed and accuracy, you won't qualify as a Ranger."

Bronco said, "Thank you sir. I've never seen speed like yours; a man has no chance pulling on you."

"You'll do fine," responded Laughlin, "see you in thirty days and we'll do it again........meantime, keep up the good work."

Back in Abilene it was late in the day; Boots and Preacher had already spent several hours searching for the camp. They knew there were several old campsites that were used to hold herds brought to Abilene until pens were ready at the stockyards. When they rounded an outcropping of rocks, they spotted smoke in the distance and rode for it. As they approached the campsite they counted six men.

Boots said, "Check your pistol; let me do the talking."

They rode up to the camp; two of the men were pointing rifles at them and one of them said, "Hold up there, keep your hands where we can see 'em."

Boots said, "Howdy boys, put your rifles down. Don't mean no harm; we're Texas Rangers."

"Show us," said one of the men holding the rifles. When Boots and Preacher pulled back their coats and exposed their Ranger badge, the stranger said, "Okay, Lem, you and Claude put your rifles down." The voice had been coming from a man in his thirties. He was rugged looking with long dark hair, a stubble beard, and appeared to be a drover. A big Colt 44 was strapped on his side.

Boots made the introductions and when he called Jerry Jack Preacher, all six men had a good laugh. The one who had been doing all the talking, said, "What's a Ranger doing riding with a Preacher?"

"Aw," said Boots, "his gun does the preaching; then he does the reading over 'em"

With that said, the laughter came to an abrupt halt as the man said in a gruff voice, "My name is Delbert Youngblood; what can we do fer you boys?"

"Looks like you boys have been in camp for maybe a week or more," stated Boots, "what's the occasion?"

"Oh, we're just drovers;" said Delbert, "waiting on a herd to come thru, see if we can sign on."

"Well now," said Boots, "that's kinda strange since the drives end here and the herds are shipped on by rail."

Realizing his story had fell on deaf ears, Youngblood responded, "What's wrong Ranger, we ain't doing nothing, ain't causing no trouble."

"Mr. Youngblood that may well be the truth" said Boots, "but we'll be back out here tomorrow. Men with no jobs soon get into trouble, tomorrow be gone."

As Boots and Preacher rode off Boots asked, "Did you recognize any of 'em from wanted posters?"

"Yea," replied Preacher, "two of 'em; the Selman brothers, Bill and Earl."

"Wanted for robbery, right?" questioned Boots.

"Right, bank robbery; what's your plan?' asked Preacher.

Boots suggested they be ready in the morning at first light. His hunch was that bunch would hit the bank when it opens and before he and Preacher had an opportunity to check on them again.

To confirm his suspicions, Boots said, "We'll be ready. They know we know about them and I told 'em to be out of town; they'll ride in tomorrow, early."

Early the next morning Cletus, Boots and Preacher went to the bank. They had a bank guard inside with a shotgun. Preacher and Cletus were across the street on roofs and Boots was lying in the bed of a wagon in front of the bank. The guard had been instructed to let the men have the money; any fighting was to be outside in the street, not in the bank.

Just like on cue, fifteen minutes after the bank opened six masked men rode up in front. One man held the horses, the other five armed with pistols, went inside. After about five minutes the men came out carrying full saddlebags. Boots had crawled out of the wagon and was hidden behind the front wheel.

The men reached their horses but before they could mount up, Boots shouted, "Texas Rangers, drop your guns, you're under arrest."

CHAPTER 5

The bank robbers immediately started firing at the wagon, BOOM; a rifle from the roof dropped one of the men. BOOM, a second shot from the roof and another man fell. Preacher and Cletus had each dropped a man. The rest of the gang was looking up at the roof when Boots stepped out from behind the wagon and barked, "Drop 'em or die!" As they pulled around to fire at Boots he got off two shots so fast it sounded like one; two men fell.

By now, the bank guard armed with his shotgun, had come to the doorway. He fired from the hip and bank robber number five hit the dirt with his guts in his hands; he had taken a full load in the belly.

The last man standing threw down his gun, fell to his knees and begged, "Don't shoot, don't shoot, I'm done."

Cletus and Preacher came down from the roofs and carried him off to jail. The five bodies were taken to the undertaker. Later on they would be put on display for pictures and viewing as was customary in the west.

Jane, who had witnessed the entire shootout through the window of the newspaper office, ran to Boots. Crying and shaking she asked, "Are you alright, were you hit, are you wounded?"

Boots just laughed then gave her a big hug and told her he was fine. Then he said, "You don't think I'm gonna get myself killed after meeting you do you?"

Jane, having been reassured that Boots was fine, went inside the bank to calm Patti down; she had been present during the entire robbery and shoot out.

After calming down from the shock of it all, Patti said, "I'm glad JoJo wasn't here, he could have been killed. I worry about him." Then, all teary-eyed, she looked at Jane and sobbed, "Jane, I think I'm falling in love."

Jane, who was looking out the bank window at Boots as he walked toward the jail said, "Yea, I know how you feel."

Jane wrote a full accounting of the incident in the newspaper; it was evident word was out about law enforcement in Abilene. Hopefully, after reading her description of the attempted robbery, outlaws, at least those who were capable of reading, would have second thoughts about the Abilene bank.

While all this was going on, JoJo was about a days ride from Abilene, Kansas. The closer he got the more he thought about what he was going to do. He thought about the days when he was growing up without a Pa'. How the kids all called him a bastard and how he wondered what his Pa' looked like and why he didn't claim him as his son. Was this guy Emmett Ryker really his father; he had to know; was he Emmett Rykers' son, or not.

As he entered town he removed his Ranger star, put it in his pocket and took his horse to the livery stable. After assuring that Puddin' was taken care of, he went to the hotel, checked into a room and took a bath. He washed his trail clothes and, while they were drying, changed into his one extra set. After donning the fresh clothes, he dusted off his hat, strapped on his pistol belt and started toward the saloon.

With each step he took the more nervous he became; this might be the first time he sees his Pa'. When he reached the saloon, he stopped outside the swinging doors, got his composure and entered. Going directly to the bar, he ordered a shot of whiskey, turned around and scanned the room, not really knowing what he was expecting to see.

Sitting at a poker table in the rear was a well-dressed man. He was neat, approximately five feet eight and maybe a hundred 'n seventy-five pounds. He had on pleated trousers, new shiny boots, and a white shirt under a blue dress coat. The absence of a hat revealed a nice brown salt and pepper head of hair fully gray on the sides. He had high cheekbones and sported a somewhat pleasant smile. The man really seemed to be enjoying the poker game. Evidently he was doing well judging by the amount of chips in front of him.

JoJo stood at the bar sipping whiskey. When a chair emptied at the table where the man was playing, JoJo walked over and said, "I see you have an empty chair, mind if I try my luck."

"No, no, set right down," said the man.

There were two other men at the table. The older of the two said, "Let me introduce the table. This is Curtis, this is Emmett and I'm Walter. What's your name?"

JoJo told them his name and took his seat between Emmett and Walter, who said. "Good, nice to know you JoJo. Maybe we can win some of our money back from you; Emmett's got most of ours.

It was Emmett's deal; as JoJo watched his hands, he could tell he was a professional. They played a few more hands and Walter said, "JoJo, you look like a Texan, where you from?"

JoJo looked at Emmett and answered, "Ft Worth, born and raised in cowtown."

Emmett's eyes quickly left the cards he was holding as he raised his head to look at JoJo and asked, "What you doing way up here in Kansas?"

JoJo shot back, "Just some personal business," then he added sharply, "what say we just play cards, no more questions?"

Left in relative quietness, JoJo played five or six more hands, cashed out and went to the restaurant for supper.

He was sitting at a table waiting on his order when Emmett walked in, went to JoJo's table and said, "We played cards together, mind if I join you for dinner."

"No," replied JoJo, "pull up a chair, I'll enjoy the company."

Emmett sat down, placed his order and started the conversation. They talked about a couple of hands that JoJo had won when Emmett commentated, "You've got a good poker face." Then, suddenly, he switched the conversation to Ft Worth and stated, "You say you were born in Ft Worth, interesting place, a man can get in some big card games there."

JoJo, ignoring the reference to Ft. Worth, said, "I notice you don't wear a gun, must wear a shoulder holster or a sleeve gun, right."

"No," said Emmett, "I quit packing about three years ago; now I just try to avoid trouble." Then returning to his prior subject asked, "How long were you in Fr. Worth?"

JoJo answered, "Left there and started drifting when I was sixteen."

Without missing a beat, Ryker pressed on, "You still got family back there in Ft Worth?"

JoJo, with irritation in his voice, shot back, "Ryker, you sure ask a lot of questions but I'll take it that you're just trying to be friendly." He got no response from Ryker so he continued, "No, no family, Ma' died when I was five. Don't know who my Pa' is; guess that makes me a bastard. Never had a Pa'; was passed around from family to family after Ma' died."

Ryker, who was listening intently, did not say a word, so JoJo went on,

"When I was old enough to leave I did, been on my own ever since. Well Mr. Ryker, it's been nice visiting with you but I'm tired and ready for an early turn in." Without another word being spoken by either party, JoJo got up and went to his room. There was no doubt in his mind; Emmett was his Pa' but he decided not to ask; he would wait for Emmett to claim him.

Rumor had it that Abilene, Kansas was a rough town; said to be full of gunslingers, two bit outlaws and drunks. The town Marshal, Jim Putnam, was in his thirties, medium built and of average height. He had been the marshal for three years. He was clean-shaven with short hair and could be mean but, only as a last resort. He had no deputies and no control of the town. It appeared it was impossible to control the streets; seemed like the marshal just let the town manage itself. Nightly, drunken cowboys would shoot out windows and beat up the townsfolk; women were not safe on the streets after dark; as Town Marshall, he simply tried to stay out of the way and survive.

JoJo went to the marshal's office to meet him. He wanted to make Putnam aware that he was a Texas Ranger and was on personal business. Jim was glad to know he was a Ranger and said, "I may be calling on you for help."

Marshal Putnam said he could find deputies capable of controlling the town folk but it was the ruffians, outlaws and professional gunslingers that were taking over the state of Kansas; those he couldn't control. Violence was everywhere, bank robberies in Lawrence, Kansas and elsewhere as well as railroads being held up clear across the state. Crime and violence were getting out of control. JoJo told Putnam he would be conducting his personal business but would lend assistance when and where it was asked for; but he didn't want it to be known that he was a Ranger. The Marshall expressed his thanks and assured him he would keep his Ranger identity quiet; JoJo retired for the evening.

The next day JoJo was walking down the boardwalk toward the saloon when he saw three men sitting on the steps of the barbershop passing a bottle around. The barbershop was three buildings away from the saloon and when JoJo started to walk past them, one of the men said, "Hold up Texas, this side of the street belongs to us. You'll have to go to the other side; if you stay over here, you'll have to crawl like a baby."

Not being amused, JoJo replied, "Well I'm too tired to walk across the street and I don't know how to crawl, so I guess I'll just stay over here and whip some ass."

All three of the men were well on their way to being drunk. The one doing the talking jumped up and swung at JoJo who side-stepped the man; drew his pistol and hit him in the teeth with the barrel. Blood and teeth flew everywhere as the loud mouth fell to the street, out cold. JoJo pointed his pistol toward the other two men, who had risen to join the fight, and said, "Boys, looks like this is my side of the street, or do you want to argue about it. Getting no response, JoJo continued, "If not, pick up snaggle-tooth and carry him on across the street to your side."

Without a word, they picked him up by his armpits and staggered across the street.

JoJo walked on toward the saloon, entered, and spotted Emmett at a poker table. He nodded his recognition to Emmett, went to the bar and ordered a shot of whiskey. As he turned his back to the bar, the swinging doors were suddenly kicked open and in stepped the man JoJo had hit in the mouth. Blood was still flowing, his gun was in his hand and it was cocked.

He saw JoJo and said, "You're gonna die Texas," as he fired his 44. The bullet went harmlessly over JoJo's head. The next sound heard were the three shots coming from JoJo's pistol. The smell of gunpowder, mixed with tobacco, whiskey and blood, created the odor of death.

The silence was ear-splitting as the patrons in the bar were paralyzed by the swiftness of JoJo's gun. After reloading, JoJo watched the door and waited for the Marshal to arrive.

When Putnam came in he took JoJo's gun and asked, "What happened, who seen it?"

Emmett walked over and said, pointing at the body on the floor, "That man came through the door and fired at JoJo. JoJo drew and killed him, fastest draw I ever seen."

The bartender said, "That's right, there's a hole over there in the wall where the slug hit when he fired."

Putnam looked around and, when no one contradicted their stories said, "Some of you boys get 'im to the undertaker, here's your gun back Texas, let's go over to the jail and fill out a report."

When they got to the jail, the marshal told JoJo to watch out for the other two men. He advised him that they all ran together and might try to ambush him. From what Emmett said, Putnam was sure as hell they wouldn't draw against him.

After passing on the advice, Putnam asked, "Are all the Rangers fast as you?"

Without hesitation, JoJo answered, "Most of 'em are faster; we live by the gun; can't afford to be slow." Then he headed for the door, looked back and told Putnam, "I gotta go send a wire to my Captain; I'll see you after awhile," then, as an afterthought added, "save me some coffee."

After JoJo left, Ryker came in and asked if he could sit down and jaw for a minute. Putnam pointed to a chair and said, "Sure Emmett, what's on your mind?"

Emmett sat down, looked up at Putnam and inquired, "That Texas boy, what do you know about him; damn he's fast."

"All I know," said Jim, "he's from Fr Worth and he's up here on personal business." Then Marshall Putnam got an inquisitive look on his face as he said, "You spent some time in Ft Worth didn't you Emmett?"

"Yea, yea I did," responded Ryker, "what's his last name?"

"It's White, JoJo White" answered Putnam.

"Well, he's either a lawman or an outlaw, his gun's too fast," said Emmett. Then he got up, walked around the jail in thought, and mumbled, "But he's a likeable kid ain't he. Well I gotta go marshal, thanks for your time. Yes sir, likeable kid," and he walked out the door. The marshal just shook his head and wondered what the hell that was all about.

The next evening JoJo went to the saloon, ordered his whiskey, turned and spotted Emmett at his favorite table. He was playing poker with three other men JoJo hadn't seen before. The man sitting in front of Emmett was a big man, dressed like a gunfighter, not a poker player. He was having bad luck and Emmett was having good luck. Each time the gunslinger lost he would swear, take a drink of whiskey and complain about his luck.

JoJo paid attention; he could smell trouble coming. The man lost again, he swore, pushed his chair back, got up and pulled his pistol on Emmett. He said, "You're cheatin' me, nobody's that lucky. You're a two bit card shark; give me back the money you cheated me out of."

Emmett remarked rather pointedly, "I didn't cheat you out of anything; you're just a bad poker player." Emmett's' right hand was under the table and out of sight when he said, "I've got a 44 pointed at your gut. It'll take you a week to die from a gut shot, but you'll die. You may shoot me, but this hair trigger will get you. Now if you're smart you'll lay your gun on top of the table, back on out of here and cool down." Emmett had certainly gotten the gamblers attention as he continued, "Come get your gun from the bartender later on or be hauled out of here now, gut shot; it's your choice."

"How do I know you got a gun under the table?" inquired the man.

"You don't," said Ryker, "just pull the trigger and then you'll know."

Beads of sweat were all over the man's face. He thought for a while, then said, "Hell, it ain't worth it," and laid his gun on top of the table. When he walked out the door, JoJo slid into one of the empty chairs left at the table.

He looked at Emmett, whose hand was still under the table and said, "You told me you don't pack anymore."

Emmett grinned and said, "I don't," then brought his empty hand out from under the table.

JoJo just shook his head, got up and said, "Gotta go, I'm hungry; maybe I'll see you in the restaurant later." He took about two steps, turned back toward Emmett and said, "Join me for dinner; for the show you just put on, yours is free." When Ryker waved his hand and nodded in the affirmative, JoJo said, "About eight then." Ryker nodded again as JoJo walked out of the saloon.

The weather was getting bad; there was blowing snow, freezing temperatures and not much movement in the city. JoJo went back to his room to clean up a bit before heading for the restaurant to fulfill his promise to buy Emmett's supper.

Emmett was already at a table waiting when JoJo entered the restaurant. He walked to the table, pulled up a chair and said, "You're early."

"Yea," remarked Ryker, "I wanted to be on time, don't get many offers for a free meal," then he smiled. The meal was served; they ate, drank wine and talked.

Emmett said, "People are talking about the swiftness of your gun. You know, it's just a matter of time till some drunk or gunfighter tries to take you out."

"Yea, I know," said JoJo, "but I make my living with my gun, that's the chance I have to take."

Emmett, who it seemed just wouldn't get off the subject, said, "Tell me about your life in Ft. Worth."

JoJo said, "I was born there, my mother died when I was five, raised by my aunt and uncle. When I got old enough I left and went out on my own. Worked as a drover, whatever I could find, that's about it."

"Where's your Pa'?" asked Emmett.

"Don't know," replied JoJo, "never met him, don't know if he knows about me."

Ryker didn't respond but asked, "You said your Ma' died when you were five.....what happened?"

JoJo, who had been reluctant at first but was now, totally engrossed in the conversation, answered, "My aunt told me that after I was born, Ma' started drinking heavily and, in that five year span, drank herself to death. Said she truly loved my Pa' and never got over his leaving."

"Did your Pa' know she was with child?" queried Emmett.

JoJo told him he didn't know and if his aunt knew, she never told him either.

Emmett, who hadn't shown any emotion, asked, "How long you gonna be here in Kansas?"

"I'll leave when winter breaks," said JoJo, "then I can ride back to Texas,"

Without any further ado, Emmett thanked JoJo for the supper and told him he needed to get back to the saloon, couldn't let the cards cool off.

JoJo sat at the table for another half hour while his thoughts rambled. He thought, 'I may as well ride on out, maybe I won't get caught in the snow. He's my Pa' for sure but he ain't gonna claim me. I miss Patti, hell, should I give it more time; maybe he'll tell me. I just don't know.' With the weather getting worse all the time, JoJo decided waiting a while longer might be the prudent thing to do.

A week had passed and he hadn't had any further meetings of consequence with Emmett. He spent most of his time in his room, the restaurant or saloon and was being careful; he was expecting the two companions of the man he killed in the saloon to try and exact their revenge.

He had walked over to the saloon after a late supper. It was approaching midnight, the saloon was crowded, girls were dancing; men were chewing, spitting, gambling and beginning to get mean.

Marshal Putnam walked in; he was making his midnight rounds. Spotting JoJo at the bar, he joined him for a shot of whiskey. Emmett was at his usual table playing poker. Suddenly you could hear gunfire and running horses coming from the street. When the riders reached the saloon, they started riding in circles in the street then up on the boardwalk firing their pistols into the air and at windows.

JoJo and Marshal Putnam went to the door, looked out and counted six mounted gunmen. Putnam with sawed off shotgun in hand, looked at JoJo and said, "Are you with me?"

"Yea," said JoJo, "let's do it."

They stepped out on the porch of the saloon and the marshal hollered, "Party's over boys; put your guns up, no need for anybody to get killed."

JoJo recognized two of the men; they were part of the ones he made go to the other side of the street a week ago. When they saw JoJo, one of them hollered, "Marshal, why don't you run along home, we've got business with Texas." The boys and me are gonna show 'im what happens when he kills one of our boys."

By now the rest of the gunmen, who surely had been filled in on the incident, all began to holler, "We're gonna pay you back fer Ike. Shoot 'em boys." As a bullet screamed by JoJo's ear, he drew his sidearm and fired. The man doing the talking was knocked out of his saddle, tumbled backwards off his horse and died in a puddle of blood. Putnam fired his shotgun; blood, skin and hair flew as his load struck one of the men square in the face. Another shot was fired at JoJo as he answered with his large bore 44 and another man paid the piper. The remaining three turned their horses, spurred hard and rode out of town at a full gallop.

Marshal Putnam asked JoJo, "Are you alright?"

"Yea, how about you," answered JoJo, "you okay?" "I'm good," said the marshal. "Let's go back in; I'll buy you a drink."

They entered the saloon, ordered a double shot while the marshal, standing at the bar, directed several men to take the bodies to the undertakers and the horses to the livery stable. He took a sip of the whiskey, looked at JoJo and whispered quietly, "If all the Rangers in Texas are as good as you, no wonder Kansas is full of outlaws. Hell, you boys are runnin' 'em all outta your state." JoJo smiled and nodded; then they lifted their shot glasses, touched them together in a toast, and drank them down.

Emmett came over to the bar where the marshal and JoJo were standing, grinned and said, "Three out of six, that ain't bad." Then he added, "In case you don't know it, Black Jack Snyder is in town."

"No, I didn't know it," said Putnam "Where is he?"

"Checked in the hotel this evening; Connie's with him," said Emmett. He came over here, said he had some unfinished business with me, paid for Connie and took her to the hotel for the night."

"Tell me about Black Jack," said JoJo.

"He's a gunfighter/gambler," said the Marshall, "takes credit for eleven men killed in gunfights, notches' his pistol to keep count. Calls himself a professional gambler, can take the drovers money easy, against someone like Emmett he doesn't do so well."

"Why is he here?" asked JoJo.

"I can answer that," said Emmett. He's heard about you, wants to size you up and he's also after me. I took a lot of money from him last time we played."

"What does he look like?" inquired JoJo.

This time Putnam answered, "He's a left handed gun, dresses nice, like a Mississippi gambler. Has Black hair parted down the middle, handle bar moustache, dark mean eyes, fairly nice looking, medium build but less than six feet tall." Putnam thought for a moment then continued, "He's quick tempered and becomes violent if he loses."

"Ever see him pull leather?" questioned JoJo.

"No," said the marshal, "but they say he's fast, couple of good guns on his list. Fast Eddie Wilson and Yank Terell; he sent them to the Promised Land."

JoJo, having absorbed all that, said, "Bartender, give us three whiskeys. Come on Emmett; join us for a night cap." Emmett agreed and thanked JoJo for the invite but Marshall Putnam begged off, said he had to get back to the jail.

JoJo and Emmett were sipping on their whiskey when Emmett probed again asking, "JoJo, what was your mother's name?"

JoJo turned and with a cold stare, looked Emmett right in the eyes and said, "Mary, Mary White; why, ever hear of her?"

Emmett's expression didn't change as he answered without hesitation, "Yea, yea I've heard her name." JoJo continued to stare. Emmett turned up his glass, drank the whiskey down and said to JoJo, "Time for me to turn in, it's late."

JoJo was confused; did Emmett know about his mother being pregnant? Had she not told him in fear he would ride away; he knew his mother had worked in Hells Half Acre; maybe he just didn't want to claim the son of a whore.

Emmett was a likeable person and he knew he could accept him and like him as his Pa'. Why won't he say I'm his son? Once again his thoughts drifted to Patti, he missed her and wondered if she was thinking of him.

After a while JoJo walked out of the saloon and went to his hotel room. Once in the room, he laid down, looked up at the ceiling and said to himself, 'Shoe's on your foot Mr. Ryker; don't expect me to bring up Ft Worth.'

The next morning came early; it was a cold, sleeting Sunday. JoJo hoped it would be an uneventful day. He went down to the restaurant, sat down at a table by his self and ordered coffee, eggs, bacon, biscuits and gravy. On the menu it read Texas Breakfast; he laughed and waited on the food, he was hungry.

The restaurant door opened and in walked a man that had to be Black Jack. He found a table, sat down and ordered. He looked all around the room until his eyes found JoJo. Then he stared until his breakfast was served and he gave attention to his food. Both men ate and occasionally caught the other ones eye. Black Jack finished first, took his napkin, wiped his mouth, got up, walked over to JoJo's table and said, "You must be the one they call Texas."

CHAPTER 6

JoJo made no reply; what Black Jack didn't know was that JoJo's hand was under the table, holding his 44 cocked with a napkin hiding it from sight.

Black Jack repeated, "I said, you must be Texas."

"Who wants to know?" blurted JoJo.

"My name is Black Jack and I figure you're the fast gun they call Texas."

"I'll proudly answer to Texas," said JoJo whose expression had never changed and his eyes had never left Black Jack's. JoJo could see he had won the stare down.

Not showing any intimidation, Black Jack questioned "What's a Texas boy like you doing up here in Kansas?"

"Eating breakfast," said JoJo, still staring at Black Jack's eyes.

"You don't talk much do you?" said Black Jack.

"Yea, I'm a quiet man," said JoJo brazenly.

"Look here Texas," snorted Black Jack, "stay out of my way, I make my living with my gun, don't get in my way."

"You make your living with that one strapped on your left side."

"Yea that's right," said Black Jack with a puzzled look on his face.

"Nice looking piece," said JoJo, "got a bunch of notches on the handle."

Black Jack started smiling, "What kind of pistol you carrying, got any notches?"

"Naw, I ain't got any notches, never done that."

"Where's your pistol?" asked Black Jack "It ain't in your holster."

"No it ain't, It's pointed at your gut and has been ever since you walked over here," said JoJo.

"I don't believe you," barked Black Jack.

"Pull the table back real slow," replied JoJo, "but be careful, it's got a hair trigger and the hammers back."

Black Jack thought for a minute and then decided he had to know. So when he eased the table back, the napkin fell off revealing the gun in JoJo's hand; it was pointing at his belly.

Black Jack said, "Very good Texas, you're one up on me but I'll be seeing you later; stay out of my way, there'll be another time," Black Jack, having been bested, turned and slowly walked away.

JoJo laughed and said to himself, 'Wonder if I should tell Emmett I used his trick." Although he had gotten the best of Black Jack this time, he knew it would not be their last meeting.

The weather conditions had continued to worsen with the sleet turning to snow. All that, along with the Kansas winds, made the weather totally miserable.

The saloon was a gathering place during bad weather and it was full. When JoJo walked in he saw Emmett and Black Jack sitting at the same table with two other men. They were playing stud and Emmett was doing well.

Emmett was sitting where he could see JoJo but Black Jack had his back to the door and had not seen him walk in. JoJo went to the bar and waved the bartender away when he tried to serve him; he could smell trouble coming.

Black Jack lost a rather large hand and became upset and belligerent. He was swearing loudly, pushed his chair back, stood up, challenged Emmett and shouted, "You're cheating me, you ain't that lucky, these cards must be marked. Get up and draw or I'll shoot you where you sit."

JoJo eased around, stepped behind Emmett's chair and said loudly, "Simmer down Black Jack, this man ain't packin'."

"The hell he ain't," insisted Black Jack, "he's got a shoulder holster."

Again JoJo stated firmly, "He ain't packin', but I am, pull on me or turn around and walk out of here."

"My fights with him not you," snarled Black Jack.

JoJo was adamant as he insisted, "I can't let you shoot an unarmed man, if you want to kill someone, try me; I'm telling you, he ain't armed."

Marshal Putnam happened to be making his rounds and entered the saloon; he was carrying the sawed off shotgun. He saw what was going on so he held the double barrel at his hip, aimed it at Black Jack and growled, "Ain't gonna be no killin' around here tonight. Party's over Black Jack, get on out of here, don't come back tonight or I'll lock you up,"

Now Black Jack was really riled as he spouted, "All of y'all are gonna pay. Texas, you put your nose in my business after I told you to stay out of my way. I'll be seeing you real soon and Ryker, you better start wearing a gun. But hear me good, gun or no gun you're gonna go down, no one cheats me and lives to tell about it."

Emmett, unshaken by the melee, said calmly, "Black Jack, I'll strap on a gun right now if that's what you want or, drop yours and we can settle this man to man here and now."

"There'll be another day Ryker," muttered Black Jack, "there'll be another day." With that said, he walked out of the saloon and into the blowing snow.

This action put the quietus on the card game so JoJo, Putnam and Emmett strolled over to the bar and ordered a shot of whiskey.

After Raines, the bartender poured, Emmett commented, "JoJo what would you have done if the marshal hadn't walked in?"

"Killed him," said JoJo.

"I don't understand," said Emmett, "it was my fight, why did you take up for me?"

"Wasn't a fair fight," answered JoJo, "you weren't armed." Then JoJo realized he was assuming something that may not be in fact, so he looked at Emmett real serious like and inquired, "You weren't; were you?"

"No JoJo, I wasn't packin' and I appreciate you stepping in for me." Then Emmett looked over at Putnam, put an open hand to his brow in a mock salute, and added, "You too marshal."

The next day the snow storm had passed; JoJo, having finished his breakfast, was sitting in the hotel lobby reading the newspaper when a young boy came running in and said, "Mr. Texas, bartender Jim sent me to get you; says there's gonna be a gunfight in the saloon." JoJo jumped up, ran outside slipped on the ice and almost fell down on the boardwalk.

He hurried to the saloon, entered thru the front door and saw Black Jack and Emmett. They were at opposite ends of the bar; facing each other and preparing to draw.

JoJo looked at Emmett; he had a pearl handled 44 in a quick draw holster; his coat was pulled away from the pistol and hand poised to draw.

Black Jack was saying, "This is more than I could hope for, you're packin'." He hadn't seen JoJo enter as he continued, "What happened? I thought Texas did your fighting for you."

Emmett said, "Not likely Black Jack, I've always done my own fighting and today is no different." He was looking straight into Black Jack's eyes when he said in a rather nonchalant manner, "I've got five good cards turned down over there on that table waiting on me; you're wasting my time with all your talk. If you want to do it, let's do it, or get out of my face."

Emmett's eyes had lost the card playing gamblers look and had transformed into the eyes of a fearless gunfighter. Black Jack said, "Let's do it," and went for his gun.

The slug from Emmett's 44 struck him in the chest; Black Jack's gun fired, striking the floor in front of his feet as he fell dead. Customers ran out of the saloon to escape, some ran for the marshal. JoJo rolled Black Jack's body to see if he was dead, it was a heart shot. Once again the presence of death was in the saloon.

JoJo looked at Emmett and said, "Didn't think you ever packed a side arm?"

Emmett smiled back at JoJo and said, "Only when I have to."

JoJo got the feeling Emmett had done this to keep him from having to face Black Jack. Now JoJo had learned one more thing about Ryker, he knew how to use a pistol.

Several days passed, the snow melted and JoJo decided it was time to go home, back to Texas. He got all the provisions he could load on his packhorse and rode over to the marshals' office. Putnam and Emmett were in the office waiting when JoJo walked in. They said their good byes, JoJo walked out and mounted up as Emmett followed him out and stood beside his horse.

Just before JoJo headed out, Emmett looked up at him and said, "JoJo, your mama was a good woman, times were hard, don't think bad about her for the way she made her living." Then he handed JoJo his pistol and belt saying, "I'd be much obliged if you'd take these." As he handed them to JoJo, he added, "Not likely I'll need 'em again."

JoJo reached out and took them, nodded his thanks and then their eyes locked in on each other. JoJo waited, he was hoping Emmett would say more but when he didn't, JoJo said, "Well, I've got to be getting back to Texas." He gave one more hard look at the man he knew in his heart was his dad, then turned his horse around and rode away.

Emmett just stood there looking at JoJo as he rode off. A single tear was rolling down his cheek. Marshal Putnam walked up beside him and said, "Did he tell you he was a Texas Ranger?"

Rather surprised by the revelation, Emmett said, "No, he didn't mention it."

The Marshall was rather perturbed by Emmett's demeanor and barked, "Hell, Emmett, you know he's your boy. He looks just like you, why didn't you tell him you were his paw?"

Emmett, still watching JoJo fade out of sight, said softly, "Didn't earn the right."

Back in Austin, Sterling was doing well. He was still working as an attorney for Lloyd Henderson, Emily's father. Sterling and Emily were very much in love; she recognized the potential Sterling had in politics. It was certain they were not going to be rushing anything, especially marriage or a family.

The governor and Lloyd had been grooming Sterling for some time now and he had learned his role; he was becoming a very popular man in Austin.

One afternoon, while Sterling was in his office working on some documents, Henderson came in and said, "We have a lunch appointment tomorrow at the Capitol; the governor wants to see us." Then Lloyd grinned and commented, "My good man, great things are getting ready to happen for you."

Sterling returned the grin and said, "Do you think he wants me to run for office; be a Senator?"

"Well," responded Lloyd, why don't you just wait and see; you'll know at lunch tomorrow."

Sterling met Emily at a restaurant for dinner that evening. When he informed her of his lunch date the next day, she broke into tears and said, "I'm so excited I can't wait to hear what he has to say."

The next day the hours passed slowly; it seemed like an eternity before noon finally came around. Sterling and Lloyd went to the Capitol and were taken directly to the Governors' office. The Governor was waiting when the secretary announced them.

As she ushered them in, the Governor rose from his chair and said, "Welcome gentlemen, it's nice to see you. How are y'all doing?" Without waiting for an answer, he continued, "how's the family Lloyd? Sterling, when are you going to ask that pretty little Emily to marry you?"

With the questions being rhetorical in nature, the Governor did not wait for an answer he simply went on with "Let's get right down to what I've got to say." They had all been standing during the 'ice breaker' comments.

As they sat down, the Governor said, "Sterling, ever since I met you I've been watching you talking with Lloyd. Young man, you are extremely intelligent and hard working; harder working than any young man I've ever seen." He paused and looked over at Lloyd, who was nodding in agreement, and added, "Sterling, in my opinion, you're what Texas needs to help promote and grow this state.

We need railroads to carry goods from Galveston Bay and other areas of the country. Progress, education and new ideas, that's what we need; grow this great state and make it attractive for outsiders."

The Governor paused for a sip of the beverages his aide had set down when they entered; it was probably bourbon. He put his glass down and stated, as he pointed to Sterling and Lloyd, "I need someone to carry our ideas to the State Legislature; Sterling, I want to see you in Congress. After we have lunch today, you will go on the campaign trail with Lloyd here as your manager."

He paused momentarily to let Sterling savor the moment; then asked, "What have you got to say?"

Sterling was pleasantly surprised even though he suspected the Governor's actions. He took the news in and said, "Sir, I'm deeply honored that you have such confidence in me; I pledge to you that I will make every effort to make your wishes and mine come true."

"Well said, my good man, well said" replied the Governor, "now let's go have some lunch."

The next day Sterling sent a wire to Stewart Coffee in Abilene. He wanted to tell him the good news and thank him for everything he had done. Sterling knew that Stewart was the real catalyst that had started him on his road to the Texas State Congress. Not knowing where Boots might be at any given moment, he asked Coffee to let Boots know the good news the next time he saw him.

Meanwhile, for Bronco, time was passing quickly on the Big Iron; he had been in Uvalde for several months and really enjoyed working on the ranch. Laughlin and Melissa treated him real nice; like family. He knew any day now, Laughlin would be putting him thru his final test before becoming a Ranger. He was looking forward to that day, but he really enjoyed ranching. Life was good; for the first time since the war, he was happy.

Laughlin had been helping stretch some wire along a new stretch of fencing when a strand broke striking him on his right hand. It was cut deep and swollen; would probably take a couple of weeks to heal. Since he and Bronco were the only two working on the fence, Laughlin told Bronco to hitch up the wagon; they were going to town for much needed Supplies.

The ride gave Laughlin and Bronco an opportunity to talk. During the ride Laughlin asked, "Bronco, you been practicing on your draw?"

"Yes sir," answered Bronco, "every night' one hundred times, just like you said."

"How are you doing?" inquired Laughlin.

Bronco told his captain he wasn't fast yet, but he was a lot faster than when he started." Laughlin laughed and said, "Before we leave town, we'll go see Uncle Bester and get you a pistol with a quick draw holster."

Due to Laughlin's injury, he wasn't packing his pistol, but he did have his rifle in the wagon. He looked at Bronco and said, "That shooter strapped to your leg, if you pull, shoot to kill; remember, a wounded man can kill you real dead. Another thing, a slower draw will kill you if your first shot misses." He let Bronco 'chew' on that for a moment, then added, "When we get back to the ranch, I want to see you draw; then we'll work on accuracy. Confidence and a belief in yourself are key to building speed and accuracy. You have to relax; the more you relax the faster you are. Boots and the others had about the same speed you had when they started practicing; now their speed and accuracy is feared throughout the state; and fear kills!"

Bronco and Laughlin's plan was to visit the jail, general store, gunsmith shop and then home. As they passed the saloon Bronco saw a familiar horse tied to the hitching rail. He was sure it was his brother's. If so he was in the saloon liquored up with some of his drifter pals. Bronco wondered why his brother was in Uvalde; but figured it was either to cause trouble or try to join up with him again.

Bronco and Laughlin stopped the wagon in front of the jail; immediately Nathan and Oral came out to greet them. "You boys too old for a horse; have to ride in a wagon?" ribbed Oral.

They all laughed, then Laughlin asked, "How's the town?"

Oral stopped laughing, got serious and said, "Three fellers rode in two days ago; been hanging around the saloon drinking. A couple of times, they've gone over to the bank acting real suspicious."

Bronco figured it was time to tell Laughlin his suspicions and revealed, "Laughlin, I think one of 'em might be my brother, Jack. I'm pretty sure I spotted his horse tied up in front of the saloon. He's no good; I shoulda told ya sooner, guess I was hoping I might be wrong but, after what Oral just said, I thought I'd better tell you now." After looking at Laughlin to see if he was upset, Bronco added, "If it is him, he's trouble; he'll probably start something with me."

Laughlin nodded at Bronco and said, "Glad you told me, that couldn't have been easy. Oral, we'll take care of our business first; then Bronco and I will visit the saloon."

They went to the general store, gave a boy their list, telling him to load the wagon; then they went to see Uncle Bester at his gun shop. Bester was a real old timer but he knew his guns. That old man could fit you with a rifle and load for long range shooting or he could give you a quick draw holster with a customized shooter; a real Ranger special. Uncle Bester was still Uncle Bester; Laughlin had known him for years; he never changed. Blue trousers stuffed inside knee high leather boots, buckskin shirt, gallowses', ten-gallon hat, long hair, moustache, no beard and reading glasses on the tip of his nose.

When they opened the door, they were immediately greeted by ole' Uncle 'B' himself. "Hello Laughlin," he, said, "I figured ya'll were about due, bet you want a rifle and pistol for this feller."

"Yes sir," responded Laughlin, "you figured right: you got one of my specials in stock?"

"Hell Captain," Bester muttered, "I always stay one up on ya; when I sell you one, I build another one." He glanced over at Bronco and said, "Here you are young feller, 44-40 Winchester lever action with adjustable rear sight and a 44-40 peacemaker pistol with a hair trigger and cutaway trigger guard."

"You got it," said Laughlin, "give him some ammo and send the Rangers the bill?"

Bester said, "Laughlin you ain't packin', what's wrong with your hand?"

"Got it caught up in some barbed wire," barked Laughlin, "it'll be fine in a few days."

They completed their business and headed for their last stop, the saloon. They entered the saloon, walked up to the bar and looked around the room.

Bronco nudged Laughlin and said, "That's my brother at the poker table by the rear wall. The two boys with him are the Tacketts; they're gunmen." He paused for a moment, then added; "probably on wanted posters."

Bronco's brother, Jack, saw him standing at the bar; he left the table and walked over to greet him. "Hello brother," he said, "how's it going?"

When he put out his hand to shake, Bronco took it and said, "Ranger McFarland meet my brother, Jack."

"Hello Jack, what brings you boys to town?" asked Laughlin.

Nonchalantly, Jack answered, "Aw, we're just sightseeing, going from town to town, you know, taking in the sights."

"Well enjoy your time in Uvalde but stay out of trouble" stated Laughlin, then in his usual style, added a bit of punctuation with, "I don't tolerate any trouble."

"We won't cause any trouble," said Jack, with a grin. He couldn't help himself, so he added, "Brother when I ride out of here are you going with me, or stay here and be a two bit star packer."

The remark was not received well by Laughlin who said, "We're going over to the sheriffs' office, then we'll be back. You and your smart mouth need to be gone; take your two pals with you. When we come back I highly recommend that you three be gone."

"Well now Ranger, you're being down right unsociable; we ain't done nothing", responded Jack.

"Jack, be gone," urged Bronco you ain't big enough to mess with the Rangers." He didn't want him dead; he was no good, but Jack was his brother.

Laughlin and Bronco went to the jail, looked at the wanted posters and found the Tacketts were wanted for armed robbery.

Laughlin said, "Oral, make Bronco your deputy; then me and him are gonna go make an arrest."

"Laughlin, you can't use your right hand," cautioned Oral.

"I know," grumbled Laughlin, "give me a scatter gun. Let's go Bronco, you arrest 'em, then we'll put 'em in jail."

Bronco said, "Let's go do it, just stand at the door and cover me."

When they entered the saloon, Bronco walked straight to where the three men were sitting. When he reached their table he made a very respectful fast draw, pointed the 44-40 at the three men and said, "Y'all are under arrest. With your left hand, quietly lay your guns on the table; anyone talks, I'll shoot 'em." Without a word, all three complied as Bronco ordered, "Let's go, move it, we're going to jail." They were marched to the jail, booked and locked up.

After they were in their jail cells, Bronco heard one of the Tacketts say to Jack, "You said he wasn't fast, that you were faster than him, you're a damn liar; all us would be dead if we'd pulled on him."

Oral said to Laughlin with a grin, "How did my new deputy do?"

Laughlin grinned and said, "Take back that deputy badge." Bronco looked at Laughlin; he thought he had not done well. Laughlin slapped him on the back and said, "When you take that deputy badge off, put a Ranger star on his chest. I'm gonna swear him in; he's ready."

Laughlin looked at the Tackett brothers and said, "Y'all are being held till the circuit judge gets here. You're under arrest for armed robbery as stated on your wanted posters." Then Laughlin looked at Jack and said, rather harshly, "Jack, you'll be held overnight then we'll let you go. There's no law against hanging out with trash but I suggest; change your life like your brother has, or you won't live long."

Bronco and Laughlin, having finished their business, got in the wagon and headed for the Big Iron. Bronco was beaming; he was a Ranger.

Laughlin said, "Bronco, You did good. That draw was smooth; tomorrow, we'll see how accurate you are." Without looking at Bronco, Laughlin asked, "What about your brother?"

Without hesitation, Bronco replied, "Not a chance, he's on his way to a short life, wish I could help him, but I guess there's no hope for him."

Laughlin said, "I'll keep you around Uvalde for awhile and when I get the opportunity, switch you and Preacher out. Boots will be good for you to train under and Preacher will appreciate the time here in Uvalde; his sweetheart is here; I suppose she'll appreciate it too."

When JoJo reached Stephenville he wired Laughlin and told him he was returning. Laughlin directed him to board a train with his horse and go to Ft Worth. The Ft Worth sheriff, Jim Elick, had been gunned down in Hell's Half Acre; he was to meet with the new sheriff, Frank Pryor. It appeared Ft Worth was in need of a town tamer; fast.

JoJo was glad he was being sent to Ft Worth. He was hoping this would allow him some time with his aunt and uncle; he wanted to talk about Emmett.

He put his horse in a cattle car while he was riding passenger. This was his first trip on a train; it was fun and exciting. He listened as the locomotive pulled away from the station. It was powerful, but slow starting. At first the power wheels would make a half turn creating a loud choo, the black smoke would boil, then another choo, the wheel turned a little faster, then choo-choo, then finally choo-choo-choo and the train was rolling.

They had to stop every thirty miles and take on water for the boilers; that's when they would be vulnerable to outlaws. Most of the train robberies occurred at water stops. The usual scenario, outlaws would rob the passengers, break in the mail car, blow up the safe and sometimes flee with as much as seventy thousand dollars. For the most part, it was the James Gang terrorizing Kansas railroads and getting away with large sums of money.

JoJo went to the dining car for lunch and sat at a table with a clergyman, Homer Rangold, and his wife Marynell. They carried on casual conversation during the meal until JoJo asked the preacher if he could question him about God. The preacher, an elderly man, said, "Certainly and I'll be glad to try and give you an answer."

With that assurance, JoJo asked, "Preacher, how do you know there's a God?"

Homer smiled and said, "I have faith. I have faith there is a God. God controls your life, everything happens for a reason. We are all gods' children. He loves us and forgives us of our sins."

"Preacher," said JoJo, "I'm a Ranger and I've killed some men, can I go to Heaven?"

"There is only one way to Heaven son," answered Rangold, "and that is thru Jesus Christ who died on the cross so our sins could be forgiven; If you have accepted him as your lord and savior, then you'll go to Heaven and have eternal life."

"Preacher," said JoJo, "I was on my way to being an outlaw, probably a gunfighter when one day something happened; instead of being cut in half with a shotgun I was given a second chance. My life changed and now I'm a Ranger, working on the side of the law."

"You see JoJo," said the preacher, "like I said, God has a plan for us all. He came into your life and gave you a chance for a new start." Homer thought for a moment and reflected, "Young man, it wasn't a coincidence that we are on this train, eating at the same table. Please remember, it's not easy walking with God, he acts in mysterious ways. When they got off at the next stop, the preacher looked at JoJo, patted him on the back and said, "God bless you son."

After Homer and Marynell left, JoJo thought to himself, 'I hope Boots and Preacher are on their way to Ft Worth, I need to talk some more about God.'

The train was about thirty miles north of Ft. Worth preparing to stop in Saginaw, Texas. As the engineer stopped the locomotive under the water tower, the chute was lowered and they began taking on water. JoJo went outside, walked to the cattle car, to see if Puddin' was riding well, when he heard the distinct sound of hoof beats and gunfire. JoJo's position in the cattle car kept him from being seen.

From his vantage point he could see six masked men; one went to the engineer, three to the mail car and two entered the passenger car. He knew the passengers were being robbed of their money and jewelry, anything of value. JoJo knew the routine; the men inside the mail car would dynamite the safe, stuff the money in bags, then come outside to their horses for their getaway. The robber holding a gun on the engineer would probably take him out; then leave.

BOOM! The dynamite exploded. JoJo had taken his Winchester rifle from its saddle holster and taken a position behind the cattle car; he was waiting for the men to come out of the mail car. The men would be in the open while mounting their horses, presenting an easy sixty yard shot.

CHAPTER 7

Suddenly, three men, with stuffed bags in their arms jumped, out of the mail car and ran for their horses. JoJo had the rifle braced on a slat in the cattle car as he took careful aim. BOOM! One man went down well before he reached the horses. BOOM! He missed. BOOM! The second man went down. The third man was on his horse and the two that were in the passenger car had also made it outside.

They located JoJo and were rapidly firing their pistols; sending lead in his direction, keeping him pinned down while they mounted up. As they were riding off, JoJo's rifle spoke again and one of the men slumped forward over his horse's neck; wounded, but not dead. The man with the engineer came running out. By now, any horse without a rider had spooked and ran off; he was on foot. One of the other riders rode by, swung him up, and they galloped off riding double.

In a span of less than three minutes, JoJo had dropped two men dead and wounded another. Also, since only one man got away carrying a stuffed saddlebag, he had saved about two thirds of the money. Although four men had escaped, one of them was wounded and most of the money was safe; all in all, it was a pretty good day for a Ranger.

After the episode was over and everyone settled down, the train restarted and continued toward Ft Worth. Once they arrived, JoJo would immediately report to the sheriff so a posse could be organized.

The train pulled in to Ft Worth and stopped at the depot. JoJo stepped down and went to fetch Puddin from the cattle car. There, standing in front of the depot, was Boots and Preacher grinning from ear to ear. Their assignment was to join JoJo in hopes of taming Cow Town, as Ft. Worth was commonly referred to.

After JoJo got Puddin off the train, he told Boots and Preacher about the robbery. The three Rangers rode to Sheriff Pryor's office, tied up their horses and went inside. Although Boots and Preacher had arrived in Ft. Worth a day before, they hadn't met the sheriff yet.

Sheriff Pryor was in his mid-thirties, approximately five foot ten inches tall, a strong muscular man. He had a dark complexion, protruding eyebrows and hard dark eyes. Frank had boxed some and sported big forearms with extremely large fists. Pryor's face still reflected battle scars from his bare-knuckle days in the ring. It was certain he was not afraid and would probably still enjoy a good fight; fist or gun.

After the usual intro's, JoJo brought the Sheriff up to par on the train robbery and asked if he was going to form a posse to go after them. Pryor said, "No use, they're already here, this is where they come to spend the money and enjoy women; they know law enforcement is weak."

Pryor saw the surprised look on the Ranger's faces and figured they were probably wondering, if he knew where they were, why were they still there? He gave them a minute to wonder then growled, "Boys, there are two bad areas in Ft Worth, Hell's Half Acre and the stockyards. Hell's Half Acre is south of town and mainly offers saloons and brothels with lots of girls. The other area is across the Trinity River north of town, at the stockyards. There are saloons, brothels and lots of money. When herds are brought in and sold, there's big money in town and, as you know, that spawns whiskey, women and trouble.

Sheriff Elick was in one of those saloons, over on Exchange Street in the stockyards, when he was shot in the back trying to make an arrest. When the drovers come to town there's always trouble. As I said, there's a lot of money and that draws gamblers, gunslingers, outlaws, whores, and card sharks."

Sheriff Pryor said he only had two deputies and they were young and inexperienced, they really weren't gun hands. He said no one wanted to wear a badge in Ft. Worth, it was too dangerous.

"Then why do you wear one?" asked Boots.

"I like a fight and I knew you boys would be coming," said Pryor, "my two deputies, you three Rangers and I, together, can do a lot to tame things down."

Pryor looked at the three Rangers rather hopefully and stated, "I'd like to start tonight if you boys are ready; if so, meet me here at six this evening."

The Rangers agreed; then walked out and headed toward the hotel. "Reckon he's as tough as he acts?" asked JoJo.

Boots remarked, "The bartender said he's tough, damn tough, just not enough help to handle all of 'em."

"Well," remarked JoJo, "we'll just give him a hand and see what he can do. Hells fire, it can't be worse than Kansas; I been dodging bullets ever since I left Texas."

"Oh, I meant to tell you," said Boots, "your girlfriend left town with a gambler."

JoJo's head snapped around as he gazed at Boots. Boots couldn't keep a straight face; he burst out laughing; he loved to have fun.

It was almost dark when the men gathered at the jail. Sheriff Pryor handed each Ranger a sawed off shotgun loaded with buckshot and a bandolier loaded with shells.

Pryor said, "Tonight I want to showcase you Rangers. When they see Rangers, it's different than seeing just a sheriff like me. They also know you can have twenty Rangers on the next train. Let's ride down to the stockyards; it's about two miles straight down Main Street. We'll stay together and carry our shot guns as we enter every saloon."

Boots asked, "Do you want to make some arrests?"

"Yea," said Pryor, "I would like to arrest Harry Davis. He's got five brothers; they all practically live in the saloon drinking all day and night."

The sheriff loaded a sixth round in his sidearm, as did the others, then he added, "Harry gets in about four fights a night while his brothers back him up. You can't take on just one of 'em; you've got to fight them all. I can take care of Harry if you boys can keep the brothers off me."

The jail sits on a high bluff south of the Trinity River. North Main Street crosses the river and leads to Exchange Street where the stockyards are located. On the south end of Main Street is downtown Ft Worth and Hell's Half Acre. Just these two areas, not to mention the rest of

Ft. Worth, is a lot of area to be patrolled by a sheriff and two rookie deputies.

They mounted up, rode down Exchange Street, crossed the river and tied up to a hitching post in front of the Western Bar. As they dismounted, Boots said, "Boys, here's what I want. Remember, we're here to intimidate so we all walk in without any conversation and walk slowly from table to table like were looking for someone. Stare down everyone we look at and say nothing; then walk out when I do."

When they entered The Western Bar it was loud; the piano man was playing, men were swearing and the ladies were hanging on the players around the poker tables. Men were pouring whiskey down, laughing and lying to each other. As the Rangers went from table to table, they had the shotgun butts down with the barrels pointed up. They Held them in the crease of their left arm, freeing up their right hand for their pistol, if needed. Their badges were exposed; they faces were stern and they stood straight up as they moved slowly through the crowd.

As everyone recognized who they were, the piano became silent, loud voices reduced to a murmur and the saloon became silent. All eyes were on the four men and the Rangers gave each person the death stare. After completing their walk around the room, they turned and started toward the door. Boots walked along side the bar and looked deliberately at the bartender; he had been frozen, with a towel in a glass, since they came in. Boots stopped in front of him, still staring, and nodded his head as all three Rangers and the Sheriff walked out the door.

Once outside, Pryor said, "JoJo, did you see the faces of any of the train robbers?" "No," said JoJo, "they all had on masks, but one of 'em was short and fat with light colored hair. His forehead appeared red above the mask, so he is probably a red faced person."

Pryor reacted to the description and remarked, "That sounds like Harry Davis. Pull your hats down boys; next up is the Maverick Bar, that's where Harry and his brothers hang out; may stir up a little trouble there."

The Maverick Bar had a stage, piano, dance floor and rooms in the balcony for the girls and their clients. It was full of drunks, poker tables and pool tables; if possible, it was even louder than the Western Bar and the smoke was so thick you could hardly see across the room. When the lawmen walked thru the door, with shotguns in hand and started their walk, they got the same reaction as they did across town; complete silence. You could have heard a pin drop; it was almost like time had stopped, except for the Rangers and Frank. All eyes followed the four men as they walked around the room. The silence continued until a short red-faced man came stumbling out of one of the rooms upstairs.

It was Harry Davis; he came down the stairs shouting, "What the hell's going on, who stopped the music?" Harry was drunk and had not yet seen the lawmen. He went to the piano player and said, "Start playing." When he didn't, Harry hit him.

Sheriff Pryor walked up to Harry and barked, "That's enough Harry, back off."

Evidently Harry was too drunk to have noticed the three Rangers in the building as he shouted, "Y'all ain't never gonna learn, the last lawman's dead; you'll be next if you keep coming in here stopping my parties."

Harry had played right into Sheriff Pryor's hands. Knowing he had backing this time, Frank said, "Harry you just threatened a peace officer, you're under arrest."

Harry, still unaware of the situation, growled, "Ain't no lawman, especially you, gonna arrest me. You'll have to whup me first; me and my brothers need to teach you a lesson." As he finished his remarks, Harry drew back to throw a punch. Frank saw it coming and threw a straight right from his shoulder that landed directly between Harry's eyes. Franks' big fist hit him with the power of a mule kick. Harry was out before he hit the ground.

Three men, Harry's brothers, jumped up from the poker tables to join in when Boots' shotgun blasted a hole in the ceiling. Four shotguns were aimed at the men as the sound of the shotgun restored the silence and made previously violent men meek.

Boots ordered, "Sit back down boys and keep your hands above your heads." Then, motioning towards Preacher and JoJo, he said, "Throw some water on Harry and then git 'im on his horse, he's going to jail."

As they were dragging Harry out the door, Boots moved over, stood beside Frank and addressed the crowd, "Alright, listen up, the Rangers are here, if there's not enough of us now, keep acting a fool and there will be." He definitely had their attention, so he went on, "There will be law and order in Ft Worth, what you saw tonight is just the beginning. We are going to clean this town up, so spread the word; the Rangers are here."

By the time the men reached the jail, the cool night air may have cleared Harry's head of cobwebs, but his forehead was swollen and his eyes were starting to swell shut; they were both black and blue.

After Harry was placed in jail, the three Rangers and Sheriff Pryor gathered to discuss the night's activities. As they sat and sipped some much needed coffee, Boots said, "Tonight we made a statement; they know we're in town and we mean business. That could be a double edged sword; we've lost the element of surprise, things could be different next time. They all agreed the rest of the night would probably be quiet since nothing had happened at The Western Bar, and the ruffians in the Maverick Bar would be massaged their bruised ego's with more whiskey and big talk.

The next morning JoJo told Boots he needed to be gone about three hours on personal business. Boots said, "Fine, take as long as you like, we've got it under control." Then, remembering last nights action, instructed JoJo to be back by dark in case Harry Davis' brothers had any retaliation in mind."

JoJo assured Boots he would return by sun-down then he mounted up and rode to an area north of the river and south of the stockyards. It was the area where his Aunt Hattie and Uncle Arch lived. They had taken him in after his mother died. He was only five at the time and barely remembered his mother.

Aunt Hattie and Uncle Arch had been nice to him. He knew they were poor and was sure his presence created a hardship; that's why he left at sixteen. When he arrived at their place, they were thrilled to see him; Aunt Hattie wept.

JoJo told them about his trip to Kansas, that he was a Ranger and how his life had changed. They expressed how proud and happy they were for him. Uncle Arch said they had no pictures of Emmett and they hadn't heard from him for over twenty years. Aunt Hattie told him that Emmett lived with his mother until he was born; then he just rode off.

"After that, Mary grieved and drank herself to death, she really loved Emmett" said his aunt, then she continued, "She had worked at

Hell's Half Acre as a waitress for only about two weeks when she met Emmett. When she became pregnant, and Emmett left her, she never went back to Hell's Half Acre, even though with the war having just ended, times were hard and a single woman had no way of making a living. That's when she turned to the bottle."

JoJo figured Emmett wasn't certain he was the father since his mother had worked in Hell's Half Acre. JoJo knew his Aunt Hattie was being kind when she said that Mary had worked there as a waitress. Besides, there was no way to prove Emmett was the father of the baby, so, evidently he just rode away from the situation. He didn't think Emmett would ever claim him, but in his own heart he knew Emmett was his pa'.

JoJo didn't know it but, in Kansas, things had changed for Emmett; he missed not being around JoJo. He wondered if he new the truth about the baby; was he the father or had he been lied to by Mary. One thing for sure, he missed JoJo.

JoJo thought and reasoned till he thought he had an answer. When he was born, Emmett left and Mary called him 'White' because she would be the one raising him, knowing Emmett didn't claim him and would never be back.

Arch said, "JoJo, I didn't like Emmett, we all knew you were his, but he wouldn't claim you. He wrote your mother a couple of times while he was in Kansas. We wrote him when she was dying and he started on his way down here but he was too late; she had already died." Thinking back to those hard times brought tears to Arch's eyes, He paused, wiped his eyes, and went on with his story, "He told me he wanted to take you with him but you were only five and couldn't live his kind of life. I told him he hadn't done anything for you. Told him to ride on out of here and don't come back; if he did, I'd kill 'im. Well, he rode off and didn't come back 'til you were nine; just rode up one day and told me he wanted to take you with him."

"Why didn't you kill him," asked JoJo.

Arch looked over at his aunt and said, "Your Aunt Hattie, the fine Christian woman that she is, wouldn't allow it, said Mary wouldn't want me to." He paused and, as he patted Hattie on the knee, looked back at JoJo and said, "I just told him no, his lifestyle was no life for you. Then I told him at gunpoint he'd better ride on and leave you alone; Hattie and I would raise you. Well, he never came back no more after that."

At that time JoJo's uncle told him his name should be JoJo Ryker; Emmett was surely his Pa'. Then Arch looked up at JoJo; he had a forlorn look on his face when he said, "Son, me and Hattie love you and tried to do what was best for you. Please don't hold it against us for not telling you sooner what we believed and knew in our hearts."

JoJo responded, "Aunt Hattie, Uncle Arch, Y'all did what was best for me and I love you both with all my heart."

JoJo rode back to the hotel, once in his room he layed back across his bed, looked at the ceiling and said 'someday Emmett you will tell me, but I won't ask you.' His thoughts soon drifted to Patti and he wished he were in Abilene with her.

Boots, Preacher and JoJo were impressed with Sheriff Pryor; there was no back down in him; all he needed was some deputies. One of his deputies was a fellow named James Lee Brock, he was new, but was a rugged individual. Brock was broad shouldered; a strong built man. He was fairly nice looking and sported a left handed rig with the usual single action 44. His weakness was women and drinking; he enjoyed his booze and sometimes took it to the extreme. The other deputy, a fellow named Roy Moore, had the makings of a good lawman; he was fearless, just didn't have any experience.

The next evening, two rangers and one deputy went to Hell's Half Acre while the sheriff, one ranger and a deputy visited the stockyards.

Boots, JoJo and Brock went into a saloon-brothel in Hell's Half Acre and one of the girls came running up to Brock. Her face was swollen and bruised; she had been beaten. She told Brock one of the men paid her to go to his hotel room. When she got there, there was a wounded man and two other men in the room. They partied all night; when they got drunk one of the men beat her up. She said when they were drunk she overheard them arguing over how to split money up from a train robbery. The girls name was Cody and she was evidently a friend of Brocks. She told them the men were staying at Hell's Half Acre's White Owl Hotel; in room 303. Brock comforted her as best he could, and then asked her to keep them informed, if she heard anything else.

Boots said, "Looks like we found your train robbers JoJo. Either Harry Davis isn't the short, fat red faced rider you saw, or these guys in 303 are part of his gang.

JoJo said, "Think so too, we're ready; we've got our shotguns, what say we go get 'em? Then JoJo looked at Pryor's deputy and said, "Brock, are you ready?"

"Let's go," said Brock, as he gulped a slug of whiskey from his flask.

When they got there, the hotel had only one stairway leading upstairs. Boots said, "When we get to the room, I'll kick in the door and holler "Texas Rangers! You're under arrest; then I'll step to my left. JoJo, you stay center and Brock, you step to my right." He waited for them to nod their understanding, then ordered, "Shoot anybody that goes for a gun. Use the shotguns and shoot to kill."

They moved into position. Boots kicked the door and as it flew open, he shouted, "'Texas Rangers' you're under arrest."

A half naked man dove for his pistol which was hanging from a chair. Boots fired one barrel of the shotgun striking him on the right side of his head; he died instantly. Another man, sitting at a table drinking, reached for his pistol; Brock eliminated him with a single blast to the face. The wounded man, Cody had alluded to, was on the couch; the fourth man was in bed naked, with a whore. They both surrendered without putting up a fight. The bodies of the two dead outlaws were hauled out and taken to the undertakers. The other two were taken to the Tarrant County jail.

The next day the Rangers rode out to the Oak Wood Cemetery, located on the north side of Ft Worth just north of the Trinity River. JoJo's mother was buried there somewhere and he wanted to find the grave. Not knowing the exact gravesite, they began searching for a marker with the name Mary White. After awhile JoJo stopped in front of a marker, it read: Mary Ryker. He was stunned, had she done this on her own before she died; had Emmett married her to give JoJo a name and if so, why wasn't he called JoJo Ryker. The puzzle between JoJo and Emmett Ryker just kept getting more and more complicated. Without a word, JoJo stood over the grave for a respectable amount of time; then suggested they return to town. He did not relay his thoughts or feelings to any of the Rangers over the mystery of his last name.

When they got back to town, Boots, Preacher and JoJo met Frank at the jail. Harry Davis and the train robbers hadn't said three words to each other; they wouldn't even give the marshal their names. Didn't make any difference, the circuit judge would sentence them, name or no name.

The Rangers were passing small talk and sipping on a cup of coffee, when a rather large man came thru the front door. He was over six feet tall, weighed about two hundred ninety five pounds and was probably on the short side of 50. He was broad across the shoulders with huge arms and a big belly; but he appeared to be very strong. He was clean-shaven and projected the image of a rugged trail boss; which he had been most of his life. His name was George Brock, Deputy James Lee Brock's Pa'.

Frank said, "Come in George; I want you to meet some Rangers." As George entered, the three Rangers stood up and shook his massive hand as Pryor introduced them: "This is Boots, JoJo and Preacher."

"Glad to meet you boys," said George, "I'll tell you, y'all got the town scared to death; fact is, the bad boys are leaving town."

Frank nodded his head in agreement and said, "George, I think you're right and, hopefully, you came in here to accept the jailer's job as one of my deputies."

"Yea," commented George, "sign me on. Not enough drives anymore to keep me out of trouble and my boy says you're a good man to work for." "Now my question is," he continued, "is my boy worth a damn, does he earn his pay?"

Without hesitation, Frank said, "You bet, along with Boots and JoJo here, he brought in that bunch that held up the train, shot 'n killed one of 'em." Sheriff Pryor watched the pride swell up in George as he added, "Come on over here, raise your right hand." As he did so, Frank swore him in and pinned a deputy's badge on him.

About that time, a young boy ran in to the office, out of breath, and gasped, "Doc Greines asks that you and the Rangers get over to his office, pronto."

Doc Greines, who had been practicing for over thirty years, was semi bald, short, over weight with a quick temper and a very low tolerance level.

Not knowing what had happened, expecting the worse, the foursome rushed over to the doc's office, guns in hand. When they entered the office, guns drawn, Greines came out of the back room, waved his hands and shook his head demonstrating his aforementioned lack of tolerance, and grumbled, "Put those damn things away, hell, the trouble ain't here, it's over at the tracks.

Still not sure about what was happening; the men holstered their pistols and followed the Doc. He led them to three beds with men lying in them. They were heavily bandaged with multiple bruises, cuts, a broken arm and cracked ribs; not all on the same man but in combination.

"Frank, look at these men," said Greines, "their damn near beat to death. Something has got to be done about that railroad bull, Ft. Worth Red." He hesitated while the Sheriff and the Rangers took in the scene; then continued, "I know the railroad hired him to keep hoboes off the train but damn it, this isn't necessary. These are good men, ex-soldiers with no money, no way to get back home except steal a ride in a boxcar........Red needs to be toned down." As he led the four men back to the front parlor of his office, he urged, "Sheriff, you need to talk to him."

"Thanks Doc," said Frank, "we'll talk to him."

They went back to the jail and Frank sent James Lee to the stockyards depot to get Red and bring him in for questioning. A couple hours later, James Lee came in with Ft. Worth Red, the famous railroad bull; he had disarmed him when he made the arrest. Red was, of course, red headed with a rough complexion. He stood six foot five and weighed in at over two hundred and eighty pounds. Red was cocky and thought that he was mean and tough. He came thru the jailhouse door swearing and complaining.

"What the hell's going on," he grumbled, "you star packers arresting me for throwing bums off the train? Hell, that's my job, that's what I get paid to do." Red was worked up and continued ranting, "Y'all hide behind your stars, pistol whip drunks and think you're tough. Let me tell you, I'm six foot five, weigh two hundred eighty five pounds and can whip any man alive." With defiance in his tone, he jerked away from James Lee and spouted, "I sure as hell ain't afraid of you boys and I'm leaving now.....git out of my way or I'll hurt you."

George had stepped over to an empty cell, unlocked it and opened the door. As Red started to walk out George grabbed him by one arm, twisted it up behind his back, walked him to the cell and shoved him inside. He closed and locked the door; Red was cussing and demanding to be let out.

Frank, who had not gotten up from the domino table, stood, removed his gun belt, layed it on the table, walked to the cell door and said, "Red, you think you're tough; you like to beat up on crippled soldiers and young men." "Well," continued Frank, "I'm gonna give you a chance to show me just how tough you really are."

Red, who sensed what was coming, looked pleased. He was accustomed to beating people up for recreation, not just his job. He was sure he could take Frank.

"Open the cell door George," ordered Frank, "lock it when I get inside."

As he entered the cell and it was locked behind him, Frank put his fists up, boxing style, and moved toward Red.

With the unwitting confidence of the bully that he was, Red said, "This will be fun; I've always wanted to whip up on a lawman."

As Red moved toward the Sheriff, Frank threw a hard jab that landed flush on Red's nose. Blood splattered followed by another jab. Reds' nose was broken. Surprised and stunned by the blows, Red shook his head and swung wildly as Frank hit him with a left hook to the ribs followed by an uppercut that snapped Red's head back nearly breaking his neck. Red was out on his feet; he stumbled toward Frank grabbing for him. Frank unleashed a savage straight right hand that struck Red on the mouth, both lips split, blood flowed and his front teeth were knocked out. Red fell, face down, to the cell floor, he was out. His body was quivering and he was in danger of swallowing his tongue.

Frank turned to George and said, "Let me out, y'all carry him over to Doc Greines. When he comes to and can walk, let 'im go. Tell Doc Greines I talked to Red."

Boots, looking over at JoJo and Preacher, said, "The bartender was right, he's tough, Franks' damn tough."

The next day Harry Davis was released from jail. He was bitter and vowed revenge; trouble was coming.

It had turned cold, the wind was blowing and street activities had moved inside. At the holding pens they were still working cattle, getting them ready for sale at the Exchange Building. Inside the saloons it was all drinking, gambling, whores and fights. When the weather was bad, Cowboys left the streets and went inside; this always created a problem for the lawmen.

Davis and his five brothers were in the Maverick Saloon. They were already drunk and the more they drank, the braver they got. They already hated lawmen and the whiskey made matters worse.

As Boots, Preacher and JoJo entered the saloon, they walked up to the bar and started talking with Troy French, the bartender. Troy wanted to stay on the good side of the Rangers so he volunteered information and kept the Rangers aware of any upcoming trouble. He told Boots that Harry had been embarrassed about Frank knocking him out with one punch and his brothers have been riding him about it.

Troy said, "Don't be surprised if it builds up to a shootout. Harry and his brothers had always been the toughest bunch in the stockyards and everyone believed they were the ones responsible for the killing of Sheriff Jim Elick. You know Elick was shot from a room upstairs and no one saw who did it. But Jim and Harry had a couple of run-ins and Harry had said he would get him. French leaned forward and whispered, "Be careful, they're back shooters."

When Harry saw the Rangers at the bar, he got up from the poker table and went directly to Boots. With his speech slurred from the whiskey, he said, "Whirzat tin horn sherf, me 'n 'ims got some unfished bidness."

"Leave it alone Harry," said Boots, "you ain't no match for him, you've already proved that."

Harry, feeling his whiskey, said, "Dis time it'll be da gun, me and my bruzzers, we'll take care of 'im."

"Go drink your whiskey and have a good time Harry. You're biting off more than you can chew," said Boots.

The Rangers left the saloon and rode back to the jail. Boots told Frank about the conversation with the bartender; they needed to find out more. All things were pointing toward one of the Davis boys being Sheriff Elicks' killer.

Frank told James Lee, "There's a chance Cody may have learned something about Elicks' murder, see if she's in Hell's Half Acre; if not, try the stockyards."

The girls routinely rotated between the two locations; they didn't stay in one brothel all the time. Previously, Cody and James Lee had some rendezvous'; still did on occasion. Brock located her, unaccompanied, in one of the saloons in Hell's Half Acre

When he asked her about Elicks' murder, she told him that Bonnie had been working at the Maverick the night after the shooting, and was in the room with Harry. Harry was drunk and told her he killed Elick; said he didn't like him. Elick was going to arrest him for robbing and killing a card shark that had won Harry's money. It seems Harry had been making remarks, saying no one cheats him at poker. Soon afterwards, the man was found in the alley with his head bashed in.

Boots told Frank he was going to arrest Harry for Elicks' murder, and try to get a confession out of him. Frank agreed; they decided to make the arrest the next day as Harry and his brothers arrived at the saloon.

Boots instructed, "We'll all go to the saloon with shotguns. Frank, James Lee and Roy will go in together; Preacher and JoJo will go in with me." Boots, being sure to show the proper respect for the Sheriff's jurisdiction, added, "Frank, It's your arrest; we're here to back you up. You need to build a strong reputation." Frank nodded his agreement as Boots continued, "You arrest Harry, if the others resist, we'll take care of them."

As expected, about four o'clock the next afternoon, the six Davis brothers rode up to the saloon, tied up their horses and went in.

When the Rangers saw them enter, Boots said, "We'll give them thirty minutes, then we go in. Frank y'all go to the bar, order whiskey, when we come thru the door turn around and tell Harry he's under arrest for murder. He's yours; we've got the rest of them."

It was time; they all walked to the Maverick Saloon. Frank, with his two deputies, James Lee and Roy, walked in with shotguns pointed straight up, butts on their hips. The saloon went totally silent. All eyes, including the Davis boys, were on the lawmen. Frank ordered whiskey; the only sound was that of whiskey being poured into three shot glasses. They picked up the shot glasses, turned them up, and sat them down on the bar as the Rangers walked in; shotguns resting on their hips with barrels high in the air.

Frank turned around, pointed his shotgun at Harry and said, "Harry, you're under arrest for murder."

Harry, who was looking at six sawed off shotguns pointed at him, three from Frank and his deputies and the other three from the Rangers, said, "I don't know why you're arresting me, but only a fool would challenge these odds."

Then he said to his five brothers, who were sitting at the table with him, "Don't do anything foolish boys, those scatterguns they're holding will cut us in half."

Realizing it was a done deal, Frank walked up to Harry, disarmed him and said, "Let's get going, you're under arrest for murder."

Boots, JoJo and Preacher went to the table where the five remaining Davis boys were sitting. Boots looked at the brothers while pointing his shotgun at them and said, "Boys, take my advice, don't bring your guns to town. If I see you in Ft. Worth wearing your guns, I'll put you in jail and throw away the key. Do we have an understanding?" Without waiting for a response, Boots advised, "You don't have time to think about it, now, do we have an understanding?" This time he waited for an answer, which was forthcoming.

Tommy Davis, may be the smartest of the six brothers, responded, "Yea, we won't wear guns; ain't fair but we won't wear 'em."

"Just Remember this boys," said Boots, "we can all get along just fine. Follow Sheriff Pryor's rules or I'll come back with more Rangers with an attitude worse than I've got." The Davis Boys remained seated as Boots pressed his point, "You boys need to call it a night and get out of town, right now."

Realizing this was not the time or the place for resistance; the five remaining Davis brothers left the saloon and rode out of town.

The next day, Boots wired Laughlin, in Uvalde, and filed his Ft. Worth report. The train robbers had been captured, Sheriff Elicks' killer was in jail and things were becoming manageable for Sheriff Pryor and his deputies.

Laughlin wired back and gave orders for them to take the next train to Uvalde. They were to drop off Preacher, pick up Bronco and go to Abilene where Sheriff Meeks was having problems again. With the lack of deputies, the infiltration of gunslinger, outlaws and more range wars, he was desperate for help. After Abilene, Laughlin instructed them to return to Uvalde by way of Del Rio.

The Rangers said their goodbyes to Sheriff Pryor and his deputies, then loaded their horses and boarded the train for Uvalde. As the train pulled away from the depot, the three Ranges went to the dining car for coffee, relaxation and a little conversation. After they sat down and their coffee was served, Boots asked JoJo if he thought Emmet Ryker was his paw.

JoJo answered, "Yea, I think so, but I don't think he'll ever claim me."

"Do you like him," wondered boots, "what kind of guy is he?"

"Yea, I really do like him" answered JoJo, "he's a loner, smart, self educated and pretty tough. He ain't afraid of anything. Yea, I like him, kinda wish I could be around him more." They could see that JoJo was pondering Emmett's motives when he continued, "I'm sure he knows I'm his boy, can't figure out why he won't claim me. Hell, maybe he doesn't like me, ashamed of me, you know, son of a whore, hell I don't know."

JoJo didn't say any more on the subject, he just drank his coffee and stared out the window. Boots and Preacher joined him and took in the scenery; they figured if he wanted to talk more about Emmett, let him bring it up.

The train stopped at Uvalde just long enough to pick up Bronco and unload Preacher and his horse. Laughlin was at the depot for a quick hello and Cyndi was there to meet Preacher, but there was no Audrey to greet Boots.

As the train pulled away from the depot heading for Abilene, Boots said, with more than a hint of concern, "Well that takes care of that, I guess I'll go see Jane when I get to Abilene." His look of disappointment turned to a big grin as he said, "she's prettier anyway."

Meanwhile, in Abilene, Fred and Glen Ray were making plans to go see their saddle maker, Enrique Palomino, to discuss some special racing saddles. Glen Ray told Angel he wanted her to go with them so she could shop for a new dress while they were at the saddle shop.

She was excited, as most women are about a new dress. She and Glen Ray had discussed marriage, but never set a date. Being Fred's little sister, once Glen Ray inherited half of the Fox spread, they both lived at the ranch; so it was almost as though they were married.

As the three of them entered town on the buckboard, Angel was dropped off at the dress shop. Since the ranch was about twelve miles outside of Abilene, they didn't come to town often; so Fred and Glen Ray went to visit with Sheriff Meeks before heading on to the saddle shop.

"Hello Cletus," said Glen Ray as he and Fred walked into the sheriff's office, "how's everything in Abilene?"

"Hello Glen Ray, Fred," responded Cletus, "you fellas need to pin your stars back on; get in here and help me. The town's filling up with ruffians again,

Not to mention strangers, gunfighters and half-breeds. You name it; we got 'em all here." Cletus paused, took a breath and asked, "What brings you boys to town?"

"Oh," said Fred, "we want to get a custom racing saddle made and Glen Ray wanted Angel to have a new dress; she's over at the dressmakers now."

Fred let that sink in then explained, "We're trying to get ready for the big horse race coming here on the first of the month. Laughlin's gonna have some of his horses here and possibly some of them Oklahoma horses will be coming in on the train. Those Oklahoma boys are still unhappy; can't get over whiskey beating Shooting Star."

Sheriff Meeks chimed in, "Boots, JoJo and Bronco are coming from Uvalde, when they get here we'll cool the town down a little, they're good Rangers."

Fred and Glen Ray walked across the street to the saddle shop and spent at least an hour talking to Mr. Palomino about the racing saddle.

Glen Ray expressed concern that Angel hadn't joined them at the saddle shop. It was getting late in the evening and if they didn't leave soon, they'd be traveling back to the ranch in the dark.

Having finished their business at the saddle shop, Fred went after the buggy and Glen Ray went to the dress shop. When he arrived there, Beatrice, the shop owner, said Angel had left more than an hour ago, indicating that she was going to visit at the hotel. Glen Ray thanked her; then went to the hotel. When he found Linda, she said Angel had never been there. Deeply concerned, Glen Ray went to the sheriff's office and made Cletus aware she was missing.

Fred and Glen Ray continued their search in town, while Sheriff Meeks rode the outskirts; they found nothing. Time passed quickly; soon it was nighttime and still no trace of her. It was becoming evident there was foul play. Either she had been kidnapped and taken hostage; or whatever else could happen to a pretty young lady.

Meeks, Glen Ray and Fred returned to the Sheriff's office; they were trying to get organized when Clifton, owner of the livery stable, came in the office and said, "Sorry to bother you Sheriff, but this might be something you need to know. Grey Eagle's horse is gone, took it without paying the boarding fee and there's a little roan horse and saddle of mine missing out of the corral."

"Who's Grey Eagle?" asked Glen Ray.

Cletus answered, "He's an Indian that's been hanging around town; used to be a scout for the Army in Ft Davis. He's been here for a couple of weeks; sleeps in the alley or the livery stable. Hasn't caused any problems but the saloons won't sell him liquor or let him inside. If Angel doesn't show up soon, we'll have to assume that Grey Eagle has her."

All the men knew if this was true, they would find her dead and abused; it was very doubtful he would take her back to an Apache stronghold in Ballinger or the Paint Rock area. However, if he did, it would be difficult to find them since Grey Eagle had grown up in the Concho River Area.

Fred, an excellent tracker, knew the trails leading to Paint Rock and the general area around the Concho. He told Glen Ray to be ready at daylight; they would need provisions and a packhorse.

Then Fred got a hard look on his face and said, "Glen Ray, if it's just you and me, we've got a chance; we can go slow and easy." Glen Ray nodded as Fred continued, "If a posse gets on his trail, he'll kill her and make his get-away. Let's hope he's taking her to the stronghold to be his woman. If that's the case, his people won't harm her and we'll have a chance to find her alive."

Glen Ray recognized the gravity of the situation as they gathered supplies and loaded the packhorse. Since there wasn't any moonlight, they had to wait until morning for any chance to pick up Grey Eagle's trail.

The Concho River area around Paint Rock was a place the Indians used to hide from the Army. The cliffs of the river were full of large caves or caverns where some of Grey Eagle's tribe remained. As Fred and Glen Ray headed southwest, Fred told Glen Ray he was certain that's where Grey Eagle was headed. If Angel was taken there, it was possible she'd never be seen again. That was Indian Territory; it was not for white men.

They rose early and headed out at dawn. As they rode on, Fred said, "Grey Eagle may ride at night, he knows this trail and realizes there may be a posse after him. We've got to stay on his heels; climb to vantage points and try to spot him." They kept riding and Fred kept talking, "When we find him, he must not know we're after him; it's our only chance to get her back alive. Food will not be a problem for him, but it will be for Angel. He'll eat frogs, snakes, snails, berries and cactus."

Fred knew he was upsetting Glen Ray with his statements, but it was the facts and Glen Ray needed to know how serious Angel's situation was so he continued, "He can go without food or water for days but Angel can't. That'll work in her favor and ours; it'll slow him down."

With this last bit of information, Glen Ray seemed to be a little relieved, so Fred added, "He'll go to waterholes, raid farm houses and steal a horse or mule for meat and other rations. If he's taken her for his women, he'll do anything to keep Angel alive; let's hope that's the case."

In the afternoon of the second day, they picked up the old Indian trail and sure enough there were tracks showing two horses traveling southwest. The area was flat with six-foot tall prickly pears, yuccas and dense undergrowth. You had to stay in the trail to travel; everything had needles. Without chaps,

a rider's legs would quickly be full of thorns from the wide variety of cacti.

Glen Ray thought about Angel and how she was only wearing a dress. It was cold at night and there would be no fires. The more he thought about Angel, the more his hate grew for Grey Eagle as he wondered, 'when will we catch up to them'.

Up ahead, undetected, Angel was sitting in the saddle, her hands bound in front of her and her horse tied to Grey Eagle's pony. She had been in a semi state of shock ever since being taken captive. Grey Eagle was drunk when he took her; like most Indians, the whiskey made him do things he normally would not do. Yet, so far, he had not violated or beaten her.

Grey Eagle and Angel continued down the Indian trail; periodically, he would climb up vantage points to see if they were being followed. Due to his involvement as an Army Scout, he could speak some English. When Angel asked why he was doing this, he said, "You my woman, we go my home, you be my woman." Angel cried and begged him to release her but he only laughed and repeated, "You my woman."

It was late in the evening when Grey Eagle saw a five foot rattlesnake cross the trail. He quickly killed and skinned it offering some of the meat to Angel. She shook her head no and said, "I won't eat it."

He said, "Me no cook, no fire, you eat raw."

Angel was starving so she tried to eat some but she gagged and threw it up. Grey Eagle took some cactus, removed the thorns and sliced it for her; he also found some roots and berries for her to eat. Having very little water, Angel knew he would soon be going for water. She prayed they would be spotted by a Calvary Patrol and hoped they were being followed by the Rangers. She kept faith that Glen Ray and Fred were coming to get her; she had to stay alive.

The next day Fred noticed the hoof prints left the trail and started across country. Evidently Grey Eagle was heading toward the secret Indian camp.

They were in the Concho River area and the terrain had changed, food was available: deer, water and turkey. It made Glen Ray feel better; now, maybe Angel was getting food and water.

Fred said, "Grey Eagle may get careless, he doesn't know we are on his trail; but, we must find them before they reach the Indian camp."

When evening came, Fred climbed a cliff and looked for a campfire. Sure enough, Grey Eagle had built a fire; it appeared he had gotten careless. The fire was for food and warmth for Angel; regardless, it told them Grey Eagle no longer felt pursued.

The campfire was about a mile away. Fred said they would leave at daylight, travel on foot and try to move into rifle range for a clean shot. They couldn't afford to miss; if they missed Grey Eagle would kill Angel to keep them from getting her back. In his mind she belonged to him and he wouldn't allow her to return if he couldn't have her.

The next morning Fred said, "Glen Ray, stay back with the horses, this is a job for one man. I'll walk; then crawl to get myself in position and then, take him out with my rifle."

Glen Ray argued, "Let me go get him Fred, she's my girl, I want him."

"No," said Fred adamantly, "I have the big rifle and I can stalk him. If you hear shots, come riding fast and go for Angel before he gets her. Don't move till you hear shots, stay hidden. I repeat, don't move till you hear shots."

Fred checked his 45-70, started walking in a crouch and traveling from tree to tree; staying in the shadows. All the tricks he had learned while hunting cats were being applied. He was getting close to the camp and could smell smoke from the fire; could it be they hadn't broken camp yet.

Fred was on his hands and knees slowly approaching the camp. Then on his belly, crawling ever so slowly; he could see the horses thru the brush but couldn't see Angel or Grey Eagle. The camp was on a small stream; he could hear water running. He continued to crawl slowly; stopping every four or five yards to view the camp.

When he was no more than a hundred yards away, he saw Angel. She was sitting next to the fire with a blanket over her head and shoulders; then wrapped around her body.

Fred lay still and stared; he was looking for movement just like when he hunted the big cats. He lay perfectly still for yet another half hour, no Grey Eagle.

Suddenly it hit him, he was no longer the hunter; Grey Eagle was hunting him. Somehow Grey Eagle sensed he was being followed; he wasn't careless after all; his fire had set a trap. Fred stared at Angel; used his looking glass and saw she was gagged and tied. She was being used as bait; Grey Eagle was waiting on him to come to her rescue. Fred thought hard; maybe Grey Eagle hadn't seen him. Maybe he's hiding; watching Angel and waiting for me to show myself; then cut me down with his rifle.

Fred gambled that he had not been seen and continued lying still waiting for movement in the brush. He prayed Glen Ray would not get anxious and come ahead. Deciding to trust Glen Ray, he lay motionless and stared at the brush around the camp. When he wasn't staring at the brush, he watched the horses; they knew where Grey Eagle was and if Grey Eagle moved they would look at him; showing Fred his location.

Several hours passed; Fred had not moved. Ants had found him and were crawling under his shirt, up his leg, on his arms and in his hair. He remained steady; he dared not move, regardless of the stings.

Finally, he saw the horses raise their head, point their ears and look across the stream. Fred knew there had been movement; it could be a deer, hogs or Grey Eagle. Apparently Grey Eagle had given in to his desire for a woman and was coming in to get Angel instead of riding away to safety.

Fred stared in the direction the horses were looking, cocked his rifle and made ready.

CHAPTER 8

Suddenly, Grey Eagle appeared; he was crouched over, moving very slowly toward Angel. Lying motionless, Fred's arms had gone numb; but, he still couldn't take a chance on moving. His neck and hands were stiff. His waiting would soon pay off; he could see Grey Eagle's head above the brush. This was his chance so he put the front site of his rifle on Grey Eagle's head and knew he mustn't miss, Angels life depended on it. His technique had to be the same as if he were hunting the big cats. He took a deep breath, exhaled and slowly started squeezing the trigger.

Slowly he squeezed, slowly, slowly, 'BOOM', the 45-70 exploded sending a 500-grain bullet directly into Grey Eagle's brain. When the bullet hit, his head exploded like a watermelon as he was knocked sideways and into the stream.

Fred got up and walked carefully to the body. Blood was running freely into the water, turning it red. As Fred went to Angel and untied her, he removed the gag and embraced her while she cried and screamed.

"It's okay little sister," comforted Fred, "it's all over, you're safe," he kept repeating.

Glen Ray came riding in at a gallop, jumped off his horse, grabbed Angel and asked Fred, "Are you alright, how's Angel?"

Fred nodded that he was fine and said, "Take care of her while I finish my job." He walked over to Grey Eagle's body, removed his knife from his side, and removed what was left of Grey Eagle's scalp; then he split him open from belly to "brisket" and left him for the feral hogs and coyotes.

Glen Ray took Angel in his arms; she looked at him and sobbed, "You won't want me anymore, he violated me." She turned her face away and started screaming again. When Fred heard what she said, he started thinking about LaQuita and praying to himself.

Glen Ray, trying to reassure Angel, said, "Everything is fine, we've got you back, that's all that matters." He knew he would have lots of work to do, if he was to help her thru the feelings she would be encountering.

Fred said, "You know, Grey Eagle could have been out of here, he could have left her behind. We would have gotten her, but he could have escaped. He had to have her so he came back for her; it cost him his life."

Glen Ray grumbled, "Yea, he might've been out of here, but he wouldn't have gotten away; I would've found him and killed him."

Having said that, Glen Ray walked over to Grey Eagle's body, pulled his pistol and started firing. He emptied his gun into Grey Eagle's remains until he ran out of bullets and then continued to pull the trigger until he realized he was out of ammo. As he holstered his shooter, he looked down at Grey Eagle and said, "God forgive me, but I hope you burn in hell."

That evening, when the sun set and camp had been established, Fred and Glen Ray prepared some camp food for the three of them. She wouldn't eat; she was still scared and very emotional; repeating over and over to Glen Ray that, after what had happened, he wouldn't want her. He held her throughout the night, assuring her it was not her fault and he would continue to love her no matter what.

Even with Glen Ray's reassurance, Angel moaned, "He has shamed me, I am no longer clean."

The days were spent traveling while the nights were spent sleepless. After several days, when they reached the town of Ballinger, Angel was no better; she continued to cry. Fred and Glen Ray were very concerned about her depression and feelings of guilt; she seemed to be getting worse. She appeared to be losing her sanity and they both hoped to get her to the doctor in Abilene and then on to her mother. Maybe then she would come out of it.

In Ballinger there was a church at the end of Main Street. Angel saw it and asked Glen Ray and Fred to take her there. They all went to a front row inside the vacant church. Immediately, Angel knelt down and started praying in Spanish. Fred knelt down beside his sister and put his arm around her. Glen Ray knelt down on her other side and closed his eyes as both men joined her in prayer.

Suddenly Glen Ray felt his pistol move. As he opened his eyes, he saw Angel. She had his pistol in her hand with the barrel pressed under her chin. Miraculously, Fred, with his sixth sense and cat-like reflexes, grabbed the barrel and pulled it out from under her chin before she could pull the trigger.

They were all in a state of shock. Glen Ray grabbed Angel, held her and said, "No baby, no baby, don't ever try that again. You can't leave me; we are supposed to be together."

Angel heard Glen Ray and questioned, "Do you still love me?"

"Yes baby," answered Glen Ray, "now even more so." He looked into her eyes and pleaded, "Don't ever try to leave me. Promise me."

Angel smiled and kissed Glen Ray; he could sense that she had turned the corner, their prayers were answered.

That night they checked into a hotel room. The next morning, Glen Ray bought a buggy and told Fred, "Let's take Angel directly home to her mother. We'll send for the doctor after we get her home." Fred agreed.

Meanwhile, the train carrying Boots, JoJo and Bronco had pulled into Abilene, right on schedule. The Rangers unloaded their horses and took them to be stabled before going to Sheriff Meek's office.

As they entered the jail, Cletus said, "I'm glad to see you Rangers. The towns getting a little too wild for me, I can use some help."

"What seems to be the trouble?" asked Boots.

"Aw, the towns full of gunslingers, paid guns, gamblers and as always drunk drovers. There was also a kidnapping; Glen Ray's fiancé was taken by that damn renegade Indian, Grey Eagle."

When he heard this, Boots inquired, "Angel? Has she been rescued, still missing, what's the situation?

Meeks replied, "Fred and Glen Ray are on the trail; expect to hear from them soon. If anyone can bring this tragedy to a proper ending, those two can."

Boots said, "I guess you're right; those two boys are an army by themselves." Boots paused; then urged Meeks to continue.

Cletus nodded and then went on, "There are a couple of ranches that are feuding over water, the owner of the Lazy-H ranch fenced off the section of his land that had water. That upset the boys over at the Double-L; they couldn't make a deal for water. That trouble has overflowed into town, resulting in a shooting here in the saloon. Witnesses said it was a fair fight."

Meeks shook his head in disgust and uttered, "Hell, you know how that goes; the boy that was killed was from the Lazy-H and was in the saloon by himself. Of course, there were several boys in there from the Double L and one of 'em, a fast gun named Slim Morgan, shot and killed the Lazy-H hand." Then Cletus got somewhat of a resigned look on his face and said, "Dammit, I don't know, maybe we can ride out to both ranches and talk with them, try to get the problem resolved without any more bloodshed."

The three Rangers agreed a face to face meeting with both parties would be a likely way to assess the depth of the problem. Since it was getting late in the day, and they had just completed a long train trip, they would check in to the hotel, get a bath, some grub and a good nights sleep. Tomorrow they would see what develops and determine a course of action.

After leaving the sheriffs' office the Rangers checked into the hotel, cleaned up and prepared for dinner. After their baths Boots went to see Jane at the newspaper office and JoJo went to see Patti at the bank; hoping to meet for dinner. They would include Bronco, even though he didn't have a girl.

They were successful in arranging the dinner engagement. Afterwards, the girls wanted to know about their trip and what happened in Ft Worth. Jane found a pen and paper for note taking; she wanted to publish the information in the newspaper.

JoJo related the events of the train robbery while Boots talked about the Miller boys. Then the conversation switched to Bronco as he explained to the girls how he happened to become a Ranger. They were impressed; congratulated him and insisted on finding him a girlfriend. Bronco blushed and said, "A girlfriend is fine, no wife though, I ain't ready for that."

The next morning Glen Ray came riding in to Abilene. Having been seen, a crowd followed him down the street towards the Sheriff's office. Everyone was asking about Angel.........you know; what happened, how is she, and many more questions.

When Glen Ray reached the sheriffs' office, he went inside and gave Cletus all the details. When he finished, he went to the doctors' office and told him to go to the ranch and treat Angel. The doctor climbed up into the buggy and rode to the ranch with Glen Ray.

When Glen Ray and Doc Jameson reached the ranch, the Doc examined Angel and said, "She's actually unharmed except for the rape and mental damage. Remember what I told Fred when this happened to LaQuita." He paused to make sure Glen Ray understood. When Glen Ray nodded his understanding, Doc continued, "Give her lots of love, keep her busy, and keep me aware of her actions." Then Doc told him that the possibility of a pregnancy was a big concern, but, if that doesn't happen, she should be alright.

Fred told his mother, Maria, not to let his sister out of her sight. He did not want her to take her life, as LaQuita did, after she was beaten and raped.

Back in town, Abilene was getting crowded. It was Saturday, the end of the month; payday for the ranch hands. Sheriff Meeks told the Rangers they would probably have work to do by midnight. That was okay with the Rangers; they wouldn't have to visit the ranches if the problems came to them.

About two in the afternoon, seven Lazy-H riders rode in and went to the Dry Coyote saloon. An hour later ten riders, from the Double-L ranch, rode in and went to the Devil's Hangout.

Cletus said, "Troubles a comin', it's been a week since Slim Morgan gunned that boy down."

Boots said, "Cletus, get us all one of them twice barrels, we're going on a shotgun patrol; I'll do the talking."

Each of the four men was armed with sawed off shotguns when they entered the Dry Coyote saloon. The seven Lazy-H riders were drinking whiskey, mingling with the girls, playing poker and generally just building up for some major hell raising.

Boots walked up, turned his back to the bar, looked out across the room and said, "Who's the ramrod for the Lazy-H?"

"I am," said a short robust young man. He was wearing tall boots with his britches tucked inside. He sported a long sleeve shirt with a vest, working Stetson, moustache and a mouth full of tobacco.

"You got a name?" asked Boots.

"Yea," said the robust one, "it's Willie Boy, what you want Ranger?" You're interrupting my party."

"Well, Willie Boy," answered Boots, "you and your men listen and listen good; no trouble and we'll all get along. I know about your man getting killed and I know the Double-L men are in the saloon across the street, but we're the law here, not you; don't start any trouble with those boys. If you do, then you've got the Rangers and the sheriff to deal with, believe me, you're no match."

"To hell with you Ranger," snorted Willie, "that boy was my brother, he didn't have a chance with that paid gun, I'm gonna get him one way or the other."

"No, you'll do nothing of the kind," snarled Boots, "if I have to, I'll put your ass in jail for making threats; got it! You boys stay in the saloon and out of trouble; any problems and I'll throw you all in jail for thirty days."

Willie appeared to have 'got it', so the Rangers left the saloon and went across the street to the Devil's Hangout. Once inside Boots said in a very loud voice, "I'm here to see Slim Morgan!"

A tall lanky cowboy, with long unkept hair and a moustache, stood up and said, "That's me, what the hell do you want?"

Boots growled back, "I'll ask the questions, you listen."

Slim, feeling his whiskey and trying to show off in front of his men said, "I ain't skeered of you ranger, I killed men before and I can kill you."

Boots gave slim a stare-down and said, "Don't be foolish, I'm not some inexperienced kid; you don't have a chance with me."

"Naw, don't reckon I do," slurred Slim, "hell, there's four of you with shotguns; too bad it's not just you and me."

Boots said to the bartender, "Were you here when Slim shot that boy? Did you see what happened?"

"Yea, I was here," said the bartender, "and I seen it."

"Was it a fair fight?" asked Boots.

"Well they both drew but the kid sure didn't want to," he answered, then added, "Slim pushed him and made him draw."

Boots said brusquely, "Mister, I'm placing you under arrest for suspicion of murder." At that point, Boots handed Cletus his shotgun and started toward Slim. When he was about six feet away, Slim made a motion to draw on Boots. With lightening precision, Boots drew his pistol before Slim cleared leather; grabbed him by the shirt with his left hand and struck him twice with his pistol; once across the face and then on top of his head. As Slim fell to the floor, out cold, Boots turned to the other men and said, "There's more of this for y'all if you want it."

Since there were no more takers, Cletus, along with the Rangers, carried Slim off to jail; one man holding his legs, another holding him under the armpits. Some of the boys from the Lazy-H, who were standing outside the saloon across the street, saw Slim being carried off. One of them was Willie Boy. He tipped his hat at the Rangers and then the group went back inside for more drinks.

The presence of the Rangers in Abilene had a calming and taming effect on the town. After six weeks, the town returned to normal.

Stewart Coffee, the attorney, and Sterling Laws' friend, went to the jail to see the Rangers. When the two walked in, the Rangers were playing dominoes; Sterling looked at Boots and said, "Boots, I've got great news for you. Your brother has been appointed to Congress. In three weeks, Congressman Sterling Law, and his bride to be, will arrive in Abilene for a visit."

Boot's face lit up as he said, "How about that, my big brother a Congressman for the State of Texas, and getting married; I'm so proud." He had to fight hard to hold back the tears of joy.

The next day the Rangers, Boots, JoJo and Bronco, rode out to the ranch to see Glen Ray and Fred. It was evident the ranch was doing well; the corrals and horse pastures were full of Morgan horses while the grazing pastures were full of cattle. Boots told Glen Ray and Fred about Sterling being a Congressman. Glen Ray informed Boots that Angel was doing fine; apparently, she wasn't experiencing any long term problems.

That evening, Glen Ray and Fred prepared a large meal for dinner. They ate beef, drank wine and enjoyed each other's company then retired for the night. The next morning the trio of Rangers rode back into Abilene.

Upon arriving, they were greeted by Roscoe Wells, one of Cletus Meeks' deputies. It seems Cletus was making his rounds the previous night and was ambushed by several riders. He was roped crossing the street; then dragged down the middle of Main Street to a spot about a quarter of a mile outside of town where he was beaten.

When the Rangers asked about his condition, they were told he had several busted ribs and was badly bruised with patches of skin dragged off parts of his body. The Doc said he'd be all right, providing he didn't get pneumonia from the broken ribs; they had bruised his lungs.

The Rangers rode directly to the Docs' office and asked to see Cletus. He was a mess; his face was swollen and skinned severely from the dragging. Boots pulled up a chair and sat down beside the bed. Cletus opened his eyes, looked at Boots and, as he tried to grin, said, "Don't look like I can take care of my town when you boys are gone."

Boots, trying to hold back his anger, inquired, "Who did it Cletus? Did you know 'em?"

Cletus, with the pain showing on his face replied, "Yea, it was Slim and that bunch from the Double-L Ranch. Guess they were paying me back for that pistol whipping you gave Slim." He groaned a little and went on, "They were all drunk and raising hell in the saloon earlier. I quieted them down on my first round at nine o'clock. When I went back after midnight, they were leaving the saloon on horseback and roped me out in the street; then they dragged me away." It was obvious that Cletus was in severe pain, but he gritted his teeth and continued, "Clifton, the stable owner, saw it happen." Meeks moaned softly and said, "He's the one that rode out and found me; I owe that man my life."

Boots eyes turned hard and his jaw squared as he barked, "Cletus, we'll get 'em; nobody drags a lawman and gets away with it."

The next morning the Rangers saddled up and rode toward the Double-L. The ranch was about ten miles from town. It was a cattle ranch owned by Louis Littleton, an old time rancher. He had been involved in some disputes with other ranchers but, up till now, it was nothing violent. Louis had started his ranch during the Indian days; he was one of the tough survivors.

The Rangers arrived at the ranch house and were greeted by Mr. Littleton who was sitting on the porch. Boots said, "Mr. Littleton, I'm Boots, this is JoJo and this is Bronco, we're Texas Rangers and we came to arrest Slim Morgan for the attempted murder of Sheriff Cletus Meeks."

Mr. Littleton got up with a puzzled look on his face and said, "What do you mean, I know nothing of this."

Boots said, "Last night, he and some of your boys were in town all liquored up; they roped Sheriff Meeks, drug him out of town and left him for dead. Meeks identified Slim as the instigator."

Littleton replied, "Ranger Boots, if this is true, then you have my apologies."

Boots nodded his understanding; Littleton motioned towards the barn and offered, "Come on, let's go to the corral, he's down there branding cattle."

When they rode up to the corral, Slim was branding a steer. When he saw the Rangers, he dropped the branding iron and stood up as if to challenge them. Before Slim could offer any other resistance, Boots drew his pistol, pointed it at him and stated, "You're under arrest for the attempted murder of Sheriff Meeks."

Mr. Littleton said, "Slim, Sheriff Meeks identified you as the one who dragged him; you shouldn't have done that. You shamed me and everyone on my ranch."

Littleton had a lariat in his hand; he swung it over his head, threw it and roped Slim. He spurred his horse, pulling Slim off his feet, as he rode off at a gallop, out of the corral and out into the pasture making a full mile circle thru the cactus and rocks. Then he returned to the corral while still dragging Slim.

When he came to a stop, Littleton, with contempt in his voice, barked, "He's all yours Ranger Boots; please accept my apology for his actions."

The Rangers tied Slim on a horse, took him to town and locked him up. He would stay there until the Circuit Judge came to town; then he'd be put on trial. They had the Doc' patch him up; they wanted him alive for the trial and sentencing. The Texas State Pen' would be his next address.

The Judge still hadn't made it into town when the day came for the Congressman to arrive. As the train pulled into Abilene and stopped at the depot; the crowd anxiously awaited the appearance of its special passenger. It seemed all the people of Abilene were there to greet the Congressman and his bride to be. Boots, along with the rest of the Rangers and Stewart Coffee, were standing on the platform in front of the depot, waiting on Sterling and Emily to step out and address the crowd.

As Sterling stepped out with Emily on his arm, the crowd let out a big cheer and Boots beamed with pride. When he saw how well Sterling was dressed and how important he looked, he thought to himself, 'That's my Bubba, you made it; you realized your dream.'

Stewart Coffee formally introduced him to the crowd. Once the cheering and applause died down, Sterling spoke for about ten minutes. The subject matter was mainly concerning the progress and opportunities in the great state of Texas. He was well received and the crowd broke out in applause several times during his oratory with a lengthy ovation at the end of his speech.

Stewart and the Rangers escorted Sterling and Emily to the hotel; they would stay several nights and then move on to another city; once the train returned.

Boots went with Sterling to his room while Emily was getting settled in hers. Not being married yet, they had separate rooms. Sterling had already discovered a politician's lack of privacy and insisted on maintaining proper moral conduct.

When they entered his room, Sterling sat on the bed; Boots pulled out a chair, sat down at the desk and proudly said, "Brother you've come a long ways. It seems like just the other day we were on that battlefield in Atlanta, you were twelve and I was ten. Now we have our Pa' that we thought was dead, I'm a Texas Ranger and you," Boots paused, he was getting a little choked up; he regained his composure and, as his voice cracked, repeated, "you brother are a Texas Congressman. I am so very proud of you."

Sterling echoed, "And I, brother Boots, am very proud of you." They were both grinning from ear to ear as Sterling remarked, "I'm in a position to make the laws that you'll enforce. It's all part of growing this great state. Believe me, being a Texas Ranger is just as important as being a Congressman. My heart swells each time I tell someone my; brother is a Texas Ranger. I'm proud of you Bubba and I love you."

They rose, hugged each other and thanked God for their blessings.

While Sterling was in town, Jane was with Boots; constantly jotting down information for her Pa's newspaper.

Shortly after Sterling and Emily left Abilene, Boots and Jane were having dinner; they were discussing Sterling's visit and his future as a congressman.

One of the things Jane asked was, "How sure are you that Sterling and Emily are going to get married, and when?"

"Oh I'm certain," said Boots, "Right now, Texas controls Sterling's life; but when it's time, they'll get married." He took a bite of his sirloin, pointed his fork at Jane and added, "He sets schedules and goals for Texas and himself; he works hard to achieve his goals; but when it reaches the point he's ready to take Emily for his wife and the mother of his children, rest assured,; it will happen."

"What about you Boots? Jane asked, "Are you on a schedule like your brother? Not waiting for an answer, she kept on in rapid fire, "Surely you must know I love you and want to be in your life? I've never felt love for anyone or anything the way I do for you. I'm miserable when you're gone; when I can't see you or talk to you. I just want to know if there's a chance for us."

Boots looked at Jane and said, "Whew, I didn't know I could listen that fast." Then, realizing how serious she was, Boots looked deep into her pretty eyes and said softly, "Jane, I care very much for you, but I'm a Ranger. I love being a Ranger and I love the State of Texas. Right now I'm a free spirit; I love the thrills and dangers involved with being a ranger. The most important thing in my life, right now, is the State of Texas and the Ranger Star."

Boots paused for a moment, and then added, "As a Ranger, I will be an important part of Texas history. I care very much for you, but at this time in my life, I'm just not ready for a commitment." Boots looked deep into Jane's eyes as he said, "I hope you understand."

Jane looked at Boots and said, "Thank you for your honesty, hopefully your feelings for me will continue to grow; in the mean time,

I will support you and continue to love you." She got up from the table, kissed Boots on the cheek, and left the restaurant.

Boots realized he had said to Jane, the same words that Laughlin had said to Melissa, in their relationship. Now, they are married and raising a family. He thought, 'I suppose it could happen, but me married, nope, not anytime soon.'

The Rangers had now been in Abilene for quite a while; with Sheriff Meeks injured, and without a crisis elsewhere, they would remain a while longer. This gave Boots and JoJo additional time with Jane and Patti.

JoJo told Boots that he and Patti had discussed marriage and she agreed, he could continue his life as a Ranger. JoJo, having grown up without parents, had probably never been loved by anyone; however, it was evident now that he and Patti were definitely in love.

It was June; summer in north central Texas was just around the corner and the days were getting hot. JoJo was sitting on the shady part of the porch when he saw the stage coming down Main Street. Bob Bell reined in the horses and stopped in front of the hotel. The guard, riding shotgun, got off and nodded as he opened the stage door to let off a single passenger.

A well dressed gentleman stepped out, brushed him self off and looked toward the jail. It was Emmett Ryker.

A surprised but pleased JoJo, started to go to the stage and greet Emmett; then he decided against it thinking; 'I'll just sit and wait, see what de does.'

Emmett picked up his luggage and went straight to the hotel. About ten minutes later, he came out of the hotel and started walking towards the jail. JoJo stared at the ground; trying not to let Emmett know he had seen him get off the stage.

Emmett stepped onto the porch, extended his hand, and said, "Hello, JoJo,"

"Well, hello yourself" said JoJo, as he stood up and shook Emmett's hand. "What brings you to town?"

"Aw, just got restless," answered Emmett, "decided to come down and look at some property that's for sale."

"What kind of property you looking for?" asked JoJo.

"Ranch property," said Emmett, "don't laugh. It's the Silas ranch; I heard the old man died and the widow wants to sell it." JoJo wasn't showing much interest so Emmett continued, "Do you know the property?"

"Yea, I do," answered JoJo, "could be a damn good ranch; has water and lots of grass, just needs attention."

"Well," said Emmett, "I'm tired of saloons, gunfights, card sharks and drunks. Been saving money for several years; now I can afford to buy a ranch and change my life style."

JoJo, looking a little puzzled, asked, "How you gonna run a ranch; you're not a rancher."

"Oh, I figure I'll hire me a good ranch hand and start with a few cattle" offered Emmett.

"Well, the ranch does have a bunch of mavericks on it. But, as you know, Silas had quit working the ranch; man there's lots of work to be done."

Emmett nodded his head in understanding then, after exchanging a few more pleasantries, they went to the hotel. As JoJo helped Ryker get checked in he said, "Emmett, I'd be obliged if you'd plan on having dinner tonight with me and a beautiful lady. Her name is Patti and I'm going to tell her all about you when I see her."

"It would be my pleasure," said Emmett, "but don't be too hard on me." Then he chuckled and asked, "By the way, is she someone special?"

"Yea, yea she is," said JoJo, "hopefully someday, with any luck, she'll be my wife."

Emmett gave him a wink; then headed up to his room as JoJo left the hotel and walked across the street to the bank. As he entered the bank, Patti saw him, got up from her desk and said, "My, my, you're all smiles today; what's made you so happy?"

JoJo remarked, "I'll tell you later; right now, plan on having dinner tonight with me and a gentleman."

"A gentleman?" said Patti. Then, teasingly, she asked, "You know a gentleman........who is he?"

JoJo stopped as he was going out the door and said, "At the present time, just a friend."

The three of them met later on that night, had dinner and indulged in some minor conversation and fine Burgundy before retiring. JoJo did not tell Patti his suspicions concerning Emmett being his dad; he thought it best to wait until he was sure himself.

By now, Sheriff Meeks had fully recovered and was back on the job. Violence in Abilene, once again, had decreased.

Glen Ray and Fred were working their ranch producing quality racehorses and providing stud service. Glen Ray and Angel hadn't married yet; Angel was still recovering from her ordeal, but was doing well.

Emmett went ahead and bought the Silas ranch; hired one of Fred and Glen Ray's wranglers and began rounding up stray cattle and mavericks.

Boots and Bronco remained the free spirits they had always been. Boots and Jane's situation had not changed. She was still ready for marriage, but Boots was not. He was enjoying the Ranger life. In fact, he and Bronco were a lot alike; they were a pair of good Rangers. Good with their guns and willing to go wherever the Ranger winds blew them.

While all this was going on, Stewart Coffee, the attorney, was staying in touch with Sterling and monitoring his political career.

There was also an upcoming horse race in Comanche. Since the development of the railroad had made traveling easier, horses in Oklahoma could be put on the train, rest in the boxcar along the way and then race fresh in Texas.

Before leaving for the race, Glen Ray had told Boots that he and Fred were going to enter Three Paws; a stallion out of Whiskey and, to date, was unbeaten. Whiskey had beaten Shooting Star, the Oklahoma Champion; now Three Paws, Whiskey's son, was the horse to beat.

Boots and Bronco wired Laughlin; told him they were going to Comanche before heading for Cowtown, Ft. Worth. After saying their goodbye's at the sheriffs office, they were preparing to mount up when Jane came walking across the street from her Dad's newspaper office. She put her arms around Boots, who was standing by War Paint, and kissed him goodbye. She had tears in her big brown eyes as she looked at him and said, "Ranger, you'd better come back to me in one piece, don't go getting yourself all shot up."

Boots grinned, put his foot in the stirrup, swung up into the saddle and said; "Count on it lady;" then he winked at her and whirled his mount around.

As they rode off, with Jane standing in the street waving, Bronco said, "Hell Boots, it won't be long till I'll be on the trail by myself and you'll be raising young-uns."

Boots replied, "If that day ever comes, that's the one that'll tame me. In the meantime let's go to Comanche." They spurred their horses and rode off at a gallop.

That night they camped on the trail; warm campfire, jerky, coffee and a warm bedroll. Boots was lying down with his head on his saddle as he looked up at the stars and said, "Bronco, we're blessed. Some day they're gonna write about how hard of a life we had." Boots paused for a moment, looked over at Bronco for a response. When none was forthcoming, he said, "Hell Bronco, this is a good life; don't wanna be no rancher or businessman, just wanna be a Ranger. Hey, that sounds like lyrics to a song;

You ever heard me sing.?

"Nope," said Bronco with a slight chuckle, "and I don't care to either," he added. Then he paused and continued, "Boots, how do you think we'll die? You think we'll be ambushed or out drawn? Hell, before the Rangers, I knew I'd meet my maker at the end of a rope." said Bronco.

Boots was quite for a moment then he said, "Preacher says Christ died on the cross; if we accept him as our Savior, we won't ever die and we'll have eternal life in Heaven."

"One thing about that," said Bronco, "there won't be any gun fighting or outlaws up there."

"Go to sleep," said Boots, "and don't disturb me; I'm gonna dream about Jane."

It was noon Friday when they rode into Comanche. Things were already starting: chicken fights, whiskey, gambling, dancing in the streets and lots of food.

Side by side, they rode slowly down Main Street sitting straight and tall in the saddle, projecting their authority; people knew the Rangers were in town.

After stabling their horses and checking into the hotel, they went to the restaurant where John Pope, the sheriff, was having lunch. They introduced themselves. When John offered them a seat, they sat down and ordered.

John was around fifty; he was short and a little over weight with balding gray hair and beard. John had hard eyes; when he looked at you, he made you feel uncomfortable. He had been a sergeant in the Confederate army and appeared quite capable of enforcing the law.

Once their meals were ordered, John said, "Glad you boys are here. There's lots of money here for the races; with more strangers arriving by the minute and me with only one Deputy, there could be trouble."

Boots and Bronco leaned forward in their chairs giving Sheriff Pope their full attention as he offered, "Even though it's been quite for a while, with only a few drunken brawls in the saloon, yesterday, three suspicious looking hombres rode in. Could be gunslingers or gamblers; hell, I don't know, maybe both."

By now, their food had been placed on the table. Boots took a bite of his steak, sipped his coffee and said, "Sheriff, we'll help where we can, but be aware, we're only here thru the weekend, and then our orders are to head for Ft. Worth."

They finished their lunch, bid Sheriff Pope good-day; then they walked over to the rodeo arena where all the race horses were being exercised and displayed.

Boots saw Glen Ray and Fred; they had set up a tent and were unloading racing equipment. Staked out next to the tent was Three Paws. The stud was a beautiful sorrel; tall and long bodied with three white "stockings", two front and one rear. He had the typical Morgan neck and was well developed in his rump and shoulders.

They looked up and spotted Laughlin coming from the depot; he and his team were leading a beautiful black stallion. The horse was magnificent; he was solid black and rippled with muscles. Laughlin led him to the set up area; then came over to the Rangers.

As he pulled up, he tipped his hat and said, "Hello Rangers, Glen Ray, Fred. I can still call you Rangers can't I?" They were pleased Laughlin still considered them Rangers and nodded their appreciation.

Laughlin, the same rugged raw-boned handsome man with just a little salt and pepper over his ears, felt the renewed camaraderie between them as he remarked, "Fred, Glen Ray, I've been looking forward to this meeting and expect a good race. That's a fine sorrel you have there, bet its 'Three Paws' I've been reading a lot about him."

CHAPTER 9

"Yes sir Captain," sparked Fred, "that's 'Three Paws' alright, but that's a fine looking horse you led in yourself."

"Yea he is Fred," beamed a proud Laughlin, "that's one of Diablo's sons, named him JJ after Mr. Fox." They were admiring each other's horse as Laughlin added, "I hear there's a chance Shooting Stars' owner, J D Blackwood, may be here with his new horse, 'Blazing Star', a son of 'Shooting Star'; if so, things could get real interesting around race time"

Sheriff Pope, who had been walking up to the group, overheard Laughlin's remarks and said, "Coincidently boys, I've got some news about 'Blazing Star'. Blackwood brought him down from Stephenville after he won a race there and he's been kept on a ranch about ten miles outside of town for the past week. Word has it, they kept him there for exercise and training; waiting for the big race. Rumor is, they'll bring him in tonight, race him tomorrow in the qualifiers, then Sunday in the finals.

Blackwood was being his usual presumptuous self, since everyone knew there would be thirty or more horses trying to qualify. There wouldn't be any "hay-burners" among them, so, qualifying was not a given.

Laughlin grinned and said, "Supper's on me boys, meet me at the restaurant; tonight at 8:00."

As Boots and Bronco started walking toward their rooms, Boots said, "This is going to be something to see, the four fastest horses in Texas all in the same race."

When the Rangers met for supper, as directed by Laughlin, they enjoyed a good meal and fellowship. Old stories were told and re-told; including the rodeo at the corral when Boots and War Paint were breaking each other.

After a great meal, and some slightly exaggerated tales, Laughlin closed the evening with a toast, "Here's to good Rangers and good horses; tomorrow, may the best horse win." Appropriately, they all raised their glasses in unison, drank down their last swallow and retired early. Tomorrow was going to be a long day.

The next day, Saturday, was a perfect day for racing. It was overcast with mild temperatures and no wind. Today's race would be a qualifying round with ten horses per race and the top three finishers going into Sunday's finals. With forty horses entered, there would be four qualifying races.

Knowing that JJ, Blazing Star, Three Paws and Whiskey were the top four horses, the officials had seeded them in separate races. Hopefully, this would guarantee that they wouldn't meet until the finals on Sunday.

The town was excited; people had traveled by train, wagon and horseback just to see, what was expected to be, Sunday's big race. All races, including the qualifiers, would be one mile in length. They were to start on Main Street in front of the bank and proceed south. One quarter mile outside of town was a group of wagons marking the outward boundary of the track. They were to ride around the wagons, circling the town and returning to the start/finish line from the north side. Twice around would be one mile. A banner, stretched across Main Street in front of the bank, signified the start/finish line.

It was noon; the horses in the first race were brought to the starting line, with Three Paws considered the favorite. Even with Fred holding him back, he won handily by ten lengths.

The second qualifier featured Blazing Star from Montague, owned by Mr. Blackwood. Blazing Star was impressive and won easily; as did Whiskey in the third race.

Then came the fourth race; featuring the black stallion, JJ, owned by Laughlin. This would be JJ's first big race; he was big, beautiful and spectacular with his flowing, uncut mane and tail. Laughlin walked him around to keep him warm before allowing his rider, Candito Jr., son of his ranch foreman, to mount him and head for the starting line.

Everyone, including Mr. Blackwood, gathered at the starting line to view JJ.

The starter's pistol sounded, and the race was on. JJ and Candito's reaction time was perfect as they immediately took the lead, they were something to see. JJ was stretched out, shiny black with long strides that increased their lead with each step. Glen Ray and Fred wanted to see how strong he would be after a half mile but didn't get the chance. He was so far ahead that Candito started pulling him up at the halfway point. They crossed the finish line well ahead of the pack; JJ had not been tested.

Laughlin grinned and said, "Well boys, whatcha think about JJ?"

Glen Ray remarked, "Hell Laughlin, he made those other horses look like mules. I think Blazing Star, Whiskey and Three Paws may well be looking at his rump all day tomorrow."

Fred said, "Huh, I just hope we can stay close enough to see his rump."

When the day's qualifiers ended and evening fell, there were lanterns glowing and tables were loaded down with plenty of food and drink. Of course, the band starting setting up and tuning their instruments in preparation for the big street dance. The horses had long been tended to and put away for the night. Everyone was anxiously awaiting Sunday.

Boots and Bronco went to the tables and filled their plates to overflowing capacity. They found a table, sat down and started eating brisket, beans, mashed potatoes and any thing else their plates could hold. Boots took time out from his eating to look up and survey their surroundings.

He elbowed Bronco and said, "Look at that table under the oak tree; see those girls with the man and woman."

Bronco looked up and remarked, "Yea, man, they're beautiful, both of 'em."

While they were looking, the girls looked back and smiled. Bronco did a double take and said, "Hey, did you see that, they're looking back at us."

"Yea I saw it," crooned Boots, "when we finish eating, let's go ask them to dance."

Bronco, who hadn't taken his eyes off the girls, said, "The one on the left is mine, I think she's pretty." The he said, rather shyly, "Boots, I'm bashful," "and what if they turn us down?"

Boots said, "Don't worry, I'll take care of it........just let me do the talking." As they quickly gulped down their meal, Boots ordered Bronco, "Let's go, remember let me do the talking."

Standing straight and tall, they walked over, trying to look impressive. As they arrived at the table, Boots took a good look at the man and woman. The man was rugged looking, about forty-five or so. He was approximately six feet tall with broad shoulders, a handle bar moustache, Stetson hat, narrow waist, calloused hands and a stern look on his face. His square jaw was framed by dark brown eyes. The lady was elegant; a pretty blond with curls hanging to her shoulders and green eyes; she was smiling.

Boots said, "Hello sir, ma'am, ladies. My name is Boots and this is Bronco, we're Texas Rangers."

The man stood up and said, "My name is Lattimer, William Lattimer. This is my wife Nora and my daughters, Linda and Joy. What can I do for you?"

"Well sir," said Boots, "these girls are breaking the law by being so pretty and not dancing. We're gonna have to arrest them and keep them in our custody for the rest of the evening."

Mr. Lattimer and his wife both laughed; Linda and Joy blushed.

Still laughing, Lattimer said, "If you can capture them they're yours. They're mean; you may not be able to keep them."

"Thank you sir," said Boots, then he looked at Joy and said, "May I have this dance?"

Boot's humorous approach had broken the ice and calmed Bronco's nerves enough for him to ask Linda. Since both said yes, the foursome danced the first of many dances and spent the rest of the evening talking and dancing.

As the festivities were winding down, they agreed to meet at noon and watch tomorrow's race.

That night, back at the hotel, Glen Ray and Fred planned their strategy for the race. Glen Ray said, "I think JJ is the horse to beat. Both Three Paws and Whiskey can handle Blazing Star, but I don't know about JJ." Fred nodded in agreement as Glen Ray continued, "We didn't get to see JJ put out any effort; Candito held him back and he still won by six lengths."

Fred said, "Maybe we should come out fast, get the lead and go inside. If we stay in on the turns, hopefully we can hold 'im off in the last half mile."

"I agree," said Glen Ray. "Whiskey's a strong finisher and so is Three Paws, get ahead, then out duel them to the finish line."

Having laid their plans for tomorrow, Glen Ray and Fred retired for the night. It's doubtful if either of them slept very well.

It was noon Sunday, Boots and Bronco met Linda and Joy at the starting line. The girls looked beautiful; they both had long auburn hair with the green eyes and beautiful smile of their mother. When you coupled that with their impeccable grooming, beautiful build and pleasant personality, Boots and Bronco would be the envy of every wrangler in town.

Finally, the horses were brought to the starting line. Bets were being placed, the excitement was high and the crowd was ready.

BANG! The starter gun sounded; the horses were off and running. JJ and Whiskey were in the middle with Blazing Star on the outside; right where Fred wanted him, Three Paws was on the inside. By the quarter mile mark, these four horses were three lengths ahead of the others. As they reached the first turn their positions changed; Three Paws was slightly ahead on the inside with the other three running even. At the second turn Blazing Star had dropped back two lengths with Three Paws slightly ahead of JJ and Whiskey.

Fred glanced over at Candito; he had not given JJ full reign. Fred was letting Three Paws run just as they had planned; get ahead and stay there. Whiskey had apparently picked up a stone and was fading. As they rounded the next to last turn, the positions remained unchanged.

They were rapidly approaching the fourth and final turn. Three Paws was on the inside running hard; JJ was gaining on him while Blazing

Star was falling back. Glen Ray had pulled up, dismounted and was checking Whiskey's hooves. With Whiskey out of the race, and Blazing Star no longer a factor, JJ and Three Paws came flying down the Main Street straightaway; fully in sight of the finish line. Fred, hoping for some reserve, turned Three Paws loose and begged "Run baby, run."

Then, as he glanced over his shoulder, JJ was coming on strong. No horse had ever gained on Three Paws after a half mile, but JJ was doing it. Fred saw Candito apply the whip and JJ responded. Soon, JJ's nose was even with Three Paws rump; then they were nose to nose. When they crossed the finish line, JJ was a half a length ahead; Blazing Star had fallen back eight lengths and Glen Ray was walking Whiskey back to the stables. JJ was now the fastest horse in Texas.

Fred and Candito paraded their horses down Main Street for their customary cool down before returning to the staging area.

In the meantime, Glen Ray had walked over to Laughlin and said, "Captain, you always had the fastest gun in Texas, now you've got the fastest horse as well, Congratulations." Before Laughlin could ask what had happened to Whiskey, Glen Ray said, "Whiskey picked up a stone; he's okay. Hell, he couldn't have caught JJ any how."

Laughlin grinned and said, "Thank you Glen Ray, sorry about Whiskey, but I'm glad he's okay." Then he looked up at the Heavens and said, "Mr. Fox, this one was for you."

Boots and Bronco were at the finish line where that had been watching the race with Linda and Joy. When the race ended, they all joined the crowd gathering around JJ and Laughlin.

When Lattimer and his wife, Nora, spotted the girls, they came over and joined the group. "I'm sure the girls won't mind," said Lattimer, "so why don't you boys come out to our place tomorrow? We can have a talk while I show you around my holdings here in Texas."

"Yes sir," said Boots, "we'll do that."

Lattimer nodded his understanding and added, "Linda you and Joy give them directions; enjoy the rest of the afternoon; but, girls, meet your mom and I around 4:00 o'clock, we'll be ready to head out by then."

Everyone agreed on a 4:00 PM departure time, then, as Mr. Lattimer and Nora walked away, she looked at him and said, "William, what do you think about the Rangers?"

Without hesitation, Lattimer responded, I've heard they're good Rangers; been some write ups in the newspaper about them, all good." "I know one thing for sure," he added, "Joy really likes Bronco."

They were silent for a few steps before Nora chimed in "You know how quite Linda is, but I can see she's interested in Boots. They're both good looking men, especially that Boots. They appear to be a little older than the girls, but sometimes that's good; glad you invited them out to the ranch."

"What about me," asked Mr. Lattimer, jokingly, "am I good looking?"

"You, William Lattimer, were the best looking man at the dance. I loved you when I met you, and I love you more now than ever." They put their arms around each other's waist and kept walking.

Boots and Bronco spent the remainder of the day with Linda and Joy. They continued dancing to music being provided by the piano, guitar and fiddle players. Fun was being had by all; Bronco and Joy seemed to enjoy each other. Even though Bronco was borderline shy and Joy was just the opposite a flirt; they had fun together.

Of course, Boots was himself as always; a free spirit, smiling, joking and always a lot of fun. He was handsome even as a youngster, but since becoming a man, it seemed he was even better looking than when he was a kid.

Boots and Bronco made sure they got the girls back to their parents by 4:00 O'clock; they didn't want to rile the Lattimers. The night passed slowly as they anxiously awaited tomorrow's trip to William and Nora's ranch.

It was a short 10 mile ride from Comanche to the ranch and they had gauged their departure time to arrive around mid-morning. From a half mile out you could see the front gate; it was impressive; a massive stone structure with large steel letters over head reading, 'LATTIMER'. Underneath that, there was a three foot circle with a big 'L' in the center. They oohed and aahed their amazement at the sight and then rode the final quarter mile at a gallop.

The huge ranch house was equally impressive; it was of partial stone and wood; well built and maintained. Everything was in place; the ranch and all of the surroundings were extremely neat. They could see the barn, corrals, bunkhouse and blacksmith shop. When they were about three hundred yards from the ranch house, they saw Lattimer come out onto the front porch. They rode on and then reined up in front of an ornate hitching post; they were told to dismount and come in, coffee was waiting.

One part of the house reflected the presence of Nora while the large study was the epitome of Mr. Lattimer; it had gun cabinets, leather furniture, Indian lances, shields, bows and arrows, quivers, a large buffalo mount and a very large mountain lion mounted in the creep position atop a log. The room was a mirror image of the owner's personality; a man of the west, a cowboy, a rancher and a man rugged enough to survive the rigors of the early west.

Lattimer seated them in his study; as Nora brought in coffee and sweet rolls. William, an astute man, having noticed Boots and Bronco looking quizzically around the room, smiled and said, "The girls are upstairs. They'll be down shortly." He sipped his cup of coffee, sat the cup on an end table, leaned back and remarked, "Boys, everything I do, I do for a reason. I've got two girls that mean everything to Nora and me. My first concern is their well-being."

Once again he slowly sipped his coffee before continuing, "It appears there's some mutual interest between the four of ya'll. They like you Rangers and it appears you two are attracted to them." Having made sure he would have their attention, he leaned forward in his chair, pointed a finger and said, "Let me make one thing perfectly clear to both of you. Ya'll are welcome to see them as long as they desire, but treat them badly, abuse or hurt one of my girls, and I will ride you down, Ranger or no Ranger, it don't matter." He paused for effect before adding, "Have I made myself clear, perfectly clear?"

"Yes sir, yes sir," said Boots and Bronco, "we can respect that."

"Now, that our little chat is over," said Mr. Lattimer, "let me tell you about the ranch. I started slow, came down here from Bowie in a wagon with my Ma' and Pa'. They decided to settle here and build this house among the Live Oaks; next to the creek. With lots of hard work, fighting Indians, battling droughts and nearly starving, we survived and now have a thirty thousand acre cattle ranch."

William had begun to reminisce as he talked on, "I always admired the Rangers, wanted to be one myself. Nora changed that and it was for the best. Slow as I am with a pistol, I'd be dead by now. Back then, our main weapon was our rifle; the Indians feared the white eyes with a rifle. You know, this town wasn't named Comanche for nothin'. There were lots of 'em, lots of raiding and killings, those were scary times."

Lattimer, realizing he had been rambling on, waved his hand in finality and said, "Enough of my talking, I'll go get the girls; then I'll have their horses readied. They want to show you some of the ranch."

The girls had come down the stairs; Boots and Bronco were waiting in the parlor. Both were beautiful; dressed in riding pants, tall boots, blouse and vest. Boots was mesmerized by Linda's beauty; she had beautiful long auburn hair with streaks of blond mixed in and natural curls hanging to her waist. Her emerald green eyes and beautiful smile were highlighted by pretty white teeth and large full lips. She had a perfect figure and a pleasant personality.

Boots and Bronco took the girls by the hand and started walking toward the corral where their saddled horses were waiting. They helped the girls mount up and rode out the corral gate as a lone rider approached them; riding hard. His horse came to a quick stop in front of the group. The man was probably twenty-six years old. He was lean with broad shoulders, a stubble beard and a working Stetson pulled down tight over dark eyes. As the dust settled, he said, "Hello Ms. Joy, Linda, where you girls going."

Joy, who was the oldest of the sisters and always took the lead, said, "Well, Merle, that's really none of your business; but, if you must, we're all going for a ride."

"Yea," said Merle, "well maybe I just better ride with you for protection, lots of things can happen; not sure these two city boys can protect you."

"No need Merle, we're in good hands," said Joy, "these men can protect us."

Linda had enough, she looked at Merle and said, "Merle, meet Boots and Bronco. They're Texas Rangers, bye Merle." The girls giggled, spurred their horses and the group rode off leaving Merle behind; wide eyed and drop-jawed.

After a distance the girls started laughing heartily. Bronco remarked, "It appears Merle has interest in one of you girls."

"Oh, don't pay him no mind; he's our foreman and he has a crush on me," said Joy.

They stopped at a spring fed pond, spread a tablecloth, opened up their picnic box and enjoyed fried chicken with biscuits and bread pudding. After lunch, they mounted up for the return trip. Boots and Linda had enjoyed each other and, it was evident, Joy was very interested in Bronco.

It was almost dark when they returned. The girls dismounted at the house and walked their horses to the corral to be stabled. As Boots and Bronco were unsaddling the girls' horses, Merle, who had been drinking, came over to the stable where Bronco was tending to Joys horse. He was letting his whiskey do his talking as he looked at Bronco and barked, "I don't care who you are, I'm telling you to stay away from Joy."

Bronco, in a calm and deliberate voice, said, "Merle, I'm sure you're not afraid of me and I admire your bravery and your taste in women. However, if you're smart, which I seriously doubt, you'll turn around and walk out of here; pull on me and they'll carry you out feet first."

Merle, and his whiskey, responded with, "The odds are against me, there are two of y'all so I'm gonna walk out of here but don't you ever get in my way or let me see you with Joy." Surely Merle was feeling his 90 proof when he stated, "If ya' do, I'll walk all over ya', Mr. Ranger Boy."

Bronco grinned as he looked at Boots over in the next stall. Boots was grinning back; trying not to laugh out loud. Merle, thinking he had won the verbal battle, hitched up his trousers, turned and staggered out of the barn.

Boots got a drunken look on his face, mockingly hitched his pants and said to Bronco "If ya' do, I'll walk all over ya', Mr. Ranger Boy." Then he broke into a roaring laughter, slapped Bronco on the back and said, "We'd better go in, I'm sure William, Nora and the girls have the dinner table set and we need to get an early start in the morning.

After a wonderful dinner and pleasant conversation, Boots and Linda retired for the evening; in separate bed rooms of course, while Bronco and Joy sat in the parlor talking. Bronco looked into Joys' big green eyes and said, "I would really like to see you again and write to you while I'm on the road." Then, in his shy school-boy manner, added, "Uh, that is, if you don't mind."

"Oh no," she said, "I don't mind, in fact I would love to see you again and I'm sure I'll miss you when you leave."

"One thing," said Bronco, "what about this Merle guy, any feelings for him?"

"No, absolutely not," said Joy. Seeing some doubt in Bronco's eyes, she quickly added, "Seriously, he's just some one who works on the ranch."

The next morning, Boots and Bronco were up before dawn. They walked to the corral, saddled up and led the horses out of the barn. As they were preparing to mount up, the ranch hands were coming out of the bunkhouse.

Bronco spotted Merle and said to Boots, "Here, hold my horse."

He handed Boots the reins, went over to the bunkhouse, stepped up on the porch and walked straight to Merle.

When they were eye to eye, Bronco said, "Merle, just wanted to let you know I'll be seeing Joy again" and then he hit Merle square in the mouth with a straight right hand that knocked him off the porch and onto his back in the dirt. Merle made no effort to get up.

Bronco looked down at him and said, "Now you hear this mister, don't mess with my girl, don't even look at her; if you do I'll come back here and walk all over you, got it?"

Bronco didn't wait for any response, he just walked to his horse, took the reins from Boots, mounted up and said, "Let's go to Ft Worth, the quicker we get there and take care of things, the quicker I can come back and see Joy."

Bronco and Boots both laughed aloud and turned their horses toward Ft Worth.

Their trail, leading out of Comanche, would take them thru Stephenville, Grandbury, and then on into Ft Worth. The first night they camped just west of Stephenville. After building a campfire, tending their horses and a beef jerky supper, they sat around the fire sipping coffee.

After a few silent moments, Boots said with a grin, "Ranger Bronco, why did you punch ole Merle? You know, William may have a warrant out for your arrest." Then he laughed and said, "You pack a pretty good punch. Maybe we should call you mule, since your punch is likened to a mule's kick."

"Aw, I shouldn't have done it," said Bronco, "but he just rubbed me the wrong way."

"Well," said Boots, still grinning, "I don't guess there was any jealousy involved."

"No, hell no," responded Bronco with a stern look on his face that slowly broke into a grin as he added, "well, maybe just a little. It was a good punch though wasn't it?"

Boots nodded yes, threw both hands in the air and said, "If we ever fight it will have to be a gun fight, you hit too damn hard for me, besides you might scar up my face and that would upset all the girls."

Bronco, deciding it was time to turn the tables, said, "What do you think about Linda? I know she likes you, Joy told me so. Hell, Ranger Boots, you've got girls everywhere: Jane, Linda, the girl in Uvalde. How do you do it; what makes you special; I will give you credit though, you're not ugly."

Bronco," said Boots, "looks has nothing to do with it; I'm smart, girls' love intelligent men. Here's some advice, get you some books and read all you can because Ranger Bronco, you're ugly, downright ugly. Now, if you couple that with stupid..........you see what I mean?"

Bronco threw his half-cup of coffee on Boots; Boots kicked some dirt at Bronco as they broke out in hearty laughter.

As they regained their composure, Boots got serious and said, "All joking aside Bronco, I'm glad you became a Ranger and I'm damn proud to ride with you."

The next day they rode into Stephenville and, as usual, made contact with the sheriff, Ray Drusky. Drusky said there were usually lots of problems when the horse races were going on, but at the present time, things were calm.

Directly a young boy came in the jail and said, "Here's a telegraph for Boots Law."

Boots reached out with his hand and said, "Here young man, I'll take it, I'm Boots."

The young boy stared at Boots' Star and blurted out, "Gosh, a Texas Ranger, that's what I want to be when I grow up."

"Well young man," said Boots, "I'll put in a good word for you. What's your name son?"

"Johnny, Johnny Longfellow," said the boy.

"That sounds like a good name for a Ranger," said Boots as he removed a cartridge from his gun belt and gave it to the boy.

The excited youngster grinned and said, "Thank you, sir, thank you. I'll keep this forever."

Boots read the telegram, then he looked at Bronco and said, "We're going to Uvalde; there's been a bank robbery and a shootout." He noticed the concern on Bronco's face, so he added; "Sheriff Fox is safe but Preacher's been shot. When it happened, my Pa' was out at the ranch with Laughlin."

The Rangers bid Sheriff Drusky a 'good day' and rode hard for Uvalde; they had to get on the trail while it was relatively fresh. When they arrived in Uvalde they met at the jail with Laughlin, Preacher and Nathan. Laughlin was nervously pacing the floor. Preacher had been shot in the shoulder; but he was lucky, the bullet passed thru without shattering a bone.

As Boots and Bronco entered the jail, Laughlin was standing and pacing the floor; he looked up and said, "Sit down boys and listen up. It was bad timing; the bank was being robbed just as Sheriff Fox and Preacher were beginning their evening walk. When they stepped out of the jailhouse, there were two armed men standing guard in front of the bank. One was carrying a rifle; he's the one that shot Preacher. Then two more came out of the bank with the money and they all rode south towards Eagle Pass. The bank, as you know, is too far away for a pistol or scattergun, so the four men rode out clean. That was six days ago."

He let them absorb the magnitude of the situation; then he continued, "A bank has been robbed and a Ranger has been shot. While Preacher is recovering, Nathan will stay here with Sheriff Fox. Boots, Bronco, you've got a lot of ground to cover; they have a big head start."

Boots said, "Captain, Bronco and I had better ride by ourselves. We don't need extra men."

Laughlin agreed then said, "I can't tell you how bad I want these men. Do your best to bring 'em in alive, but remember, they shot a Ranger." He knew they got his meaning as he looked sternly at them and said, "You boys can't wait, you need to ride now!"

Nathan came over to Boots and said, "Boys be careful, they're killers."

"Thanks Pa'," said Boots with a grin as he mused, "four to two; that makes it about even." Then, with seriousness befitting the situation, he said don't worry Pa', we'll get 'em…….. dead or alive."

They didn't take a packhorse, just stuck a double barrel shotgun on their saddles and rode. The plan was ride to Eagle Pass, get supplies and inquire about strangers; especially men with money.

Shortly after leaving Uvalde, heavy rains caused more loss of time. When they finally arrived in Eagle Pass, the rain had stopped but the streets were muddy. The mud, heat and humidity made it hard on their horses so they decided to rest them at the stables and get an early start in the morning.

After taking care of the horses, they decided not to pay Sheriff Crenshaw a visit. He was young and inexperienced; they knew he would be of little or no help, so they went to the Cantina instead. It was almost empty. There was a small card game, some bar girls and a couple of cowboys drinking at the bar; so they ordered whiskey and sat down at a table.

Boots turned up his glass and said, "Bartender, bring me another shot and that redhead at the end of the bar." He and Bronco, as was customary when first entering a saloon, had removed their badges.

When the bartender served the whiskey, the redhead approached the table, stopped, and said, "My, my, handsome, it's gonna be a pleasure helping you pretty boy."

Boots flashed his boyish grin and replied, "Sit down beautiful; Let me buy you a drink."

She sat down on Boots' lap, ran her fingers inside his shirt and said, "You like; maybe we go upstairs."

Boots said, "Yea, me like, but I need to ask you some questions. Have you seen four strangers in here recently? They're cousins of ours."

She got that pouting look on her face and spouted, "You no spend time with your cousins, you spend time with me, you pretty, I show you plenty good time."

Bronco was enjoying the scene when a young cowboy stepped thru the cantina door. He was a tall, well built man, dressed in black with silver spurs, vest and a pearl handled pistol tied down in a quick draw holster; he appeared to be about twenty-five years old.

Bronco noticed his strong facial features, clean-shaven face, and dark, curly shoulder length hair under a black Stetson. He looked at the girl sitting on Boots' lap, flashed her a big smile and said, "Carmelita, get over here, you know you're my girl."

Boots and Bronco were sitting at the table; their Ranger badges still in their pockets as the man walked over, reached out and took Carmelita by the arm.

As he pulled her off Boots' lap and to his side, he put his arm around her, looked at boots and growled, "She belongs to me, I suggest you boys ride."

Boots calmly looked the man in the eyes and said, "We've been riding, gonna rest for a while."

"Not here," said the man, "mount up and get out of town."

Boots replied, "Ain't happening, we'll leave when we decide; not until."

Bronco, wanting to ease the situation, said, "Set down mister, let me buy you a drink, you can have your girl."

The cowboy grinned, sat down and said, "Hell, why not... get me that drink." He introduced himself as Ryder McCoy, sometimes cowboy, sometimes gambler, and sometimes gunslinger. Then he said, "Today I'm a man protecting his woman and getting a free drink."

Boots, not wanting to blow their cover, introduced himself and Bronco as cowboys looking for their cousins.

Ryder mumbled, "There were four men thru here the other day, didn't stay, had a few drinks, visited the girls and then rode south towards Mexico."

The bartender had brought the three men a round of drinks and set them on the table. Ryder took a sip of his, put the glass down and said, "They didn't look like wranglers; mean looking bunch. The leader called himself Butch, that's all I remember."

He took another drink from his glass, gave a knowing look at Boots and Bronco, then spouted, "Hell you boys aren't looking for your cousins, y'all are lawmen, that's why I backed off."

"You're right," said Boots, "I would appreciate it if you kept it quite. We think those men held up the bank in Uvalde and wounded a Ranger."

"I don't hold to that kind of stuff," said Ryder. "If I can help, let me know."

Boots said, "We're not supposed to go into Mexico, but we'll go in a ways. Too much time has passed since the hold-up; I think they're headed for Monterrey. They have money and if they go deep into Mexico, hell, it may be six months or a year before they come out." Boots finished his drink and added, "But, eventually they will come out and you can help by alerting us if you see 'em; besides, there will be a reward."

Ryder said, "I make my money by playing cards, don't usually hire my gun out to nobody, but if you boys need some help down this way, I'd be glad to throw in with Rangers."

The Rangers spent that night in Eagle Pass; rested the horses, loaded up on provisions and then mounted up for their journey across the river. When they left, it was early morning and the sun felt good on their shoulders. They would ride for three days inside Mexico while heading for Monterrey. After that, if no contact or trail, they would return and be forced to play the waiting game.

After crossing the Rio Grande and riding about a quarter of a mile into Mexico, they heard hoof beats coming from behind. It was Ryder. He was mounted on a solid black gelding and riding hard toward them. He pulled up, stopped where they were waiting, and said, "Thought I might ride along, hell I know both sides of the river, maybe I can help."

Boots looked at Bronco, who was nodding his approval, as Boots said, "Glad to have you, an extra gun down here is appreciated."

They spurred their horses and continued at a walk looking for signs of four horsemen.

They hadn't gone far when Ryder said, "There's a bandito gang down here that runs the border from Laredo to Eagle Pass and sometimes all the way to Del Rio. They're headed by Rene Alvarez; if you can locate him he'll probably have some information. He likes the Rangers; knows the ones called Baby Ranger and Shotgun?"

"Yea," said Boots, "Glen Ray told us about the shootout in the Streets of Laredo; he's the one they call Baby Ranger and Shotgun, is my Pa'."

They continued their slow walk trying to pick up a trail. It appeared the outlaws had used an old Indian trick by dragging a bushy limb behind their horse virtually wiping out their tracks. The three continued to talk as they rode.

Bronco asked, "Where you from McCoy?"

"Kansas mostly," answered Ryder, "but I've been around."

"What brought you here, wondered Boots; "are you running?"

"Yea, but not from the law," said Ryder. "I was eighteen; in a saloon playing poker and winning big. A wrangler, who's Pa' owned the biggest ranch in four counties, was losing big. He was a sore loser; you know the type, probably using his Pa's money. He went for his gun; we both drew and fired; he missed, I didn't. Killed him graveyard dead with one shot. The law said it was self-defense and turned me loose."

Ryder began to roll a smoke and continued, "His Pa', along with his ranch hands, didn't see it that way; they were gonna hang me so I jumped in a boxcar and rode the tracks all the way to Eagle Pass; as far away from Kansas, and a rope, as possible." He lit his cigarette, took a puff and added, "Don't have any family. Ma' and Pa' both dead, died with the fever so I just drift, you know, a free spirit." He took another drag on his hand rolled and said, "I try to stay out of trouble; play a little cards, chase women and practice with my pistol. Always admired you Rangers, heard lots of tales about y'all and your fast guns. Kinda feel honored, you boys letting me ride with ya."

Boots said, "I was raised to be a Ranger, but Bronco here, kinda has a background like yours; ain't that right Bronco."

"Yep," said Bronco, "if I hadn't joined the Rangers I'd likely be dead by now."

They had been riding for three days without any trace of the outlaws when Boots turned and said, "We'll go back to Laredo, might pick up a trail or get a lead from someone."

One days ride from Laredo, they spotted vaqueros riding out about an eighth of a mile on each side of them. Suddenly six banditos appeared in front of them; they appeared to have come out of nowhere. Some had their pistols drawn and others were aiming their rifles.

CHAPTER 10

What appeared to be El Jefe, the boss, hollered "Ola hombres, what you think you do in Rene's Mexico?" Boots and Bronco had their badges out of sight and in their pockets; Rangers weren't supposed to be in Mexico. "Senor Ryder, Rene knows you, but who are your amigos," asked Rene.

Ryder said, "These are Texas Rangers, they're friends of the Baby Ranger and this one's paw is Shotgun."

"You know my friend Baby Ranger? Asked Rene, "Oh he's plenty fast with his peestol. Shotgun mucho bravo, I like theem both," said Rene.

"Rene," said Ryder, "four men robbed the bank in Uvalde and wounded a Ranger......these Rangers are down here looking for 'em."

"What you do wif theem?" asked Rene, "you no Ranger."

Ryder answered, "Yea I know amigo; just trying to help a little."

Rene looked over at Boots and said, "We no see the bad men; if we do, we keel theem and keep the dinero, right?"

Boots said, "Sorry Rene, I need to recover the money, but one thing's for sure, these boys are going back, dead or alive and we don't care if they're dead."

"Ranger man Boots," said Rene, "We been in Del Rio, but we look good when we get to Laredo and see if we find, we know where to look, you don't, we find, we look good. We go now to our hideaway, we come see you soon. Amigo," he said, looking at Ryder, "you gonna be Ranger too?"

"Well Rene," said Ryder, "don't know, ain't been asked, besides the Rangers probably wouldn't have me, hell you won't have me."

Rene laughed and said, "You pretty good; maybe you do good, they take you; remember, you no shoot Rene and I no shoot you." Without any further conversation, Rene shouted, "Adios amigos," as he spun his mount around, slapped his horse on the rump with his sombrero and spurred him towards Laredo.

Boots said, "We might as well ride on in to Laredo, we can nose around a few days and see if we can get some leads. If Rene doesn't turn up anything, maybe Marshall Starrett has heard something."

Ryder said, "I need to make you aware of something. There are four wranglers from the Dos W Rancho, north of Cotulla, and when they come to town they raise hell. I've had some run-ins with them, there's bad blood between us. I whipped John Provost, the eldest brother in a fistfight. It was over a cantina girl, embarrassed him and now the four of them are out to get me."

Boots grinned and said, "Don't worry, if they go after you, me and ole Bronco will throw you in jail where you'll be safe from the mean ole hombres."

"That's it," said Ryder with a grin, "no more talk. I knew I shouldn't have brought it up; I can take care of myself, but of course if there're four of them, maybe you could lend me Bronco."

All three had a good chuckle as they continued on towards Laredo. When they arrived and the horses were stabled, they checked into the hotel for a hot bath and shave. They would spend a couple of days; if nothing turned up, they would head for San Antonio. Could be, instead of Monterrey, the outlaws had gone there to spend their money.

Boots and Bronco had a fresh change of clothes in their saddlebags; Ryder didn't. The Rangers changed into their clean clothes; Ryder washed his and hung them out on the balcony to dry. He told Boots and Bronco to go ahead to the saloon without him; when his clothes dried he would join them for drinks.

The Rangers left the hotel room, went to the cantina, sat at a table and ordered whiskey. It was a typical cantina, poker tables, long bar with spittoons and rooms upstairs for the ladies to conduct their business. The tables were full, as usual, but the mood was quite, unusual for a border town saloon. Boots and Bronco talked with the bartender, the girls and customers, about the hold up in Uvalde. They had no luck; either no one knew anything, or they weren't talking.

After a while, Ryder came in, sat down at the table and ordered whiskey. When he finished his drink, he got up and said, "I've got to go to work; it's time to make some money. You know, just riding with you Rangers don't pay nothing." He laughed and walked over to a poker table with an empty chair, and took a seat.

Around 9:00 PM, Marshal Luke Starrett came in. He was making his rounds but decided to have a drink with the Rangers. They made idle talk, finished their drinks, and then bid each other good night. Ryder remained at the poker table, the Rangers went to bed and Luke finished his rounds; the night was uneventful.

The next morning promised to be a hot South Texas day; a day when you tried to stay out of the sun. Around mid-day, the Rangers and Luke Starrett were sitting on the porch of the jail hoping for a breeze when four mounted men came into view; walking their horses down Main Street.

Luke asked, "Where's Ryder? That's the McKnight brothers and two hands from the Dos W Rancho up by Cotulla; trouble's coming."

Luke stood up and motioned for the men to come over to the jail. They rode up and stayed in the saddle when Wilbert, the older of the two brothers, said, "Hello marshal, you want to see us?"

"Yea, I do," said Luke. "This is Wednesday, what are you boys doing in town in the middle of the week. You don't have a supply wagon with you."

"Me and the boys don't work on the ranch anymore," spouted Wilbert, "we quit."

"Y'all got another job," queried Starrett.

"No," Wilbert answered, "thinking we might go to Mexico for awhile; we're healed well enough to enjoy the senoritas and tequila for a while."

Wilbert's younger brother's name was Bobby; the other two riders were Wesley and David.

Luke said, "You boys stay out of trouble while you're in town, ya hear; remember, idle time can get you in trouble." Without another word, they turned their horses and rode off towards the saloon.

When they were beyond hearing distance, Bronco asked, "Did you see how they looked us over?"

"Yea, I did," replied Boots. "We'll make the afternoon rounds with Luke; then spend some time in the saloon; by then they'll have some whiskey in their guts and will probably be feelin' brave."

Around three o'clock, when Luke, Boots and Bronco entered the saloon, it became real quiet; all eyes were fixed on the Rangers. Everyone wondered why they were there. The three of them stepped up to the bar and ordered whiskey. The bartender's name was Richard Mouton but everybody called him 'Dick'. He was rather short with dark curly hair, very intelligent, talented at pool and cards. He could also play the guitar and sing. His only drawback was his short temper.

One night, as Luke recalled, Dick was drinking with some drovers when they asked him to play and sing; so he did. One drunk didn't like his singing so Dick busted his guitar over the drover's head. Since it was his only guitar, he wouldn't let the drover back in the saloon until he bought a replacement guitar. Luke tolerated him because he could get info from the girls.

When Dick brought Luke and the Rangers their drinks, Boots said, "Hey Dick, any idea why Wilbert and those boys quit the ranch?"

"I'm not sure," he answered, "but Rosie was upstairs with Wilbert; I'll see if she knows anything."

Dick called Rosie over to the bar and they went into his office in the backroom. He returned shortly and told Boots that Wilbert had been left some money by his Pa' and was going to party until he was broke again.

About that time Ryder came walking into the saloon; Wilbert saw him, got up from the table, pulled his pistol and hollered at Ryder, "Hey cowboy, I told you there would be another day. This saloon can't hold the two of us." He walked toward Ryder with gun drawn and said, "Get outside, get on your horse and ride."

Without saying a word, Ryder turned and walked out the door. Wilbert followed him out and snarled, "That's right, now get on your horse and ride."

Ryder went to his horse and climbed in the saddle. Wilbert turned, went back inside the saloon laughing and spewed, "No guts. I wish he'd pulled on me so I coulda killed 'im."

Ryder's horse was a great big black gelding named 'Bad Moon'. Once on Bad Moon, Ryder spurred him hard, jumped up on the boardwalk and burst thru the swinging doors running over Wilbert. Still mounted he crashed into the table where Wilbert's compadres were sitting; scattering them all over the room. As he turned and dismounted, he ran over, picked up Wilbert and said, "I guess one whipping wasn't enough for you." Then he started punching Wilbert, who gave no resistance; he was half out already.

Suddenly, Dick ran around the end of the bar with a sawed off scattergun and stuck it in Ryder's belly. Ryder started grinning and said, "Now Dick, don't shoot me, you know I was just having fun."

"Fun hell," shouted Dick, "You ride your horse in here, tear up my bar and then.......Oh what the hell." Dick started laughing and said, "Come on, I'll buy you a beer." The he turned to the other men and snorted, "Out, get out of here and I mean now before I unload on you." They gathered their hats; drug Wilbert out the door and rode off. Boots looked at Luke and Bronco; they all laughed as they joined Dick and Ryder for a drink.

When they sat down at a table, Dick poured them all a shot of whiskey then Boots asked Dick if he thought the money those guys were spending could have come from the bank robbery.

Dick answered, "Absolutely not, the money Wilbert had was probably for a few steers he rustled off the Dos W Rancho."

They all finished their drinks, told Dick they would see him in a couple of days, and walked out of the saloon.

As they mounted their horses, Bronco looked at Ryder and said, "Let me ask you a question – were you mad back there in that saloon or just having fun?"

Ryder grinned and said, "I was having fun, old Bad Moon here was mad, weren't you boy," with that being said, Ryder patted his horse on the neck and they rode back to the jail with Starrett.

Unbeknownst to the Rangers, there were four men camped deep inside Mexico. They were the men that held up the Uvalde Bank and wounded Preacher. The small gang included the leader, Toby Williams and three members; Clyde Bellows, Hershel Reynolds and Buffalo Jack.

Clyde is mean and a killer; Hershel's fresh out of prison and Buffalo Jack's a drifter and bounty hunter. He got his name hunting buffalo for the railroad and was known to be an expert marksman. He had one of the new fangled scopes on his rifle; he didn't know what it was called, he only knew that, when you looked thru it, the target got bigger making him deadly at long range!

The group was sitting around the campfire; they were in a bad mood. They had been hiding in the Mexican hills for a couple of weeks, had money to spend, but were steadily growing restless.

Buffalo said, "Toby, lets get out of here, I ain't afraid of no Banditos or Rangers. I need a woman and some whiskey."

Toby responded, "Shut up Buffalo, I'll say when we leave, not you."

The other men joined in with Buffalo saying, "Toby, we're all ready to get out of here."

Toby, not wanting to lose control of the gang, said, "Alright, we'll ride to Eagle Pass and then split up. Four riders together draw too much attention. We'll leave in the morning."

The next morning, as they mounted up and rode toward the border, Toby said, "Boys, remember one thing, if we get caught and that Ranger dies, we all hang together." Just to make sure they understood his meaning, he added, "I know Buffalo shot 'im, but it don't make no difference, they'll hang us all." Then, to drive his point home, he continued, "I don't know about y'all, but I'd rather die fighting than doing the dance of death at the end of a hangman's rope."

Although they realized the perils they might face, they rode on towards the border and Eagle Pass.

On the second day, the four outlaws reached the Rio Grande and split up as planned. Buffalo Jack was going to Laredo; Clyde, Hershel and Toby were undecided.

The Rangers, along with Ryder, were still in Laredo. It was mid afternoon; Boots and Bronco were at the jail talking with Marshall Starrett, while Ryder was in the saloon, playing poker.

Bronco told Boots and Luke that, unless the gang was going to rob again, which was unlikely, they would have split up by now; with the banks money and no women or booze, they'll soon get careless.

Luke agreed; they'd be edgy from hiding out and, with the money they got from the bank job, they'd want a woman and some booze. He assured them they'd show up somewhere as he said, "You boys hang around Laredo for five or six more days; I expect I'll get a wire from someone that thinks he's spotted one or all of 'em."

About an hour later Ryder walked into the jail and said, "Boots, a fella rode in about three hours ago. He's filthy; looks like he's been on the trail for a while. Calls himself Buffalo; he's a big man, ugly, dirty foul mouth and getting louder with every drink. He's already been upstairs with Sarah; she's the only one who would service him, he's so damn filthy you can smell him twenty feet away."

Boots said, "Go back to the saloon and tell our friend, Dick the bartender, to try and talk to Buffalo; see if he can find out anything. Tell him to pour the whiskey to him. We can't go over there, everyone knows we're Rangers; if he's one of the hold up men, he'll take off soon as he sees a badge."

Ryder went back to the saloon, gave Dick the message then sat at an empty table so he could observe. Dick did a good job keeping Buffalo's glass full of whiskey and, as expected, Buffalo got louder and meaner the more he drank.

Finally, Dick said, "You better tone it down a little; the sheriff will be coming thru here making his rounds anytime now."

"Let 'im come," stammered Buffalo, "if he says something to me I'll take care of him. Sheriff's are cowards hiding behind a badge or their old men like that one over in Uvalde."

Dick continued to prod him as he said, "You must be talking about Oral Fox, Sheriff of Uvalde. Look out for him, he's old but he's got one hell of a reputation."

"Yea," bragged Buffalo, "well not any more." Realizing he had said too much, Buffalo turned from the bar and looked around the room.

Ryder, being young and good looking, as always, had attracted several of the girls to his table.

Buffalo stumbled toward Ryder's table and said in a drunken manner, "Cowboy, you may have all the looks, but look here girls, look what I have."

He reached in his shirt and pulled out a sock stuffed with money and said, "Now, who is the best looking, the broke cowboy or ole Buffalo?"

Trying to avoid a confrontation, Ryder got up from the table and said, "They're all yours Mr. Buffalo. I'm leaving." He walked by the bar and told Dick, "Keep him here, don't let him leave."

Back at the jail they were anxiously awaiting a report from Ryder. They didn't have long to wait; Ryder walked in and said, "I'll bet all the cash I have that he's one of the bank robbers." He briefed them on the action at the saloon; it was decided they would make an arrest.

Boots said, "Luke, you and Ryder wait outside, one at the front door, one at the back. Bronco and I will walk in with our badges on display. We'll say nothing; just go to the bar. If he's one of 'em he'll try to get out and make a break for it. Take 'im when he comes out. Remember he wounded a Ranger. Don't be gentle and don't be careless, he's dangerous."

Ryder and Luke got into position as Boots and Bronco walked into the saloon. Dick shouted "Hello Rangers, come on over, drinks on me."

Immediately, Buffalo Jack pushed the girls away from the table, stood up and staggered toward the door. As he walked out the door Luke stepped in front of him with pistol drawn and said, "Hold it Buffalo, you're under arrest for attempted murder and bank robbery."

Buffalo dove from the boardwalk and landed on the ground under the hooves of two horses tied to the hitching post. Luke fired and missed. Buffalo drew his pistol and fired striking Luke in the arm. By the time Boots and Bronco reached the door, Buffalo was up and trying to mount his horse. Bronco was first through the door as Buffalo swung around on his horse and started to point his pistol at Bronco. He wasn't fast enough; Bronco put two slugs in his chest. Buffalo slumped forward, slid off the horse and hit the ground dead. His shirt had come open and blood stained bills fell on the ground. The slug had passed thru the money before striking him in the chest.

Boots grabbed Luke to help him but he refused and said, "Just a flesh wound, I'm okay."

Boots looked at Bronco and remarked, "Good job, one down, three to go."

The next day, as was customary, Buffalo's body was placed in an open pine casket and propped up in front of the undertakers for display and photos. Boots wired Laughlin and informed him that it was apparent the gang had split up and were probably traveling alone.

Buffalo's horse was led to the stable and cared for; his saddlebags, saddle and rifle were taken to the jail. The next day when the Rangers and Ryder arrived at the jail, Luke said, "Boots, I'm making you a present, maybe you can use it while chasing the rest of the gang." He motioned towards a gun rack and said, "Look in that buckskin pouch over there."

Boots went to the gun rack, picked up the pouch and removed the buckskin cover; inside was a custom built Sharps 45-70 rifle with a telescope sight mounted on it. It had an extended barrel for long range shooting. The sight was something new Boots had heard about but had never seen.

Luke said, "Weapons go the sheriff to be auctioned, but I figured you could put this one to good use. It Belonged to Buffalo, he don't need it anymore, figure it might come in handy some day."

Boots put the rifle back in its soft case and uttered a single word, "Thanks."

As he touched the brim of his hat, Luke understood.

The next morning, Boots and Bronco were leading their horses out of the livery stable when Ryder rode up. Without dismounting he said, "Howdy boys, y'all 'bout ready to ride?"

"Yea," said Boots, "We're going to San Antonio; you riding with us?"

"Naw," said Ryder, "I'm going back to Eagle Pass, there's a little senorita over there that I'm hankering to see."

Boots and Bronco laughed, and then Boots said, "You ever decide to pin on a star, the Rangers will have you, in the meantime stay out of my rifle sight." They grinned at each other; then Ryder rode away.

The Rangers mounted up and rode to the marshal's office. As they got there Luke came out onto the porch holding a telegram. "You boys will want to hear this," he said; "Got a wire from Laughlin. Three men held up the Grandbury Bank; posse ran them down. Killed two and wounded the third.

Starrett paused for a moment, looked at Boots and said, "The wounded one confessed to the Uvalde bank job; said the other two, and Buffalo, were his partners. He didn't know Buffalo was dead."

"Oh yea," Luke said as he raised his index finger in the air, "Laughlin said you boys are to hang around Laredo until he decides where your needed next; and that's fine with me," Luke added, "things are a lot more peaceable when you boys are around."

Back in Abilene things were going well for Emmett Ryker. Progress on the ranch was slow, but Emmett was relaxed and enjoying his new life outside the saloons. JoJo spent a lot of time at the ranch helping and educating Emmett about ranching.

One afternoon they were stretching barbed wire for a new fence, when Emmett said, "Let me buy you a drink of water and let's sit for a while under that shade tree over yonder.

"JoJo, who was sweating profusely, anxiously answered, "I'll drink to that."

They went to the wagon for water; then sat under the tree for a work break.

The two men commented back and forth about the weather and fence building. Then, after a long pause, JoJo said, "Emmett, why did you give me your pistol and holster back there in Kansas?"

Caught by surprise, Emmett paused before answering, "JoJo, I didn't want to wear it any more and thought you might like it."

JoJo responded, "Well I appreciate it, that's the first thing anybody ever gave me."

"Listen JoJo," said Emmett, "that's a good little girl you're seeing. Why don't you and Patti get married? Get out of the Rangers before some back shooter kills you." JoJo remained silent as Emmett continued, "Get married, start a family, have a future. Don't do like me, live your life and have nothing."

Sensing the work break was over, the two men got up as Emmett added, "By the way, I'm going to town tomorrow; maybe Patti can join the two of us for dinner. It'll be on me; gotta pay you some how fer all the hard work you've been doing."

JoJo told Emmett he'd ride in a little later; see what Patti's doing and, if possible, they'd join him at the restaurant about six.

The next day Emmett rode into Abilene and went to Stewart Coffee's law office. His visit lasted about thirty minutes; then he went to the restaurant in hopes of meeting JoJo and Patti for their dinner date.

About six fifteen, JoJo and Patti walked into the restaurant; Emmett thought to himself, 'What a fine looking couple they are.' Patti was glowing; it was evident she loved JoJo, and the way he looked at her, beaming with pride, it was obvious the feeling was mutual.

The three of them enjoyed a fine dinner; then ordered wine. During casual conversation Patti asked Emmett about his family.

Emmett, looking a little uncomfortable, said, "Oh I got a brother up in Ada, Oklahoma, that's about it, don't have much of a family."

Not knowing the history between Emmett and JoJo, Patti queried, "Were you ever married?"

JoJo was looking at Emmett and trying to read him just as though he was playing poker.

Emmett hesitated for just a moment, then answered, "Had a wife, she died, don't like to talk about it. Ain't done a lot of things right in my life."

Patti could tell Emmett was a little put out by her inquiry, as he got up from the table, put on his hat and said, "Well, I've got to get back to the ranch. You two have fun; have some more wine." Emmett tipped his hat, kissed Patti on the forehead and walked out the door.

Patti looked at JoJo and said, "I'm sorry I got too personal and caused him to leave." JoJo waved it off as incidental. Patti got a curious look on her face and uttered, "JoJo, I'm confused, why did he pick Abilene when he left Kansas? Are you telling me everything? Y'all could pass for father and son."

JoJo looked down at his plate for a moment then raised his head, looked directly at Pattie and said bluntly, "If I'm his son, he's never said so. All I know is I sure do like him." Then JoJo laughed and said, "I like him; but I love you."

Patti blushed slightly and blurted out, "JoJo, do you mean it? You've never said it before."

"Yea," laughed JoJo, "I know I haven't ever said it before, but you're my first and last love."

The two hung around the restaurant, laughing and talking for several hours, before returning to their respective quarters. JoJo went to the Hotel, Patti to her luxurious ranch house. Emmett apparently had returned to his ranch after his abrupt departure from the restaurant.

A week passed and JoJo had not seen Emmett in town; which was strange, In fact, it was so strange, he became worried and told Patti he was going out to check on Emmett, but he'd be back soon.

As JoJo rode up to Emmett's ranch, he read the name on the gate, "Aces High Ranch". He smiled and said to himself 'He bought it with aces and named it after his poker hand.'

He was expecting to see Emmett on the porch or riding out to greet him; it didn't happen. When he got to the house, he dismounted and walked in; no Emmett. He walked back out and went to the stables to see if Emmett's horse was gone, when a single rider came up from the south pasture. It was Buster; a young wrangler that worked for Emmett.

Buster was very fond of JoJo and, because he was a Ranger, showed him great respect. Buster was a slender eighteen-year old, fairly nice looking and much more mature than most eighteen-year olds.

"Hello Ranger JoJo," said Buster, as he rode up.

"Hey Buster," replied JoJo, "how you been doing? Seen Emmett around or did he get lost on this big ole ranch."

"Mr. JoJo," said a puzzled Buster, "Emmett's been gone four days. He left a note on the table telling me to take care of things. Don't know were he is or where he went, said to get you if I needed some help."

JoJo's mind was filled with thoughts, but he couldn't reason what was going on so he rode back to town, found Patti and told her what had transpired.

Patti asked, "JoJo, do you think he's okay? Where could he have gone?"

JoJo, obviously puzzling over the situation, said, "I don't know Patti, we'll just have to wait and see; Emmett's hard to figure out."

For the next three months Emmett did not return. JoJo spent time at the ranch; helping Buster do the necessities and all the time praying for Emmett's return. Another three months passed and no Emmett.

JoJo wired the Sheriff in Kansas, inquiring about Emmett. He received a telegraph saying no one had seen or heard from him; whereabouts unknown.

JoJo was continuing to oversee the ranch. He sold some bulls, started an account at the bank, deposited the money in Emmett's name and continued to wait, worry and wonder.

JoJo, the Ranger, could wait no more, if he could track an outlaw, surely he could find Emmett. Remembering Emmett had a brother in Ada, Oklahoma, he decided to wire the town sheriff and inquire about anyone named Ryker.

Ada was a small town; Sheriff Johnson sent a wire back saying the local hardware/general store owner, Wayne Ryker had a brother named Emmett.

Hearing this news, JoJo wired Wayne asking for information about his brother, Emmett. The return wire read: BAD HEART – IN FT WORTH – HEART DOCTOR.

JoJo told Patti he was leaving for Ft Worth; he needed to get some answers. He kissed Patti good-bye, saddled up and rode toward Ft Worth. Patti watched him ride out of sight; tears were rolling down her cheeks. She knew how much JoJo was hurt by the disappearance of Emmett.

As JoJo rode he thought about his Ma' and wondered if he would find Emmett on Hells Half Acre; returning to the life he had always lived, playing poker.

When JoJo arrived in Ft. Worth, it was mid-day so he rode to his Aunt Hattie's house. When he arrived, he told her and Uncle Arch why he was there. They knew nothing of Emmett's whereabouts and Arch reminded JoJo he had told Emmett never to come back or he'd kill him. JoJo left and rode to town.

As he rode by the funeral parlor; the undertaker was standing outside on the porch. He was a skinny, middle-aged bald headed man dressed in a dark navy suit. He had white skin and looked cold to the touch. His name was Perkins.

JoJo asked if he had heard of Emmett Ryker. "Yes, yes I have," said Mr. Perkins. "Why do you ask?"

"I'm a Texas Ranger," replied JoJo, "Tell me what you know about him."

"Well sir," said Perkins, "he was living in a room in the hotel and seeing Doc Greines just about everyday; had a bad heart."

"Do you know where he is now?" asked JoJo.

CHAPTER 11

"Yes," said Mr. Perkins, "he's over there in the Oak Wood Cemetery. Strange fellow; didn't say much. He bought a headstone from me, paid for his burial and died of a heart attack all by himself up there in his hotel room."

JoJo dipped his head and said, "Thank you sir; you've been helpful." JoJo was almost in shock, so many unanswered things. With Emmett dying by himself, he felt great sorrow and hurt.

He mounted his horse, slowly rode toward the cemetery and tied up at the gate. He was searching his mind for possible answers as he walked around looking for his Ma's grave. When he found it, there was a freshly covered grave and headstone directly beside her's. As he got closer he could almost read the fresh headstone on the new grave. The inscription was blurred by some dirt that had blown over the words so he reached down and brushed it away. As his eyes focused on the revealed letters, they read:

EMMETT RYKER
HUSBAND OF MARY RYKER
FATHER OF JOJO RYKER

JoJo stood over the grave as tears came to his eyes; then he knelt down on one knee and cried openly.

After a long while he gathered himself together, stood up, put his hat back on and. in the Ranger way, touched the brim of his hat, nodded and walked away.

As he rode back toward Abilene he came to the conclusion that Emmett left Kansas because of his health. Then, when he came to Abilene, he changed his way of life but his health worsened. Probably saying to himself, 'I ain't never done nothing for this boy and I ain't gonna burden him with my problems now', so he rode off into the sunset to die alone.

Several days later, JoJo rode up to the bank in Abilene and was greeted by Patti. Before he could dismount, she anxiously asked, "Did you find him?"

"Yea, I found him," he answered.

"Was he alright? She wondered, "Tell me about it."

"Patti," said JoJo, as he grabbed and held her tightly, "he's dead, my Pa's dead."

"Your Pa," she said curiously, "Did he tell you he was your Pa?"

"Yea," he answered, "in his own mystical way he did." JoJo could tell Patti wanted to know the whole story, so he added, "It's a long story. Let's go to the restaurant and I'll try to tell you the entire complicated story."

They went to the restaurant, sat at a table and ordered. JoJo started telling Patti about his Aunt Hattie, Uncle Arch and his Ma' as Stewart Coffee came thru the door, went directly to their table and said, "JoJo, I heard you were trying to find Emmett? Did you find him?"

"Yes," said JoJo, with his head down and looking at his plate. "Yea I found him; he's dead Stewart, buried up in Ft Worth."

"Oh JoJo, I'm so sorry," said Stewart almost in a whisper. After a few minutes more of condolences, Stewart said, "JoJo, I do need to make you aware of something."

"Yea," said JoJo, "what's that?"

Stewart sat down, took off his hat and said, "Before Emmett left Abilene, he came to my office and created a will. Said if he didn't return, I was to give the will to you. JoJo, he made you the sole heir to his ranch. It's paid for and he said to tell you it was a wedding present for you and Patti."

Meanwhile, out on the trail, Boots and Bronco were about fifty miles east of Abilene. After Buffalo Jack, the bank robber that shot and wounded Preacher, had been dealt with, Laughlin directed them to hang around Laredo for a while.

After about a month, they were sent on patrol to Ft Worth where they stayed for about two months before being ordered west to Abilene. The trip had been unusually peaceful; no major problems.

As they approached Abilene Bronco said to Boots, "Bet you'll be happy to see Jane when we get there."

"Yea I will," he answered, "kinda missed her." Not wanting Bronco to think he was soft, he asked, "How about you Bronco, what you gonna do? I thought you would have swung over to Comanche for a couple of days and seen Joy Lattimer."

"Naw," said Bronco, then he added jokingly, "ole Merle might whup up on me. I'll leave her alone till we can both go to Comanche."

Boots laughed and quipped, "You may be scared of Joy, but you ain't scared of no Merle, you already showed that. I'm not sure I want you falling in love though, you're too good a compadre, I like riding with you."

Bronco said, "Never mind about me and Joy, what about you, Jane loves you, how you gonna handle that situation."

"Don't worry," said Boots, "I care, care a lot, but this Ranger's gonna 'Ride the Ranger Winds' for a long time."

When they arrived in Abilene they checked in with Sheriff Cletus Meeks informing him they would be in Abilene for a while; then continue their patrol on to El Paso and Del Rio; wherever duty called. The purpose of the patrols was to make their presence known in an effort to prevent problems.

Cletus was pleased the Rangers would be in town for a spell and suggested they meet at the restaurant for steaks later that night. They were in general agreement, so Cletus said, "Boots, you bring Jane, JoJo can bring Patti; they've asked about you boys every day you've been gone."

They picked a time and met as planned: Cletus, Boots, Jane, JoJo, Patti and Bronco.

They had a wonderful time; trail stories were told and JoJo told them about Emmett. He said it was impossible to tell all the stories since they were together last. Jane had her notepad and was busy taking down tidbits of information for stories in her Pa's newspaper.

After JoJo's stories wound down, Jane said, "Bronco, don't you have a lady friend? I don't like seeing you alone." Bronco was a big, tough, rugged man, but he was shy and bashful around the ladies.

Without waiting for Bronco to answer, Boots asked, "Jane, how much does it cost to place an ad in the newspaper?"

"If it's for the Rangers, there's no charge," she answered.

"Good," said Boots, "then place this ad: WANTED, DEAD OR ALIVE, Girlfriend for a Big homely looking Ranger; answers to the name of Bronco; rough around the edges, but probably trainable."

Everyone laughed, Bronco blushed then Jane said, "Y'all that's not funny, quit pickin' on Bronco. He's a handsome man and I've got just the girl for him; my cousin. I'm gonna write her a letter of introduction and the next time y'all are in Ft Worth, Bronco, you better go see her. If you don't, I'll whup up on your stubborn, shy Ranger head when you return to Abilene."

About two hours after finishing their meal, the conversation had dried up when Cletus said, "I hate to leave good company but I've got rounds to make."

Bronco spoke up and said, "I'll go with you Cletus; it's Saturday night and I don't have a girl to walk with, so I'll just walk with you."

"Fine, fine," barked Cletus, "glad to have the backup."

They slowly made their way down one side of Main Street; peering carefully into dark spots and alleys. It was after ten; most places were closed with the exception of the hotel, restaurant and saloons. At the end of the street they crossed over and started back down the other side. They had reached an area about five yards form the saloon, when they heard loud noises coming from inside. As they got closer, they heard loud cursing, tables and chairs being thrown around and glass breaking. Not knowing what to expect, they walked to the swinging doors, and peered inside.

There, standing on top of a pool table, was a large man holding a pool cue like an axe handle. On the floor was a man lying face down with his head in a pool of blood. There was blood gushing out of a large cut on his forehead. Another man was rolling around on the floor trying to get up. He was bleeding profusely from cuts above his eyes and his nose appeared to be broken. Standing on the floor, next to the pool table, was a fourth man with a cue stick in one hand and a knife in the other; he was trying to hit the man on the table.

Un-noticed, Cletus eased through the saloon door, backed up to the bar and shot one barrel of his shotgun into the ceiling. For a moment, the entire saloon seemed to go mute; all sound had ceased.

Cletus, in a raspy voice, growled, "That's it boys, everybody cool down."

As he realized he had their utmost attention, he continued, "What's the problem here, don't make me hurt someone."

The man on the table said, "I beat 'em all and when I tried to collect, they wouldn't pay up; then the three of 'em jumped me."

Bronco, who had entered the saloon behind Cletus, stepped up to the man with the knife and pool cue, and said, "Mister, Drop the cue stick and the knife right now. When the man didn't respond immediately, Bronco added, "I can get rough if you push it."

"I ain't dropping nothing," said the stranger, "see what he done to my friends, I'm gonna beat him to death or cut 'em. Now get outta my.............." He never got it all out before Bronco, who was standing at an angle facing him, threw a big right cross that landed hard against the man's head. The punched knocked him over a table, face down on the floor. The fight was over in one punch.

Then Bronco turned to the man on the pool table and said, "Come on down, don't make me come up after you."

The man looked at Cletus, who was pointing the shotgun at him, looked at the man Bronco had just knocked out, and decided to give up.

Two men went to the Doc's office to be sewn up before going to jail. The other two just went straight to jail and were placed in separate cells.

This was the last ruckus for a while in Abilene as far as ruffians go; however, things were heating up in the romance department. JoJo and Patti had decided to tie the knot. At Patti's request, the wedding would be kept simple with Boots acting as Best Man and Jane the Maid of Honor.

Once they made up their mind, nothing could hold them back as the wedding took place just a few days later. After the usual wedding reception and partying, JoJo and Patti took a couple of days off for a whirlwind honeymoon. Afterwards, it took about two weeks for everything to return to normal.

Patti was working at the bank; JoJo was taking care of Ranger duties and tending to the ranch. They were both very happy.

One day at lunch time, JoJo rode to the bank. He told Patti he was going to the ranch to help Buster repair a fence that was down and, since it was Friday, he would join her in town later for dinner. Afterwards, they could take the buggy back to the ranch for the weekend.

It was a quiet day in Abilene, until around two-thirty, when three men rode into town heading down Main Street. Boots and Bronco had left town and were on their way to Comanche. Cletus was at the stockyards; there were no deputies on duty; the setting was perfect for a robbery

The three strangers rode to the bank, pulled their bandanas up over their nose and dismounted. One man stayed outside and held the horses while the other two entered the bank; pistols drawn.

Once inside they told the customers to lay face down on the floor; then they walked around the counter to the safe. Patti was working along with a male employee named Lester. The intruders handed them some bags they had brought in, ordering them to be filled with money. The robbers weren't aware the bank President, Mr. Murray, was in his office and armed with a pistol. Murray heard the robbers, pulled his pistol, opened the door and fired. He was firing rapidly as the robbers returned fire filling the room with lead.

As Murray ran out of ammunition and was wounded, the robbers ran out the door, mounted their horses and rode away, moneybags in hand. Patti lay dead, face down on the floor; she had been hit in the neck.

Sheriff Meeks wired Boots and Bronco, telling them to return to Abilene. He only told them there was a dire emergency; none of the details. Simultaneously, a rider was sent to the ranch for JoJo.

JoJo rode into town full out; his horse was lathered and exhausted. He had almost ridden him to the ground in his efforts to get to Patti. When he got to the undertakers, she was still laid out on a table; there hadn't been time for embalming or placement in a casket.

JoJo ran to her and fell across the body crying, "Why, why? First Emmett, now Patti; why? why?"

He would not let the mortician touch her. He pulled a chair up beside her, sat down, held her hand and continued to cry shamelessly. Finally after several hours, Sheriff Meeks was able to get him away from the body and back to the hotel. Suddenly, as fast as they had started, the tears stopped

Suddenly JoJo became silent, no tears, no talking, it was as if his mind had left his body.

Two days later Patti was buried in the town cemetery and JoJo still hadn't said a word. In fact, he hadn't spoken since leaving her body at the funeral home.

Sheriff Meeks stayed with JoJo all during the burial ceremonies. JoJo remained silent throughout. Once the burial was complete, Sheriff Meeks led JoJo to the sheriff's office and said, "JoJo, set down, let's talk. I'm hurting with you, let's talk."

JoJo stood at the window looking toward the cemetery. Slowly he turned, walked to the domino table, removed his badge, laid it on the table, turned, walked out the door and headed toward the saloon. He hadn't spoken a word.

Once in the saloon, he went to the bar and layed enough money down for a bottle of whiskey. Without speaking, he went to a corner table and drank until he passed out. The bartender sent for Cletus. Cletus entered the saloon, took one look at JoJo, shook his head, picked JoJo up and carried him off to jail. He was really worried about JoJo as he put him in a cell to sleep it off. Cletus didn't sleep much that night, he simply watched and worried over JoJo with a few cat-naps in between.

The next morning, Cletus received a telegraph that the bank robbers had been captured and were in the Sweetwater jail; waiting on the circuit judge. Cletus woke JoJo and told him the good news.

JoJo immediately got that strange, distant look on his face; it was evident he wasn't right; Cletus figured he was in shock. Finally JoJo spoke and said, "Gimme my gun; I'm going to the ranch."

Cletus breathed a sigh of relief; figuring JoJo might be coming out of it. JoJo left the jail, went to the livery stable, mounted his horse and rode off toward the ranch. Once out of town, he turned his horse, spurred him to a full gallop and headed straight toward Sweetwater.

When he arrived, two days later, he rode slowly down Main Street directly to the jail. The day was coming to an end. Sweetwater was a small town with one deputy and a local sheriff. JoJo figured the sheriff had gone home and the one deputy would probably be alone.

When he reached the jail, he stepped up onto the boardwalk; the boards creaked as he approached the door. When he tried the door knob, it was locked so he knocked and said, "Open up."

The deputy peeped out and said, "Oh, It's you JoJo, just a minute and I'll let you in." When the deputy opened the door, JoJo stepped inside, drew his pistol and hit the deputy a hard blow on top of the head. The deputy, Mika Reynolds, went down hard, real hard.

The men in the cell jumped up and started hollering for help. JoJo pointed his Colt 44 at the men in the cell and opened fire. When he had emptied his pistol; their bodies lay on the floor, crumpled and bleeding. The smell of blood and gunpowder filled the air as he reloaded and again fired all his rounds into the bodies lying on the floor.

JoJo holstered his pistol and looked at the deputy lying on the floor in a pool of blood. As he walked out he hoped he hadn't hit the deputy too hard and prayed he would be alright. He feared the worse, knowing he had really hit him hard. JoJo quickly got to his horse, rode down Main Street and out of town. He figured he would head west thru the badlands and cross the Rio Grande into Acuna, Mexico.

Back in Abilene, Boots and Bronco had just arrived and were consulting with Sheriff Meeks. Cletus informed them about the bank holdup and how the tragedy of Emmett and now, Patti's death, his bride of only a few weeks, had affected JoJo.

The jail door opened and in walked the runner from the telegraph office. The boy handed Cletus a telegram. When Cletus read it, he sat down at the desk lowered his head and moaned, "Oh my God. JoJo went to Sweetwater, shot the three robbers in their cell and hit a deputy over the head. The deputy lived long enough to identify JoJo as the attacker."

Boots usual smile turned to a look of deep concern. He said, "Damn it, damn it, guess who'll be sent out to bring him in."

Within a short time a telegraph arrived. It was from Laughlin and read: 'Boots and Bronco bring him in – get Fred for tracking – no posse, we're not going to hunt him down like a dog.'

Boots and Bronco spent a restless night before leaving the next morning with a fully loaded packhorse; they headed for the JJ Ranch to get Fred.

As they rode along silently; they traveled slowly, their hearts weren't in the chase.

Finally, Bronco broke the silence and said, "Why did that deputy have to die, there's no choice, they'll hang him for sure."

"Oh Yea," said Boots, "you don't hang Rangers."

"The Judge won't have any choice, if we bring him in, he'll have to hang 'im." said Bronco.

"Yea," said Boots, "you're right, he'll hang alright, if we bring him in." Bronco wasn't positive, but he thought Boots had put a lot of emphasis on the "if". But he wasn't sure what that meant.

When they reached the ranch, they made Glen Ray and Fred aware that Laughlin wanted Fred to help them track JoJo. Fred said, "Hell, I don't want to bring him in, you know he didn't mean to kill that deputy."

Boots said, "Nobody ever said being a Ranger, even part time, was going to be easy. Laughlin has sent us; he knows if anyone has a chance of bringing JoJo in for trial, it's us."

Fred said, "Yea, you're right, but honestly where he's heading we might not find him. We'll leave today, head for San Angelo and straight to Acuna; figure he thinks we expect him to head toward Presidio, but my hunch is Acuna."

They mounted up and headed toward San Angelo. After several days they arrived and went to the general store where they inquired about any possible lone rider buying provisions for the trail. They were told a man had been in the store a few days ago, bought a packhorse and loaded it down with supplies for maybe two weeks.

Boots knew that, from San Angelo, JoJo could have either gone west into New Mexico or south into old Mexico. They stayed with their hunch and rode toward Acuna.

All the time the Rangers were riding, they were hoping JoJo would get to the Rio Grande and cross over into Mexico before they caught up to him.

About twenty miles out of San Angelo Fred picked up a trail of two horses. The tracks indicated one horse was following the other with the trail horse loaded down, probably a packhorse.

That night they camped, built a fire, ate jerky, drank coffee and talked. Boots said, "Fred, you can probably understand what JoJo is going through since you lost LaQuita."

"Yea, I can," said Fred. "I'm not over it yet. The loss of LaQuita made me want to die, it's a pain you can't describe and revenge doesn't take away the hurt." Fred recalled his encounter with Shortee, Laquita's killer, and said abruptly, "Hell boys, I've been thinking about it, I found the trail, now I'm going home. I ain't gonna bring that boy in to be hanged."

The next morning as they broke camp, Fred said, "Vaya con Dios," and rode away toward Abilene.

Boots and Bronco rode slowly and tried to follow the tracks. Boots said, "How you feel about this Bronco?" Bronco said, "I just pray he's across that river and never comes back, he was a good Ranger."

Slowly they tracked, wasting as much time as possible. Finally after several days, from a high ridge about two miles out, they could see the small town of Acuna.

Boots turned to Bronco and said, "You setup camp and wait for me. I'm going to Acuna." Perfectly understanding Boots' meaning, Bronco offered no argument.

He wondered just exactly how Boots would handle the situation if he found JoJo. He knew what he would do if it was him going into Acuna and he found JoJo. He would tell him to stay across that river pronto and then he would turn and ride hard and fast to Abilene; then make out his report that JoJo was in Mexico and out of Texas jurisdiction.

As he started setting up camp, Bronco watched Boots ride down the hill toward Acuna. He had no idea how long he would have to wait on Boots, but he did know that Boots lived by the Ranger code and hoped JoJo was already in Mexico.

Boots was riding toward the river when he spotted smoke from a smoldering campfire. The sun was setting; the dry desolate area took on a new look with the shadows extending to the mountains in Mexico and the orange sunset sinking like molasses in the western sky. Night creatures were waking up to start their night. He heard coyotes howling and saw javelinas going to water in the river; quail were gathering in coveys under bushes in preparation for another perilous night.

Unafraid Boots rode up to the campfire. JoJo's horse was hobbled, the packhorse was grazing, but JoJo wasn't at the camp. Boots squatted down, picked up the coffee pot, poured a cup and sat, waiting on something to happen. He knew JoJo was watching and he was dead if JoJo desired.

CHAPTER 12

From behind a tall yucca, with the sun to his back, JoJo slowly stepped out, looked into Boot's eyes and said, "I knew it would be you." Then, as if he read Boots' mind, continued, "Boots, those three guys had it coming, they killed my Patti. I know I did wrong, but they killed her."

Boots said slowly, "That deputy you hit in the head, he died too, and he didn't have it coming. JoJo, I gotta take you back."

JoJo looked down momentarily, then he looked back at Boots and said, "You ain't gotta say no more, they'll hang me for killing that deputy for sure; don't matter that I didn't mean for it to happen; I just pray the Lord will forgive me."

"Damn it, I thought you'd be in Mexico by now," said Boots.

"No, never did like Mexico," said JoJo.

Boots said, "You know I've always loved being a Ranger, now I'm not so sure, but I'll have to take you in, it's my duty."

"Yea I know," said JoJo "ain't nothing left for me to live for. Emmett's gone, Patti's dead and I ain't gonna hang." Then JoJo squared his shoulders to Boots, cleared his coat tails away from his gun and said with conviction, "Do your job Boots, ain't no need of talking, just gonna make it worse, do your job."

Boots, reluctantly, stood up to face JoJo. He always thought JoJo just might be faster on the draw than he was.

"Damn it, why didn't you cross that river?" asked Boots as he stood up to face JoJo.

They stood thirty feet apart staring into each others eyes for what seemed like an eternity. Finally JoJo said, "I want to thank you for being my friend, we rode good together but the time has come to end it, come get me Boots."

"I ain't drawing," said Boots. "Damn it, I can't shoot you, I ain't pulling on you JoJo."

"Then I will," said JoJo as he drew and fired.

Boots could almost feel the bullet as he heard it whiz past his head. Instinctively, he drew and fired; the bullet struck JoJo in the chest. As JoJo fell forward to his knees, Boots dropped his gun and ran to him; he was still alive. Boots fell to his knees, grabbed JoJo, held him up and said, "I always knew you were faster than me."

"Yea, maybe faster," said JoJo with a half grin on his face and blood running out the corner of his mouth. "But I missed," he added.

"No JoJo, you didn't miss; you wanted to die," said Boots as he watched JoJo's eyes slowly close, he was dead. JoJo was now with Patti and Emmett, he had a look of contentment on his face.

Boots held JoJo close to his chest and cried for several minutes; then he arose, put JoJo on his horse and led him back to the high ridge where Bronco was waiting.

Neither man spoke as they dug; then lowered JoJo into a shallow grave.

Boots said a prayer; then reached into his pocket, pulled out JoJo's Ranger badge that he got from Cletus's office, bent over, pinned the badge on JoJo's shirt and slowly covered his grave. Accepting what had happened would take some time. Other than the prayer, not a word had been spoken.

Once the burial was finished, they mounted up and slowly rode away. After about thirty yards, Boots turned his horse around, looked at the grave, reached up, touched the brim of his hat, nodded his head and rode away. He could feel the cold Ranger Winds blowing on his backside and knew the quickest way to forget death was to ride away.

Well into the next day the silence had not been broken; finally Boots turned to Bronco and said, "Why haven't you asked me what happened?"

Bronco continued to ride with eyes fixed forward and said, "Figerred you'd tell me iffun ya' wanted me to know."

Boots stopped his horse, stared into Broncos eyes and said, "He wanted to die." Bronco remained silent as Boots continued, "Let's just leave it at that…; then he paused and added, "Don't ever ask me anything more."

As Boots and Bronco continued north, the skies became dark and it started raining. The mood was somber, Boots' face reflected the sorrow he was feeling for the loss of his friend.

When they reached Abilene, Boots told Bronco to wire Laughlin then file a report with Sheriff Meeks. With that said, he rode to the newspaper office to see Jane.

When he entered, Jane ran to him and said, "Are you okay? You look terrible."

Boots replied, "I need to be with you, we need to be alone." The next morning, after having breakfast, Jane said, "Boots, you have the right to grieve but you must leave it behind. JoJo's body is in that grave but you know his spirit is in Heaven with Patti and Emmett."

Boots had his head down, obviously in pain as Jane assured him, "Baby, you must carry on with your life. You told me once that only a few select men could meet the rigorous requirements of a Ranger's life. You knew it wouldn't be easy. You met the challenge, not only as a Ranger, but as a real man. Remember, you were sent after someone who had broken the law and committed murder. Enforcing the law wasn't just your job; it was also your duty as a Ranger."

Boots had clearly heard what Jane said and knew she was right. He was hurting inside and wondered if he had it to do over, would he ride away. Jane's words, and his integrity as a man, reassured him he would still do his duty.

Jane had comforted Boots much like his mother did when she was alive. He was glad she was in his life, it would help him forget.

Back in Eagle Pass, trouble was brewing. A young fellow, who would turn out to be Henry Tillman, was causing havoc. He was adding notches on his pistol by raiding campsites and forcing drovers to draw on him. Since drifting in from Arizona, he had carved eleven notches on the pearl handle of his pistol. It was evident he was trying to build a reputation as a gunfighter. About this same time, Ryder McCoy, who had been working on a ranch near Kingsville, returned to Eagle Pass when the ranch work dried up.

It was late in the afternoon on a midsummer day in south Texas. The sun was bearing down; it was a good day to be inside. Ryder was sitting in the saloon playing poker with some wranglers from nearby ranches. As usual, the saloon had plenty of customers with girls and poker games. The swinging doors of the saloon swung open and three men entered. Ryder heard spurs jingling; probably large Mexican spurs with rowels.

One man came in first; the other two, a few feet behind. The man in front was about five feet ten inches tall and of medium build. He was well dressed; complete with leather batwing chaps and leather gloves. His pistol was a pearl handled Colt 45 nestled in a cut-a-way, fast draw holster. He sported a thick moustache and his stride reflected a cocky attitude; his image projected that of a 'gunfighter'.

The trio walked to the bar, bellied up and ordered whiskey. One of the men spat into an already full spittoon causing spit, mixed with tobacco juice, to splash all over the floor.

The one in the leather chaps appeared to be the trio's leader. He looked at the bartender and said, "You and the girls stay, keep our glasses full." Then he turned from the bar and in a loud voice growled, "My name is Henry Tillman – this bar ain't big enough for all of us, everybody out but me, the girls and my boys."

Slowly all the men started to leave the saloon except for Ryder and the three wranglers with him at the poker table. Ryder had not looked up from the cards he was holding when Tillman barked out, "I said everybody! That includes you poker players, let's move it……now!"

The three wranglers with Ryder slowly got up and eased toward the door. The saloon was now vacant except for Tillman, his men, the girls and Ryder. Ryder, who was sitting with his back toward the men at the bar, made no effort to move.

Tillman, obviously irritated, grumbled, "Hey you, you deaf? If you ain't, you'd better have a damn good reason for still being here."

Still sitting at the table shuffling cards, Ryder broke his silence and said, "Ain't finished playing poker yet. You boys want to play a few hands?"

When Tillman and his two companions walked over to Ryder's table, with their guns drawn, Henry said, "Do you know who I am?"

Ryder, still shuffling the cards, shook his head and said, "Nope, can't say that I do."

Henry, with his pistol pointed a Ryder's head said, "Tillman, Henry Tillman, that's my name. Mean anything to you now?"

"Nope," said Ryder, "never heard of you."

"Mister, I control everything around here. This is my territory," said Tillman. "If you want to stay alive, you'd better make tracks."

"Mr. Tillman," said Ryder, "it's awfully hot outside and I just ain't ready to leave."

"That's it," said Tillman. "Wade, you and Homer teach this tin-horn a lesson and then throw 'im out."

Wade grabbed Ryder by the shirt. When Ryder kicked him in the crotch, he let go and fell screaming to the floor. Homer landed a round house right to the side of Ryder's face knocking him out of the chair. As homer tried to stomp his face, Ryder caught his boot, twisted hard and sent Homer crashing hard to the floor.

As soon as Homer went down, Ryder jumped up and kicked Homer flush in the face knocking him backwards; his eyes were swelling shut by the time his head hit the floor. With blood spurting out of his nose, his part of the fight was over; he was done for the day.

Wade, who had finally managed to get up, swung at Ryder striking him on the shoulder. Ryder responded with a hard left hook and then a devastating straight right. Wade dropped to one knee; he was all but out.

Ryder looked down at the two men on the floor and said, "Come on boys teach me a lesson, I'm a slow learner."

"Shoot 'im, Henry," shouted Wade, "shoot 'im."

Tillman said, "Hold it Wade, fights over, you boys get outta here." Henry could see Homer's eyes were swelling shut as he told them, "get a room at the hotel." Then he holstered his pistol, looked at Ryder and uttered, "Sit back down stranger, I'll join you for a drink." The bartender brought a bottle and two glasses. Henry filled Ryder's shot glass and they both turned bottoms up.

Henry said, "You know how to take care of yourself with your fists. Are you any good with that shooter?"

"Fast enough to stay alive," remarked Ryder.

Henry laughed and said, "Well then, hopefully we won't have to pull on each other. I've got some things I'm working on; maybe we can do something together." Before Ryder could answer, Tillman added, "You'll be hearing from me, gotta go patch up my boys. You'd be obliged to look out for 'em, you embarrassed 'em.

Tillman started to leave, stopped and snorted, "By the way, you got a name, like to know who I drink with."

"McCoy," said Ryder, "Ryder McCoy."

Several days had passed. Ryder was leaving the restaurant after eating breakfast and paying for his meal. When he walked outside to where his horse, Bad Moon was tied, he saw Wade and Homer riding down the street. Ryder stood next to his horse, looking over the saddle, as the men rode toward him. He was hoping they wouldn't see him and ride by.

Not a chance. Wade spotted him as they reigned in their horses. He had two black eyes and his face was still swollen from the kick Ryder gave him. Wade said, "Look what I found Homer," as he pointed at Ryder.

Ryder said, "Ride on by boys, no need for someone to die."

"Oh don't worry 'bout us," said Wade, "you're that someone who's gonna die." Wade, still on his horse, drew his pistol and fired; he missed.

Ryder returned fire striking Wade in the belly. As Wade slumped forward he cried out, "Oh my God Homer, I'm gut shot;" then he leaned over the saddle horn and rode off with Homer helping him stay in the saddle.

Ryder turned and started walking toward the sheriff's office. The sheriff, Johnny Gonzales, was in his twenties, new to the job and inexperienced. He had heard the gunshots and was running toward Ryder. Ryder put his hands up and said, "Hold on now Sheriff, it was self defense, he shot first."

Two men, who had been seated on the restaurant porch, saw the shootout and told the sheriff it was, in fact, self defense.

Ryder had planned on riding up to Uvalde in hopes of seeing Boots and Bronco but, because of the gunplay, he told the sheriff he would stay in Uvalde for a while; wanted Homer to cool down. He was pretty sure Wade, being gut shot, was probably finished and he didn't want anymore killing.

Several days passed; no Homer. Ryder packed his saddle bags, tied them on Bad Moon, mounted up and started for Uvalde. He was in no hurry; had a lot of thinking to do. His mind kept drifting back to how it was when he rode with Boots and Bronco. Maybe a Rangers life is what he wanted. With the lifestyle he lived, surely there would be more gunfights. He was hoping Boots would be in Uvalde so he could talk to him.

About midday on the fifth day of traveling, Ryder rode into Uvalde. He thought how different it was from Eagle Pass and Laredo. Uvalde was a clean town and seemed friendlier. As he rode up to the sheriff's office, a peg legged man and an old geezer were sitting on the porch in the shade. They were enjoying the breeze and staying out of the hot sun.

Ryder pulled up and, without dismounting, said, "Howdy men, names Ryder McCoy, I'm looking for a Texas Ranger named Boots."

The peg legged man said, "He ain't here, can I help you?"

"Is your name Shotgun?" asked Ryder.

"Yea, that's right," said Nathan.

"Then you're Boots Pa", barked Ryder, "he's told me a lot about you."

Nathan and Oral, the old geezer, got up as Nathan said, "Climb down, come inside and we'll have some coffee." They went inside; Oral poured coffee and introduced himself as they began talking.

"Why you looking for Boots?" asked Nathan.

"Oh, I helped him and Bronco on a chase into Mexico; kinda liked what I saw of a Rangers life. Wondered if Boots could put in a good word for me; think I'd like to be a Ranger."

Nathan told Ryder he would take him out to the "Big Iron" ranch and introduce him to Captain McFarland. Ryder acknowledged his appreciation as Nathan added, "Captain is a fair man and we always need more Rangers."

Back in Eagle Pass; Wade, as Ryder expected, had died five days after being gut shot. Homer was vowing revenge and Tillman was boasting he would add another notch on his gun the next time they saw Ryder.

Henry, who, after meeting Ryder, was considering asking him to join his gang, was planning a train robbery north of San Antonio; but the death of Wade made it impossible for them to join forces. Homer was vengeful and Ryder had embarrassed Henry and his men; his action could not go unpunished.

Meanwhile, Nathan and Ryder rode out to the Big Iron to see Laughlin. As they were approaching, Laughlin, sitting on the porch, spotted them as they rode thru the main gate. He got up, went to the yard gate and waited for them.

As they pulled up, Laughlin said, "Hello Nathan, ya'll get down. Who's your prisoner?"

"No prisoner," said Nathan, "feller who wants to talk about a job with the Rangers. Names Ryder McCoy; says he rode with Boots and Bronco on a ride into Mexico."

"Ya'll come on in"; responded Laughlin, "we'll have a cup of Melissa's coffee. As they were entering the ranch house, Laughlin remarked, "Acquainted with Boots and Bronco you say, them's good Rangers, proud to have 'em."

They walked into the kitchen where Melissa was baking cookies; Audrey Fox was with her. Laughlin introduced everyone and said, "Audrey is spending some time with Melissa; they're working on a church project."

Ryder was trying not to be rude and stare at Audrey, but he thought she was beautiful. As she brought coffee to the table, she asked Ryder if he was a Ranger.

"No ma'am, I'm not," he said, "but I sure hope to be."

When Melissa heard what Ryder said, she looked at Laughlin and said, "Laughlin, hire this handsome young cowboy, looks like he'd make a good Ranger." Then she paused for a moment before adding, "Audrey, don't you think Ryder would improve the appearance of our Rangers?"

Audrey blushed and said, "I sure do. Laughlin you better hire him or Melissa and I'll whip up on you."

Laughlin, who was not about to enter the ladies conversation, said, "Nathan, you and Ryder join us for dinner, then ya'll spend the night in the bunkhouse. In the morning I'll ride back to town with ya'll; want to check on Oral and Preacher."

After dinner, the men sat on the front porch, sipped coffee, and talked. The girls cleaned the kitchen, then went into the parlor and visited.

Melissa said to Audrey, "That Ryder is a nice looking young man, don't you think?"

"Yes, he's nice looking," then she added, "a very interesting man,"

Melissa said, "Most interesting men have an interesting past. If he hangs around here his past will show up."

"I'm betting he's here to find out about being a Ranger," said Audrey.

"Why are you saying that," asked Melissa.

"A free spirit on the move, not afraid of danger and walking on the right side of the law," said Audrey. "Well anyway, I sure hope he stays," she added.

Melissa warned, "Be careful, remember, ladies love outlaws like babies love puppy dogs."

Laughlin, Ryder and Nathan were still sitting on the porch talking. When Laughlin asked Nathan how he had been doing, he replied, "Real good, been taking a lady from church to dinner occasionally. Don't know what the boys are going to think about me seeing someone."

Laughlin bellowed, "Nathan, you have two fine boys. Boots and Sterling wish the best for you, it'll be fine."

Laughlin asked Ryder about his life and Ryder said, "What you're going to hear I am not real proud of, but it was my way of survival."

"I was born in Kansas, not much family, and like most boys it was a cattle drive at fourteen where I learned to be a man. Became a good poker player; don't have a drinking problem and found it easy to take a drunks money. Then one day I beat a man out of a large sum of money. He said I was cheating and drew on me; I beat him. The bartender and other witnesses confirmed it was self defense but, come to find out, the dead mans Pa' owned the biggest ranch in four counties. When he sent men after me, I jumped a boxcar and rode it to San Antonio; then on to Eagle Pass where I stayed for about three years; that's where I met Boots and Bronco."

Ryder paused to catch his breath then continued, "My trouble started brewing there when a fellow named Henry Tillman and two sidekicks came into town. Tillman, trying to build a name for him self, had killed six or seven men, not gunfighters, just drunks and young cowboys. He notches his pistol after each killing; then he brags about it trying to build a reputation as a gunfighter. Just like in Eagle Pass, he always has a couple of men with him for protection."

He sipped his coffee, saw that Laughlin and Nathan were listening attentively, so he added, "Tillman tried to have his men rough me up for not leaving a saloon; but that backfired when they lost the fist fight. Two days later they tried to gun me down in the street. I gut shot one of 'em; don't know for sure, but I suspect he died. Sheriff Gonzales seen the fight and told me I'd best get out of town, so I decided to come to Uvalde and talk to Boots about becoming a Ranger."

Laughlin chewed on his story for a moment, then said, "Boots and Bronco are in Abilene. Boots can recommend you, but I do the hiring."

Laughlin eased to the edge of his chair, leaned forward, looked intently at Ryder and bluntly asked, "You ain't trying to hide behind a star and get away from Tillman; are you?"

"No sir," said Ryder, "I fight my own fights."

Laughlin gave him an understanding nod and said, "I'm aware of Tillman; as a matter of fact, I was planning on sending a couple of Rangers to Eagle Pass to check out his activities." McFarland eased back in his chair, rubbed his chin in deep thought and said, in a half whisper, "I could use another Ranger." Then, not wanting to give McCoy the wrong impression, remarked, "Boots and Bronco will be here in about ten days. You understand I'll need to discuss you with Boots; can't guarantee a thing."

"Thank you sir, I understand" said Ryder, "In the meantime, Captain, I'd be much obliged if you could point in the direction of some work, I'm flat broke."

"Yea, sure" said Laughlin, "I can hire you on right here at the ranch. Candito, my foreman will put you to work." Then with a smile, Laughlin continued, "If you work out; I just might keep you on as a wrangler; good wranglers are hard to find, Rangers come easy."

Nathan, whom Laughlin had been looking at all the while, took the joke as a compliment, grinned back and laughed softly under his breath.

The next day Nathan started back to Uvalde and Ryder started working on the ranch. As Nathan rode, he thought back to when Audrey was seeing Boots. He knew for sure Ryder would be seeing her and he recalled how she had looked at him. Nathan chuckled to himself and said out loud, "This could get very interesting, hell; it could get down right exciting."

The week passed quickly and Ryder was enjoying the work on the ranch. When Sunday morning came around, he had asked Laughlin if he could go to church with them. Laughlin said he had plenty of wranglers to handle things and that Ryder could ride in with him and the family.

Laughlin, Melissa and young Sam all climbed into the buggy and headed for church with Ryder trailing behind on horseback. Ryder told his horse 'Bad Moon' to act right or he would be tried, convicted and shot right there in front of the church, which was something new for both of them.

When they arrived at church, Laughlin stopped the buggy in front of Jerry Jack and said, "Ryder this is Ranger Jerry Jack, the one known as 'Preacher'.

"Really glad to meet you," said Ryder, "I've heard stories about you. They say you preach to outlaws before you arrest 'em."

Preacher grinned and said, "You heard right, but I'm still a Ranger; also studying to be a minister. Fact is, Brother Morgan, the minister here is teaching me."

Audrey saw Ryder and immediately came over to welcome him. She looked beautiful; Ryder was overwhelmed.

Audrey said, "Come on," and grabbed Ryder by the hand. "You're going to sit with me during services and take me to the covered dish lunch afterwards." Ryder had the shakes; no other woman had affected him like Audrey.

Church services were soon over and the congregation went outside under the shade trees for the buffet lunch. They had filled their plates when Audrey said, "Look, there's Grandpa Fox.

Grandpa, Grandpa," said Audrey, "come join us." She found a table and saved a space for Oral. When Oral reached the table, he hugged her, was introduced to Ryder, said hello and then they all sat down.

Oral said, "Mr. McCoy, what do you think of my granddaughter? Pretty ain't she?"

"No sir," said Ryder, "she's down right beautiful; and I'd be right proud if you'd call me Ryder."

Oral nodded his okay and said, "Probably wonder why she's not married eh! Well I'll tell you why. She's had lots of boyfriends but I take care of that."

Oral got a real intimidating look on his face and grumbled, "You see, when they come to town on the weekend to court her, me and Nathan ride out to meet 'em and take 'em to jail for the weekend. Then we turn 'em loose on Sunday night and run 'em outta town. Nobody's gonna git my granddaughter."

"Grandpa," said Audrey as she shoved Oral on the shoulder, "quit making up stories, you'll run Ryder off for sure." Ryder liked Oral; he hoped Laughlin would accept him as a Ranger. He could see this as a good life. When the luncheon ended and the clean-up was completed, it was time to load up and start back to the Big Iron.

Ryder said goodbye to Audrey and asked if he could see her next time he was in town. Audrey replied, "I would be disappointed if you didn't come to see me." Ryder grinned as he mounted up; he felt good.

Several days later, Nathan was riding down the lane to the Big Iron Ranch. Laughlin saw him coming, greeted him at the yard gate and asked, "What brings you here Nathan?"

"Well sir," said Nathan, "there's three fellers in town, dressed like gunfighters and asking if anyone knew where to find Ryder McCoy. Captain it's that feller Tillman from Eagle Pass. Do you want Oral and me to take care of it; we can."

"No," said Laughlin, "stable your horse and spend the night here; in the morning me, you and Ryder will ride into town."

From the bunkhouse Ryder could see Nathan's horse. He had a feeling that Henry would pursue him and figured that's why Nathan was talking with Laughlin. Ryder started walking toward the ranch house where Nathan and Laughlin were sitting on the porch. When he reached the yard gate, Laughlin said, "Come on, join us; we were just getting ready to come gitcha; we need to talk."

Ryder stepped towards the porch, looked at Laughlin and asked, "What's up."

Laughlin's face grew stern as he said, "Henry Tillman and two of his men are in Uvalde questioning your whereabouts."

Ryder, standing on the ground looking up at Laughlin and Nathan, looked down at the ground for a moment, then looked up and said, "I knew they would come after me. Didn't think they would come to Uvalde though, this being District Headquarters for the Rangers. I'll mount up now and go face them, or I can ride on, whatever you require."

"No," said Laughlin, "we'll all three ride in together in the morning. You'll be wearing a star; I'm swearing you in as my deputy."

The next morning Ryder was up early and waiting on Laughlin in the bunkhouse. Nathan walked in, told Ryder to come join them in the 'big house' for breakfast. After breakfast, Laughlin swore Ryder in as a deputy; then they mounted up and started to town. As they rode Laughlin instructed them to say nothing, let him do all the talking. He said, "As of now they have done nothing wrong, but I'll give them a warning and they'll probably leave town."

Upon arriving in Uvalde they went to the sheriff's office to speak with Oral. Oral told them the men had been hanging out at the saloon but weren't causing any trouble.

It was mid-afternoon; Tillman and his two companions were still in the saloon.

Laughlin said, "Oral, you stand guard outside the saloon by the horses. Nathan, you and Ryder go to the bar with me. Stay there until needed; I'll see if we can handle this without any bloodshed."

They entered the saloon and all three went to the bar; Laughlin told the bartender no drinks. Nathan asked, "Is that them over by the window playing poker."

"Yea," said Ryder, "the one in the middle is Tillman."

Laughlin walked over to the table where Henry and his men were sitting. Their eyes had followed the Rangers when they came in and were now fixed on Laughlin as he stood next to their table.

Laughlin's eyes turned steel blue, his jaw squared, he looked each man in the eye and then he spoke, "I'm Ranger Laughlin McFarland.

I hear you boys are looking for my deputy, Ryder McCoy, back there leaning on the bar."

"Look Ranger," said Tillman, "we knew ole Ryder back in Eagle Pass, just wanted to look him up and have a drink. Guess he told you about back shooting one of my men. Now, we got no hard feelings, hell Wade weren't no good no how."

Laughlin said, "Tillman, no more talk out of you. I know who you are and what's been going on in Eagle Pass. I was planning on sending a couple of Rangers down there to investigate these so called self defense killings I've been hearing about."

Tillman said, "Now Ranger, I haven't broken the law and you can send all the Rangers down there you want to, especially if they're all like that back shootin' Ryder. He shot my man and then ran to you Ranger boys to hide him."

Laughlin was getting impatient and madder by the minute when he growled, "Tillman, he whipped both your men in a fist fight and then killed on of 'em several days later after they shot at him. Sheriff Gonzales was a witness; knows it was self defense and no charges were filed. Now I'm tellin' ya, talks over, you boys aren't welcome in Uvalde. Get up, get out, get mounted and ride."

"We ain't done nothing," said Tillman, "and we ain't leaving. See these notches on my gun? There's seven of 'em, nobody pushes me around, not even a Ranger."

Laughlin took a step back from the table so he could have all three men in front of him and said, "Ryder, come arrest these men, they're going to jail."

Ryder, who was hoping be could get involved, grinned, walked over to the table, drew his pistol and said, "Everybody put your hands on the table." Then he walked around behind the three men and disarmed them, one by one. When it came to Henry, Tillman said, "I'll get you Ryder, you're gonna die."

Ryder grabbed Tillman by the hair, slammed his face down on the table and continued to hold his head down as blood began to spill from his mouth and nose. Then he barked at Tillman, "Anytime you want to try me I'm ready, I'm not a drunken cowboy. How about now, if the Captain here," motioning toward Laughlin, "gives me the word, I'll let you up and we can get it on right now, brave man. I'll give you your gun back; you won't have to look for me, I'll be right here in front of you."

Laughlin stepped up to the table and said, "Not this time Ryder, back off, you and Nathan go lock 'em up." Oral joined them as they locked the three in separate jail cells.

As Laughlin left the jail to mount up, Oral followed him out and asked, "What do you want me to do with 'em?"

Laughlin answered, "I'll be back in five days and we'll see what kind of attitude they have; I'll make up my mind then." He mounted up, looked down at Oral and said, "Tell Ryder to keep wearing that deputy's badge. He handles himself well; but, I just might have to work on his tactics a little"

Back in Abilene Sheriff Meeks received a telegram from Laughlin. The wire simply read: **Boots come to Uvalde.**

Cletus knew where to find Boots; he would be at the newspaper office with Jane. Since the death of JoJo, Boots spent most of his time with her; he was bothered very deeply by the situation surrounding JoJo's death.

Cletus opened the door to the newspaper office, stuck his head in and, grinning ear to ear, said, "Telegraph for Mr. Boots; no more laying around here and getting soft, back in the saddle," he urged, "your boss wants you in Uvalde."

Boots read the telegram, looked at Jane and said, "I'm leaving today. I'll come by after I'm saddled and say goodbye." Boots walked out the door and headed for the livery stable.

Jane looked at Cletus and said, "I'm worried about him, he's really sad and hurting bad."

Cletus replied, "Honey, don't worry. Laughlin knows what he's doing; he's putting him to work."

After leaving Abilene, Boots slowed War Paint to a walk. He looked at the red hills that were so fresh and clean from an overnight thunderstorm. He could smell the crisp fresh air as it entered his nostrils. It was a beautiful day God had created, but he was hurting. He couldn't erase the vision of JoJo standing in front of him; then watching him die in his arms.

If the same thing that happened to Patti would've happened to Jane, he wondered how he would have reacted. He had no answer so he shouted out, **'Why, JoJo, why didn't you just cross that river and stay in Mexico'.**

War Paint layed his ears back as if Boots was upset with him. With a halfhearted grin Boots said, "It's okay ole pal, you've done no wrong, your saddle partner is just losing his sanity, talking to himself."

The ride to Uvalde was long and lonesome, but it gave him time to clear his mind. As Boots rode into Uvalde late in the day, he saw Sam tied in front of the jail. He knew Laughlin was in town, so he dismounted, tied up and entered the jail.

Laughlin was alone at Oral's desk; sitting and doing some paper work. He heard Boots enter, turned from the desk, got up, shook Boots hand and said, "Sit down at the table; I'll get us some of Oral's coffee."

Laughlin poured the coffee, sat down at the table and said, "We need to talk. Son; I put you in a very difficult situation when I selected you to go get JoJo. I'm sure you knew I would." Boots was staring Laughlin in the eyes as he continued, "Boots, you're my best Ranger, you're like a son to me. You're known as the Ranger that adheres to the code, that no man is above the law, not even a fellow Ranger."

Laughlin leaned closer, put a hand on both of Boot's shoulders and said, "I'm sure you wished he had crossed that river, hell, I would've, but he didn't, so you took the only honorable option available."

Boots removed his hat, looked at the floor and said, "Laughlin, he outdrew me, he wanted to die. He was a good Ranger, what a waste." Boots rose from the chair, put his hat on and walked to the door, turned to Laughlin and said, "Please, let's not ever talk about this again;" then he tipped the brim of his hat and walked out.

Boots checked into the hotel, bathed, shaved and had a good meal at the restaurant. Then he went directly to the hotel and had a good nights sleep, his first since the incident. The next morning he met Laughlin and Ryder for breakfast.

After breakfast Laughlin, pointing to Ryder, said, "Boots, I want you to meet our newest Ranger, Ryder McCoy. Let's go over to the office and I'll swear him in. You boys will be partners for awhile."

Ryder was shocked; he couldn't believe it. They went to the jail and after the short swearing in ceremony, Laughlin gave him his badge and said, "Ryder you'll be riding with my best Ranger; learn from him."

Boots shook Ryder's hand and responded with, "Remember I told you one day you might want to be a Ranger, well congratulations, you're one now."

After the congratulations ran their course, Laughlin went to the cell door, opened it, let Tillman and his two men out and said, "You boys get on your horses and ride, don't come back to Uvalde. You aren't welcome here. If I hear of anymore killings in Eagle Pass these, two Rangers will be coming to see you."

Tillman opened the door to walk out, stopped, looked at Ryder and snarled, "It ain't over."

Laughlin grabbed Tillman by the collar and said, "Go while you can, one more word and you go back in for thirty days." The trio walked out, mounted up and rode off at a gallop.

Soon afterwards Nathan, who had been out at Hondo taking care of some business, entered the jail, walked over to Boots, shook his hand and said, "I'm proud of you son." Boots said nothing, he just nodded his head.

That evening, Ryder and Boots made the rounds for Oral and Nathan. As they were walking the streets, they saw Audrey going into the restaurant with Oral. Ryder said, "Boots, I hope we don't have a problem. I've been calling on Audrey. She said at one time you and her were in a relationship."

Boots laughed and said, "Nice girl. You have my blessing, just be careful, her grandpa is the Sheriff of Uvalde and it sounds like Tillman has a dislike for you." He paused then asked, quizzically, "What happened?"

CHAPTER 13

"Long story," replied McCoy, "he tried to muscle me around; I fought back and killed one of his men in a shootout. It all happened in Eagle Pass where Tillman spends most of his time." Ryder took a breath and continued, "Tillman likes himself; he's trying to build a reputation as a gunfighter so he picks his targets carefully, you know, wranglers, saloon drunks and the like. He's boastfully proud of his seven notches on that pearl handled 45 he carries."

"Sounds like he ain't gonna give it up with you. Watch your back," said Boots.

Boots and Ryder spent the next three days at the Big Iron ranch with Laughlin. Boots knew Laughlin was keeping him there for observation; Laughlin wouldn't send him out until he was emotionally prepared.

During supper on the fourth day, the threesome was in the bunk house when Laughlin said, "Be ready to saddle up in the morning. Sheriff Starrett of Laredo has been shot." When Boots and Ryder gave him an inquisitive look, Laughlin added, "He was riding with a posse and caught a bullet in the leg."

Boots and Ryder made ready to ride; it was mid-summer and the temperature in Laredo would probably be around a hundred and six degrees.

In an effort to avoid the burning sun, that could melt a rider and his horse by midday, they left Uvalde before sun-up and rode slowly, resting their horses often. Bad Moon and War Paint appreciated their kindness.

They abandoned the stage trail and were riding on the open range with plans to stop at Herman Fox's ranch. As they neared the Fox ranch several riders rode hard and fast toward them. It was Herman's wranglers. After catching up to Boots and Ryder, they rode in with the Rangers.

As they reached the ranch house, Fox greeted them and said, "Boys, looks like we got some trouble brewing again. Lost about thirty-five horses the other night to rustlers; Luke formed a posse and went looking for 'em. When he found them, a gunfight followed and Luke took a bullet in the leg."

Boots questioned Herman about the severity of Luke's wound. He was told it wasn't real bad but Luke would probably walk with a limp.

After expressing their relief regarding Starrett's gunshot, Herman said, "My boy, Billy was riding with the posse when Luke was shot. After being wounded, Luke appointed him as his deputy; Billy is in town now acting as sheriff till Luke recovers."

The Rangers had not stepped down. Herman gestured with his arm and urged, "You boys dismount; I'll take care of your horses while ya'll wash up and then we'll have supper."

During supper Herman told Boots and Ryder that things were getting out of hand; horses and cattle were being stolen and stages were being robbed. He figured the bank would be next.

Then Herman chuckled and said, "Old Bob Bell told me times are changing; said in the old days robbers were poor; used old worn out black powder pistols. This last time, however, he said one of the robbers had a pearl handled 45, was clean and dressed well."

Boots looked at Ryder; they both were thinking the same: Tillman.

They finished their meal and Boots said, "Herman, thanks for the dinner, we need to turn in. Got an early get up tomorrow, want to ride in and talk to Billy."

The next morning, they skipped breakfast and headed out early. From the ranch to town was a half day ride. By the time they reached the Laredo jail, the temperature was already above the century mark.

When they tied their horses up in front of the jail, Billy stepped outside onto the porch. He was six feet tall with dark hair and handsome but manly features. The man had a way about him that projected authority as he greeted them with a "Howdy Rangers, good to see you."

Boots replied, "Hello Billy, you look good wearing that star, you should keep it on, you look like a lawman."

Billy laughed and said, "Me and Luke known each other for a spell and I help out from time to time. You know, I always wanted to be a lawman, a Ranger as a matter of fact but Paw needed me on the ranch so I became a rancher instead." His laughter got a little louder as he added, "Hell, I'll probably live longer as a rancher."

Boots, who had joined in the laughter momentarily said, "I don't know about that, don't sell yourself short, I've seen you in action, you can ride with me anytime you choose."

They all walked into the jail and sat down at the table as Boots asked, "Ok Billy, now tell us what exactly is going on."

Billy let out a deep sigh and answered, "It could be Vaqueros stealing the horses and cattle; then taking them into Mexico, but the stage robbers aren't Mexicans. You see, even though they were masked, Bob Bell got a good look at 'em; said he could identify their horses and one of them sported a real fancy shooter.

Boots said, "Billy, I don't think any Mexicans are involved." Then he glanced over at Ryder and continued, "I'll bet Henry Tillman held up the stage and those horses and cattle are on a ranch south of Eagle Pass. The bank is probably next."

Ryder nodded his head and said, "I agree, it's got to be Tillman and his two misfits."

"Ryder, do you know where Tillman's ranch is," asked Boots.

"Yes," said Ryder, "I've ridden by it, about ten miles west of Eagle Pass."

The front door of the jail opened and Luke Starrett came hobbling in. "Hello boys," he said, "you need another man to play dominoes?" Then he laughed and spouted, "I can't sit a horse, but I can ride a chair with the best of 'em."

Boots said, "Glad you came in. I needed to talk with you." Seeing the Rangers were serious, Luke grabbed a chair as Boots continued, "We're going to Henry Tillman's ranch in Eagle Pass to look for some stolen horses and cattle. I'd like Billy to ride with me and Ryder; think you can handle things while we're gone?"

"Yea, sure," said Luke, "I'll appoint our blacksmith as a deputy till Billy gets back."

"Fine, then we'll leave in the morning," said Boots, "it'll have to be a slow ride in this heat."

The next morning they watched the sun come up out of the east. It was a beautiful sunrise; a cinnamon sky, much like an artist would paint. By eight o'clock it was already pushing eighty degrees; another unbearable day was on its way. The trio rode slow, resting and watering the horses whenever possible.

Since the slow riding gave them time to talk, Ryder said to Billy, "I see you've got a Springfield 45-70 in your scabbard."

"Yes Sir," said Billy, "Pa' gave me this rifle and I grew up shooting it."

"Can you hit anything?" asked Ryder.

Boots said, "Ryder, let me answer that question for you. Sheriff Starrett said Billy's deadly at long range and has never been beaten in competition."

Billy grinned and said, "Yea, every now and then I get lucky and Sheriff Starrett's very kind with his words."

They continued their journey with light conversation when Boots said, "I have a question for you Billy; what was Herman like as a young man?"

Billy got a proud look on his face as he answered, "He was a fighter of Indians and Mexicans; made and enforced his own laws. They tell me he was good with his gun and his fists. In fact, the old timers tell a story about him when he was a young man."

Billy pushed his chest out a little further as he continued, "It seems that after dark one night, three men pulled Papa in between two buildings and beat him up pretty good. Time passed and then one day, when Papa was in town, he seen one of them fellers at the barbershop getting a shave. Well, so the story goes, Papa reached in his pocket and pulled out two steel tub handles. He had shaped them to fit his fists; which made himself a pair of brass-nucks."

Billy paused to make sure Boots and Ryder were still paying attention. When he was satisfied that they were, he added, "There was a hundred pound sack of potatoes sitting outside the barbershop. Papa put on his brassnucks, picked up the sack of potatoes and went into the barbershop. As he entered, he threw the sack of potatoes on the fellers lap, jumped up on him while he was still in the chair and worked him over with his home made brassnucks. They say his face was a mess; those nucks cut him everywhere he got hit. Anyway, they call Papa the little Banty rooster; 'cause like the Banty, he's mean and loves to fight."

It was growing late in the evening and they were looking for a place to bed down for the night. Shadows were beginning to cover the ridges, the sun was setting in the west as the sky turned orange; it was beautiful. You could hear the coyotes yelling and' on occasion, javelinas could be seen darting through the brush. Rabbits were beginning to appear and look for their evening meal.

Ryder said, "No jerky for me tonight, we're going to have rabbit."

They stopped and built a campfire. A little later, as Ryder came in with several rabbits, he grinned and said, "This shotgun has its uses, outlaws and rabbits."

That night they ate rabbit, drank coffee and went to sleep early. The next morning was an awesome change, you could see clouds building up in the west and there was lots of lightening in the clouds.

Boots saw Billy looking at the clouds and said, "What do you think?"

Billy replied, "We'll be alright, storms thirty miles away."

Boots liked Billy. He didn't say much but when he did, he was direct and to the point; spoke with authority. They mounted up and started toward Eagle Pass; they expected to get there late in the evening. Billy was riding a paint horse named Dan and sat the saddle well.

Boots said to Billy, "I hope there ain't no Apaches down here close to the river; they'll want mine and your horse for sure, they love paints."

Ryder said, "They wouldn't be able to get ole Bad Moon; can't nobody ride 'em but me."

They continued to ride and talk, which was good for Boots; he couldn't dwell on JoJo. The storm all but missed them; just a little shower that cooled things down. They rode into Eagle Pass at sunset.

Boots said, "Ride in line and stay together. We'll get a room, supper and then head for the saloon. Ryder, since you know people here, see what you can find out about Tillman."

Ryder nodded in the affirmative as Billy said, "I'll get the horses stabled then meet ya'll at the restaurant if you'll carry my rifle and saddlebags to the room?"

Yea sure," said Boots, as he and Ryder were removing the saddlebags from their horses.

Boots and Ryder washed up in the room while Billy washed up at the livery stable; then they all met at the restaurant.

After eating Boots suggested they go over to the saloon and see what they could find out about Tillman. As they made their way, Boots asked, "Ryder, didn't you have a girlfriend working in the saloon?"

Ryder answered, "Yea, Carmelita. She'll tell me everything she knows."

When Billy and the Rangers entered the smoke filled saloon, there was loud profanity, flowing whiskey, drunks, overflowing spittoons and bar girls. Most of the poker tables were full and there were several men at the bar, so they sat down at a table and ordered whiskey.

Boots, having noticed that three of the men at the bar had gulped their drinks, walked out of the saloon and quickly rode away, tapped Ryder on the shoulder and said, "Those three must have seen our badges and high tailed it; probably Tillman's men."

About that time, Carmelita came down the stairs, spotted Ryder, and moseyed over to their table. Ryder got up, took her by the arm and they went upstairs. After a while, Ryder rejoined them at the table and said, "Tillman's got about twenty men at his ranch."

He took a drink from the glass of whiskey he had left on the table, and then continued, "When they come to town and get drunk, they brag about how much money they have and how good Tillman treats 'em. Carmelita said they sell the stolen cattle in Mexico after they've changed the brands. I've seen a running iron in action, they can change any brand. Now at Tillman's ranch, it's free range, no fences; but he's probably got 'em herded up by the river."

At this point, McCoy paused, finished his whiskey, wiped his mouth with his sleeve and remarked, "I'm pretty sure I know where they'll be."

"Good," said Boots, "we'll ride out at first light; maybe we can catch them changing brands." Boots looked at Billy, put his hand on his shoulder and said, "Maybe you can identify some of your animals."

Billy nodded in the affirmative. The threesome retired early in anticipation of their early morning ride.

The next morning as they were riding towards the Tillman ranch, Ryder said, "Boots, let's circle down by the river; they'll be watching and may approach us. After we've seen the herd we can head for Tillman's ranch house."

Boots agreed so they rode along the river, as Ryder had suggested. When they came upon a herd of horses and cows Boots said, "Billy, ride on in amongst them and check the brands; Ryder, you watch for Tillman's men."

Billy was making his way thru the herd when he yelled out, "Hell, they're all ours, most of the brands ain't been changed; the others have been altered."

"Come on out of there," said Boots, "let's go see Tillman."

They had ridden about a hundred yards when twelve men came riding towards them, spurring hard. Not wanting to tip their hand, Boots cautioned, "Keep your pistols holstered, let 'em come on in."

The men pulled up about twenty yards in front of the Rangers. They were all rugged, dirty looking men; a couple of them were drunk. The leader was a big man, six foot, two hundred and fifty pounds or more. He was wearing batwing chaps, a cowhide vest and a wrangler's hat. He had the sleeves of his long sleeved shirt rolled up to his elbows. His gun was tied down; gunslinger style.

The man had dark brown eyes, long hair and a moustache; he was dirty and un-groomed. As they rode up, he said, in a loud voice, "Well boys it looks like we caught us some rustlers." He was looking directly at Boots when he uttered, "You know what we do to rustlers out here? We hang 'em; ain't that right boys?"

Boots took his Ranger badge out of his pocket, pinned it on his shirt and said, "We're Rangers, take us to Tillman."

The dirty one was having none of it as he barked, "My name is Big Ben Johnson, I'm the head wrangler here and I ain't taking you to Mr. Tillman. Me and the boys are going to hang y'all; the boss will be proud of us."

Boots nudged his horse into a walk until War Paint and Big Ben's horse were nose to nose. Boots face hardened and his neck swelled; you'd think the veins were trying to jump out of his skin. He looked into Big Ben's eyes and said, "Johnson, you may have us out numbered and you may even kill us, but hear me and hear me good; I assure you, you'll be the first one to die. I'll put a bullet in your heart before y'all get me. Now if you're ready to die, make your play, if not, take us to the ranch house."

Big Ben stared at Boots; beads of sweat were popping out on his face. It was evident he was chewing on what Boots had said. He continued to stare for a while longer, then turned his horse and said, "Let's take 'em to Tillman; he can kill 'em."

When they reached the ranch, Tillman came out of the house putting on his pistol. He was dressed in tight pants, blousy shirt with a vest, high top boots and had his long blond hair combed and in place. You could see he wanted to be a gunfighter. He stood on the porch looking out at the riders; then he said, "Well, well, what have you boys brought me? Seeing McCoy in the group, he barked, "Hello Ryder, I see we meet again. I told you it wasn't over. What are y'all doing on my ranch?"

Big Ben spoke up, "We caught them snooping around the herd in the south pasture."

The south pasture you say," replied Tillman, "what were you looking for: everything has got my brand on it."

Boots answered, "Maybe so and maybe not; either way we're gonna get a warrant and come back out here for a look at your entire stock."

"That's fine," said Tillman, "only thing that don't have my brand would be some stray mavericks we haven't branded yet."

Tillman let that settle with the Rangers before continuing with, "Whatever you do, don't bring that back shooting Ryder out here. If you do, I'll shoot him down like a dog, just like he did my man."

Ryder glared at Tillman; then turned his horse and followed Boots and Billy out the gate. After they rode clear of the ranch, Boots reigned up and said, "Be alert. Tillman may send men out to bushwhack us; check your rifles."

As Tillman watched the Rangers ride off, he said to Big Ben, "Take care of 'em; don't let 'em reach town alive. When it's done, take their bodies across the river and bury 'em."

The Rangers had reached an area with a dry creek on their left and a ridge on their right when Boots said, "Be ready, if they're gonna hit us, this is a likely spot."

The words were barely out of his mouth when seven riders came over the ridge riding hard with their guns drawn. Boots shouted, "Ride for the creek and take cover."

They raced for the creek, dismounted and pulled their horses in behind some boulders before getting in position to fire. Billy was lying behind a log with his 45-70 resting across the top. Tillman's men were over two hundred yards away and closing when Boots heard Billy's rifle speak and saw a rider knocked off his horse.

The remaining six reigned up, still about two hundred yards out, when Billy fired again. Another rider fell; the other five dismounted and ran for cover. Shots were being exchanged when one of Tillman's men, trying to get closer, ran towards a large rock. Boots dropped him with his 44-40 leaving only four.

Ryder hollered at Boots, "Stay put and pick 'em off when they move; we got cover they don't."

Billy shouted back, "I'm going to show you how we shoot turkeys." He took aim over the top of the rock, where one of the men was hiding, and barked, "Watch, when he sticks his head up, he's mine." Billy continued to aim just above the rock; then a head came up and, BOOM! The 45-70 spoke. The man's head blew up like it was a cantaloupe.

The other men witnessed the headshot, and hollered, "Let's get out of here; he'll kill us all with that rifle." As they ran for the horses, Billy was taking aim as Boots said, "Let 'em go; we'll tie the dead ones on their horses and haul them in to the undertakers."

As they headed toward Eagle Pass, leading the horses with their dead, Ryder said to Billy, "That was nice shooting. Sheriff Starrett was right; you are deadly with that rifle."

Billy grinned and said, "Yea, I guess I do alright."

Ryder pushed his hat forward over his eyes, scratched his head, and asked, "How'd you learn that head shot anyway?"

Billy said, "When I was a boy and would go turkey hunting, Papa didn't want me to tear up the meat so I'd only take head shots."

When Ryder asked how was that possible, Billy answered, "When you see a turkey you get ready for your shot; then you gobble. The turkey will stick his head up, looking for the bird that's gobbling; then you shoot his head off and save all the meat. Papa use to send me turkey hunting with just one bullet and I doggone sure couldn't go home with no turkey."

Boots grinned, Ryder scratched his head, and they all three continued on towards Eagle Pass. When they reached town, all the townsfolk followed them down the street to the undertakers. They left the bodies, told the undertaker to bill the Rangers; then Boots went to the telegraph office. He sent a wire to Laughlin that read: FOUND RUSTLERS AND CATTLE – FOUR RUSTLERS DEAD – GOING AFTER GANG LEADER TOMORROW – IT'S TILLMAN

When Boots joined the others at the sheriff's office, he said, "Luke, we're going out tomorrow to arrest Tillman. We can file attempted murder on him now; then, after we skin a couple of cows to check the altered brand, we'll also file charges against him for horse and cattle rustling."

Luke responded with, "I'm going with you, I can damn sure sit a horse, and I owe them boys; one of 'em shot me in the leg. Besides, you'll need an extra gun."

Boots laughed and said, "We might just send Billy out there. Hell, the way he shoots, he can probably take care of 'em by his self."

"I told you about Billy," said Luke. "How did he do with that big bore?"

Boots grinned, "Three of them boys at the undertakers were shot with a 45-70. Does that answer your question?"

The next day had all the promise of a scorcher; it was already hot at seven in the morning when the Rangers rode toward the Tillman ranch. They were careful as they rode with one man riding point in an effort to avoid another ambush.

The ride was uneventful. When they reached the ranch it appeared to be deserted. The Mexican cook greeted them as they rode up to the house. Ryder asked him, in Spanish, where everyone was.

He identified himself as Lopez and said, in broken English, "All zee men zay leeve las night; zay no fight Rangers. Meester Tealman, he also leeve last night, he go south towards za reever and Mayhico."

Boots, reacting immediately, said, "Ryder and I will go to Mexico. Luke, you and Billy go back to Laredo. We'll get provisions from Tillman's kitchen."

Lopez, by telling the Rangers where Tillman and his men were, had tipped his hand; it was apparent he didn't think much of Tillman or his men.

Boots had picked up on this so when he told Lopez to fill their saddlebags for the long trip, the cook said, "Be careful senor, he have freeeends in May hico zat he supplies weef zeee stolen cows."

Luke and Billy had already taken off for Laredo when Boots and Ryder headed for the river. It was already midday and the heat was overpowering. As they rode across the river, which was shallow and hardly moving, Ryder asked, "How far in can we go?"

Boots answered, "Not very far. Hopefully we can pick up a trail soon, catch Tillman and bring him back." He could see Ryder was wondering what the plan was if they didn't find Tillman's trail quickly, so he added, "If he reaches the ranch, or ranches, that he sells to before we catch him, we'll have to turn back; too many guns and we have no authority."

Ryder nodded his understanding and they continued to ride; following an old Indian-Mexican trail. At the end of the day Boots said, "We'll bed down tonight then start back. We can't go any deeper, it's too dangerous."

They set up camp without lighting a fire; ate dried jerky and drank water. Their water supply was getting low and they had not passed any wells. After hobbling the horses so they could graze all night, they retired for the evening.

Ryder, who was in a talkative mood, said, "I can't believe I'm a Ranger. I'm proud I met you and Bronco back in Eagle Pass. My thoughts about life have totally changed. Before I just existed; now I'm part of something, something that will do down in history. I plan on growing old with the Rangers."

He continued to ramble on about the Rangers and their place in history; then he said, "That boy Billy would be a damn good Ranger. Can you believe how he can shoot that rifle?" Ryder heard Boots snoring; he grinned, closed his eyes and slowly dropped off to sleep.

When they arrived back in Laredo, Boots told Billy to go back to his ranch, get his wranglers and fetch his horses and cows from the Tillman ranch.

Then he said "Luke will ride in the buckboard and go with you to make it official."

Hearing this, Luke barked, "Hell no, I'll ride; told ya my leg was healed enough for me to sit a horse."

Boots grinned, held up both hands to back Luke off, then went to the telegraph office and sent a wire telling Laughlin: TILLMAN IN MEXICO. SEARCH CALLED OFF. STARRETT TO ARRANGE FOR WANTED POSTERS.

Boots and Ryder were in the restaurant having lunch when Ryder asked, "What do we do about Tillman?"

Boots said, "He'll show up when he needs money. We'll hear about him when he comes out of Mexico; then we'll go get him."

A young boy from the telegraph office came in the restaurant, walked to where Boots and Ryder were sitting and said, "Ranger Boots, I have a telegram for you."

Boots said, "Thank you," and gave the young boy a cartridge from his belt.

The boy said, "Thank you," then turned to walk away, stopped, looked back and asked, "Mr. Boots, did you really shoot another Ranger? You didn't, did you?"

Boots felt the dagger in his heart, his face flushed and once again he could see JoJo falling forward. He paused for a moment before answering the boy and then he said, "Yes young man, I did. I'm not proud of it, but it had to be done." The young boy lowered his head, turned and walked away.

Boots watched the boy until he was outside the restaurant, then he snapped, as if he had been in a trance, and said, "Better read this telegram." After reading the telegram, he remarked, "Laughlin wants us to hang around Laredo for a while; he wants Tillman brought in as soon as possible." He folded the telegram, put it in his vest pocket, and continued, "Laughlin figures Tillman will return to the area in a couple of weeks; he'll be needing some money and we'll probably hear about a robbery somewhere around here."

After leaving the restaurant they started walking to the sheriffs' office; there intentions were to sit on the porch in the shade and absorb the southeast wind. To get to the sheriffs office they had to pass the livery stable. As they walked by, Ryder looked in on the horses that were being stabled and said, "Dammit Boots, that roan horse in there, the one with the stocking on his left foot, belongs to one of the bushwackers."

Boots said, "Well now, let's just go in and find out who he belongs to."

A young stable boy was busy cleaning the stalls when Boots approached and asked if he knew who owned the roan. The boy said, "Yes sir I do. Came in last night; belongs to a big fellow with a beard. He was wearing a black hat with a tan shirt and black vest. I think I saw him go in the saloon with two fellers about an hour ago."

Boots said to Ryder, "I need a shot of whiskey, how 'bout you?"

Ryder nodded and they headed for the saloon. As they entered, they stepped up to the bar and ordered whiskey. It wasn't crowded, only a few men, girls and the bartender. The Rangers turned their back to the bar and surveyed the room. There he was, sitting at a table with two men and a saloon girl. When the two men spotted Boots and Ryder; they got up. One went to the back of the room; the other to the end of the bar.

Boots said to Ryder, "Stay at the bar, watch my back, I'm gonna go talk to the one at the table." When Boots approached the table, the girl, anticipating trouble, got up and left. Boots stopped and asked, "Mister, do you own that roan with the white stocking over at the livery stable?"

"Don't know anyone with a horse like that," said the man angrily.

Boots' jaw squared as he glared at the man with penetrating eyes; much like a wild animal just before it springs on its prey, then he said, "That's a damn lie, the boy at the livery stable said it's yours."

The man standing at the end of the bar was approximately thirty feet from Ryder; the other man had made his way to the door and created a cross fire on Ryder and Boots.

Suddenly the man at the table said, "We didn't get you the other day, but we damn sure will today." He went for his gun as he was standing and said, "Take 'em boys.

CHAPTER 14

Boots gun hand was a blur as he pulled his pistol and fired. The man was shot in the chest and knocked backwards over the table. The man at the bar reached for his gun; Ryder was faster and his 44 colt bucked as the shot hit the man in the throat. He fell forward to his knees, fired his pistol harmlessly into the floor and fell face first on the saloon floor. The man at the door turned and ran out of the saloon. He mounted up and rode quickly down the street; spurring and whipping his horse in an attempt to get away.

Billy heard the shots from inside the jail and ran out on the porch, rifle in hand. The man, heading out of town, was about two hundred yards away when Ryder ran into the street and hollered, "Take him Billy! Don't let him get away!"

Billy rested the rifle next to one of the porch posts, aimed and fired; the rider rolled out of the saddle. Ryder went back inside the saloon. The smell of gun smoke, whiskey and blood could not mask the stench of the two dead men who had relieved themselves in death. Silence filled the room.

As Luke came in the door, Boots walked over to Ryder and asked, "Luke, is the other one dead. We need one of 'em alive to question the whereabouts of Tillman."

"Boots," Luke answered, "he's stone cold dead. You know Billy and his rifle."

"Yea," said Boots, "I know; a head shot." Luke nodded as Boots continued, "These men were the ones that got away when we were ambushed."

"I can't believe they were stupid enough to come into town," said Ryder.

"It don't figure," said Boots. "Either booze or women, maybe both."

Luke asked, "Boots, what's your thoughts on Tillman?"

Boots replied, "I think he'll continue to shoot drunken cowboys; form a small gang and rob stages or small banks. I don't think he'll try railroads until he gets organized." He nodded toward Ryder and said, "Tillman knows he's hot and Rangers are after him, so I think he'll just slash and run. Eventually, he'll form a pattern and we'll figure him out."

Back in Uvalde, Jerry Jack, known as the Preaching Ranger, had been mostly inactive. Under Brother Morgan, he was studying to become a preacher and, even though he was a Ranger, he was dating Morgan's daughter. Laughlin had him staying close to Uvalde to help Oral and Nathan, if need be.

Oral was in his seventies and, even though he was still sheriff of Uvalde, most of the work was being done by Nathan or Jerry Jack.

Oral had left early in the day leaving them the town. It was around three in the afternoon and the stage from San Antonio, due at noon, had not shown up. The old timer Bob Bell and a shotgun guard were carrying passengers and a strong box holding cash for deposit in the Uvalde bank.

It was late August and the heat had been severe most of the summer. Nathan and Jerry Jack were sitting on the jail porch hoping to catch a cool breeze when Nathan said, "I think we'd better ride out a ways and see if the stage has broken down. Something's wrong; Bob Bell is always on time."

They mounted up and rode east to investigate, taking the San Antonio trail. About ten miles out of Uvalde they saw the stage. It was off the trail; the horses had wandered off and were grazing. Nathan and Preacher spurred their horses hard toward the stage. Bob Bell had suffered a gunshot to his side; the guard was dead and the only passenger was also lying in the trail dead, fifty yards from the stage.

When they dismounted, Nathan climbed on the stage; Bob was alive but bleeding badly so they moved him inside the coach. After making Bob as comfortable as possible, they loaded up the dead and tied their horses to the stage. Nathan drove while Preacher tended to Bob.

When they arrived in Uvalde, a crowd was waiting in the street along with the doctor, who had anticipated trouble. Bob was taken to the doc's treatment room while some of the men took the stage, with the bodies, to the funeral home. Preacher told Nathan that Bob was able to talk and had said they were ambushed by three men, out by Coyote Flats. They all wore masks but, one was well dressed and had a fancy pistol. Bob said he was the one who stripped the passenger of his belongings; shot him in the head; then shot the guard as they rode off.

Nathan said, "It sounds like Tillman, he was probably the one wearing the fancy pistol."

"Bob said he was carrying five thousand dollars in cash and they got it all; shot the lock plumb off the strong box," said Jerry Jack.

Word had reached Oral, so he was in town. Oral, Nathan and Preacher met up in the sheriffs' office to make plans for a posse while a rider was sent to the Big Iron to notify Laughlin.

The two Rangers, Nathan and Preacher, wouldn't let Oral ride with the posse so they rounded up six men and started their pursuit. The posse rode out to the site where the holdup occurred and picked up a trail leading south towards Eagle Pass.

By this time, back in Uvalde, Laughlin was at the jail with Oral, analyzing the situation. He told Oral to stay on the alert in Uvalde; he would have Boots and Ryder leave Laredo and ride to Eagle Pass; where they would stay until something developed. Meanwhile, Nathan, Preacher, and the posse could continue their tracking.

Boots received the telegram from Laughlin and, in a short while, he and Ryder were on the trail to Eagle Pass. As they rode, they were talking about Tillman when Boots said, "It's evident Tillman's trying to become famous; hell, he proved that when he shot everyone in the stage robbery. But you know, his quest for recognition may well be his down fall."

Ryder, who had been quiet, spoke up and said, "You may be right; reward posters are already being posted, that'll help." They were nodding in agreement with each other as Ryder continued, "Someone, hell, maybe one of his own men will give him up for that reward money."

Boots chimed in, "My bet is the posse will follow him to the river. I think he's staying just over the river in Mexico." They rode on for a ways as Boots continued, "Ryder, when we get to Eagle Pass, maybe your friend Carmelita knows where to find Rene and his Banditos; if so, we'll go see him. If we tell him the reward money goes to him, he'll find Tillman no matter where his is in Mexico. I can promise you, two thousand dollars will get Rene's attention." They continued to pass the time with small talk knowing the 70 mile ride to Eagle Pass would take more than two days.

Three days later, the trail the posse had been following, led them to the Rio Grande. The Rangers figuring Tillman and his men had crossed over into Mexico and, since they had no authority across the river, headed back to Uvalde.

Meanwhile, Tillman and his three man gang rode into the little town of Benavides. It consisted of a make shift saloon and flop house with girls and a few adobe stick buildings. The town had a working well and that's what kept the town in existence. Tillman decided to have his men set up camp behind the saloon where they could lay low for several days.

Members of his gang consisted of Frank Hernandez, Willard Johnson and Pedro Hernandez. Frank was a two bit hired gun, Willard was dumb but mean and Pedro was a killer, knife or gun. Tillman, who knew there would be a price on his head, had to keep them in money or they would turn on him for the reward.

Later that evening, after Tillman had split the take from the stage robbery, they were in the saloon drinking rot gut whiskey. Frank, after a few drinks, said to Tillman, "Why did you kill those people on the stage? Now we'll be hung if we get caught."

Tillman grinned and said, "I like to kill, it makes me feel good, I've killed ten men. I'm fast and mean and I want some Ranger notches on my gun."

Frank said, "You sure you're fast? You're not just a back shooter are you?"

Tillman flared as he looked at Frank and barked, "You want to see if I'm fast......... pull on me."

Frank stared at Tillman, lowered his head and murmured, "Forget it; we can't be killing each other."

In Eagle Pass, Ryder spent some time with the saloon girl, Carmelita. She told him that Tillman was somewhere across the river. Said he usually comes back to rob and kill then retreats. She also said she would get word to Rene and his Banditos about the reward money. Ryder had told her to make sure Rene knew that Tillman had to be alive in order for him to collect the reward.

With Bronco in Abilene, Nathan and Preacher in Uvalde, Starrett and deputy Billy Fox in Laredo and Boots and Ryder in Eagle Pass, the Rangers had Texas blanketed. If Rene flushed Tillman out of Mexico, they could make contact quickly, regardless of where he surfaced.

Rene Alvarez and his Banditos were camped at an abandoned mission in Mexico; which was now being used as a saloon. Felipe, one of the Banditos had returned from Eagle Pass and relayed Carmelita's message to Rene from Ryder. When Rene heard the news, he grinned then said, "Rene and hees Banditos get mucho dinero; we bounty hunters. We get two thousand American dolares for catcheeng greengos."

If Tillman surfaced in Del Rio, Rangers were standing by in Uvalde. Although Laughlin knew his chances of showing up in Abilene were slim, he saw fit to put Bronco on the alert.

Bronco was standing outside the telegraph office reading Laughlin's telegram when Jane, who was looking out the news office window, spotted him. Wondering what the latest had in store, she crossed the street, approached him, and asked, "Any news from Boots?"

"No," said Bronco, "he and Ryder are over in Eagle Pass on the lookout for this Tillman character."

Wanting to hear more, she responded, "Come on Bronco; let's go over to the restaurant and get a cup of coffee; I need to talk to you."

As they entered the restaurant and sat down to order coffee, Jane said, "Bronco, I'm really worried about Boots. You know I'm in love with him and the thing that happened with him and JoJo is breaking my heart." She was nearly in tears as she asked, "Do you think he's alright; will he ever get over it?"

Jane lowered her head as Bronco put his hand on her shoulder and responded, "We're all concerned about Boots and wonder how we would have reacted if Laughlin had chosen one of us instead of Boots." Then Bronco put his hand under Jane's chin, lifted her head, looked into her eyes and said softly, "Jane, Laughlin is no fool, he knows Boots is his strongest Ranger and that's why he was selected. Boots will never forget what happened, but he'll get over it."

Bronco could feel the tension going out of Jane's face as he continued, "Boots has a right to grieve for his friend but he knows, if he had done what JoJo did, one of us would have been sent after him; hell, it could've even been me." Jane's eyes were now free of tears and she was holding her head up looking at Bronco as he said reassuringly, "All I can tell you is to believe in Boots, support him and be there for him; do that and he'll be fine. He's strong, the strongest of the strong."

"Thank you Bronco," said Jane, "I feel much better now."

Meanwhile, back in Benavides, Tillman was in camp practicing with his pistol. His men were sitting in the shade watching him draw and fire. Tillman loved the attention, so he was really trying to show off. He would stand in front of a yucca plant, as though it were an adversary, draw his pistol and fire several rounds into the cactus; then he would walk away, turn and fire a few more slugs into it. After each series of mock shootouts, he would hold his 45 up, spin the cylinder, reload, twirl the big shooter and holster it; grinning as though he had just wiped out a group of Texas Rangers.

After several episodes of "shoot the cactus", Frank Hernandez, who really doesn't like Tillman said, "You're pretty good alright, but that cactus don't shoot back. Besides, them Rangers ran you out of Uvalde; you damn sure didn't scare them."

Tillman's face turned red with anger as he blurted out, "I ain't afraid of any man, especially no Ranger."

"Oh Yea" said Frank, "word is two Rangers are in Eagle Pass right now; one of 'em is that Ryder McCoy fella. Why don't you run him and his partner outta Eagle Pass, the same way they ran you outta Uvalde."

Tillman's ego wouldn't let him back away from the situation, so he barked, "Why not? Be ready tomorrow morning, we're going to Eagle Pass." The more he thought, the braver he got as he continued, "but I won't just run 'em outta town, I'll kill 'em, both of 'em." True to his word, Tillman and his men headed for Eagle Pass just after sunup. The ride would take them a couple of days.

Boots and Ryder were still in Eagle Pass; it was the seventh day of their stake out. The late summer heat was still around and, by midday, it was unbearable. There was little activity in the streets; most people were inside. The few who braved the heat, were sitting in the shade hoping to catch a breath of southeast breeze that flirted by every once in a while.

About a half hour before sunset Ryder and Boots were walking down Main Street toward the restaurant. At the far end, four riders were slowly walking their horses down the middle of the street.

Ryder stopped, stared at the riders and said, "Boots, that's Tillman and his gang."

Their shotguns were at the jail about a hundred yards away; all they had were their pistols. Boots said to Ryder, "Cross the street and get between the buildings; we need to create a cross fire."

Tillman saw the Rangers so he and his men spurred their horses hard and went riding down the street firing at the Rangers. As they got closer, Tillman and one of his riders dismounted and took cover behind a wagon; the other two attempted to ride by the Rangers and get behind them.

As they rode past, Boots and Ryder each rolled a man out of his saddle with a single pistol shot.

Tillman and Frank were behind a wagon firing at the Rangers. One of the men, shot from horseback, wasn't dead; without getting up, he fired hitting Ryder in the back and knocking him to the ground; he was hit hard. Boots heard the shot, turned and placed three shots into the fallen rider.

Suddenly Tillman darted out from behind the wagon, ran to his horse, leaped into the saddle and turned to ride away.

Frank stood up and yelled, "Tillman, you yellow bellied bastard, come back here and fight." Then he aimed his pistol and shot the horse out from under him; sending Tillman tumbling to the ground.

Boots, who had stepped out from behind his cover to get a shot at Tillman, left himself in the open. Seizing the opportunity, Frank turned and fired at Boots; striking him on the inside of his thigh. As

Boots turned and fell to one knee, he fired. The bullet knocked Frank backwards; he was dead.

Boots leg was bleeding badly but it wasn't broken. The bullet had passed thru muscle and flesh; the bones were intact. He limped out to the middle of the street and squared up to Tillman, who had just gotten up from the fall.

Boots holstered his pistol and barked, "Tillman, you don't like Rangers. You want a reputation and a Ranger notch on that fancy gun of yours. Well mister, here's your chance; make your play."

Tillman started shaking, his hands were trembling.

Boots continued, "It's your choice; you can try me now, or I take you in and let you swing on a rope." As Tillman stood there, sweating silently, Boots calmly added, "Make up your mind Tillman, my patience are wearing thin."

Tillman thought for a minute then desperately reached for his gun. The barrel of the big Colt hadn't cleared leather when Boots' slug hit him in the chest. The force of the slug knocked Tillman backwards as his gun went flying out of his hand. The fancy pearl handled 45, was lying in the dirt with its seven notches shining in the sun. There would never be eight. The reputation Tillman so desperately desired died in the dirt roads of Eagle Pass.

As a crowd was quickly gathering, some men carried Ryder to the doctor's office. Boots' leg was cleaned and bandaged but Ryder wasn't so lucky. The slug had gone deep in his back and imbedded close to his spine; it was bad. For over an hour, the doctor tried to remove the bullet. He was not successful so he decided to place Ryder in a buggy and take him to San Antonio where there was better medical care.

The doctor said there was an experienced surgeon, from back East, who had relocated to San Antonio; said he had the skills required to remove a bullet next to the spine.

Boots questioned the long trip to San Antonio, wondering if Ryder could make it. The Doc' said, "We don't have a choice; one slip and he's dead, or at best, completely paralyzed. Take him to San Antonio; I'm just not good enough."

A buckboard, with a makeshift bed in the back, was set up for Ryder; War Paint and Bad Moon were tied to the rear. While Boots handled the team, the Doc' cared for Ryder.

They traveled day and night as fast as Ryder's condition would allow; the going was slow. The trip took the better part of three days with the team stopping in small villages along the way for any available supplies or medicines.

The surgeon in San Antonio, Tom Lauderdale, was on standby; he had been alerted by telegraph before they left Eagle Pass. He knew time was running out and each wasted minute placed Ryder closer to death.

After the War Between the States, Lauderdale had recognized the need for medical advancement. It was this fact that inspired him to attend medical school where he graduated with a degree in surgery. Doc' Lauderdale was fairly short and of medium build. He was in his mid fifties and balding on top with extremely intelligent looking eyes; he was very energetic.

When the team arrived in San Antonio, they were led to the doctor's office. Some men prepared a stretcher, carried Ryder upstairs to the treatment room and placed him face down on an operating table; immediately, the doctor started his procedure. Ryder was given Laudanum in an attempt to ease his pain; it had little effect.

About an hour later, Lauderdale, drying his hands with a bloody towel, came down the stairs to his office, where Boots had been waiting. He wiped the sweat from his brow and said, "I got the bullet; it was lodged next to the spine." He shook his head and added, "You know, you just can't tell about back wounds."

A worried Boots anxiously asked, "Doc', tell me straight out, what are the odds for his recovery?"

Doc' rubbed the back of his neck and answered, "He may recover completely or he might have nerve damage." Lauderdale could see the anxiety in Boots' face so he quickly added, "Either way, if we keep the infection down, he will recover. We'll just have to wait and see about any other damage."

With that bit of assurance, Boots queried, "Any idea how long his recovery might take."

Lauderdale answered, "Of course that depends on the severity of the damage, but he'll need to be here in my office for at least three weeks, then we'll see." Then, in an effort to ease the tension, Lauderdale grinned, chuckled and added, "He won't be riding off with you on any chases for a while, that's for damn sure."

Boots said, "Much obliged Doc", the Rangers will pay your fee, make sure he gets the best care available."

Doc' Lauderdale stared into Boots eyes and said, "Due to you Rangers, the State of Texas is growing and becoming civilized. There'll be no charge. I appreciate what you boys are doin' for Texas."

Boots, having received a wire from Laughlin instructing him to stay with Ryder until he recovers, was spending time at the sheriffs' office. The sheriff's name was Vernon Franks. He had taken over as sheriff, about six months ago, after the previous sheriff retired early, saying it was too dangerous.

Vernon was in his early thirties. He had been a wrangler on the Montana Trail Drives and, having worked as a deputy in Kansas and Amarillo, was also a seasoned lawman. He was six feet tall with broad shoulders and narrow hips. He had large arms and very big fists; with his blond shoulder length hair, he resembled Wild Bill Hickock. Boots liked Vernon and would accompany him on his nightly rounds.

Two weeks had passed since Ryder was brought to San Antonio to see Doc Lauderdale. The Doc' had done an excellent job; Ryder was already walking and well on his way to a full recovery. It would, however, be several more weeks before he could saddle up on Blue Moon.

One afternoon while Boots and Vernon were sitting on the front porch of the jail, the stage arrived from Austin. When it stopped in front of the Plaza Hotel, the guard started unloading luggage and a large trunk. The stage driver was Raymond Bell, son of Bob Bell; he opened the door to the coach and helped a female passenger step out.

Boots and Vernon froze; they stared at the lady passenger as if they were hypnotized by her beauty. She was in her twenties, had long honey blond hair and, due to her long legs, was above average in height. She was well built and moved gracefully. While identifying her bags she turned, looked at Boots and Vernon while flashing a flirtatious smile behind beautiful blue eyes that could be seen sparkling and dancing all the way across the street. Then, much too soon, she turned and followed the porters into the hotel.

Boots looked at Vernon, Vernon looked at Boots. Finally Boots said, "Did you see that?"

Vernon said, "Sure I did; we must have looked like two country bumpkins the way we were staring."

Boots didn't care, he just asked, "Wonder who she is," then he paused momentarily and added, "I'm going over to the hotel and find out."

"No, sit down," said Vernon, "I'm fairly certain that's Jeanette McDonald, the singer that's been advertised over at the Silver Dollar saloon. She's the owner of a traveling entertainment troupe from back east."

"A traveling troupe?" said a startled Boots.

"Yea," replied Vernon, "I heered a rich fella, named Sam Dutton, went to Arizona and seen Lilly Langtree in the Bird Cage saloon; he was so impressed with her, he came back and built a theatre; named it the Silver Dollar and he's bringing in entertainment. Jeanette McDonald is the singer/owner of her group; they traveled all the way from Boston to San Francisco." Dutton signed a contract for her to perform here while she's on her way to New Orleans.

Boots said, with obvious excitement in his voice, "Let's go over to the Silver Dollar. I'm gonna get you, me and Ryder tickets for the show. It'll be his get well present." Boots started towards the Silver Dollar, waved Vernon on and said, "Come on, let's go while they still have tickets."

With that said, off they went for tickets. After purchasing three seats in the front row, they went to see Ryder. As Boots and Vernon entered the room where Ryder was recuperating, Boots started dancing around the room, laughing and holding up the tickets.

Ryder, a bit confused, put his hands in the air as if to ask, what the hell is this. Boots gave him a big smile and said, "See these, these are tickets for the Silver Dollar. Me, you and Vernon are going to see Ms Jeanette McDonald. She's come all the way from San Francisco, just to sing and dance over at the 'Dollar'."

Boots continued to do his mock dance around then he stopped, put his thumbs under his armpits, stuck his chest out and crooned, "She's already seen me and Vernon; we can tell she likes us. Wait till you see her Ranger McCoy, she's beautiful." He pranced around in his 'Royal' posture before adding, "I bet she falls for me, Ranger Boots Law, also known as the Heartbreak Kid."

Boots, still performing his 'shadow dance', finally stopped and barked, "Come on partner, we've got to get you healed and cleaned up. The show's Saturday Night, that's tomorrow. It's your get well present."

For the first time in a long time Boots was beginning to act like he did before the incident with JoJo. Ryder was still in a little pain from his wounds, but was sure happy to see Boots so excited.

For the rest of Friday, Boots, Ryder and Vernon were like kids waiting on Christmas. None too soon, Saturday evening finally arrived; it was time to go see Ms. Jeanette McDonald.

They had washed their clothes, trimmed their hair and brushed their hats. They cleaned up pretty good and were a pair of handsome Rangers. Not to be outdone, Vernon was all decked out as well; with his long yellow hair and handle bar moustache, he was a handsome sheriff. They entered the Silver Dollar, took their seats, ordered whiskey and anxiously awaited Jeanette.

Finally, after three whiskeys, a midget dressed in a suit appeared on stage. His oiled hair was parted down the middle; he sported a heavy waxed moustache which was twisted and pointed straight out. The Silver Dollar was lighted by coal-oil lanterns and candles. Smoke filled the air and the crowd was chanting: We want Jeanette – We want Jeanette. The little fellow had a megaphone in his hand and, as he raised it to his lips, shouted, "Ladies and gentlemen, the Silver Dollar is proud to present, all the way from San Francisco, Ms Jeanette McDonald, the sweetest canary of them all." The crowd applauded and the stage curtains parted.

There she was, dressed in an emerald green strapless gown, with a peacock feather in her hair, Ms Jeanette McDonald. Her long honey blond hair was shining and her blue eyes were dancing as she let them roam around the crowd. She had a tiny waist, well developed buxom and firm rounded hips. Her tall spiked heels made her legs appear even longer than they were. She was more woman than any man in the room had ever seen.

The piano started playing as she danced across the stage and started singing. Her voice was beautiful and, together with her looks, she had the crowd mesmerized.

After three songs, she left the stage, but would return again for the second half of the show. The three lawmen looked at each other and smiled. Boots said, "Did y'all she how she looked directly at me when she was singing?"

"It wasn't you," said Ryder, "she was looking at me. I could feel it."

Vernon chimed in, "Y'all are both wrong, she was looking at me." All three laughed heartily; they were having a good time.

When the second half of the show started, Jeanette appeared in a red strapless gown that was even more eye catching then the green one. This time, when she started singing and moving, she was greeted by three drunks reaching up on the stage in an attempt to touch her.

Vernon rose up from the table, walked to the drunks and motioned for them to sit down. When they complied, Vernon turned to Jeanette, smiled, tipped his hat and returned to his table.

Boots said, "Good job sheriff, but next time, send in the Rangers."

Vernon puffed up his chest and spouted, "I'm now her hero. I can tell she likes this Texas lawman. Don't have 'em like me on the West Coast."

Boots and Ryder smiled and gave Vernon a 'get out of here' wave of there hands.

After Jeanette's final act, everyone gave her a standing ovation; then most of the crowd went to other rooms to gamble while some slipped in to one of the three little bedrooms next to the card tables.

The lawmen stayed at their table, ordered whiskey and discussed the show; however, their conversation centered mostly around Jeanette's stunning beauty.

When the show ended, Jeanette went backstage, freshened up and then came out to the tables where the crowd was sitting. She greeted well wishers but, it was evident, she was making her way to Boots, Ryder and Vernon's table.

As they watched her working her way towards them, Ryder said, almost painfully, "My God, I think she's coming to our table."

When Boots turned to look he knocked over his whiskey glass spilling it all over Ryder's lap. "Damn Boots," responded Ryder, "look what you've done. You did that on purpose, didn't you? Geez, here she comes."

As she reached their table, they all stood up in military fashion, as if it were a General inspection.

Her smile lit up the room as she said, "Evening fellas; may I join you men for a drink?"

While Ryder and Vernon just stood their like manikins, Boots said, "You certainly may," as he pulled out a chair and helped her sit down.

Now that they were all seated she said, "Sheriff, I'd like to thank you for removing those drunks. One never knows how far they might try to go."

Vernon said, "Aw shucks ma'am, there weren't nothing to it." Once said, he thought, that must have sounded like a real hayseed.

Boots filled the momentary silence and offered, "Allow me to introduce us. I'm Ranger Boots Law, this is Ranger Ryder McCoy and the Sheriff here is Vernon Franks."

"Oh, it's so nice to meet you," said Jeanette "I've heard all about how wild Texas is and how brave you lawmen are."

She turned to Boots and Ryder, got a quizzical look on her face, and said, "Hmm, Boots and Ryder, I read the newspaper in Austin. Are you the two Rangers who were in the Eagle Pass shootout? As Boots and Ryder nodded the affirmative, she added, "My goodness, the paper said both of you were wounded."

Jeanette had a special way about her, everything she said was with emotion; she was also tantalizing with her eyes and body movement. Although she was sharing her conversation among the lawmen, she was honing her attention in on McCoy as she said, "Ryder, may I call you Ryder? The paper said you were badly wounded."

Ryder grinned and said, "Yea, I took a bullet in the back; Boots was hit in the leg. I was brought here for treatment and recuperation under Doc' Lauderdale's care."

When Jeanette asked how his recovery was coming, Ryder answered, "Well thankfully, I can come and see pretty ladies dance and sing, but it'll be a couple more weeks before I'm ready to ride the range."

Jeanette smiled, showing perfectly straight, ivory white teeth, and said, "I'm sure life as a Ranger is exciting, but you could get killed any day; aren't you afraid?"

Ryder laughed and said, "Ma'am, I'm more afraid sitting here talking to you than I am facing down outlaws."

"Oh Ryder, you make me blush," babbled Jeanette in a refreshingly girlish manner.

Not to be left out of the conversation, Vernon jumped in and asked, "How long will you be here before moving on?"

"We usually stay two weeks and do three shows a week, she answered, "then, after San Antonio, it's on to Corpus Christi, Galveston and finally, New Orleans; then we make the return trip to San Francisco."

Not wanting to appear overly anxious to continue their first meeting, Jeanette stood up and remarked, "It's been my pleasure. I hope to see you again. Just think tonight I met the Texas Rangers we read about in magazines back east."

Realizing the conversation was over, the men stood up as Jeanette said goodnight, turned and walked away. The smell of her perfume still lingered in the room long after she had departed.

When she was gone, they looked at each other, and then Boots said, "Ryder, I believe you're the winner. I think it's you she likes."

Ryder smiled and said, "I hope so, I truly hope so. She is beautiful."

The next day, while Ryder was lying face down on the examining table with Doc Lauderdale changing bandages, he caught the scent of perfume and heard footsteps coming up the stairway; he knew immediately that it was Jeanette's perfume. He tried to turn his head sideways so he could see the doorway, when Doc Lauderdale said, rather harshly, "Be still, I'm trying to clean this wound."

About that time, in walked Jeanette; she looked at Doc Lauderdale and said, "I'm here to check on the condition of a handsome Ranger named Ryder McCoy. Is he here?" then, in her tantalizing way, she laughed.

Lauderdale looked up at Jeanette and said, "Pretty lady, I'm just about finished with him, then he's all yours."

"Thanks Doc'," said Jeanette. "But do you think he'll be strong enough to buy me dinner tonight?"

Ryder said, "I can answer that. You durn right I will, meet me in the restaurant at seven."

Jeanette walked over to the head of the table, put her hand in Ryder's hair and said, "Bye Ryder, don't be late," and walked out.

Ryder looked at Doc Lauderdale, smiled and said, "I'm better already."

About an hour later Boots came to the doctor's office to see Ryder. "Hey Ryder," said Boots, "how you feel today? I thought I'd come by to see if you wanted to have supper tonight with me and Vernon."

Ryder was sitting in a chair, he ducked his head momentarily, then looked up with a big smile and said, "I sure would, but I got other plans."

"What do you mean 'other plans', asked Boots? Hell we're saddle pals, why can't you eat with us?"

"Because Ms. Jeanette McDonald came over here and asked me to take her to dinner. What do think about that? Looks like you ain't the Heartbreak Kid anymore."

Boots looked at Ryder and said, "Don't forget which fork to use, don't talk with you mouth full and hold your pinkie up when you take a drink."

Ryder remarked, "Hey, it's just dinner, why I gotta be so formal?"

Boots gave him a side glance and said, "Hell man, I know you're in love; maybe I'd better ask Laughlin for a new partner. Just imagine, a lovesick Ranger out on an outlaw chase." Boots broke into full laughter and added, "Pal, I'm just envious, she's so damn beautiful; y'all have a good time and I'll see you later." Then, not quite ready to stop raggin' on Ryder, Boots mumbled as he walked to the door, "I guess me and Vernon will just have to catch outlaws and rescue pretty ladies by ourselves."

The evening finally came. It was only half past six and Ryder was already in the restaurant waiting for Jeanette. As she came thru the door, every head in the restaurant turned to look at her. Her pace was brisk and frisky; she was both elegant and teasing as she walked to the table.

Ryder rose from his chair, helped her get seated and then sat down. While her hands were resting on the table, he laid his hand on hers, looked into her eyes and said, "Hi pretty blue eyed girl, you look very beautiful tonight."

Jeanette blushed slightly as she said, "You look very brave and handsome yourself, Ranger McCoy."

They ordered wine, drank and conversed; first about Ranger life and then, about her life as an entertainer. She said she was born in Chicago; her parents were entertainers and she had been dancing and singing for most of her life. At the present time she was traveling from city to city; usually staying in a city for about two weeks before moving on to the next one."

Ryder, who had been listening intently, said, "Sounds like an exciting life."

"No, not really," she said, "I always travel alone by stage or train. "It's a fast life, though not very exciting." "Except of course, when I meet a Texas Ranger or two," she added with a mischievous grin.

Ryder, tried to be nonchalant as he asked, "Do you have someone special?

"No not really," she answered, "I do meet lots of men, but they're not very interesting."

Pressing his luck, Ryder queried, "How about me; am I interesting?"

"Well, I'm not sure" she replied, "and, I must say, I've never met a Texas Ranger before, but I'm certainly looking forward to getting to know you better."

Ryder, believing he had gone about as far as he dared on their first encounter, finished out the night with small talk. They enjoyed the evening, bid each other a goodnight, and retired to their separate lodgings.

CHAPTER 15

Back in Uvalde the long hot summer days were giving way to cool autumn nights. Laughlin, as usual, was up at daybreak having a cup of coffee before starting his daily routine of tending to Sam. With coffee cup in hand he walked out on the porch; the eastern sun was just beginning to peek over the horizon. He took a deep breath and said, "Lord, thank you for this day."

When he finished his coffee, he set the cup down and started walking towards the corral. As usual, Sam was expecting him and had already begun trotting around the corral; showing his excitement to see Laughlin. Laughlin opened the corral gate and spoke, "Hello big fellow, how you doing this morning?" Laughlin enjoyed his mornings with Sam and Sam enjoyed the attention, not to mention his hay and rubdown.

From the day he got the big colt from Herman Fox, Sam and Laughlin began sharing a special relationship. Sam was now fourteen years old and had never been ridden by anyone but Laughlin.

While Laughlin was brushing Sam's still powerful body, and combing his mane and tail, he stopped for a minute and said aloud, "Sam old pal, we've ridden many a trail together. You've always been sure footed and, no doubt, saved my hide more than once." It was obvious that Laughlin was reminiscing as he continued, "Remember that rattlesnake down by the Frio River; and how about that time you out ran a raiding party of Indians, down on Comanche Flats?"

Laughlin looked around, to see if anyone was in hearing distance, then said, "What the hell, I don't care who's listening." As he continued, "Sam, sometimes when I walk by you here in the corral, your eyes tell me that you yearn for just one more adventure. Just you and me out there in God's country; yea, I guess we wouldn't ride as fast as before, you may have lost a step or two and I suspect my gun hand might be a tad bit slower." Then he placed the brush on the rail, looked at Sam and said, "I love you old pal and I'll always take care of you." Laughlin turned and walked out of the stall to the corral gate. As he closed it behind him and started walking toward the house, he could smell the breakfast that Melissa was preparing.

Sam's eyes were focused on Laughlin and his ears were standing up as he trotted up and down the corral fence, nickering. Laughlin continued to walk away; he could here Sam's sounds of affection as he reached up and wiped tears from his eyes as if specs of dirt had blown into them. He truly loved that horse.

Meanwhile, Jeanette's two week engagement in San Antonio had passed by quickly; she was preparing to leave for the next city, Corpus Christi. Her impending departure saddened both her and Ryder. Since meeting, the two of them had spent most of their free time together. But now it was time for her to go; Ryder, Boots and Vernon were at the stage to see her off.

Jeanette had tears in her eyes when she hugged Boots and Vernon and said goodbye. Then she turned to Ryder, gave him a kiss on the cheek, hugged him tightly, and said, "I'll write to you. Keep yourself safe."

Her gear was loaded onto the stage as she climbed into the coach. The driver released the brake; spoke to the team of horses, and off they went. The trio of Boots, Vernon and Ryder, stood in the street watching the stage until it was clear out of sight.

Ryder turned to Boots and said, "Didn't think I could ever feel this way about a woman."

Boots smiled, put his hand on Ryder's shoulder and said, "Let's go saddle up. Doc' says you can ride again."

War Paint and Bad Moon, having spent several weeks at the livery stable, were frisky and ready to run. Ryder had to be careful; he didn't want to reopen his wound. They road for about an hour; Ryder told Boots he was fine and ready to get back to work.

Laughlin had sent word for them to return to Uvalde as soon as Ryder was properly healed, so they left San Antonio the next day, heading west. They alternated between a walk and a slow gallop to keep the horses fresh and allow them an opportunity to talk.

During one of their walking interludes, Ryder said, "It's going to be hard for Jeanette and I to continue a relationship. I have to be very careful not to fall completely in love. Although I have strong feelings for her, her lifestyle and mine don't mix."

Boots chimed in, "I know what you mean. Being a Ranger makes it almost mandatory that you're single. You know I care for Jane, but if we were married, she would want me to leave the Rangers." They walked their horses around a rather large puddle of water left over from a recent cloudburst as Boots continued, "Best thing we can do, is remain free spirits; we'll get old soon enough." Then he thought momentarily, changed the subject and said, "I know we're traveling cross country to Uvalde, but it'll still take two days; lets go by the Fox Ranch, its on the way."

"Yea," said Ryder, "they're good folks. Sure do like Billy." Then, as if he suddenly remembered, spouted, "Say Boots, I've never seen Fred shoot, you say he's good. How would you compare Billy to Fred?"

Boots answered, "Hard to say, they're both deadly." He paused, and then added, "Man, I wouldn't want to live on the difference." They continued walking their horses as Boots said thoughtfully, "You know, their personalities are quite different. Fred jokes, brags and has fun but Billy goes straight to the point and doesn't talk a lot; he's kind of scary when he has that rifle in his hands."

It was just getting twilight when they arrived at Herman's ranch and were invited to spend the night. The invitation was well received since it was Ryder's first long ride after taking a bullet in the back.

Donnie Rae had prepared a nice supper; Boots and Ryder did her proud, they both ate double helpings. Later they sat on the porch and listened to Herman tell stories about building the ranch and the Indian attacks. He told about children being taken captive and how they were never the same when rescued. He said women captives were either raped and mutilated or taken to the Indian's camp to be used for pleasure and domestic slaves. Sometimes the Indian women wouldn't accept them and often killed the captives out of jealousy. Also, Herman said it was a known fact that Indians had no resistance to alcohol. Even though it drove them crazy, the first thing they looked for during a raid, was alcohol.

Herman paused, and then continued, "You know, our ranch house was attacked several times but we were able to fight 'em off. Billy and his rifle would take out several of 'em; bodies would be lying all over the place. During a lull, we would stop firing so they could pick up their dead and wounded; then they would ride off. Indians feared the white man with a rifle and would soon give up the fight, especially if someone like Billy was in the house with a rifle."

After a couple of hours of Herman's tales, they retired for the night. The next morning began with biscuits and gravy, sausage, eggs and lots of Donnie Rae's coffee.

When Boots finished his breakfast, he said to Donnie Rae, "That's the best breakfast I ever had; will you marry me?"

Donnie Rae blushed and said, "I've already got two men to take care of, don't need another one."

Herman agreed, "Not only is she a good cook, but she's almost as good with a rifle as Billy; and she can outride both of us."

The Rangers saddled up, filled their saddlebags with food prepared by Donnie Rae, offered their appreciation, then mounted up and headed towards Uvalde. The day was starting out real pleasant with the smell of autumn in the morning air. The recent rain had 'greened' everything up and Comanche Flats was beautiful.

It was the beginning of the mating season for the white tail deer. Occasionally they would see a buck chasing a doe or one with his nose on the ground, trailing. About a hundred yards in front of them, partially exposed, stood a magnificent buck. He was in full rut and his neck was swollen to the max'. He looked strong and proud; man was he beautiful. He had been staring at them for some time when suddenly he bolted and began running in and out of the brush, sometimes leaping for long distances.

Boots stood up in the saddle, watched the big buck bounding out of sight and said, "Wasn't that something. He was beautiful; a definite keeper."

Ryder, in an attempt to be philosophical, said, "Boots, did you ever notice that, in wildlife, the male of the species is always the prettiest. Now why can't it be that way for humans?" then he grinned.

Boots laughed and said, "I'm perfectly happy the way it is. I don't want to be prettier than my woman." Then he turned in the saddle, looked at Ryder, and said, "Speaking of women, I think I'll tell Audrey about you and Jeanette when we get to Uvalde. What do you think about that old saddle pal?"

Ryder looked serious for a moment; then said, "I don't rightly know how to handle this, but it's a good problem to have. Maybe I'll do like the Indians, have me four or five squaws."

Up north, Bronco was still in Abilene; he had been ordered to stay there assisting Sheriff Cletus Meeks after Boots left for Uvalde. Things had been fairly quiet except for Saturday nights when wranglers came to town drinking and raising hell.

Bronco and Meeks were sitting around the jail one morning discussing the recent trend; train robberies. It seems that more gold and currency was now being transported by rail than the banks kept in their vaults. In fact, an organization called, The Pinkerton Detective Agency, had been hired to pursue such gangs as: The James Boys, led by Jesse James, The Younger Brothers, led by Cole Younger and The Wild Bunch, led by Butch Cassidy and the Sundance Kid. There were handbills and reward posters being posted in every town and berg west of the Mississippi.

The two continued to banter back and forth when a young boy ran into the jail and shouted, "Telegram for Ranger Bronco Wilson."

Bronco put up his hand and said, "That's me son, thanks." As the boy handed him the wire, he reached and took a bullet out of his gun belt and handed it to the boy; a gesture he had learned from Boots.

Bronco read the wire, looked up at Cletus and said, "I've been ordered to meet Boots and Ryder in Ft. Worth; then it's on to Bowie and points north."

"Did Laughlin give you any details," asked Cletus.

"Just that there has been some Indian activity around Bowie and north towards the Red River," answered Bronco. As he got up to leave, he added, "I suppose Boots will brief me when we meet in Ft. Worth; you gonna be okay here."

Cletus said, "Yea, me and the bartender can handle the drovers alright and I don't think we have a problem here with the train robberies; the hot spots seem to be farther up north....... in Kansas and Missouri."

Bronco gathered provisions, said his farewells to Cletus, and headed east. It was still early morning and Ft. Worth was almost a four day ride.

Bronco, Boots and Ryder arrived at the Cattleman's hotel in Ft. Worth within hours of each other. Boots and Ryder had left Uvalde a week before Laughlin wired Bronco in Abilene.

After taking care of their horses, they got a bite to eat; then retired to their hotel room for a good night's rest. Boots briefed Bronco on the situation in Bowie. Apparently, small bands of Indians in Oklahoma were leaving the tribal grounds, riding south across the Red River and raiding in Texas. They were stealing horses, burning cabins, killing and terrorizing whites all along the river as well as around Spanish Fort. Recently, a white girl had been taken captive during one of the raids north of Bowie, just outside of Spanish Fort.

The next morning, the three Rangers took the first train to Bowie. It was mid-morning when they arrived; the late fall weather had brought them overcast skies, blowing wind and a light drizzle. The trio unloaded their horses next to the depot and adjusted their saddles preparing to ride. They could smell the acrid smoke, bellowing out of the locomotive, as they heard the familiar sound of the train leaving the depot; choo...choo...choo...choo, choo...choo...choo...choo.

They stood watching the caboose until it drifted down the rails and out of sight. Bronco shook his head and said, "Amazing, I don't see how anything that big and heavy can move at all, much less as fast as it does."

"Hell," said Ryder, "who knows, one day we might be flying."

They all had a good laugh; then Bronco blurted out, "I'll stick with the horse."

Just then, Wylie Bill Coleman, a Ranger from the Northern District, rode up to the depot. They briefly discussed the situation; then, rode north towards Spanish Fort.

As evening approached, they rode into Spanish Fort, stabled their horses and rested for the night. The next morning they were saddling up when Ryder approached Boots and asked, "What do you know about this Wylie Bill?"

"Why do you ask?" queried Boots.

"He's not very likeable," said Ryder, "he's a know it all and not very friendly."

Boots said, "Yea, I know. He's not from our district and Laughlin says he has a reputation of being a mean hothead; but he knows the area and Laughlin wants us to bring the girl back alive, so I guess we're stuck with him, likeable or not."

They mounted up, with Wylie leading the way, and went towards the Baker cabin where the family had been slain and the girl kidnapped. When they arrived at the homestead, the house and barn had been burned and were still smoldering. It had been two days since the Indian raid. Wylie and some men from town had found the remains the day following the attack.

Nothing was said for a few minutes; then Wylie broke the silence and stated, "The father and the two young boys were mutilated; then thrown into the pigpen for the hogs. They cut off the father's head, scalped him, then placed it on the gatepost."

Boots could see that Wylie, who was as tough as they come, was having trouble as he recalled the carnage of the raid but, even though he was troubled, he continued, "There was blood in the yard and on the porch as well as the walls and floor inside the cabin." Wylie then shook his head, spit out his chaw of tobacco, and added, "The linen on the bed was soaked in blood. The mother had been raped, stomach split open and partially skinned. Me and some of the town folk buried the remains out behind the barn."

Wylie gathered himself and told Boots "With the lead the Indians have, they're probably going to steal more horses then cross the Red River before heading to their tribal grounds in Oklahoma." Then he spat, wiped his mouth and growled, "The girl, Cindi, is sixteen and they'll probably take her to their camp as a wife rather than kill her. I've never seen anything as brutal as what was done to that family."

You could still smell the dried blood; flies were buzzing around and the odor of death penetrated the air.

Wylie, who had bit off a new chaw, spat again, wiped his mouth on his sleeve and said angrily, "The son's-a-bitches are Comanche's, and we're gonna get the bastards."

Without another word, the Rangers headed towards the Red River and whatever dangers lay ahead.

It was drizzling, but it was easy to pick up the trail. It appeared there were six horses. One set of tracks were deeper than the others; Cindi was probably riding double behind a brave.

The sun was setting in the west as they reached a place called Herring Point. Smelling smoke; they dismounted and eased up to a viewpoint looking down in the hollow; that's where the smoke was coming from. It had grown dark and the flames from the fire allowed them to see into the camp. Suddenly Cindi started screaming and crying out.

It was evident the Indians were beginning to take turns with her. The Rangers were lying in the grass, staring at the camp, when Wylie, still lying flat, shouldered his 45-70 and aimed. Boots, realizing he was aiming at Cindi, pushed the rifle down and whispered harshly, "What the hell are you doin'?"

Wylie, with a hardened look on his face, said, "I'm gonna kill her; put her out of her misery."

Boots growled, "To hell you are, we're gonna try and save her. I give the orders here not you. We're gonna spread out; you drop a brave around the campfire; then we'll start shooting. Maybe they'll panic, forget the girl and ride off without her."

Wylie grudgingly agreed and waited for a brave to appear in the light of the campfire. A moment later he fired, dropping a brave face first into the fire. When the other Rangers started firing, the Indians ran to their horses and fled with Cindi riding behind a brave.

It was too dark to track the Indians; besides the drizzle had become a downpour and would wash away the horses' tracks. They decided to camp right there in the hollow and start their pursuit the next morning. Their plan was simple; follow the Red River. According to Wylie, there was a shallow crossing about twenty miles north.

After they pitched camp, Ryder asked, "Wylie, why were you going to shoot Cindi?"

Wylie scowled and said, "You don't know much about Indians do you boy. That girl will never be the same; she'll be crazy. Whites won't accept her because she's been with the Indians; her life may as well be over now."

Boots interrupted harshly and said, "Maybe so, but all the same, we're gonna try and save her. Now let's get some sleep, I'll take first watch."

The next morning they were up early and riding along the south bank of the Red River. They had picked up some horse tracks and estimated them to be a day old. There were at least six horses; so it appeared they were following the raiding party.

Late that evening, once again they dismounted and crept toward the smell of smoke. Soon they came upon a clearing; there were three tepees with a campfire. Three squaws were tending the fire and cooking a couple of rabbits.

Boots whispered to the others, "There's no horses in camp; that means the braves are out and Cindi is probably in one of the tepees."

They returned to their horses, mounted up and rode into the camp. The startled squaws gathered in one of the tents. Wylie, who spoke Comanche; dismounted, walked to each tepee and looked inside. Cindi was not in camp. He turned to the squaws and loudly asked about the white girl. The squaws, while still huddled with each other, shook their heads no.

Wylie walked away, mounted his horse, pulled his pistol and shot the three squaws. It was a total surprise and not sanctioned by the Rangers. Boots hollered at Wylie, "What the hell are you doing? Why'd you do that?"

Wylie was grinning as he holstered his pistol, looked at Boots and said, "I saw what they did to that family, if you want to ride with me you'd better toughen up."

Boots looked Wylie in the eyes and said, "We're going to ride with you till we find the girl. If you ever do that again, I'll kill you." The two men looked at each other for what seemed like an eternity. Nothing was said; the stare Boots gave Wylie was a silent understanding.

As the day came to an end, God blessed them with a beautiful sunset. The western sky was turning a beautiful orange as the sun disappeared behind the horizon. They set up camp under some large pecan trees and built a campfire; it would take a bit of the chill out of the night air.

Boots was about thirty yards from the campfire watching and listening. A task they would alternate through the night.

Ryder said to Wylie, "Let's go check the hobbles on the horses." They both rose to their feet, poured out what was left of their cold coffee and walked toward the horses. After checking the horses, Ryder said, "Wylie, I'm gonna give you some advise. Don't push your luck with Boots; he's ram-rodding this chase, not you."

Wylie looked at Ryder and said, "Oh yea, what's he gonna do, shoot me like he did his partner, JoJo."

Ryder unleashed a straight right hand to Wylie's jaw that nearly broke his neck. The blow sent him flying backwards, landing on his back. Ryder immediately straddled him, reached down, got a hold of Wylie's bandana and jerked his head up. They were almost nose-to-nose as Ryder looked into Wylie's glazed eyes and said, "Don't you ever bring that up again. If you do, a 44 slug will hit you; not my fist." Ryder slammed Wylie's head to the ground, rose up, turned and walked back to camp.

The next morning was cool and over cast. As Boots saddled up he thought about Cindi; and silently prayed that she was all right.

They continued along the trail that ran beside the riverbank. Once again, it was late in the evening when they smelled smoke. Riding carefully and quietly, they saw a wagon with two mules grazing and a man tending his campfire. Not taking any chances, they rode into the camp with rifles in hand. Boots identified himself and the other men as Rangers.

The man was in his forties, short, medium build, top hat, and long beard. He was dressed in a worn out continental suit; said his name was Happy Slocom, a peddler, trader and medicine man.

Boots asked, "How do you survive here in Indian territory?"

"Tis simple," answered Happy, "so long as I supply the Injuns wif farwater, they won't kill me."

Boots said, "Makes sense." Then he added, "We're looking for a raiding party with a white girl. Have you seen 'em?"

Happy replied, "Matter-a-fact, I shore have, 'bout two owersago. They took muh whiskey barrel; ther wuz a girl 'bout sixteen wif 'em. She looked real bad, like she wuz outta her hayed. Her eyes were op'n but it didn't peer she-as seein' inathing. I pity her when nay stop-n-camp, wit tat whiskey they'll party and get mean whif-er."

"How far ahead of us are they," asked Boots.

"Purt neer two owers, ah guess," said Happy, "they won't go ina further tuhday. They'll drink till they plum pass out."

Boots said, "Boys, we'll probably get to them as the sun sets." After a two-hour ride they heard gunfire, whooping and hollering just ahead of them. They stopped their horses, dismounted and gathered for instructions as Boots said, "I'll take Wylie with me; we'll creep up close enough to see how many are in camp and try to spot Cindi. Y'all wait for us to return; if you hear gunfire, come riding hard."

Under the cover of darkness, Boots and Wylie crouched over and got to within forty yards of the camp. A large fire was going and it appeared four of the Indians had already passed out from the whiskey. Those four were lying on the ground motionless while the other two were taking turns with Cindi. This time Cindi wasn't hollering, she didn't make a sound.

Wylie said, "See that, she's already lost her will; she's in a state of shock and probably doesn't even know what's going on. She'll never be any good, she won't heal and she's crazy; better off dead."

Boots said, "Shut up Wylie, we're going to lay here and watch till the other two pass out and then we're going in."

Another thirty minutes had passed when the two remaining Indians sat down. Their heads bobbed, they drank from the jug, their heads bobbed and they drank from the jug; moments later, they passed out.

Boots said, "Let's go back to the horses."

When they reached Ryder and Bronco, Boots told them the Indians were passed out and Cindi was tied to a tree. Then he said, "We're going to mount up with pistols drawn and ride into that camp while they're sleeping. Don't give 'em a chance; if any of 'em lives, he'll try to kill Cindi."

They mounted up, rode hard into the camp and began firing at will. Two of the Indians made it to their feet before the pistol fire cut them down.

Boots dismounted and went to cut Cindi loose from the tree. When he did, she went into a crazy rage, fighting, screaming and clawing. Boots held her tight, hugged her and tried to quite her down. As he held her he saw Wylie shooting and scalping the Indians. The last one was still alive when he was scalped.

Wylie had the look of a mad dog; he was holding a bloody knife and six scalps.

Boots looked at Wylie and ordered, "No more, it's over."

Wylie dropped the knife and the scalps. He had a wild look in his eyes as he said, "She's got to be killed; she has evil spirits in her head, no one will help her, she's crazy; she must be killed."

CHAPTER 16

As Wylie drew his pistol to fire at Cindi, Boots turned to block her body with his taking a bullet in his left shoulder. Instinctively, Boots drew his pistol and fired; Wylie fell face down; dead as he hit the ground.

When Ryder and Bronco rushed to Boots, he said, "Take care of Cindi, I'm alright, it didn't hit any bone."

After securing Cindi, who continued to scream and shake uncontrollably, they made Boots as comfortable as possible; knowing the bullet had to come out.

Ryder laid his knife in the hot coals of the camp fire. When it was red hot he told Boots to bite down on his glove as he stuck the hot knife in the wound. It made a sizzling sound as it touched flesh and blood. The bleeding stopped immediately. Ryder removed his bandana, bandaged the wound and then helped Boots to his feet. Boots hadn't made a sound.

They wrapped a blanket around Cindi, put her on the horse with Ryder and rode toward Spanish Fort with a dead Ranger draped over his horse. They rode all night hoping to get out of Indian Territory before daybreak.

When they reached Spanish Fort, a crowd gathered and followed them down the street to the sheriffs' office. Ryder and Boots took Cindi inside the office while Bronco took Wylie's body to the undertaker.

A few moments later a middle-aged man burst into the sheriffs' office. When he saw Cindi, he bellowed, "That's her alright. I'm her Uncle, that's Cindi."

Boots said, "Good, we need to get her some clothes; then you can take her home."

"Take her home!" exclaimed the man. "I ain't taking her home, she ain't my responsibility; besides she may be diseased and she'll never be right. They never get over being with the Indians, evil spirits enter their head; she'll be crazy. I don't want her, nobody will, she's better off dead."

Boots face turned to stone, his neck swelled, his fists clenched, his eyes were dancing as he fixed on the man's eyes and said, "You are a miserable excuse for a man, get out of this office and keep going. Don't let me see you again, next time I'll beat you to death. You don't deserve to be alive."

Boots, Ryder and Bronco stepped out on the jail porch with Cindi. Cindi was shaking badly and holding on to Ryder.

Boots, addressing the crowd that had gathered, said, "This is Cindi, she was taken captive by Indians after they killed her family. She needs a home and someone to care for her. Is there anyone here who will help her?"

Everyone in the crowd of twenty-five or more lowered their eyes and looked at the ground. There was complete silence, Boots eyes surveyed the crowd but received no response. Finally a middle-aged woman wearing a bonnet and print dress looked at Boots and said, "You Rangers had no right bringing her back here, you should have killed her. None of us are going to take her, probably diseased and she's crazy, always will be crazy, Injuns do that to 'em."

Once again Boots bristled and became angry and emotional. He shouted at the crowd, "Y'all want me to shoot her; well I might just shoot all of y'all instead." With that said, he drew his pistol and started firing into the air. The crowd panicked and ran into or over each other in an effort to get away.

Quickly the crowd was gone. Cindi was still shaking in Ryder's arms as Boots turned, looked up toward the heavens and said, "Help me God, show me the way, I don't know what to do."

The sheriff of Spanish Fort, Willard Cox, who had been in Nacona when the Rangers brought Cindi in, returned shortly after the episode in front of the jail. He suggested putting Cindi in a cell where she would be safe; he would have his wife feed and care for her while she was recovering.

The Rangers agreed and Ryder led Cindi into the cell. He sat and tried to talk to her but she only stared blankly, as though she was in another place.

Willard said, "Why don't you boys go on over to the restaurant and get a bite; I'll stay with her, besides, we need to keep her locked in the cell for awhile so she don't run away." The Rangers took Willard's advice and went to the restaurant.

Willard sat in the cell for a while; talking to Cindi, assuring her she was going to be safe. He had the door to the jail locked when he heard a loud knock and voices calling his name. He got up, locked the cell door behind him, and went to see who was knocking. It was a group of six local ladies from town.

Eleanor, who had elected herself spokesperson, said, "I'm here representing the town folk. We want that girl out of here before something happens. Everyone knows she's crazy, the town doesn't want her here."

As she was speaking to Willard, a noise came from inside the jail cell. Cindi was murmuring and making noises. Willard fumbled with the keys as he hurried to unlock the door.

When he opened it, he saw Cindi hanging from a shredded blanket. She had tied one end of it around her neck, stood on the chair Willard had been sitting in; the, apparently, she had tied the other end around the jail rafter, kicked the chair out from under, and hung herself.

The Rangers had seen the crowd and were returning to the jail when Willard discovered her. Boots pushed the ladies who were blocking the door aside, and the three Rangers stepped inside. They removed their hats and stared at the scene in front of them; a sixteen-year old girl hanging from the jail rafters.

Boots, with tears in his eyes, still looking at Cindi said, "Well boys, I guess God had seen enough and decided to call her home. May she rest in peace!"

He turned, looked at the women standing in the door with the crowd behind them, and said, "Y'all should be real proud of yourselves, the Indians didn't kill that girl, y'all did; now you vultures can get out of my sight. Cut her down gently boys."

Meanwhile, about noon in an upstairs room above the Red Dog Saloon back in Ft. Worth, Joe Don Sutton, ex-bouncer, was facing his daily task of trying to wake up. He opened his eyes and looked at the ceiling as rays of sunlight were finding their way thru tattered curtains and across the filthy make shift bedroom floor.

He swung his legs around, put his feet on the floor, raised himself up, and sat on the side of the bed. When he noticed he was fully dressed and still had his boots on, he began to laugh, and then he squeezed his temples as an excruciating pain hit him right between the eyes. This was his usual morning ritual after a night of hard drinking and barroom carousing.

Joe Don was twenty-one years old, going on seventy. He was about six feet tall, had broad shoulders with very strong muscular arms and a lean narrow waist. With his strong, square jaw, rugged facial features, protruding cheekbones and cold dark brown eyes, Joe Don had the features of a formidable foe. His hair was brown, straight and hanging to his shoulders; he was liked by the ladies and feared by the men.

He sat for a while on the side of the bed, remembering when his paw was alive and owned the Red Dog Saloon. After his death, it was taken over by Will Driskell, the owner of three other saloons in Ft. Worth. Joe Don thought about his growing up in the saloon and how Dalton, his paw, had told him he didn't have a mama and not to ask any questions. In the alley behind the saloon, Joe Don had seen his paw beat more than one man senseless. In his teens, when Dalton was drunk and feeling mean, he would beat Joe Don with his fists. Once his paw beat a man to death and made him drag the body to the livery stable and leave it in a horse stall.

When Joe Don turned sixteen, Dalton made him the bouncer at the Red Dog. It was his paw that encouraged him to drink, cheat at cards, be mean, fight, and kill. He succeeded; Joe Don was mean and soon became a feared man in the stockyards and Hell's Half Acre.

Late one night in the Red Dog, Dalton was drinking his whiskey and, as usual, became mean and violent. Joe Don was also drinking at the bar when Dalton cursed and struck him with the back of his hand.

Joe Don had enough, he didn't flinch, and said, "Paw, don't ever hit me again."

Story goes that Dalton laughed and said, "I've been hearing stories about how tough you are boy, but you'll never be able to stand up to me."

Then he came out from behind the bar and hit Joe Don flush in the face. Blood spurted from the cut on his eyebrow but Dalton never landed another punch. Joe Don beat his Paw to death while the customers looked on, afraid to interfere.

Joe Don, who was still sitting on the bed as his thoughts returned to the present, reached under it and pulled out a bottle of whiskey. He turned it up, filled his mouth, gargled and spat. Then he turned the bottle up again and drank several ounces, causing bubbles to appear inside the bottle. He let out a loud belch, capped the bottle and slid it back under the bed. Feeling refreshed, he rose and walked over to a chair where his gun belt was hanging. After strapping it on, he pulled the pistol and checked the load; then he looked at the three notches on the handle, put his hat on, went downstairs to the bar and said, "Good morning world, what a hell of a night."

After a few more shots, he went over to the White Owl Saloon on Exchange Street for his daily amusement which consisted of shooting pool, playing cards, drinking whiskey and playing with the girls. Melba, his favorite girl, enjoyed attention, especially watching men fight over her.

As usual, she was sitting next to Joe Don while he was playing poker. She would bring him whiskey, snuggle next to him, occasionally kissing and biting him on the ear.

This went on for a while when Joe Don said, "Woman, leave me alone, now's not the time, these cards are being sweet to me."

She became bored and whispered in Joe Don's ear, "See that cowboy that just came in and is standing at the end of the bar."

Joe Don took his eyes off the cards, looked at her and said, "Yea, what about him."

"Well," said Melba, "Last night I was upstairs with him. First he wouldn't pay, then he hit me."

Joe Don grinned, got up from the poker table, walked to the cue rack and removed a stick. He reversed ends, holding it like an axe handle as he walked toward the cowboy. When he was close enough, he hit the cowboy in the back of his head, knocking him to the floor; then he struck the cowboy over and over with the stick until he broke it in half. Then with the heel of his boot, he stomped the man in the face, followed by kicks to the ribs and stomach.

After the beating, he reached into the pocket of the badly beaten and unconscious cowboy, and removed two dollars. He kicked the cowboy one more time before walking over to Melba and handing her the two dollars. As he turned and headed back to the poker table, he noticed that others in the saloon had been watching. He pointed at the fallen cowboy and said, "That's what happens to anybody that messes with Melba."

Then he picked up his money from the table, reached over, grabbed Melba by the arm and said, "Come on baby, let's go upstairs, fighting turns me on."

Two days later, Joe Don walked into the White Owl saloon and went directly to the bar. Three men were standing there drinking whiskey as he walked up behind them, pushed two of 'em apart and leaned on the bar

One of the cowboys he shoved aside said, "There's room for all of us here at the bar friend; what's your problem?"

Joe Don barked, "This bar belongs to me; nobody drinks here when I'm around."

One of the other cowboys, a tall slim fellow said, "I ain't moving; bartender give me a drink."

Joe Don responded loudly, "Maybe I didn't make myself clear mister; I'm Joe Don Sutton, the meanest man in Ft Worth, now get outta here."

When no one moved quick enough for Joe Don, he grabbed the tall fellow by the back of his head, slammed his face on the bar, knocking him out; then drew his pistol and started pistol whipping the other two wranglers. They were cut on top of the head, across their faces, nose and forehead. Quickly helping each other up, they ran full speed out of the saloon.

Joe Don went into a rage and bellowed, "Nobody messes with Joe Don." Then he emptied his pistol into the ceiling, walls and floor. In an instant the saloon was empty.

The next morning he was sleeping off another hangover when Melba came to his room. She leaned over his bed and shook him awake. Joe

Don looked at her, grinned and said, "This is nice, room service, crawl in beside me."

Melba said, "Later Joe Don. I came to warn you. That cowboy you beat up the other night lives in Weatherford; his paw owns a big spread over there and, word is, he's bringing in some of his riders to take care of you."

Joe Don grinned, pulled her in bed and said, "I need to thank you."

Later in the day, Joe Don saddled up and rode to Sheriff Pryor's jail. It sat on top of a bluff over looking the river. When he walked in the jail and Sheriff Pryor looked at him a little sideways, Joe Don grinned and said, "Bet you never thought you'd see me in a jail."

Pryor grinned and said, "Nope, I thought maybe over at the undertakers, but never here, what's the occasion?"

Joe Don said, "You know I try to lead a nice peaceful life but everyone picks on me."

Pryor grinned again and shook his head. He knew eventually there would be a showdown between him and Joe Don.

Joe Don continued, "I've got a bunch of ole cowboys coming over from Weatherford to see me. It seems the cowboy who jumped me the other night in the White Owl, ran back to his paw in Weatherford. Now I'm told the old man and some of his riders are coming to get me."

Pryor grinned again and said, "Looks like you got yourself a problem, hope you get it worked out."

"No," said Joe Don, "they've got the problem; 'cause, if they ride in here after me, I'm not hard to find. I thought maybe you could ride out to the county line and send 'em home. If not, there's gonna be some shooting and the first one to die will be the old man. Think his name is Laxon, Corey Laxon. Tell ole Cory if he comes to town, be prepared to die."

Joe Don looked at Pryor, tipped his hat, walked out the door, mounted up and rode to the stockyards to meet his two buddies, Jim Tuttle and Kurt Strange. They're almost as mean as Joe Don; making their living cheating at cards, rolling drunks and stealing. Jim's only five feet tall with a stocky build, full head of red hair, a moustache and snuff stained teeth. Now Kurt is six feet tall, of medium build with a full head of brown hair and a trimmed beard. He tries to stay groomed;

considers himself a ladies man. Both men are mean and good with a pistol; but fear Joe Don.

After their usual 'howdy's', Joe Don told them about the threat of men coming and said he needed some backup; said for them to be armed with shotguns and he would make sure it happened in the saloon.

It was Friday; the evening sun was setting in the west, painting a beautiful, peaceful picture to the end of day in a Texas cattle town. Soon it would be dark and things would no longer be peaceful, the night was going to roar like a mountain lion.

Joe Don, Kurt and Jim were at Sam's Saloon over on Exchange Street, sitting at a table drinking whiskey. Kurt and Jim were drinking heavy, trying to settle their nerves before the expected gunfight.

Joe Don had an evil grin on his face. His eyes were glassy and he had the look of an animal about to spring on its prey. He was getting high off the anticipation of a gunfight and death.

About an hour after dark, the Laxon riders, seven of them, came riding down Main Street with the boss, Corey, leading the group.

They tied up in front of the White Owl Saloon, went inside and lined up at the bar. Mr. Laxon was fifty or so but in good shape. He was a tall muscular man with gray hair, a white moustache and hazel eyes. He had a stern, all business look on his face; as his eyes scanned the bar, he turned to the bartender and said, "I'm looking for Joe Don Sutton, is he here?" When the bartender nodded in the negative, Laxon barked, "Send someone to fetch 'im; tell 'im Corey Laxon and his boys are here."

A young wrangler volunteered. He ran over to Sam's saloon, entered, walked briskly up to Joe Don's table and said, "Joe Don, Corey Laxon and six of his men are at the White Owl and they sent me here to fetch you."

Joe Don grinned and replied, "Go tell 'im I don't take orders from the likes of him. Tell 'im where to find me."

The wrangler hurried out the saloon doors and headed toward the White Owl. When he arrived, he told Laxon exactly what was said; then advised him where he could find Joe Don.

In the meantime, Joe Don told Kurt and Jim to get in position on either side of the saloon doors. He said, "I'll sit in the back of the saloon against the wall. There will be no talking, just shooting; we'll have 'em in a cross fire;

Remember, the old man is mine. Don't quit shooting until they're all dead or have cowered out and run for it."

Simultaneously, Corey Laxon was telling his boys when they get to Sam's saloon, they were to follow him inside, but he wanted Joe Don for himself.

Sam's saloon was empty except for Sam, who was the owner, Joe Don, Kurt and Jim. Everyone else had cleared the bar fully knowing that a deadly gunfight was imminent.

When Corey and his boys arrived at Sam's, Laxon pushed the swinging doors open, and stepped inside. Sam ducked behind the bar to avoid flying bullets. Laxon continued to walk as his men followed.

Joe Don had hidden his pistol under the table; it was cocked and in his hand. When Corey was halfway across the floor, Joe Don jumped up and fired his pistol; killing Laxon with the first shot. He continued to fire into the surprised men as he heard a tremendous blast. Kurt and Jim had fired both barrels of their scatterguns at the same time. Four of Laxon's men took the full charge of the two shotguns and hit the floor dead.

The other two men managed to get out the door; however, one fell dead before he could reach his horse while the other one managed to ride away, wounded and bleeding badly. The entire shootout had only taken a few seconds. Six men were dead, and one was badly wounded.

Joe Don and his men had escaped the ruckus, unmarked. Laxon had managed to clear leather, while his cowboys had never drawn their guns; they were still holstered.

Sheriff Frank Pryor, who had been alerted, rode the mile and a half from his office to Sam's. He slid his horse to a stop in front of the saloon, dismounted and charged across the boardwalk, bursting into the saloon. It was obvious he was too late. The presence of death could be felt and smoke from the gunpowder filled the air. Joe Don was sitting at a table with his men, casually drinking from a bottle of whiskey; celebrating his victory.

Pryor looked at Joe Don and said, "Keep your hands on top of the table, all of you. Then he turned towards the bar and asked, "Sam did you see what happened?"

Sam, who was probably in his sixties, was a frail gray haired man who had tended bar on the north side most of his life, looked over at Joe Don and said, "Yea Frank, I did."

"What happened," asked Frank keeping his eyes fixed on the trio at the table.

"Laxon and his boys," answered Sam, "came in after Joe Don but got more than they bargained for. Joe Don, Kurt and Jim shot 'em down." He pointed towards the four bodies lying dead on the floor, and continued, "Besides Laxon and these three, one's in the street dead, the other rode off wounded and bleeding bad, he probably won't make it either."

Pryor drew his pistol, walked to Joe Don's table and repeated, "Keep your hands on top of the table;" then he walked around behind the three men and relieved them of their pistols.

By this time James Lee and George, his deputies, entered the saloon just as Frank was saying, "Joe Don, until I get some answers about what happened here, you and your boys are under arrest." James Lee and George led them outside and took them to jail.

As they left, Frank turned to Sam and asked, "Sam, was it a fair fight?

Sam lied and said, "Yea, they came in here to get Joe Don; hell, the ole man had his pistol in his hand, but he never got off a shot." Then Sam got a real quizative look on his face as he asked Pryer, "Did you see Joe Don's eyes?"

"Yea," said Frank, "same look as a killer's. He's gonna be a problem."

The next morning, Boots, Ryder and Bronco arrived in Ft. Worth riding south from Spanish Fort. As they rode into town, Boots said, "Y'all go to Sheriff Pryor's office. I need to wire Laughlin our report; then I'll join ya'." Ryder and Bronco dismounted in front of Frank's office and went inside.

After his usual welcoming, Frank introduced them to his deputies, James Lee and George. Then he poured each of them a cup of coffee and said, "You boys are a day late. I sure coulda used y'all last night. Had six men killed with one, riding off wounded, that we haven't found."

Ryder said, "Six men killed? Who done that?"

"Three of 'em did it," said Frank, "they're in a cell in the backroom now."

"I've got to see these men;" said Ryder. "Who are they?" he asked.

Frank picked up the keys and said, "Come on, I'll show ya; gotta let 'em go anyway, witness said it was a fair fight; self defense." As they walked to the backroom, Pryor continued, "One of 'em, Joe Don Sutton, is meaner then hell. Local boy; when he was sixteen, he beat his paw to death with his bare hands."

Pryor unlocked and opened the cell door as Boots, Ryder and Bronco went in to witness the release. When Joe Don seen the Ranger badges he said, "Well look here boys, ole Frank's called the Rangers in on us, ain't you boys skeered;" He mocked.

Frank said, "Sit down and shut up bird-brain, I've come to let you out."

Joe Don sat down, put on his grin and said, "Sorry you Rangers missed the party last night, it was exciting."

Frank had Kurt come out first. James Lee led him out; then George led Jim out.

When Joe Don came thru the cell door where Boots, Ryder and Bronco were, he stopped, stared at the Rangers and said, "I'm the meanest man in Ft Worth. This town belongs to me; get in my way or try to slow me down, and you'll rue the day."

Boots looked at Ryder and Bronco, they were grinning, he smiled back, winked and said, "Think we can handle him?"

While this was all going on, Jeanette McDonald was back in Dallas. She had one more night remaining on her two-week engagement; then it was on to Ft. Worth for two weeks before heading to Oklahoma then back to California.

To her surprise, she often times found herself thinking of Ryder. It seemed every town was the same. The Mayor and wealthy businessmen were always trying to entertain her but she would have no man in her life since meeting Ryder. She made a special effort to find out about the Texas Rangers and had come to this conclusion; they were well-respected men living a dangerous and exciting life while taming Texas.

To her surprise, she found herself at the telegraph office wiring the Sheriff in Ft. Worth, inquiring about Ranger Ryder McCoy's whereabouts.

A little while later she received a response saying he had been in Ft Worth for two days. After reading the wire, she smiled and felt a warm feeling coming over her. She was anxious to see Ryder.

After their brief meeting with Joe Don, Boots, Ryder and Bronco had spent the rest of the day with Sheriff Pryor. They had all decided to have dinner at the Cattleman's Restaurant on North Main.

As they were walking down the boardwalk towards the restaurant, Ryder saw a poster taped to a lamppost. It read, 'Coming soon and appearing at the White Owl saloon, Ms. Jeanette McDonald.' Ryder snatched the poster from the lamppost, read it and exclaimed rather loudly, "She'll be here in two days. Can you believe it, what luck! Laughlin don't you dare send us anywhere. How about that? I see her in two days......and she'll be here for two weeks." Ryder let out a big whoop, slapped his leg, and then did a little dance down the boardwalk.

Boots looked at Pryor and Bronco and said, "Hope we don't get in any gunfights, he'll be useless for the next two weeks." Boots laughed and hollered at Ryder, who was still dancing down the boardwalk, well ahead of them.

As Ryder was celebrating the good news, Boots shouted, "Hey, wait for us, it says here she'll be accompanied by her husband, the piano player."

Ryder stopped, turned around, gave Boots a shocking look and said, "I didn't see that on the poster."

Boots couldn't keep a straight face and they all burst out laughing. When Ryder realized he had been had, he slapped Boots on the back and resumed his promenading all the way to the restaurant.

They entered the restaurant, were seated, and ordered a sirloin steak. The dinning room was rather large. Over in a dark corner, sitting at a table, was Joe Don and his two companions, Kurt and Jim.

Frank gestured towards them and said, "There's Joe Don and his boys; keep your eyes on 'em."

Ryder questioned, "What's wrong with that guy? Is he crazy?"

"Yea," said Pryor, "crazy mean."

Joe Don and his boys finished eating; then remained seated, drinking whiskey. When Joe Don saw the lawmen, he whispered something to his companions; then they got up from their table and headed toward the Rangers and Sheriff Pryor.

Joe Don was wearing his intimidating cocky grin as he slowly approached their table. Kurt and Jim were standing hip-shod behind him as he pushed his hat back on his head, looked at the lawmen, curled his lip and said, "You boys stay out of trouble ya hear, don't want no trouble in my town." Then he turned and strutted out of the restaurant with his two lapdogs trailing obediently behind.

Boots looked at Sheriff Pryor, shook his head in disgust and said, "That boys on borrowed time. He's riding with the devil."

Time passed quickly for everyone but Ryder. When it was time for the stage to arrive, bringing Jeanette from Dallas, the Rangers gathered at the stage stop with Ryder anxiously awaiting its arrival. Finally it came down North Main and reined to a stop where everyone was waiting.

Jeanette was inside waving at the Rangers and the crowd; Ryder rushed to the stage, opened the door and helped Jeanette step out onto the ground. She was dressed in a pale blue dress with a pink lace blouse, long gloves and hat tilted to the side with what looked like a peacock feather stuck in it. Her cheeks were rosy, her long blond hair was shiny and her beautiful blue eyes were complimenting her tantalizing smile; she was gorgeous.

Ryder held her hand as they walking toward the boardwalk with Boots and Bronco carrying her luggage. The sound of charging hoof beats made Ryder turn as a cowboy reined his horse to a sliding stop between the stage and Jeanette; it was Joe Don.

Sutton looked at Jeanette, removed his hat and said, "Pretty lady you'll be seeing a lot of Joe Don;" then he slammed his hat back on his head, spurred his horse and rode off with dirt and dust flying from the horse's hooves.

Jeanette looked at Ryder, who was burning with anger, and wondered, "My goodness, who was that."

"Trouble," replied Ryder, "that was trouble, stay away from him, I think he's possessed."

Without another word, the Rangers helped Jeanette check into the Hereford Hotel. They carried the luggage to her room; then Ryder remarked, "You must be tired, we'll let you get some rest."

Jeanette put her hands on her lovely hips and asked bluntly, "Now wait a minute, you don't think you're going to walk away without asking me to dinner tonight, do you?"

Ryder beamed and replied, rather bashfully, "No Ma'am." Then he boldly asked, "Lovely Lady, will you have dinner with me tonight?"

Jeanette said, "No," teasingly, "but I will have dinner with all you Rangers. Say about eight, at Cattleman's?" She led the Rangers to the door, paused and said, "Don't be late; gentlemen never keep a lady waiting." She blew a kiss as they walked away.

When the Rangers were out of hearing distance, Boots said to Bronco with a sly and mischievous grin, "Did you hear that Bronco, all of us. I'm still not sure which one of us she'll choose?"

Bronco, continuing the charade, said, "I don't know, but I do know me and you are the best looking."

Ryder just smiled and took the joking in stride; he knew Jeanette liked him; he could see it in her eyes.

The Rangers, bathed, shaved, shined their boots, washed their clothes, dusted their hats and prepared for their dinner date. Ryder stopped by the barbershop and had the barber dust him with talcum. Boots and Bronco refused to associate with him as they walked down the boardwalk to the restaurant.

It was eight o'clock and the Rangers were seated in the Cattleman's Restaurant with their eyes fixed on the front door in anticipation of Jeanette's arrival.

The door opened and in walked Jeanette, as always, when she makes an appearance, all eyes turn to her and a hush comes over the crowd. Ryder got up from the table, walked to her, put his arm in hers and led her to the table.

Jeanette said, "Hello Boots, Bronco; and Ryder, it was sweet of you to show me to our table."

Ryder grinned and said, "Thank you ma'am, don't want you to think all Rangers are ill-mannered and don't know how to act in a ladies presence." Jeanette laughed and sat down at the table.

They drank wine, dined, drank more wine and discussed her show; scheduled to begin the next evening. During the evening, it was evident Jeanette really enjoyed her time with Ryder the most.

After dinner they walked her back to the hotel and promised they would attend her show the next evening. Jeanette gave all of them a kiss on the cheek and then said, "Good night."

As the Rangers walked back to their hotel Ryder asked, "Have y'all ever been in love?"

Boots said, "No, absolutely not."

Bronco echoed, "No, me neither. Neither one of us is dumb enough to fall in love."

Ryder said, "Then I must be dumb 'cause I think I am in love. I'm numb all over."

Boots laughed and said, "Fool, it's all that damn wine you drank."

Ryder with a slurred voice said, "How much longer is it till tomorrow night."

Boots answered, "Oh my God, maybe it's not the wine. He is in love!"

Nothing more was said as the Rangers went to their hotel rooms for the night; making sure Ryder, the slightly drunk, lovesick Ranger, got safely tucked into bed.

While the Rangers were having a great evening with the lovely Jeanette, Joe Don was over in the White Owl saloon drinking and playing poker. Paulette, a new girl, was serving drinks. She was a pretty brunette; always smiling and very well built.

Joe Don ordered whiskey; when she brought his drink to the table, he pulled her down on his lap and asked, "What's your name baby?"

She replied, "Paulette," squirmed and said, "please let go of me."

To which he replied, "How about you and me going upstairs? You'll like old Joe Don."

Paulette pulled herself free, and turned to walk away. This embarrassed Joe Don; he jumped up from the table, grabbed her by the arm, spun her around and kissed her. Paulette fought him off, pulled away and slapped his face so hard you could hear it clear across the room.

CHAPTER 17

That did it, Joe Don hit her flush in the face, breaking her nose and cutting her upper lip severely. Then he picked her up, cradled her in his arms and carried her upstairs to have his way with her. Everyone in the saloon was afraid of Joe Don and offered no help for Paulette

After finishing with Paulette, Sutton continued to drink and played poker all night. It was around four in the afternoon when he finally awoke. He was in his room fully clothed; he smelled of smoke, whiskey and had the body odor of a pig sty. He crawled out of bed, went to a wall basin, poured water over his head and in his face; then he ran his fingers thru his hair, put on his hat and went downstairs for more whiskey. After turning up several shots, he remembered the singer, Jeanette, would be appearing later that night. He looked at himself in the bar mirror, grinned, and said, "She's gonna like me, yes sir she's gonna like ole Joe Don."

Soon it was evening and time to attend Jeanette's performance. She had arranged for the Rangers to be seated in a reserved area near the stage.

The introduction was made, the stage curtains opened, the piano started playing and Jeanette appeared. She was dressed in a baby blue gown trimmed in pink and white. She was beautiful and so was her voice as she sang and danced to several songs on stage. She continued to sing as she came off stage and went from table to table tantalizing the crowd.

Standing at the back of the room was Sheriff Pryor. His deputies, James Lee and George, were positioned on each side of the room.

Jeanette walked to the Ranger's table, sat down on Ryder's lap, sang to him, and then returned to the stage. When she finished her last song, the crowd gave her a long and loud standing ovation while hollering for more.

A drunken Joe Don Sutton had staggering thru the door just in time to see part of her last song. When Jeanette disappeared back stage, he spied his buddies, Kurt and Jim, sitting at a table; so he joined them. Joe Don was drinking whiskey straight out of the bottle and, in his drunken stupor, was making a complete fool of himself.

After changing from her stage costume, Jeanette left her dressing room and joined the Rangers at their table. They were in the process of telling her how much they had enjoyed the show when Joe Don started walking towards them.

Ryder saw Sutton coming and blurted out, "Here comes trouble."

Boots motioned to Ryder and Bronco as he said, "Let's try not to ruin Jeanette's night, let me handle it."

Joe Don staggered up to the table, looked at Jeanette, removed his hat, bowed and said, in a drunken slur, "Ah like ya honey, lesh me-n-you party." Then he put his hand on Jeanette's shoulder and said, "C'mon baby, alla wimmon likes sho Don. Lesh go dance."

As he reached down to pull her out of her chair, she said, as friendly as possible, "No thank you, I'm with these gentlemen."

Before Boots could respond, Ryder barked, "Mister take your hand off the lady, she's with us and it's time for you to leave."

Joe Don straightened up, tried to focus his drunken eyes on the Rangers and said, "She don't know 'bout choo Rangers. Does she know one of y'all killed hish partner?"

Like a cat, Boots sprung to his feet, grabbed Joe Don's holstered pistol with his left hand and began pistol whipping him. Sutton fell to the floor; he was bleeding badly from gashes in his scalp and forehead. Boots continued to beat him after he went down; it took Sheriff Pryor, Ryder and Bronco to pull him off.

Sheriff Pryor's deputies picked Joe Don up off the floor. Blood was flowing heavily from his head and face; his shirt was torn and soaked with blood. He was semi-conscious as George and James Lee carted him off to jail for a lock up and treatment.

Boots was still furious and had to be restrained for several minutes. Finally he regained his composure, sat down at the table and said, "I'm alright. Ms. Jeanette, I apologize, please forgive me."

Jeanette, in an effort to calm him down, took Boots by the arm and said, "Come on, let's dance."

When they were on the dance floor, Bronco looked at Ryder and said, "Sutton must know about JoJo, Boots would have beaten him to death if we hadn't stopped him."

Several days passed, the Rangers had attended every performance by Jeanette and Joe Don was still in jail. Ryder and Jeanette had shared every possible moment; it was obvious, Ryder was falling in love.

After a week, Sheriff Pryor let Joe Don out of jail with a stern warning; any more trouble and he would get a thirty-day lockup. Boots had humiliated Joe Don like never before and his hatred for Boots, and the Rangers, increased every day he was in jail; he was certain to want revenge.

Jeanette's two weeks in Ft. Worth had passed quickly; it was time for her to move on to her next engagement, which was in Oklahoma.

The last night was special; Ryder spent the night in Jeanette's room. They were in love; but knew the romance would have to be at long range. A tearful goodbye was shared the next morning as Jeanette boarded the northbound stage for Oklahoma.

Joe Don had been planning revenge ever since his pistol-whipping by Boots. He had kept Kurt and Jim, his drunken buddies, at his side; he knew he would need an alibi when he killed Boots. His plan was to remain in the White Owl Saloon, playing cards with Jim, while Kurt ambushed Boots. That way he would have lots of people to witness his presence and support his alibi.

The ambush was to take place when the Rangers went to the restaurant for their evening meal. Kurt was to shoot thru the window and kill Boots while he was having dinner with Ryder and Bronco.

The time had come for Joe Don and his two buddies to execute their plan. The trio: Joe Don, Kurt and Jim were in the White Owl sitting by the window drinking whiskey. They could see the restaurant; so they watched and waited for the Rangers. Shortly after dark, Joe Don saw the Rangers enter the restaurant. He told Kurt to wait fifteen minutes; then get in place by the alley window and take his shot at Boots.

Joe Don told Kurt, "I'll be playing cards with Jim, and Melba will swear you were upstairs with her."

So no one would see him leave, Kurt left thru the back door of the saloon. He crossed the street and went down the alley to the rear window of the restaurant. The Rangers were already seated at the table enjoying their meal. He pulled his forty-four, centered the sight in the back of one of the rangers and squeezed off a round. The Ranger fell forward face down in his own dinner plate. Kurt ran back to the saloon, rushed thru the backdoor and up the stairs to a room where Melba was waiting for him.

In the restaurant all the customers had scurried for cover. Boots ran out into the street looking for the shooter. Ryder was tending to Bronco; it was of no use, he was dead; shot in the back.

Ryder cried out as he held Bronco, "Why? Why? Why did they shoot Bronco?"

Boots returned to the restaurant, looked at Ryder and said, "That bullet was meant for me; I think we both know who did it."

Bronco's body was at the funeral home and people from near and far came to pay their respects. At Laughlin's direction, his body was to be taken to Austin where he would be buried near Captain Beasley's grave.

Bronco was laid to rest with a full Ranger ceremony. A large number of people paid their respects; it was a very sad day.

Immediately after the burial, Boots and Ryder took the next train back to Ft Worth; their hearts were filled with vengeance in mind. Upon their return, Sheriff Pryor met them at the depot.

"Boys," he said, "I'm glad you're back; I need to fill you in on what I found out." As they headed towards the jail, Pryor continued, "Hell, I think we all know who is responsible, but they all have witnesses saying they were in the White Owl when the shot was fired. One thing is kinda suspicious though, Kurt's face is all swollen up; looks like somebody whipped up on 'im, but he claims his horse threw him into the stable gate.

Pryor paused for a moment, then asked, "Boots, what's your take on this?"

Boots answered quickly, "Frank, I think the wrong man was shot and, now that you've told me about Kurt, I believe he's the shooter. Joe Don probably beat the hell out of 'im because he was drunk and shot the wrong man. Hell, we both know the shot was meant for me."

"I agree, the bullet was meant for you," said Pryor, "now all we've got to do, is prove it." Boots shook his head in agreement as Pryor continued, "The pistol whipping you gave him, not only humiliated him, it damaged his reputation. A worthless piece of trash like Sutton can't let that go. I'm going to bring Joe Don in for questioning with you and Ryder present, but let me ask the questions."

Pryor sent his deputies, James Lee and George to bring Joe Don in for questioning. In a short while, they walked into the sheriff's office with Joe Don in custody; they had disarmed him.

When Joe Don entered the room and saw Boots, the look of hate and rage could be seen in his eyes. Apparently the ass-whipping Boots gave him hadn't done much to change his disposition as he looked at Boots, displaying a half smiling smirk, trying to intimidate. He continued his irritating manner and said, "Hello Rangers, Pryor got y'all in here for questioning too?" Then he looked directly at Boots and barked, "Boots, I hear you kill Rangers."

Pryor and Ryder had to tackle Boots; he was leaping toward Joe Don.

Sutton laughed and said, "See there sheriff, he's violent, better watch out for him."

Ryder and Pryor took Boots outside and tried to calm him down. Boots said, "You don't need to say anything. I let him get to me. I'm okay now. I'll restrain myself; let's go back inside."

Once inside, Pryor seated Joe Don at a table; the Rangers sat across the room while Pryor circled and asked, "Where were you when Bronco was killed?"

"In the saloon playing cards with Jim, ask him," said Joe Don. "The bartender will vouch for me, so will everyone in the bar. Hell, why would I want to shoot that Ranger, he ain't never done nothing to me. I suppose he's arrested lotsa men. Maybe it was one of them; sure as hell wasn't me."

Pryor told his deputies, "Give him his gun," then he looked at Joe Don and said, "Get out of my office, but don't leave town."

When Joe Don left, Boots said, "Bring in Jim, question him and turn him loose; then arrest Kurt; I'll take it from there."

As suggested, Jim was brought in, questioned and let go.

Boots said, "Now let's go arrest Kurt for murder."

Joe Don, Jim and Kurt were in the saloon drinking heavily. Through the saloon door came Pryor, Boots and Ryder; pistols drawn. When they surrounded the table where the three men were seated, Boots said, "Kurt, you're under arrest for the murder of Ranger Bronco Wilson."

Kurt, thinking he had a sure-fire alibi, looked surprised as Boots barked, "Boys, get his gun; you two fellas sit right where you are and keep your hands on top of the table."

Kurt, still thinking he was home free, said, "I ain't done nothin'; I was upstairs with Melba, she'll tell ya, I never left the room."

"Shut up," said Boots, "we know better. You'll hang for killing Bronco and I'll play music while I enjoy watching you perform the Death Dance."

Pryor and Boots grabbed Kurt by the arms and drug him off to jail as he protested and claimed his innocents. Ryder, still pointing his pistol at Joe Don and Jim, backed out of the saloon and into the street.

When Kurt was locked up, Boots pulled up a chair, turned it around, sat down with his arms draped over the back, and said, "Kurt, you're buddies don't want to hang so they ratted on you; both said you were drunk, feeling mean and shot Bronco." Kurt appeared a bit shocked, but he wasn't convinced Joe Don and Jim had turned on him, so he clammed up as Boots went on, "Witnesses verified Joe Don and Jim were in the saloon when the pistol shot was heard, but no one knew where you were."

Kurt was getting a little nervous, but was still defiant as he said, "Bull-crap, you're making this up Ranger, I was with Melba."

Boots shrugged his shoulders, got up from his chair and said, "They claim you did it because you hated Rangers; they have alibis, and you don't. Besides, Melba said you didn't come into her room until after the shot was fired."

"That ungrateful bitch," said Kurt, "she's lying."

Boots said, "Kurt, she may be an ungrateful bitch, but she's not lying; and, as for those buddies of yours, they'll just ride out and never be seen again. They'll be free and you'll be over there in Boot Hill."

Boots had finally hit a nerve as Kurt blurted out, "Those rotten bastards, they're not going to make me take all the blame."

Kurt, who had been sitting on the edge of his cot, began cursing and pacing back and forth in his cell. Suddenly he stopped, put his hands on the bars of the cell door and said, "Okay, I killed him but it wasn't my idea; Joe Don made me do it. Hell, you know him; if I had refused he woulda killed me."

He paused, looked at the lawmen, then went on, "Boots, it was supposed to be you; he hates you for the beating you gave him." Now Kurt was desperate; in an attempt to gain some sympathy, he barked, "Dammit, I was drunk, the lighting was bad and I shot the wrong person. Joe Don nearly beat me to death when he found out it wasn't you. Look at me; he really banged me up."

Realizing he was getting nowhere, Kurt lowered his head and, with resignation in his voice, said, "They ain't gonna put all the blame on me. Joe Don wants you dead; if I swing they'll swing with me."

Boots turned, looked at Pryor and Ryder, then said, "Boys, let's go over to the saloon. I want to arrest a couple of fellas for murder."

Boots was the first one in the saloon; Ryder and Pryor were behind him. He stopped and stared directly at Joe Don, who was sitting at a table with Jim. Without taking his cold stare off Joe Don, Boots said, "Boys don't let anyone out the door."

Boots maintained his stare as he slowly walked towards Joe Don. When he was six feet away, he firmly, but calmly said, "Joe Don, you and Jim are under arrest. With your left hand, put your pistol on the table."

Jim's hand was shaking badly as he removed his pistol and laid it on the table. When Joe Don didn't respond, Boots said, "Jim, walk on over to Sheriff Pryor, you're under arrest."

Boots eyes had never left Joe Don's when he said, "I gave you a chance to surrender and you didn't. Now stand up and make your play."

The smirk on Joe Don's face had turned into a look of concern as Boots continued, "You've tried to build a reputation of being bad; beating up women and drunks. Well, here's your chance to show how bad you are.

Joe Don didn't know exactly where this was going, but he knew he didn't like it.

Boots didn't let up as he urged, "Come on, maybe you want me to turn my back so you can back shoot me. Come on bad boy Joe Don, show me what you've got, face me and pull, you'll die quicker; if not, then maybe I'll just beat you to death."

Boots was getting hotter by the minute. Joe Don knew he had to make a move soon or face more humiliation.

Boots moved a few paces closer and bluntly stated, "Mister, you made the worst mistake possible; you had a Ranger killed. Not only that, he was my friend, now I'm gonna show you what bad really is."

Joe Don slowly stood up, reached for his shot glass and turned it up as if to take a drink; then he threw it at Boots and started his draw. He never cleared leather; Boots had drawn and was pointing the gun at Joe Don's chest. Sutton's eyes were the size of saucers as he began to tremble.

Boots said, "Put your right hand in the air and, with your left, unbuckle your gun belt and let it drop." When Joe Don did as he directed, Boots said, "Kick it over to the Rangers." Then he unbuckled his own gun belt and threw it to the Rangers behind him.

With his eyes still staring at Joe Don, Boots barked, "Now that everybody's seen how slow your gun hand is, here's your chance to show 'em just how bad you are with your fists."

When Joe Don didn't move, Boots continued to egg him on, "Come on bad boy, this is for Bronco."

As Boots walked forward, Sutton lowered his head and charged. Boots grabbed him by the hair of his head, brought his knee up and smashed him in the nose. Blood began pouring from his nose as Boots threw a straight right. If Joe Don's nose wasn't already broken, it was now.

The blows knocked Joe Don backwards up against the bar. He was trying to hold himself up when Boots grabbed him around the neck with his right arm and pushed his head back against the bar. While pinning him on the bar, Boots threw seven or eight hard left hooks that dug into Sutton's liver and probably broke some ribs. When Joe Don fell to the floor, Boots pounced on his arms with both knees holding him down. Sutton's mouth was split wide open; both eyes were damn near swollen shut and blood was spurting everywhere but Boots just wouldn't quit. He had his fingers in the corners of Joe Don's mouth pushing and tearing flesh, all the time saying, "You back shooting son of a bitch. You're dead."

Sheriff Pryor, realizing that Boots would probably beat Sutton to death if he wasn't stopped, began pulling him off. When he was finally able to get him off Joe Don, Boots got one last kick in; landing it on Joe Don's left ear, partially tearing it off.

Pryor held Boots back; he told Ryder and some men, who were in the bar, to take Sutton to jail and put him in the same cell as Kurt and Jim. They were also told to get Joe Don some medical attention. They wanted him in good shape for the hanging.

After a night's sleep and a good breakfast Boots and Ryder went to the sheriffs' office. Pryor was completing his arrest report including what charges the men were being held on. Frank looked at Boots when he came in and said, "Coffee's in the pot."

They both declined, then looked in the cell where the men were. Joe Don was lying on the cot; he had bandages around his ribs, stitches on his face and his ear had been sewed back on; he was nearly unrecognizable.

Pryor said, "Read this and if you agree, sign it." It read: Joe Don Sutton, charged with resisting arrest and murder; no bail. Boots looked at Frank, nodded his head, and signed the report.

Pryor gave Boots a sideways glance and said, "If I ever go bad, I hope you're not the one they send after me."

Boots grinned and replied, "Frank, if that ever happens, I hope I'm not the one either."

With no further business at hand, the Rangers shook Pryor's and his deputy's hand; then walked out, mounted up and rode toward Uvalde.

The first night they set up camp and talked a little about Bronco. Ryder said, "I'm sure gonna miss him, he was a good saddle pal."

Boots responded, "Yea, I agree, but remember what they always say, 'The quickest way to forget death is to ride away from it.'"

After all that had happened, Boots' thoughts drifted over to Abilene and Jane.

The Rangers had Bronco's horse, Puddin', unsaddled and were leading him back to Uvalde. He would be turned out on the Big Iron; never to be ridden again. After several days they reached the ranch; Laughlin met them at the gate, and while Ryder and Boots watched from their saddles, Puddin' was turned loose in the corral.

Boots was still watching Puddin as Ryder turned, looked at him, and said, "Well Boots, there'll be an empty saddle in the old corral tonight." Then he looked up towards the heavens and softly whispered, "Rest in peace Bronco."

After spending some time with Laughlin and filling him in on all the previous activities, they retired for the night. The Rangers would stay in the bunkhouse with the crew from the Big Iron.

The next day, Boots left the ranch and rode toward Uvalde; he was going to see his Pa' and Oral. It was a beautiful day, slightly overcast with the temperature in the seventies; a good day to be alive. As he rode he began talking to War Paint, saying aloud, "War Paint ole pal, I've lost two good friends, JoJo and Bronco. I'll never get over JoJo, I think about him every day and I pray to God each night. Don't know why things happen the way they do, they say its God's way and he has a plan for all of us."

Boots, talking to War Paint as though he were his saddle mate, continued, "Bronco had just found himself and was living a good life; he was a God fearing man and a good Ranger. Guess maybe God took him home to be by his side. Sometimes old pal, I feel like mounting up and just you and me start riding, maybe go to California. My life has changed a lot since I was on that battlefield back in Atlanta. I found Pa, met Jane and oh yea, found you."

The mock conversation he was having with War Paint was making him feel better, so he continued, "What do you think my friend, reckon we can get Laughlin to send us to Abilene so we can see Jane? Listen to me rambling on, God's been good to me." Then he looked up at the beautiful cloudless sky and said, "Thank you God for this day and thank you that I'm alive to enjoy what you've provided. – and tell JoJo and Bronco we'll join 'em some day; riding heaven's ranger winds together again."

When Boots reached the sheriffs' office Nathan and Oral came out on the porch to meet him. "Get down boy," said Oral, "get down and come on in, let's talk. You've got a lot to tell us from what we've been hearing."

Nathan was beaming with pride as he looked at Boots and said, "Son, I'm glad to see you, you're looking good, come on in."

Boots got down and walked inside; he noticed Oral was moving a little slower than when he had last seen him. He seemed to be bent over a little.

"You doing alright Sheriff Fox?" asked Boots.

"Yea," said Oral, "doing fine. Be eighty my next birthday." Then he asked Boots, "Think I'll make it?"

"I sure do," said Boots, "I wouldn't want to run you a foot race or draw against you."

Oral grinned and said, "Thank you son; you make an old man feel good."

Boots turned his attention to Nathan and asked, "Pa, how about you, how you doin'?"

"Aw," said Nathan, "Oral and Laughlin work me to death. That's why they look so good and I'm skinny and sickly."

Oral laughed and said, "Boots, he's got a lady friend; she's the one that keeps him busy, skinny and lookin' sickly, not me or Laughlin."

Boots laughed and replied, "Good for you Pa. I'm proud for you."

Oral wondered, "Boots, Audrey's been asking about Ryder, how's he doin'?"

"He's fine," replied Boots, then he changed the subject and said, "You got any of your good coffee left Oral."

Oral chuckled and said, "Thanks boy, I can see you've got a lot more sense than your Pa; you recognize good coffee."

Nathan grinned and held his coffee cup out towards Oral as he poured Boots a cup. Oral looked at Nathan and said, "I oughta make you go over to the restaurant and get yours; but since your boys here, I'll pour you a cup."

Nathan 'haw-hawed' and when his cup was full, said, "Thank you Sheriff Fox, it's an honor to drink your fine coffee."

They talked idly for a while; then later Boots left the sheriffs' office and returned to the Big Iron.

He was sitting on the bunkhouse porch with Ryder when the young man from the Uvalde telegraph office delivered a telegram. It was for

Ryder; he accepted the wire, thanked the boy, and then gave him a quarter and a cartridge from his gun belt.

The young man was thrilled, not by the quarter, but by the Rangers cartridge.

The telegram was from Jeanette; she had read about a Ranger being killed in Ft Worth and was worried about Ryder's safety. It said she would write him a long letter and mail it to the sheriffs' office in Uvalde. Ryder grinned; he felt a warm feeling coming over his body as he folded the telegram and remembered their last night together in Ft Worth.

Ryder, in his elated state of mind, left the telegram on the porch banister as he left Boots sitting alone. Boots spotted the forgotten telegram and, even though he knew he shouldn't, the temptation was too great; he read the telegram and went looking for Ryder.

He found him down at the corral, taking care of Bad Moon. Boots, on the outside of the corral, leaned his arms on the top rail and looked in where Ryder was brushing Bad Moons' mane and tail.

Boots tipped his hat back on his head and, with a sly grin, said to Ryder, "Well lover boy, it seems you've got a woman problem. Jeanette is sending you a letter to the sheriffs' office and Oral says that Audrey is asking about you. Looks to me like you've got yourself trapped in a box canyon, can't shoot your way out of this one.

Then Boots pulled his hat back down over his eyes and mumbled, "Gonna be worth watching how you handle it." Boots was laughing as he turned and walked away from the corral whistling "My Darling Clementine".

Ryder, with a serious face, shouted, "Damn it Boots; it ain't funny."

Boots continued to walk and whistle. Laughlin saw Boots leaving the corral and went to meet him. They reached each other about halfway between the house and the corral.

Laughlin stopped Boots and said, "Melissa has invited Nathan, Oral and Audrey out to the ranch tonight for dinner. She's also requested you and Ryder join us. Be sure you tell Ryder."

Boots said, "Yes sir Captain, I sure will." Boots turned and walked back toward the corral." This was getting better all the time.

CHAPTER 18

Ryder had seen Boots talking with Laughlin and said, with anxious hope in his eyes, "Captain sending us somewhere, are we leaving?"

Boots with a sly, cocky grin said, "Nope. We're invited for dinner at the big house and guess who some of the other guests will be?"

Ryder pulled off his hat, wiped his brow with his shirtsleeve and said, "Tell 'em I'm sick. I'm real bad sick, I can't be there."

Boots broke out laughing and said, "You're not sick now, but you will be when you tell Audrey about Jeanette."

That evening when they gathered in the dinning room, Melissa seated Audrey next to Ryder. A lovely dinner had been prepared and everyone was having a great time, except for Ryder of course.

A couple of times, when Audrey placed her hand on Ryder's, he pulled away. As the evening passed on, it became evident to Audrey, that something was wrong.

After dinner, everyone moved to the front porch to enjoy the cool evening breeze. Ryder took Audrey by the hand and said, "Let's walk down to the corral and check on Bad Moon."

When they were out of hearing distance, Audrey stopped, put her arm on Ryder's shoulder and turned him toward her. She looked him in the eyes and said, "Ryder, what's wrong, you're different. Have things changed?"

Ryder, hat in hand, looked at the ground, shuffled his feet and said, "Audrey, I've found someone else and I think I'm in love."

Audrey immediately broke into tears, turned and ran towards the ranch house.

When Melissa heard her crying, she ran out to meet her. "What's wrong, are you alright," she asked? "Did Ryder hurt you?"

"No, I'm not alright," said Audrey, "and yes he did hurt me. He's in love with someone else."

Ryder was afraid to return to the porch; he walked to the corral and into Bad Moon's stall. He didn't know what to expect; Oral might be upset and draw down on him, so he hid out in the stall.

A few minutes later, in walked Boots. He had a swagger to his walk and was grinning. Ryder, who wasn't grinning, asked, "What's happening? What are they saying?"

Boots said, "Captain and Oral are plenty hot; they're going to have wanted posters made with your picture on 'em: Five-thousand dollar reward. Wanted: Dead or Alive, 'The Heartbreak Kid'."

Finally Boots got serious, looked at Ryder and said, "Melissa's got Audrey calmed down, she's hurt and mad but she'll soon get over your mean heartless butt," and again Boots strutted out of the stall whistling a tune; only this time it was 'Home on the Range'."

Laughlin, realizing that Boots and Ryder had spent a lot of time in the saddle the past few months, advised them to hang around the ranch and take it easy until the results were in from Joe Don's trial in Ft Worth. After about two weeks Laughlin received a telegram, it read: Joe Don and Kurt Strange to hang. Jim – twenty years. Hanging will take place in ten days on gallows across from the courthouse.

Laughlin ordered Nathan, Boots and Ryder to accompany him to witness the hanging; they would ride to San Antonio; then take the train to Ft. Worth.

When Jeanette read about the upcoming hanging, she sent a wire to Oral requesting that he inform Ryder that she would be in attendance. When Oral received the telegram he smiled; regarding Jeanette, he harbored no ill feelings towards Ryder.

After a two day ride from Uvalde, the Rangers boarded the train in San Antonio. Upon their arrival in Ft. Worth, they checked in at the Hereford Hotel; then went to see Sheriff Pryor. The sheriffs' office sat discreetly on a tall bluff across from the courthouse. About thirty yards outside the jail, under a very old and huge live oak, a two man gallows was being erected.

When the Rangers entered the jail, as usual, they greeted each other with the customary handshake and tipping of their hat.

As Sheriff Pryor was introduced to Laughlin, whom he had never met, he was impressed and said, "Sir, I've heard a lot about you and I'm honored to finally meet you here today."

Laughlin smiled and said, "Thank you Sheriff, It's my pleasure; now; if you don't mind, I'd like to see your prisoners."

Pryor unlocked the door and took them into the room where there were six individual cells. The three prisoners were each in a cell of their own; isolated for security purposes.

Joe Don was sitting on his bunk; leaning against the wall. When he saw the Rangers he smirked and said, "Rangers, Yea, I thought I smelled something."

Laughlin stepped up to the cell door, looked at Joe Don, squared his jaw and said, in a low but distinct voice, "Justice will soon be served." Then Laughlin's eyes began to dance with the look of a wild animal about to spring, as he added, "Mister, when you swing from the gallows, pray nothing goes wrong; you really don't want me coming after you." Laughlin continued to stare into Joe Don's eyes, who finally couldn't take it any longer and lowered his head.

They left the room; as Laughlin heard the door being locked behind them, he stopped, looked at Pryor and said, "See you at the hanging." Then he pointed toward the cell block and barked, "Be sure those low-life's are there;" then they walked out of the office.

The next morning, Joe Don was awakened by the sound of hammers and men sawing. The gallows would be finished by early evening; he and Kurt would hang the next day at noon.

Outside, the crowd was already gathering. People were camping on the courthouse lawn with wagons drawn as close to the gallows as possible. Some had been there for a week. Folks were climbing trees in an effort to peer through the windows at the condemned men.

As Joe Don stared out, he looked back on his life; all he had ever known was crime and violence. First fighting with his Pa'; then, finally, beating him to death. He recalled his card playing, whiskey drinking, whoring around, and pistol whippings. He remembered he had never read a bible or been inside a church. His only desire was to be noticed and that had cost him his life. He began to wonder what dying would be like; then he grinned and thought 'tomorrow I'll know'.

The next morning, when he heard the bags of sand stopping at the end of the rope to test the gallows, he said to him self, "The sound of death is drawing near."

Joe Don and Kurt received their last meal, but neither of them ate a bite. Since being in jail, there had been a distinct separation between Joe Don and Kurt, they weren't even speaking.

At eleven-thirty, a preacher entered the cell room, sat down outside Kurt's cell and began to pray for him. Kurt reacted violently and said, "Get away from me, I don't want you here;" then he shouted, "Sheriff, get this man out of my sight."

Without being told by Sheriff Pryor, the preacher moved to Joe Don's cell, sat down and asked, "Then brother, may I pray for you?"

Joe Don came to the bars, sat down on a chair, looked the preacher straight in the eyes and said, "I don't know Jesus, tell me about him and this God of yours."

The preacher looked at Joe Don and began, "God is the beginning and the end. He sent his only son, Jesus, to die for us and absorb our sins. There is only one way to Heaven, and that is thru Jesus. If you believe in God, and accept Jesus as your savior, through him, you will be granted eternal life."

Joe Don questioned, "How is that possible? I have sinned, stolen, and murdered. He couldn't possibly forgive me."

The preacher responded, "My Son, when Jesus was being crucified and dying on the cross, he forgave a sinner who also was being crucified along side him. If, in your heart, you believe in God and accept Jesus as your Savior, you will go to heaven. That's the only way to salvation."

Joe Don began to sob quietly then said, "Preacher, even if I do, it's too late for me; I only wish I had known about God earlier in my life."

The Preacher softly said, "Joe Don, time doesn't matter. Only you, and God alone, know what is in your heart; truly believe and this very day, you will enter the gates of Heaven and walk with him for eternity."

Joe Don, who was now sobbing aloud, said, "Preacher, will you walk and stand with me today at the gallows?"

The preacher said, "Gladly, and God will walk with you also."

The crowd had seen the preacher enter the jail and knew the time was near. People were everywhere, shoulder to shoulder, crowding the gallows; in trees and on rooftops. Young kids were sitting on the shoulders of their fathers or brothers. The streets were lined with people waiting to pass by and view the dead while they were still dangling from the hangman's noose.

Sheriff Pryor and his deputies came to get Kurt and Joe Don; their time had come. With their hands bound behind their backs, Kurt struggled and resisted; cursing and kicking at the deputies.

Joe Don stood quietly and said to Sheriff Pryor, "I have asked the preacher to walk with me; is that okay?" Pryor nodded his head yes and they started the death march. As they climbed the steps of the gallows, up to the deck, Kurt was still resisting; swearing and cursing lawmen and Rangers alike.

Joe Don, after taking his position, looked out at the crowd waiting to see him die. The Rangers were directly in front of the gallows looking up at the men when Ryder, surprised, whispered to Boots, "Would you look at Joe Don, his expression has changed. I don't see hate as before." Boots agreed with Ryder as a noose was placed over Kurt's head and pulled into place.

When the Sheriff asked Kurt if he had any last words, he said defiantly, "Yea, all of ya' can go to hell, death to all y'all lawmen. I'm just sorry I didn't kill more of y'all, especially Rangers." The hood was slipped over his head and he shut up.

Sheriff Pryor then asked Joe Don if he had anything to say. Joe Don looked at the Rangers and said, "I'm sorry for what I done to that Ranger and I pray for forgiveness of my sins. The preacher standing beside me has shown me the way. I have accepted Jesus Christ as my Savior and I'm ready to bear the burden of my sins."

When Joe Don finished saying his piece, Sheriff Pryor asked, "Do you want the hood?"

He said, "No Sheriff, I want people to see that I am happy and at peace with the Lord." Then he turned to the preacher who was standing at his side, looked into his eyes, and said, "Thank you preacher man; I'm ready to go now."

The hangman pulled the rope, the floor opened and the men dropped. The hangman's rope stopped their fall, breaking their necks. Their bodies twitched, their legs kicked and their body functions were involuntarily relieved; they were dead.

Ryder thought to himself and remembered what he had heard a man once say about a hanging; he said it was a ghastly sight. Ryder, agreed, it was that; a ghastly sight.

Laughlin turned to the Rangers and said, "I'm gonna go find that preacher, ya'll wait here." When he walked behind the gallows and didn't find the preacher, he asked around; but no one knew him or where he went.

Laughlin returned to the Rangers and said, "Find that preacher and bring him to Sheriff Pryor's office; I've got to meet him."

The Rangers spread out throughout the crowd, looking and asking about him. They had no luck, no one knew him or had ever seen him before so they returned to the jail and went inside where Laughlin was waiting.

Boots looked at Laughlin, with disbelief in his eyes, and said, "Laughlin, the preacher is not to be found, it's as if he vanished into thin air."

There was complete silence for a full minute then as if on cue, all the Rangers looked up toward the heavens, wondering if they had witnessed some kind of Devine intervention.

Remembering that Jeanette had wired Oral that she would be in Fr. Worth for the hanging, Ryder went to the telegraph office to see if there was word from her, There was indeed a telegram from Jeanette; it read, 'Train broke down, waiting on repairs, be there in two or three days.'

Ryder gave Boots the news; when Boots told Laughlin, he smiled and said, "Me and Nathan will be going back to Uvalde." Then with a wink, he added, "You and Ryder hang around here till I send for you."

When Boots told Ryder the good news, he was grateful and so excited, he said, "Come on, let's go over to the general store. I need some new duds."

Boots, acting serious, asked, "You ain't getting married; or are you? If you ain't, then why you getting all duded up?"

"Shut up," said Ryder, "you're just jealous, let's go to the store."

Jeanette wasn't due to arrive by train until noon the next day; however, Ryder was up at daybreak. He wasn't about to miss her arrival.

It was a beautiful day; clear skies with a slight breeze and temperatures in the seventies; a perfect day to spend with a perfect girl. Ryder scrubbed and shined his boots; he had on new black britches, a red double breasted shirt and a black Stetson. After wiping it with a wet rag and reshaping it for hours, he had that Stetson looking new. He topped the outfit off with a black bandana, neatly tied around his neck. He was clean shaven, and had trimmed his shoulder length hair before stopping off at the barber shop for a dusting with talcum powder.

Boots said, "I'd better go with you to meet the train; in your state of mind, I doubt if you can find the depot." Boots refused to let up his ragging on Ryder.

Ryder, not to be outdone by Boots, said, "No you won't; as trashy as you look, she won't get off the train. You're a disgrace to the Rangers: dirty and all smelly, I'm gonna deny knowing you."

Boots laughed, it was fun seeing Ryder so excited. They left the hotel to meet the train and Ryder tried to stay ahead of Boots, partially for fun and partially in anticipation of seeing Jeanette.

The train arrived on time; they could hear the blowing of the whistle a half-mile from the depot. The engineer eased it down and stopped the passenger car at the center of the platform.

As Ryder ran towards the passenger door, it opened and Jeanette stepped out. She was beautiful with her pale blue dress, pink blouse and plumed hat.

Ryder said, "Hi Jeanette, my God you're beautiful."

Jeanette, sounding surprised, remarked, "My goodness Ryder, you look really nice. I've missed you." Then she looked past him and said, "Hi Boots; how are you?"

Ryder, not wanting to let Boots get a word in, said, "That's not Boots, that's some tramp that just got out of a boxcar."

Jeanette laughed and said, "Boots, as usual you look very handsome." Then she turned, looked back at the door and said, "I want y'all to meet my little sister. This is Linda."

Boots and Ryder shifted their eyes from Jeanette to Linda. Boots' mouth dropped open. Linda was an absolute knockout, probably around twenty-three with long blond hair that extended to her waist. She had beautiful hazel eyes that sparkled in the sunlight. She wore a blue corduroy skirt with a white lace blouse and bolero vest made of matching blue corduroy.

As Boots helped Linda off the platform, Jeanette said, "Linda will be traveling along with me; she's a singer and will be part of my show."

Boots and Ryder were speechless, especially Boots as Jeanette continued, "We'll be staying at the Hereford Hotel. Now, gentlemen, if you'll help us to our rooms, we can meet at Cattleman's for dinner, say seven o'clock."

Boots and Ryder couldn't have been happier as they quickly accepted.

After getting the girls to their hotel room, they were riding down Main Street when Ryder said, "Jeanette gets prettier every time I see her and how about that sister of hers, she's also beautiful, wouldn't you agree Boots?"

"Yea, I guess she's alright," said Boots, trying not to show his excitement.

They continued their ride and when they got to the general store, Boots stopped War Paint at the hitching post, and dismounted. Ryder asked, with a knowing grin on his face, "What are we stopping here for?"

Boots said, "Shut-up. Do you think they have a black shirt like that red one you bought?"

Ryder broke out in laughter and said, "Yea, and some britches and the barber shops right over there across the street."

At seven o'clock, they met at Cattleman's for dinner. Jeanette and Ryder were wrapped up in each other while Boots and Linda had a fun time.

Boots, who had strong feelings for Jane, realized it was just his first meeting with Linda, but she did something special to him; She made him feel comfortable and warm all over. As the evening ended, the girls were back in the hotel when Boots found him self already missing her and hoping for a next time.

Linda and Jeanette would be performing down town at the Majestic Theatre for at least two weeks. Boots and Ryder were hoping there wouldn't be any reason for them to leave while the girls were in town.

Making the most of the situation, Boots and Ryder were with the girls everyday during the next two weeks. Linda was an educated young lady with a wonderful sense of humor; laughing all the time and enjoying the teasing she constantly gave Boots. He wondered if he was out classed, being a Georgia farm boy and all.

He apparently had nothing to worry about since she believed everything he told her. Sometimes he made up Ranger stories and, when questioned, would swear he was telling the truth. It got to the point where she would ask Ryder to verify Boots' tall tales; of course, he did. They had lots of fun together, all four of them.

The two weeks passed quickly; the girls' next stop was San Antonio. Boots and Ryder helped them board the train, exchanged good-byes and watched the train pull away with Jeanette and Linda hanging out the window, waving. It was evident that Ryder and Jeanette's relationship was growing stronger and, apparently, one was developing between Boots and Linda.

Back in Uvalde, Laughlin took the wagon into town to pick up ranch supplies at the General Store. Oral and Nathan didn't see Laughlin or they would have gone over to the store to help load the wagon.

When Laughlin came out of the store with his arms filled with flour and other items, he heard a loud young voice say, "Hey Ranger, I need to talk to you."

Laughlin, standing at the rear of the wagon, looked out to the middle of the street. He saw a young cowboy standing there staring at him so he stepped out from behind the wagon, squared up on the young man, and sized him up.

He wasn't much more than a boy, maybe eighteen. He was dressed in tight pants, tucked in the tops of his boots, and a blue long sleeve shirt with a black vest. He was slender built and clean-shaven with short hair and a black Stetson hat pulled snuggly down on his head. His eyes were brown and reflected an odd combination of fear and hate.

They were standing in the street, about twenty yards apart, when the young man said, "My name is Johnny Bellows. Right here, in this very street, you and two of your Ranger friends gunned my Pa' down. Now he didn't have a chance, but I'm gonna kill ya."

Laughlin looked the young man in the eyes and said, "I did kill your Pa', it was just me and him; he called me out. You're right about one thing, he didn't have a chance. I'm much faster than he was, but he did have a choice; he could have walked away and still be alive."

Laughlin's eyes took on their steel gray death stare as he said, "You also don't have a chance, but you do have the same choice he had." Laughlin paused to give the kid time to think, then snorted; "It's your play."

When nothing happened, Laughlin, with his eyes still glaring at the young man, ordered, "With your left hand, reach over, get your pistol and drop it on the ground."

Johnny was looking into Laughlin's eyes hopelessly trying to stare him down. After a long pause Johnny started trembling, reached over with his left hand, pulled his pistol from the holster, dropped it on the ground and started whimpering. Laughlin walked to him, put his arm on his shoulder and said, "You did the right thing son; you're under arrest but you're still alive."

Oral and Nathan had stepped outside the jail when they heard the confrontation. Laughlin motioned them over and said, "Take Johnny to jail and keep him there for three days; get some grub in his belly then escort him to the county line." Then he looked at the kid and ordered, "Son, when they let you out, go home and find another line of work; you're not cut out to be a gun-fighter."

Laughlin returned to his wagon, turned it around and started toward the ranch. About two miles outside of town, he stopped under a tree next to a running creek. This was the spot he and Melissa had used for a picnic several times when they were courting; it was a special place. Sitting in the shade of the giant Live Oak, he thought about how blessed he was by having Melissa, Sam and the ranch as he said aloud, "Thank you God for all your blessings and for keeping me safe today." Laughlin knew his life as a Ranger had made him many friends and enemies alike.

The young gunman Johnny Bellows was a prime example. He wanted to kill Laughlin for shooting his Pa' eight years ago. Laughlin, realizing he could have been ambushed at long range and gunned down by a Winchester, looked up and once again said out loud, "Thank you Lord."

Three days passed and, as Laughlin had directed, Oral and Nathan brought the boy his horse before releasing him from jail. Oral had Johnny's gun belt and pistol in his hand when the three of them left the jail and mounted their horses.

As they rode toward the county line, Oral looked at Johnny and said, "Son, you're a lucky man. You almost pulled leather with the fastest gun in the west. Your Pa' got what he deserved; he was trying to build a reputation as a gunfighter; he was no match for Laughlin and neither are you."

When they stopped at the county line, Oral handed the boy his gun and holster. As Johnny reached for it, Oral took hold of his arm, looked directly into his eyes and said, "Son, take my advice, when I give this gun back to you, put it in your saddlebags; don't wear it and put aside any thoughts of revenge, you'll live longer."

As Oral and Nathan turned their horses and started a slow walk back to Uvalde, they noticed Johnny putting his rigging into his saddlebags; it was a good day to be alive.

Back in San Antonio, it was around midday. Jeanette and Linda were sitting in a restaurant, relaxing and having lunch, when Jeanette said, "Little sister, tell me about Boots."

Linda smiled and said, "I've only known him a short time but I wish he was here, I already miss him." Then she got an inquisitive look on her face and asked, "Do you think he has someone else?"

Jeanette laughed and said, "As good looking as those two boys are, and being Texas Rangers living the dangerous life they're exposed to, yea, they've got girls, probably lots of girls."

Linda looked disappointed as she asked Jeanette, "What are your thoughts about Ryder?"

Jeanette gathered her thoughts and replied, "You know; when I travel from town to town and perform, I meet lots of men. Now Ryder is the first real man I've met. He's exciting and fun to be with; even like a little boy at times but he can change instantly into the most rugged man I've ever known."

Jeanette finished her after dinner tea, patted her voluptuous lips with a white linen napkin, and said, "I've never been in love, so I don't know how it feels; but I do know this, I've never, ever, felt this way before about any man."

Linda, responding in kind, said, "I know what you mean; I think about Boots every minute of the day. I pray he's safe; God, I wish I could hold him now."

Jeanette laughed and said, "Girl, we're not very smart. We could have just about any wealthy man we desire, and we're falling for two Rangers making a dollar-fifty a day."

Linda, almost choking on her last sip of tea, laughed and said, "Yea big sister, you're right, but they are men, real men." Then she added, "Let's write 'em a letter and mail it to the sheriffs' office in Ft Worth, maybe they're still there."

They were in fact still in Ft Worth, sitting on the front porch of the Tarrant County jailhouse, passing time when Ryder said, "Boots, I can see you really like Linda, but how's this gonna affect you and Jane?"

Boots reached in his pocket, pulled out his knife and started sharpening it on a wet stone he had in his hand. He paused, thought for a moment and said, "Damned if I know. Jane's ready to get married, start a family and I'm not."

He drug the knife over the wet stone, shook his head and continued, "I know Jane loves me and will wait for me to either get shot up or settle down." This was difficult as he paused once again, pointed his knife at Ryder and said, "I really don't know how Linda feels; hell, she could have any man she wants. Why would she want me with all those rich dudes chasing her? He went back to sharpening his knife as he went on "I will say this though, she really makes me feel good."

"Even more so than Jane?" asked a wondering Ryder.

Boots paused and said, "Yea, yea, reckon so, hell of a mess I've got my self into; ain't it?" Then he laughed and blurted out, "Let's go over to Sam's place; you can buy this troubled soul a beer, just don't let me cry in it."

While the Rangers were having their personal problems, Texas and the west was having its own. More track was being laid by the railroads, as miles of barbed wire were being strung. Ranchers would fence off their property to keep other ranchers from grazing their land. This allowed them to fatten their own cattle for shipping by rail. Without the long cattle drives, herds suffered little or no weight loss, creating more profit per cow.

Two things were said about the West; it was changed by barbed wire, but won with a Winchester.

Laughlin had continued to fence his property but, due to his position in the Rangers, he encountered little opposition. Not so true with other ranchers. Primarily because of barbed wire, there were violent range wars all over the state. In fact, it got so bad; a law was passed forbidding a man to carry wire cutters in his pocket.

None the less, fences were being cut, torn down and range wars were wide spread. New Mexico Territory, Arizona, Texas, Oklahoma were the major hot spots, but other areas like Kansas and Wyoming were also involved. Progress was good, but with progress comes problems.

As the railroads came across the country, water towers had to be set up every thirty miles for the steam powered locomotives to take on water. The railroad companies had to hire people to dig wells, build water towers and man the sites. As a result, small towns were started by families at these stops creating more problems with the ranchers.

After the civil war one ranch in particular, the King Ranch in Texas, had 146,000 acres and was growing daily. Lots of things affected the ranches but none more than drought and the Texas fever tick.

The battle for land was evident, some ranchers were bought out by the railroad; others by larger ranches, such as King's, or burned out if they refused to sell. Laughlin had kept the Rangers at long range unless called for by ranchers requesting help. Most of the feuds settled themselves or were successfully handled by the local sheriff or marshals.

Cattle sales continued to bring large sums of money to Ft Worth. With money came growth and trouble. Sheriff Pryor now had six deputies and, at times, that wasn't enough. North Main was now about two miles long and led from downtown Ft Worth to the stockyards on Exchange Avenue.

Of course, South of Ft Worth, Hells Half Acre was still thriving with its saloons, gambling and brothels. The stockyards had all of that along with murder, rape, robbery and known outlaws. In addition, drovers would celebrate bringing in a herd; get drunk and fight with anyone, sometimes each other. The Sheriff kept his jail, better known as Pryor's Hotel, full of pistol whipped drunks and ruffians.

Most of them were wranglers who would get drunk, ride their horses inside the saloons, grab the women and ride off with them. Some of the cowboys had their favorite lady and would kill each other for her companionship.

Rumors had it that Butch Cassidy and the Sundance Kid had recently spent some time in Hells Half Acre; however, since there hadn't been any disturbances, Sheriff Pryor let it lay. He figured, let 'em have a good time and they'll move on. Besides, since the hanging of Joe Don, no one had risen to take his place as the king of the stockyards. Pryor had been around a long time and knew to avoid confrontations if possible; to do otherwise meant bloodshed; Pryor was smart.

One night Ryder and Boots were making their rounds in the stockyards. When they entered the Red Dog saloon, there was a fight taking place; a fistfight and a good one. Boots and Ryder watched the action, waiting on the fight to end; making sure there was no gunplay. Finally one of the cowboys knocked the other to the floor and was kicking and stomping the downed cowboy. That's when Boots, with scattergun in hand, walked over, grabbed the cowboy by the back of his shirt, and barked, "Get off him, fights over."

The man spun around, saw Boots and said, "I've done whupped him, may as well whup you."

Boots cocked both hammers on the scattergun, pointed it at the cowboys chest and snorted, "As I said, fights over, or else we'll see how many holes this double ought buckshot will put in that two dollar shirt you're wearing."

The cowboy, realizing he was looking at a Ranger, backed off.

Boots, with his scattergun still pointed at the standing man's chest, said, "A couple of you fellas carry this man over to the Doc's office." Then, as he poked the other cowboy in the chest with the double barrel, growled, "You, mister tough guy, get on your horse and ride. If I as much as see you in Ft Worth again, I'll put you in jail and throw away the key; now move."

When Boots and Ryder walked out of the saloon to continue their rounds, Ryder looked at Boots and said, with a grin, "Well done Ranger Boots, well done."

Boots looked at Ryder and joked, "You reckon we could learn to sing and dance; then we could join the troupe with Jeanette and Linda? This Ranger life is boring." They both laughed heartily and continued their walk down Exchange Avenue.

Back in Uvalde, Laughlin was sitting on the front porch watching the day come to an end. The sunset was beautiful; God had out done himself with all the colors of the rainbow. The sun was setting beneath the high thin clouds; creating a beautiful picture beyond anything man could capture on canvas.

Suddenly, his attention was diverted from the sunset by a distant lone rider; riding full out towards the corral. Laughlin smiled, he knew it was Sam on his pony, Cyclone.

Sam was now twelve years old and his pony was out of Samson and Princess. He was a true dapple gray like his Pa', Sam; and, like his Pa', he was big, powerful and fast. That's why Sam had named him Cyclone. As Sam reached the corral, Laughlin could see Trailer, his dog, still trying to catch up. Wherever Sam and Cyclone went, Trailer followed.

Laughlin smiled and said to himself, 'Lord, I don't know which ones the prettiest picture, your sunset or my boy riding across the pasture; however, thank you for both of 'em."

Laughlin waited on the porch; he knew Sam would take care of Cyclone first; rub him down and brush him, then give him oats and hay. After about twenty minutes, Sam and Trailer came out of the corral and started walking towards the ranch house. Trailer spotted Laughlin sitting on the porch and broke into a run; he was excited to see Laughlin as he ran up on the porch, sat down beside him and started licking his forearm with affection. Laughlin grinned and said, "Trailer, someday you'll learn that you can't keep up with Cyclone. Reckon that's why Sam named you Trailer, you're always behind the two of 'em."

As Sam reached the porch he said, "Hi Pa," and sat down beside Laughlin.

Laughlin remarked, "Sam, that horse of yours sure can run and you're a pretty darn good rider."

"Yes sir," said Sam, "I like to ride and Cyclone can really run fast. That's why I call him Cyclone." Sam stood up, looked at Laughlin seriously, and said, "Pa', do you know what the boys in the bunkhouse call me?"

Laughlin said, "No, but I hope it's good." Sam got a big grin on his face and said, "It is. They call me Dusty; wanna know why?"

CHAPTER 19

Laughlin said, "Sure do son; why do they call you Dusty?"

"Well Pa'," said Sam, "it's because when me and Cyclone ride, we leave a trail of dust behind. Pa', I like that name, can I use it for my nickname?"

Laughlin said, "It's alright with me; but I imagine to your mother, it'll always be Sam."

"Great," said Sam, "from now on my name is Dusty. What do you think about that Trailer?" Trailer reared up on Dusty and licked his face.

Standing several feet away, behind the front door screen, Melissa had been eavesdropping. She smiled and said, "Thank you lord," with tears of happiness running down her cheeks.

The next morning at the breakfast table Laughlin and Melissa had finished breakfast and were sipping on a second cup of coffee. Sam had been finished for some time, but had not asked to be excused.

Laughlin, who was enjoying the moment, knew Sam was trying to get up enough nerve to talk with his mother about his nickname.

Finally Sam said, "Mom, you know Ranger Jerry Jack?"

Melissa said, "Yes I do. Why do you ask?"

"Well," said Sam, "his nickname is Preacher, right?"

"Yes, that's right," said Melissa.

Laughlin, acting as though he didn't know what was coming, was trying not to show any emotion.

"Mom, I have a nickname," said Sam. When Melissa didn't say anything, Sam continued, "The wranglers in the bunkhouse call me Dusty, and I like it."

"Why on earth would they call you Dusty, asked Melissa? I make you take a bath and stay clean, don't I?"

"Oh mom, it's 'cause everywhere me and Cyclone go we leave a trail of dust."

"Oh, I see," said Melissa, "what does your father say about you wanting to change your name?"

"He said it's alright, right Pa'," as he pleadingly looked at Laughlin, who put his hands up as if to say…..'leave me out if this.'

Melissa smiled and said, "Alright Sam, we'll call you Dusty. Your Pa' named you after his horse and I wasn't thrilled about that; so, Dusty it is." Now young man," said Melissa, "go clean up Dusty's room and get your chores done."

"Thanks mom, thanks dad," said a happy Dusty, "Now, I can't wait to tell the boys in the bunkhouse that I have a nickname, Dusty McFarland. I like it, maybe one day it will be Ranger Dusty McFarland."

After breakfast Laughlin went to the corral and entered the stalls to take care of Sam as usual; but, this morning as he opened the door to Sam's stall, he said, "Good Morning Sam, today we're gonna take a ride into town."

Immediately, Sam's ears stood up and he nickered, as if he understood what Laughlin said.

When Dusty saw Laughlin saddling Sam, he walked to the corral and said, "Pa', you taking Sam for a ride?"

"Yep," said Laughlin, "get a saddle on Cyclone; we're goin' to town."

They saddled both horses, mounted up and started toward Uvalde. Dusty was only twelve but there was no doubt he was Laughlin's boy. He was slender with broad shoulders and had his Pa's dark hair as well as his penetrating blue eyes. Laughlin was six foot tall and, the way Dusty was growing, it appeared he would be taller than his Pa'. Dusty had a happy personality and, had it not been for the bunkhouse boys calling him Dusty, he would have probably been called Happy.

The day was beautiful and the temperature was mild, a great day to be shared by father and son. As they rode, Dusty began to ask Laughlin questions.

He asked, "Pa', are you really the fastest and most feared gun in the west, like everyone says?"

Laughlin responded, "Son, my job requires me to know how to use a gun and my life depends on how fast I am."

"I know," said Dusty, "but just how fast are you pa?"

"Son," he said, "I don't know how you would measure that; let's just say I'm fast enough to still be alive."

Dusty chewed on that answer for a moment and then said, "Okay Pa'; that makes sense." They rode on slowly and suddenly Dusty asked, "Pa', when are you gonna get me a pistol and teach me how to shoot?"

Laughlin looked at Dusty rather firmly and said, "Dusty, don't ask me about that again. When you're ready I'll come to you." Then Laughlin's stern look disappeared and changed into a smile as he said, "You are ready for a rifle though, that's why we're going to town."

"A rifle," shouted Dusty, "oh boy, let's ride. I can't wait,"

"Hold on, hold on, I promised old Sam a nice easy walk to town and back, no running."

As usual when they turned down Main Street toward Uncle Besters Gun Shop, Laughlin sat erect in the saddle and projected an image of authority.

Dusty watched his father and tried to mimic everything Laughlin did. Like father, like son.

As they rode by the sheriffs' office, Oral, who was sitting in a chair on the front porch, said, "Hello Laughlin, who's that new deputy riding with you."

Dusty beamed and said to Oral, "I'm Deputy Dusty McFarland."

Oral grinned and said, "You shore do favor a young feller named Sam I used to know."

"Nope, ain't him. I'm Dusty," said Sam.

"Well Dusty," said Oral, "when you get through helping your Pa', come on over and I'll see if Dusty is any better at dominoes than Sam was."

Dusty assured Oral he would as he and Laughlin went to Uncle Bester's gun shop. "Hello Laughlin, how you doin'", greeted Bester as they entered his shop. "How's little Laughlin?" he continued, looking at Dusty. "What can I do for you, need a new six gun?"

"Naw," said Laughlin, "need a rifle for Dusty; he's ready to have one of his own."

Bester, as he reached over to his rack and pulled out a 25-20 Winchester, said, "I've got exactly what he needs, this is just right for 'im."

Dusty's eyes lit up; it was love at first sight.

Laughlin paid Bester; as Uncle B. handed Dusty several boxes of ammunition, he said, "Ammunitions on me. Son, you listen to your Pa', he's the best."

Dusty said, "Thank you sir, and I will listen to my Pa'. I'm proud of him."

Without any further ado, Laughlin and Dusty rode out of town toward the ranch. After Dusty had placed his 25-20 rifle in one of his dad's old scabbards that was hanging from his saddle, he said, "How 'bout it Cyclone, I have a rifle; now me, you and Trailer can go hunting."

When Laughlin overheard Dusty, he grimaced and said, "Not so fast sonny boy, you've got a lot to learn about safety before I turn you loose with a rifle." Then, in order to ease any harshness in his comment, he added, with a smile, "Now don't be asking me when you can hunt; I'll tell you when you're ready."

When they reached the ranch Dusty said, with excitement, "I want to show Mom my rifle; can I Paw?"

Laughlin responded cautiously, "Sure, but remember this, treat every gun as if it were loaded. Remove your rifle from the scabbard, work the lever and leave the chamber open."

Melissa was in the kitchen baking a cake when she heard them ride up. As she opened the screen door to greet them, trailer, who hadn't accompanied them to town, shot past her, started jumping with excitement and circling Dusty; he was really excited to see them. Dusty held the rifle out for Trailer to see and said with a big smile, "Look Trailer, Pa' bought me a rifle. Soon we can go on a real hunt."

Melissa stepped out on the porch, smiled and said, "My, what a nice rifle; did you thank your dad?"

Dusty thought for a moment, then answered, "I'm not sure; I've been pretty excited." Then, in case he hadn't, almost shouted when he said, "Pa', thank you, thank you."

Laughlin nodded his 'you're welcome' and said, "Take our horses to the corral; I'll be down shortly to care for Sam. Let me have your rifle, I'll put it on the rack above the mantle." Dusty, who had already opened the chamber, handed the rifle to his dad.

As Laughlin walked to the house and entered the kitchen, Melissa was standing with her back turned but he could see she was wiping her eyes with a towel. Laughlin, suspecting what was bothering Melissa, walked up, put his hand on her shoulder and said, "Melissa honey, what's wrong?"

She turned to Laughlin and answered, "Oh Laughlin, one day he wants a nick name, the next day he gets a rifle. Laughlin he's growing up too fast, I'm losing my baby." Melissa was fighting back the tears as she continued, "He walks like you, talks like you, looks like you and the next thing you know, he'll want to be a Ranger, just like you."

Laughlin took Melissa in his arms and softly whispered, "Now don't you worry, he'll always be your baby. Boys never want to leave their mamas."

As Laughlin spoke, he was already dreading the day when Dusty would ask to become a Ranger. Laughlin knew it was just a matter of time; probably just six years away, when Dusty turns eighteen.

In San Antonio, it was Sunday; Jeanette and Linda's two week engagement had ended, the mayor, Tom Bergheim and the newly elected sheriff, Ben Crenwell had asked Jeanette and Linda to have lunch prior to leaving town the following Monday. The girls had sat through the luncheon engagement and found themselves truly bored. Both men were single, fairly nice looking, but truth be told, the girls were thinking about Boots and Ryder.

After lunch, Jeanette and Linda returned to their hotel room; once inside Jeanette said, "Linda, you were almost rude to those men."

Linda said, "Me? I was almost rude, you were down right rude."

Then, as they both broke out in laughter, Jeanette said, "We both know where our hearts were, with Boots and Ryder."

"Yea," said Linda, "let's take the train and go back to Ft Worth."

"Good idea," said Jeanette, "but first, I'll send a telegram and see if they're still there, if so, we'll go visiting."

In Ft Worth, people were going to church; it was a beautiful, quiet, sun filled day at both the stockyards and Hell's Half Acre. Boots and Ryder were sitting on the front porch of the jail when Sheriff Pryor came out of his office and said, "Come on boys, I'll buy you a Sunday dinner."

Ryder quickly responded, "Best offer I've had today. Let's go Boots."

Boots, who had been unusually quiet for the first part of the day said, "No, y'all go on, I need to take care of something; it's kinda personal."

Ryder barked, "Alright, suit yourself: Pryor, can I have his steak since he's turning it down."

Pryor laughed and said, "You can have anything you're big enough to eat."

As Frank and Ryder walked towards the restaurant, Boots got up, tightened the cinch on War Paint, put his feet in the stirrup and swung into the saddle. He rode down the bluff, north of the jail, and crossed the Trinity River to the Oak Wood Cemetery.

The cemetery was beautiful. It had big oak trees with a special area dedicated to Confederate Soldiers with large monuments and mausoleums. There were also statues of Confederate Soldiers dressed in full battle uniform and a large area of graves only sporting head stones. War Paint was walking at a slow pace as if he was honoring the dead.

Boots was searching and reading headstones as he rode. Then there it was right in front of him; a marker reading:

Husband – Emmett Ryker Wife – Mary

Father and Mother of JoJo Ryker

Boots mind drifted back as he remembered how JoJo had ridden many miles to find his Pa' and how hurt he was when he found out Emmett was dead. Boots swung out of the saddle, dropped the reins, removed his hat, went to one knee and said out loud, "Mr. Ryker, I loved your boy like a brother. We were saddle pals and we rode the Ranger Winds wherever they took us. He was proud of you and loved you very much; but when he lost you and then, two weeks later, Patti was gunned down, it was as if he had nothing to live for.

Boots was wrenching the brim on his hat as he added, "What he did to those three men in the Sweetwater jail was wrong according to the law; but I would have done the same thing." "Now," Boots continued, "He really felt bad about the deputy; that was an accident, your boy had no quarrel with him. All of us Rangers knew Laughlin would send one of us to bring him in; I knew it would be me. Mr. Ryker, you'll never know just how much I was hoping he had crossed the Rio so I could turn around and come back."

Boots was fidgeting; trying to find the words and wishing Ryker were here in person to hear them. As the phrases formed in his mind he blurted out, "When I asked him why he hadn't crossed the river, he simply said he didn't like Mexico. But I knew he really just wanted to die. Sir, your son was faster then me; he missed me on purpose. Yea, he wanted to die, but only by a Ranger's gun. You lost a fine son and I lost my best friend. I don't know why things happen the way the do; I just know God controls our lives. I just wanted you to know how sorry I am that it had to be me.

Tears were welling up in Boots' eyes as he slowly came to his feet and then, expressing his true inner feelings at the tragic loss of JoJo, he remarked, "Many times I have wished he hadn't pulled his shot and it was me laying there. It would have been easier dying then living with the fact I killed my best friend. Sir, I just needed to talk to you and I pray that someday, JoJo and I will, once again, ride the Ranger Winds."

With that, Boots looked up at the heavens, tears rolling down his cheeks, and said, "I miss you JoJo." Then he put on his hat, mounted up, looked at the two graves, nodded, tipped the front of his hat and rode away.

When he returned to the hotel Ryder, who was waiting in the room, greeted him with, "I've got good and bad news."

"Okay," said Boots, "let's hear it."

"Well, the good news," remarked Ryder, "is the girls want to come to Ft Worth to see us."

"Hey," said Boots, "that is good news." Then he got that curious, but anxious look on his face as he asked, "Now, what's the bad news?"

Ryder let out a loud sigh and said, "The bad news is we have a telegram from Laughlin; we're to get on the next train to Uvalde for re-assignment."

Boots, a little disgusted, slapped his leg and barked, "Damn! Alright, I'm gonna wash off some of this trail dust; then wire Laughlin that we'll be on the first train out in the morning. Meanwhile, you wire the girls with our best regards; tell them our situation and that we'll stay in touch."

"Regards," said Ryder, "Hell, I'm gonna give Jeanette my love."

Bright and early the next morning, Boots and Ryder boarded the train heading south for Uvalde with stops in Waco, Austin and San Antonio before reaching Uvalde. All toll, the 380 mile trip would take about twenty hours. Without bucking any headwinds, Old 97 could average around 25 miles per hour. Any additional time would come from routine stops at small town Depots or to take on water for her boiler.

When the Rangers arrived in Uvalde, they disembarked, retrieved their horses from the stockcar, and met with Laughlin at the sheriffs' office. Oral and Nathan were also in attendance.

Laughlin told them he was sending them after a Buffalo soldier, Sgt. Bob Hackett. Boots had met him back when he and Preacher took a herd of horses to Ft Stockton."

When Boots heard the assignment, he said, "Yea, yea I remember him, nice guy; hell of a soldier. What did he do?"

"Well it seems," said Laughlin, "he beat a soldier to death with his bare fists; happened over at Ft Clark. Word is, he lit out with the troops chasing him but they lost 'em."

Oral was pouring everyone a cup of his "famous" coffee. Laughlin took his and said, "They've already sent several patrols out but haven't had any success, soooo, the Military has asked us to help bring him in."

Without hesitation Boots exclaimed, "Ryder is all I need, two men are enough." Without waiting for Laughlin to respond, Boots continued, "We'll go to Ft Clark, find out what happened and interview some of the Buffalo soldiers that served with him."

Boost sipped on his coffee, looked up at Laughlin and said, "Hell, he's black, how's he gonna hide. My bet is he's with the Indians, they respect the black soldiers and have either taken him in or, for sure, have offered aide."

Laughlin said, "That's why I'm sending you, you're smart and I know you'll find him. Better take a pack horse, go down to the livery stable, may want a mule if you're going into the Big Bend area."

As they got up to leave, Laughlin told them to prepare for an early morning departure and then they were to meet him, Oral and Nathan at the restaurant for supper.

Knowing it could, and probably would, be a long chase, Boots and Ryder stocked up with jerky, coffee, munitions, two large goat skin water flasks, ponchos and bedrolls. After securing everything for the night, they met at the restaurant as planned.

During supper, Boots remarked how Sgt Hackett had told him the Buffalo Soldiers were only given old and sickly horses, worn out uniforms and guns; said all the good stuff went to the white troops. Then he recalled how the Indians had a respectful fear of the black soldiers because they were brave, fought to the death and had the heart of a buffalo.

After dinner, Laughlin, Nathan and Oral went to their respective homes while Boots and Ryder retired to their rooms. As Boots lay on the bed with the lamps turned out, he started thinking about Jane and then about Linda. He knew Jane was in love with him and wanted to get married; but, Linda was fun and exciting and, like Boots, a free spirit. With Linda, he could see her when the opportunity presented itself; they could maintain a long range relationship. On the other hand, Jane was in love; Boots wasn't.

As he continued lying there, he wondered 'How long would Jane wait?' That was the unknown and now, with Linda in the picture, he was really in a pickle and wasn't sure if he loved anyone.

Then his thoughts changed to Ryder; would he get his heart broken? Boots couldn't see Jeanette wanting to settle down; besides, she had men with money pursuing her.

The long train ride had tired them both. Ryder was already snoring as Boots rolled over and faded off into a restless nights sleep.

The next morning they mounted up and started toward Ft Clark with the packmule tied to War Paint. On the second day, they reached the Fort and went directly to company headquarters.

The fort was commanded by Captain Jackson, with Lt Benson serving as his second in command. Boots and Ryder met individually with both the captain and the lieutenant.

The Captain, in his fifties, was a career soldier and, it was evident, was waiting on retirement. Conversely, the Lieutenant was in his twenties, arrogant, unfriendly and full of himself. The Captain, as was reported by his Lieutenant, told the Rangers that Sgt Hackett was a trouble-maker. He further stated that he, himself, had no personal involvement with Sgt Hackett until the death of one of his troopers.

When Boots and Ryder met with Lieutenant Benson, he was, very arrogant and somewhat belligerent. He said Sgt Hackett was a trouble maker, created unrest among the black troopers and constantly challenged authority.

Boots detected a Yankee accent in Benson's speech patterns. When asked where he was from, Benson replied "New York," then quickly added, "I attended West Point."

Boots wandered quietly to himself; a West Point graduate, here at Ft Clark, one of the most remote forts in the southwest, doesn't make sense. As Boots' thoughts returned, he told Benson he wanted to meet with the Buffalo soldiers with no military involvement.

Hearing this request, Benson quickly and abruptly barked, "I can't allow that, I must be present."

Boots, without knowing if he had the authority, stared firmly into the Lieutenants eyes and growled, "Sir, you are interfering with an investigation ordered by the State of Texas; you will not be present."

Benson lowered his eyes, turned and walked toward the door; then he stopped and mumbled, "I'll summon them to their quarters; but I warn you, they're all liars."

When Benson, left Ryder said, "Can we really do that, make him stay out of our meeting?"

Boots smiled and said, "Looks like we just did."

When they entered the Buffalo soldiers barracks, there were approximately twenty-five men present; all ages, young and old. Their uniforms were faded and torn; they had been patched several times. Some fit, some didn't, and their boots were worn out; they were nearly barefoot. There wasn't a fat trooper in the barracks; they were all lean and thin, some even gaunt.

Boots looked at Ryder; he could see Ryder was shocked and angered by what he was seeing. Then Boots turned his attention towards the soldiers and said, "Hello men, my name is Boots Law and this is Ryder McCoy, we're Rangers."

One of the older men in the back said, "My name be Otis Washington. I's remembahs you Mr. Boots. Yo wus jus a young'un and ya brungus some hosses to Phoat Stockton. I's wif Sgt Hackett, we's rode out to escoat yu uns an da hosses tuh da phoat"

"Yes sir," said Boots, "I remember you and Sgt Hackett; y'all retrieved some horses the Indians had stolen from us."

"Yas sir," grinned Otis, "n we brought back da Injuns ponies to, but wuddun no Injuns on 'em, day all dead," then he laughed.

Boots sat down at a table and said, "Otis, come on over here and sit with me. I want to hear about Sgt Hackett."

Otis joined Boots and Ryder at the table, sat down and said, "Whut's youse wants to know. Sgt Hackett is a good man and a good soldier."

"Well," said Boots, "that's not what Lt Benson says; said he was a trouble-maker."

"No, suh, he weren't no trouble-maker. He jus spoke out and tried to get some things fo us. Looks here at us, looks how weez dressed, worn out uniforms 'n shoes, we gets the white troopers ol' shoes. Our hosses are ol', sickly, dem hosses youse brings ova, we dint gets nones uf 'em, white troopers gets 'em."

"Tell me about Hackett and Benson," said Boots.

"Aw, Benson hates all us blacks, special Sgt Hackett. When Sgt Hackett he ask for hosses or cloes, Lt Benson cuss him sompem terble, tells 'im to shut up, tells 'im hees lucky to be live. Sais lots uh his reltives done died to helps free us, sais we shuall be shot dade."

Boots said, "Lt Benson was a West Point man. What's he doing out here?"

"He ain't no West Point man, sais he is. He likes da bottle, it got 'im runs off fum West Point. Whens he gets drunk, he gets 'Bull', one uh his troopers, to use da whip on us. Takes us 'bout two miles down sout of da phoat. Gots a tree in a clearin', ties whoever to da tree, den Bull yooz da whips while da Lootenant he watches." Then Otis grinned, showing his broken and tobacco stained teeth, and said, "Bull, he dohn do dat no mo."

"Why not," asked Boots, "who stopped him?"

"Sgt Hackett done did," answered Otis, "when day took our Sgt to da tree, we's hid and followed 'em to watch see whut da gon done. Day tied Sgt Hackett face fust to da tree, rope 'round his wrist and 'rapped 'round da tree. Bull tore off Sgt Hackett's shurt and he starts lashin' 'n cuttin' da Sgt's back widis bullwhip. Lt Benson he sats on his hoss watchin' 'n drinkin' fum a whiska bottle 'n was sayin', 'Boy, when youse learns to keep yo mouf shut, Ize gon' stop da whippin.' Bull musta hits 'im twenta or thirta times but Sgt Hackett he never mades a soun'. Then it looks a sif da Sgt pass out, his hade wents limp and 'is laegs collapses. Lt Benson he saise cut 'im loose and let 'im lay; day'll say dat 'is hoss drugs 'im to dead."

When Otis paused, Boots urged him to continue. Otis thought for a moment then said, "The Sgt, he a smot ole dog, he ain't pass out; so when Bull cuts 'im down an' da Sarge falls to da groun', he grabbs boata Bulls laegs and pulls 'em outs fum unda 'im wif Bull fallin' on 'is back. Sarge hops on tops of 'im, like a mount'n line. Din he stawts beatin Bull 'n da face wif boat hands, din Sarge tooks da whip and rans da han'le down Bulls troat, kills ol' Bull wif 'is own whip."

Boots queried, "What did the Lieutenant do then?"

"Nuttin'," answered Otis, "beins da cowad 'e wuz, 'e turns 'nd runs 'fo Sarge could get im. We comes outta da bushes and gives Sarge one of our hosses and he rides away in a hawd run."

"What happened next," asked Boots?

"Aw," said Otis, "nex day da Sarge he don' make row call; Bull was missing; Lt Benson actes like he don't 'no nuttin. Lata in da day daise finds Bull 'n da lieutenant saise Sgt Hackett he killed Bull 'n wuz missin'. Day tries ta finds da Sarge, but he to smawt, so day gives up afta ten daise."

Otis stopped for a moment, got a strange look on his face as if a light had just come on, and said, "Mista Boots, youse Rangas dun been sent outs here to gets da Sarge?"

Well sort of," said Boots, "we were sent to investigate a killing and that's what we're gonna do. Now Otis, I believe you boys know where Sgt Hackett is, but I ain't gonna ask you to tell me."

Boots and Ryder stood up from the table; as Otis rose, Boots took him by the hand and said, "Thank you, you've been very helpful."

Then Boots looked at the other men in the room and said, "Men, I've heard lots of good things about the Buffalo Soldiers. Your courage is not only admired by the Indians; it's also greatly admired by the Texas Rangers. We salute the Buffalo Soldiers and, like the Rangers, ya'll will be part of Texas' history. With that said Boots and Ryder stood tall and gave a Military salute to the group.

When the Rangers walked outside the barracks, Boots said, "Let's go back; I want to see the captain and lieutenant again."

They had only walked a few paces from the barracks when Boots remarked, "Ryder, are you thinking the same thing I am?"

Without explaining Ryder answered, "Sure enough, what are you gonna do now?"

"I'm gonna give Lt Benson something to worry about," said Boots.

When the Rangers entered the headquarters, the captain and lieutenant were anxiously awaiting them. They went to the captains' office and were asked to sit down. The Captain sat at his desk with Lt Benson standing next to him.

"Rangers, how about a cigar and some whiskey," asked the captain?

"No thanks," said Boots, rather sternly.

"Very well," said the Captain, "did you learn anything that might help you catch that killer, Hackett?"

Without being asked, Lt Benson chimed in, "I can answer that. All they heard was a bunch of lies, all them boys are liars."

Boots stared directly at the Lt. and said, "Mister, it's my job to find out who's lying, and that I will do." He turned his attention towards the Captain and stated, "Something's bothering me," Boots paused, and then continued, "I have a couple questions I'd like to ask."

"Certainly," said the captain.

Boots asked, "Are the Buffalo Soldiers in the same Calvary as the white troopers?"

"Certainly," answered the Captain, "although, they do have their own regiment and fight together. Why do you ask?"

Boots stood up from his chair, looked the captain in the eyes and said, "Then why in the hell ain't they treated the same? They're wearing rags, worn out boots and their horses are pitiful."

Without taking a breath, Boots turned his attention to Lt Benson, stared him down and barked, "When I return, count on it, you and me are gonna get better acquainted."

That ended the conversation. As Boots and Ryder mounted up and rode out of the fort, Ryder asked, "What's next, where do you think he is?"

"Being black he can't hide," answered Boots, "he's either in Mexico or in the Davis Mountains with the Indians. We'll go to Del Rio and hang around till we get a lead; right now I'm not sure which way to go."

They arrived in Del Rio and went directly to see the sheriff, John Tatum. John had been the deputy until one night when the sheriff was back shot in the saloon.

They entered Tatum's office, identified themselves, and then inquired about Sgt Hackett. Tatum was a short man and wasn't very big; he looked more like a banker than a sheriff. He was bald but had a long handlebar moustache and was said to be a fair hand with a pistol. Tatum knew very little about Hackett; fact is, all he had was the wanted poster he showed the Rangers describing Hackett.

A bit disappointed, Boots and Ryder left the sheriffs' office and went to the saloon for a drink. Maybe they could pick up some information from the bartender. As customary, they had removed their badges before entering the saloon.

After entering the saloon, they stood at the bar sipping whiskey and carrying on a conversation with the bartender. Boots told the bartender they were looking for an old army buddy of theirs, a Buffalo soldier, and asked if he had seen or heard about him.

The bartender, who wasn't friendly and reluctant to give out any information, said, "Nope, haven't seen him, would remember a black man, don't see many of 'em around these parts."

A young girl overheard the conversation and said, "I know where one is, how much you pay."

Boots reached in his pocket, pulled out a silver dollar and dangled it in front of her.

She grabbed it from him and said, "He's in Presidio with my sister Maria; they're going to Mexico."

Boots looked at Ryder and said, "That's a long hard ride, let's get started."

In Presidio, Sgt Hackett and Maria were making plans to enter a small village in Mexico where she was born. Her mother and father were there and she knew Hackett would be safe; the Army wouldn't enter Mexico.

There had been some heavy rain up river causing the Rio Grande to rise. Maria and Hackett were waiting for the waters to subside so they could cross. The Sarge had met Maria some time ago when the Buffalo Soldiers were patrolling along the border. She worked in the cantina in Presidio and they would see each other whenever possible. Maria knew Hackett had killed Bull; but, she was willing to hide him and live together in Mexico.

After several days, Boots and Ryder finally reached Presidio; a typical border town not big enough for anything but a cantina and a few adobe buildings.

As they entered the town, Boots said to Ryder, "If he's here he'll be in the cantina with Maria. I'll go in first, and then you come in with your pistol drawn; ready to shoot."

Both men dismounted, and then Boots walked to the cantina doorway and stopped; allowing his eyes to adjust from the bright sun to the dark room.

The cantina was empty except for two old Mexicans and a girl. The girl came to him and said, "Buy me drink gringo."

Boots responded, "Why not. What's your name?"

"Maria, Maria Lopez. Have a seat; let me go to the bar and I'll get you some good tequila, not this watered down mesquel."

When she reached the bar, she ducked behind it as Sackett stepped out of a room behind the bar. Boots, who had seated himself facing the bar, had his pistol hidden in his lap under the table.

CHAPTER 20

Sarge said, "I knows you don't I? You dat young man I met drivin' a herd of horses to Ft Stockton."

"Yes sir, that's right," said Boots.

"Well now," said Hackett, "from what I've heard, dat young man grew up to be da best Ranger of 'em all."

"Don't know about that," said Boots, "but I have grown up."

About that time Ryder, as planned, stepped inside with pistol drawn and pointed at the Sarge.

Hackett looked up, saw the gun and blurted out, "Now don't you gets nervous, I gots no quarrel with you boys."

Boots motioned Ryder to holster his sidearm and said, "Sgt Hackett, come on over and sit down. Ryder, see if there's a shotgun behind the bar." There wasn't, only Maria.

Hackett joined the Rangers and said, "I must be pretty impotant if you Rangers comes after me." Then he laughed and said, "Y'all sho nuf found me, knew dem army boys couldn't do it."

Boots stared into the Sgt's eyes and bluntly asked, "You kill Bull."

"Yes suh," said Hackett, "I sho did."

"Why'd you do it?" asked Boots.

"Cause he needed it," said the Sgt. "he weren't no count, a drunk and hated us Buffalo Soldiers."

"How did you kill him?" asked Boots.

"I beat on 'im some, then I stuck the handle of his bullwhip down his throat, tried to make him eat it, but he died first. I guess you boys are gonna take me in and they'll hang me for sho, but I'll go peacefully. I got the one that needed it; got no quarrel with nobody else."

Boots said, "Sarge, stand up."

Hackett stood up slowly, not knowing for sure what was about to happen.

Boots said, "Turn around."

He turned slowly until his back was towards Boots.

"Stop," said Boots, "now, take off your shirt."

Hackett unbuttoned his shirt and slowly pulled it off exposing his bare back. His back was covered with scars that were obviously caused by a bullwhip; it was a gruesome sight.

Boots took a good look then said, "Put your shirt back on." When Hackett had done so, Boots stood up, reached out, took the Sgt's hand in his and said, "You're one helluva man. Good luck in Mexico with your bride; but stay on that side of the river, don't ever come back; you hear me?"

"Yas suh, I show do, I show do," said Sarge.

Boots and Ryder walked out of the cantina, mounted up and started walking their horses toward Del Rio.

Ryder, with a big smile on his face, said, "I'm proud of you Ranger Boots, but just one question; why did we have to ride all this distance, if you were gonna let him go?"

Boots, without turning his head, staring straight ahead said, "Just needed to see the scars."

Jeanette and Linda, who were now in Austin, performing nightly, wired the sheriffs' office in Uvalde. They were hoping word could be sent to Boots and Ryder advising them of their whereabouts. The telegram was sent with an ending that read: 'be careful, we both miss y'all.'

After sending the telegram, Linda looked at Jeanette and said, "This is crazy. I can't get Boots out of my mind. I think of him all the time and I have dreams about him in a shootout. Can you believe it, I think I'm falling for that damn Ranger."

Jeanette said, "Maybe, maybe not; but they are different from the other men we've met."

Linda thought about what Jeanette said, then remarked, "You know, you're right about that, they're real men. Live by the gun and could possibly die by the gun." She continued to pry the deep reaches of her mind and continued, "Boots is fun loving, hell sometimes he acts like a little kid but he can charm you to death; then strap on that six shooter and face any man living. You're right Jeanette; I've never met a man like him before."

Jeanette responded with, "I know, Ryder is the same way. That's why I fight my feelings for him; any day could be his last day to be alive."

The girls continued to reminisce about their Rangers; while back in Uvalde, Laughlin had been giving Dusty lessons in proper gun handling and shooting techniques. The lessons included instructions on how to sit on the ground with his legs crossed and his elbows on his knees for accurate long range shots. Laughlin explained how important sight picture was. Dusty was a good listener and a fast learner; impressing Laughlin with his quick learning ability and accurate shooting. Dusty's 25-20 wasn't a big caliber long range rifle, but at a hundred yards or less, a good marksman could drive nails with it.

Laughlin told Dusty to be ready to ride by mid-afternoon. They were going deer hunting and, if successful, they could make some deer jerky.

Dusty's excitement grew as Laughlin said, "This will be your deer, I'm not shooting; but," Laughlin grinned broadly and added, "don't get buck fever on me and miss your first deer."

Dusty assured him he wouldn't as they rode toward a shallow creek crossing where, on numerous occasions in the past, Laughlin had seen deer. They dismounted about a quarter of a mile from the crossing; easing their way slowly and silently towards their destination.

Once there, Laughlin and Dusty sat down behind some scrub brush about sixty yards from the creek. Laughlin whispered to Dusty, "When you see the deer, wait for him to give you a good unobstructed shot, aim for the neck and squeeze the trigger slowly. Don't panic or hurry your shot; you'll only wound the deer. Remember, you owe it to the animal to make a clean kill."

The two of them sat there silently and still for what, to Dusty, seemed like hours. Just as the sun was disappearing over the horizon, a buck appeared. He was slowly and cautiously walking the edge of the stream, as all deer do.

Laughlin had placed the sun at their backs with the southeast wind in their face. The buck, which had not seen nor smelled them, had his head down drinking water as Laughlin whispered to Dusty, "When he raises his head, take 'im."

After a few excruciating seconds, the buck raised his head; Dusty remembered what his Pa' had told him: aim, aim, aim, pull slow, pull slow – Bang!, the little 25-20 spoke.

The buck was down; Dusty had made a perfect shot. Laughlin shook his hand and said, "Good shot son; are you excited?"

Dusty, almost shouting, said, "Yea, my hearts beating really fast and I'm shaking. Did I do good?"

"Yea son, you did good. I'm proud of you. Now let's go get your deer and I'll show you the second part of the hunt; gutting, skinning and drying him in the smoke house for jerky."

The deer was a young fat six point; after field dressing, he was thrown across Cyclone. Dusty had to ride double with Laughlin as they returned to the ranch. When they reached the house, Dusty jumped down and ran in the house hollering, "Ma', Ma', come look at my deer!" Then he dragged her out onto the front porch to view his kill.

"My, my," she said, "We've got another man in the house. One's a Ranger and one's a hunter."

"Yea Ma'," shouted an excited Dusty, "one shot, my first deer. Pa' said I did good."

"You did do good," said Melissa. "I'm very proud of you."

Laughlin, attempting to corral the excitement, said, "Come on let's get started; the funs over, now the real work begins."

After the deer was skinned, Laughlin cut thin strips to hang over the smoldering ashes which, earlier that day, he had prepared in the smoke house.

After everything was done and they were having supper with Melissa, Laughlin looked at Dusty and said, "Son, you grew up some today. I'm proud of you; you showed discipline and it brought you success. Now I can let you hunt by yourself; but only with my permission and you can only shoot what I approve."

Laughlin took a bite of the fresh back strap Melissa had prepared and continued, "We'll start with porcupines; we need to get rid of all of 'em on the ranch."

"Why Pa', what harm do they do?" asked Dusty.

"Son, if a young calf sees a porcupine he'll smell it. When he does he gets needles in his nose. Then when he goes to nurse on his mother, the needles stick her in the milk bag and she won't let him nurse. Results.....a dead calf; starves to death."

Laughlin continued, "Porcupines and coyotes, if you see a cougar, get away. Come back and tell us where you saw it and we'll get Mr. Bledsoe's hounds and try to track it." Laughlin smiled and said, "Your favorite, Ranger Boots will be showing up in a couple of weeks. Gonna tell him about your deer and your rifle?"

"You bet I am, he'll be proud of me just like you. Boy I sure do like Boots." Dusty thought to himself, 'Maybe someday when I'm a Ranger I can ride with Boots.'

Boots and Ryder had been making their way back to Uvalde, but at a slow pace.

On the return trip from Presidio they stopped in Del Rio for a couple of days to rest after the long ride and hours in the saddle. They discussed their route back; they could take the stage road straight to Uvalde.

With the soldiers at Ft Clark, Ft Davis and Ft Stockton, the Indian problems had all but ceased. Their biggest danger would be when small raiding parties came from the mountains in Mexico. The Indians would leave their sanctuary in the mountains, cross the Rio Grand and raid along the border; then flee back across the river to the safety of the mountains.

Most of the time it would be raiding parties starting out from south of Del Rio; then running along the river toward Laredo.

As they were leaving Del Rio, they met a wagon driven by a farmer with his wife and five children in the wagon. The man saw the Rangers and pulled up on his running team of mules. The mules were lathered and it was evident they had been running and pulling the wagon for awhile. Once he got his team stopped, he shouted, "Injuns, Injuns, they attacked our farm house. Burned the barn, stole my two horses, set the house on fire! I got two of 'em with my Winchester then they rode off with the horses. Lucky to be alive sure enough; praise God we're alive."

Boots asked, "How many were there?"

"Seven or eight, but I got two of 'em. Those two won't steal and burn nothing anymore."

"Which direction did they go?" asked Boots.

"South," said the farmer, "they left riding hard and leading my horses."

Boots said, "Take your family into town. Tell the sheriff what happened and ask him to wire the Uvalde sheriff's office that we are in pursuit. We'll try to run them back across the border before they do any more harm."

The farmer and his family drove the wagon off towards Del Rio.

Boots said to Ryder, "This sounds like Three Fingers. He hides in the mountains in Mexico and ventures out to steal horses, burn barns and kill babies, doesn't take hostages, likes to torture. They say he'll only fight when things are in his favor. Indians still fear the white man with a rifle, that's why he fled after two of his warriors were killed. My thoughts are he'll ride along the river, steal horses and burn, but won't stay long enough for the soldiers from Ft Clark to catch up with him. We're not far behind and can probably catch up to him and chase them back to Mexico. In Mexico he has the banditos to fear and, as usual, he'll disappear into the mountains to their unknown stronghold. We should be chasing four or five Indians leading horses. Hopefully, we can catch up to them before any more attacks are made."

The Rangers continued to ride and soon found the burned cabin and barn. It was still smoldering. Boots told Ryder they were at least eight hours behind the raiding party. He added they needed to make contact now, catch 'em off guard. They know the soldiers from Ft Clark will be two or three days behind them. Three days of raiding and then they would hightail it to the mountains across the river.

Ryder said, "What's the plan? There's five of them and only two of us."

Boots said, "We'll ride hard, climb up vantage points and try to make visual contact. Surprise is on our side, they will be expecting troopers, not two Rangers. If we get in a gun battle try to protect our horses and shoot theirs out from under them. That'll make a whole lot of difference. Hopefully when they see us, they'll ride for Mexico thinking we're with the troopers."

287

After about four hours of riding they rode upon a high knoll and visually scanned the area. In the distance, on the expected route of the Indians, they spotted smoke.

They rode full out towards the smoke and, when in viewing distance, the remains of a burned cabin could be seen. As they rode closer a young boy was sitting on the porch staring forward; it appeared he was in shock.

Two bodies were in the yard, the remains of his Maw and Paw. They had been mutilated; it appeared from the blood trail, they were shot in the house then dragged out in the yard and tortured.

The woman was nude, looked like they slashed her repeatedly with a knife and scalped her; the man was nude, Indians probably took his clothes then he was tortured and mutilated. It appeared he had been castrated while alive and then dismembered and scalped.

Boots and Ryder approached the boy carefully and cautiously. The boy was in a mild state of shock, but after recognizing he was safe he began to come out of the trance he was in.

His name was Anthony Hardin and he was twelve years old. Anthony said they only had one gun in the house and it was a shotgun. His Paw probably saw the Indians coming and locked himself and his Maw in the house. Tried to fight off the Indians but had no chance. Anthony said he had ridden to the river to fill up water pouches. At the river he heard gun shots and by the time he arrived at the cabin the Indians were gone.

Boots and Ryder told him they were Texas Rangers and were in pursuit of the raiding party.

Anthony said, "I want to go with y'all. I'm a good rider and my horse is fast, I can keep up."

Boots looked at Ryder and said, "We don't have a choice; if we take him back they'll kill again, if we stay after them we'll catch up to them soon. Anthony, can you shoot a rifle?" asked Boots.

"Guess I can. I would use Pa's shotgun to hunt quail and rabbits. It can't be much different."

Boots said, "When we catch up with them your job will be to hold the horses. We'll do the shooting." Boots asked Anthony if they had whiskey in the house.

Anthony said, "No, but we had some jugs of wine in the cellar."

Boots looked toward the cellar, the door was opened; he hoped the Indians drank the wine quickly, that would slow them down. They dug shallow graves behind the burned house and buried the two bodies. Anthony didn't cry but he promised his Maw and Paw he would get the Indians no matter how long it took him.

Boots thought to himself, 'Reminds me of myself when I was twelve years old and on that battlefield back in Georgia, the boy has spunk.

The three of them mounted up and rode away at a gallop following the well laid trail left by the Indians.

Boots knew of Three Fingers; he had heard the story how two of his fingers were shot off during a raid on a settler's cabin.

They rode until the sun set and the darkness of night settled around them. Boots gave instructions, no fires, one person on guard all night, watching the horses.

Ryder took the first watch. Boots and Anthony spread their bedroll and laid down with their heads resting on their saddles. In a while Boots and Anthony started talking.

Anthony said, "Ranger Boots, when we catch those Indians are we gonna kill them?"

"Yea," said Boots, "or run them across the river and back into Mexico."

Anthony said, "When we see 'em, can I have a gun? I'm gonna kill 'em for what they did to my Ma' and Pa'."

Boots said, "I'll give you a pistol, but you leave the killing to us, remember, your job is to protect the horses."

Anthony said, "Boots, when you shoot 'em I'm gonna scalp 'em with my knife." Anthony had a skinning knife in a buckskin pouch tied on his side; he patted it and said, "Ain't no Indians gonna slip up on us."

"Why not?" asked Boots.

"Cause my horse Smokey can smell 'em, he was stolen by the Indians once, but he broke free and came home. He hates them and when he smells 'em he goes wild."

Boots said, "That's good to know." Boots smiled and said to himself, 'I'll let him believe that.'

About midnight Boots relieved Ryder and took over the watch. Boots found a large tree close to where the horses were hobbled and grazing. He sat there on his butt, leaned his back on the tree and laid the sawed off shotgun across his lap. He knew the scattergun loaded with double ought shot was the best weapon to be used at night.

Boots knew that if the Indians knew they were being followed they would double back, come in at night and try to steal the horses. Five of them against two men and a boy; not being out gunned Boots knew Three Fingers might try to steal the horses.

Sometime about two in the morning Boots heard Smokey stomping and pawing the ground with his front hoofs. Smokey nickered, reared up and tried to run, but he was hobbled. The disturbance he was making had disturbed War Paint and Bad Moon; now they were skittish about something.

Ryder and Anthony had been awakened; Boots heard Anthony say, "Ranger Boots, Indians, Smokey smells Indians."

Suddenly Boots could see the outline of two men beside the horses. They were trying to remove the hobbles. When the horses were out of the line of fire, Boots fired one barrel of the shotgun and heard a loud scream as a body dropped to the ground.

Boots sprang to his feet, ran toward the horses and saw someone running. Boots aimed, fired the other barrel of the scattergun and watched the image fall. By this time Ryder and Anthony had reached Boots.

Boots turned to Ryder and said, "There must have been only two sent to steal the horses. Chances are, after losing four of their party, the rest of 'em will ride hard and fast for Mexico. We'll pull off the chase and head to Uvalde in the morning." Boots asked, "Where's Anthony? I thought he was here with us."

It was very dark but Boots could see movement in the area where he shot the second Indian. Boots said, "Come on, that one may still be alive."

They ran toward the downed Indian and found Anthony kneeling over him; he was removing the scalp and in his hand was the scalp of the other Indian. Boots looked at Ryder and said, "Like I said, this kids got spunk, he ain't no ordinary twelve year old."

In a few days the trio reached Uvalde. They rode directly to the Big Iron ranch to meet with Laughlin.

When the Rangers and Anthony rode thru the front gate, Dusty saw them; he jumped on Cyclone and rode full out to greet them; Trailer wasn't far behind. Dusty pulled Cyclone up to a stop and said with a big smile, "Hi Rangers. Who's that with you?"

Boots said, "Hello Sam," but was quickly corrected.

"My name's Dusty now, no more Sam. Do you like my nickname?" he asked.

"Sure enough; Dusty, that's a good name. Well Dusty," said Boots, "I want you to meet Anthony. How about you taking him down to the bunkhouse and get some vittles in 'im; he's a might hungry. We'll be down after we see your Pa'."

"Sure enough," said Dusty, "come on Anthony, let's go."

As they rode away you could hear Dusty asking Anthony about the two scalps hanging on his belt.

Boots and Ryder joined Laughlin who was waiting on the front porch of the ranch house.

"Hello boys," said Laughlin as they dismounted.

"Hello Captain," said Boots and Ryder almost in unison.

"Come on up and sit down, I'm anxious to hear about Sgt Hackett and the boy that rode in with y'all," crowed Laughlin.

As Boots and Ryder sat down on the steps, Boots said, "Captain, I didn't bring Hackett in, far as I'm concerned what he did was justified."

"Where is he now?" asked Laughlin.

"Mexico," said Boots.

"So be it," said Laughlin, "let's leave it at that. Who's the boy?"

"Anthony Hardin," said Boots, "Ma' and Pa' were killed by Three Fingers and his raiding party. We were on their trail; they burned a cabin outside Del Rio and stole the horses; the father, mother and three children barricaded themselves in the house. The father cut two of 'em down with his long rifle then they moved on to Anthony's place. He was at the river getting water when they attacked. We took 'im with us as we pursued ole Three Fingers. We were camped when two of 'em slipped in to steal the horses. I got both of 'em with my scattergun. My thoughts are they'll take what they have and ride back to Mexico. He lost four warriors, weren't but six or seven to start with."

"What about the boy" asked Laughlin?

"He's alright, no fear, scalped both them Indians before we knew it. Said they killed his folks, took that skinning knife on his side and scalped 'em both. Got upset cause we didn't go after the other two, said someday he'll kill Three Fingers, said he wouldn't forget."

Laughlin said, "Y'all go down to the bunkhouse, get 'im cleaned up then come up here for supper. I'll see if some of Dusty's clothes will fit 'im. By the way, it's Dusty now, not Sam."

Boots and Ryder laughed and Ryder said, "Yea, we've already been informed."

Laughlin went inside and informed Melissa they would have guests for dinner: Boots, Ryder and Anthony.

"Anthony?" asked Melissa, "whose Anthony?"

Laughlin said, "Sit down and I'll tell you about him. He's twelve years old and an orphan, no family." Laughlin filled Melissa in on what had happened; leaving out the more gruesome parts of the story.

Boots, Ryder and Anthony left the bunkhouse and walked to the ranch house for their supper engagement. They were greeted by Melissa and seated in the dining room.

Laughlin said the blessing and they began a fine meal prepared by Melissa.

After eating supper Melissa asked Anthony to join her on the front porch. Dusty was following Boots around and Laughlin knew to stay out of the way and let Melissa spend time with Anthony. After conversing with Anthony for an hour or so, Melissa called Laughlin and Dusty to the porch.

She said, "Dusty, Anthony will be spending the night in our extra bedroom tonight, will you show him around and help make him comfortable please."

Dusty's eyes lit up and he said, "Sure will. Come on Anthony, follow me."

Laughlin looked at Melissa and smiled. She looked back at Laughlin and said with a tear in her eye, "We've got to talk."

After the boys were in their beds Laughlin and Melissa went to their bedroom to prepare for bed. They laid down; Laughlin turned the kerosene lamp out and laid his head back on his pillow.

Melissa said, "Laughlin, it's so sad that Anthony has no kin, no home and he's only twelve years old. We've got to help him. Laughlin, please say he can stay here. We can put him in the bunkhouse, send him to school with Dusty and let him learn ranch work. He's such a nice looking boy; strong, blond hair, green eyes, and intelligent. Guess what he asked me to do? He asked me to pray for his mother and father, to tell them he loved them."

The darkness of the bedroom hid Laughlin's' smile, he knew all this was coming; he loved his wife.

The next day Boots wanted to go into town and see his Paw, Nathan. Laughlin asked him to take the buckboard and carry Melissa, Dusty and Anthony to town. Melissa wanted to buy both the boys some new clothes.

After arriving in town Melissa and the boys went to the General Store; Boots to the sheriffs' office.

Boots, Nathan and Oral drank coffee while Boots brought them up to date on his recent female experiences. They laughed, joked, talked and had a good time.

Melissa and the boys completed their shopping and started walking to the sheriffs' office. As they were walking, she heard sniffling, she looked at Anthony; he was crying. Melissa asked, "Anthony, what's wrong? Are you alright, why are you crying?"

Anthony looked up at Melissa with tears streaming down his cheeks and said, "Ma'am, I ain't never had store bought clothes before. My Ma' always made 'em for me. Thank you. When I get a job I'll repay you."

Melissa said, "You can repay me by wearing them Sunday when we all go to church."

"Wow!" said Anthony, "we're going to a real church with a piano and singing. I like to sing." Melissa nodded as they proceeded on to the jail.

Melissa entered the sheriffs' office with the boys at her side. Boots, Nathan and Oral all jumped up when she came in. She said, "Sit down boys; go back to your dominoes."

Oral said, "Does Laughlin know you're hanging out with those two fellows?" Pointing at Dusty and Anthony.

"Yea," said Melissa, "the town girls were looking in the window at them over at the General Store."

The boys both blushed and then Dusty said, "Wait till you see the girls in church."

After saying their goodbyes, they all loaded up in the buckboard and rode back to the ranch.

When they arrived at the ranch, Dusty jumped out of the buckboard and said, "Come on Anthony, let's go saddle up Cyclone and Smokey. I'll show you around, wait till you see our race horses."

When Sunday arrived, Laughlin, Melissa, Dusty and Anthony went to church. Melissa introduced Anthony to Brother Morgan and then he, in turn, introduced Anthony to the congregation.

When Brother Morgan said 'Let's turn to hymn number 147 in our song book,' Melissa handed Anthony a book. The piano started playing and everyone was singing including Anthony. Melissa looked at his hymn book and it was upside down; she realized he couldn't read but was singing along in a beautiful voice. Evidently his mother had taught him songs by singing with him.

After the services they were having their usual covered dish lunch and several people came over, welcomed Anthony and commented about his beautiful voice.

Anthony said, "Thank you, but Dusty sings better than I do."

"No," said Dusty, "just louder."

About that time Brother Morgan came over and said, "I would like to extend an invitation to you boys to be members of our choir."

Dusty looked at Anthony, Anthony looked at Dusty; then they grinned and said together, "Yes sir, we like to sing."

After lunch they returned to the ranch. The boys ran to the barn, saddled up and went exploring.

Laughlin said, "Tonight Anthony can stay in the bunkhouse with the boys, we'll fix him a good bunk. He'll enjoy the wranglers."

Melissa frowned and reluctantly said, "Alright, but they better not pick on him or they'll have me to deal with."

For the next two or three weeks Anthony spent his nights in the bunkhouse and his days with Dusty. Several times Dusty would sleep in the bunkhouse; the two of them were becoming good friends.

One morning after breakfast Dusty excused himself and said, "I'm going to the bunkhouse to see Tony."

"Tony?" asked Melissa.

"Yes ma'am," said Dusty. "Now Anthony's got a nickname just like me. Tony Hardin and Dusty McFarland, Rangers of the future," and he grinned at Laughlin as he walked out the door.

About mid morning Laughlin strapped on his holster and pistol, walked to the barn where Ryder and Boots were helping clean the stalls.

He said, "You boys get your pistols and meet me out behind the barn."

Boots and Ryder knew what was going to take place; Laughlin was going to practice his draw and shooting. Dusty and Tony sat on top of the rail of the fence to watch. Laughlin had a backstop about fifteen yards in front of him with six bottles sitting on a rail.

Boots and Ryder stood behind Laughlin to watch as he drew and fired.

Laughlin squared up to the target, his eyes hardened, he reflected deeply with concentration and then with unbelievable speed drew and fired six times; hitting all six bottles.

Tony was shocked; he hollered, "WOW! WOW, did you see that Dusty?"

Dusty said, "Sure I did. That's my Pa'. He's the fastest Ranger ever."

Ryder had never seen Laughlin draw and he hoped he would never be on the receiving end of what he had just witnessed. Laughlin's speed was only surpassed by his accuracy. Ryder had heard stories regarding Ranger Laughlin McFarland but had dismissed them as exaggerated myths. He now realized they were downright conservative.

Boots and Ryder took their turns and it was obvious Boots was considerably faster than Ryder. In fact, Boots was a respectable second, only to Laughlin. Ryder, on the other hand, needed some work.

Laughlin continued to dazzle them with speed and accuracy for the next 30 minutes before ending the practice session and heading for the house.

Boots and Ryder headed back to town, while Dusty and Tony finished cleaning the stalls.

When Laughlin entered the Ranch House, Melissa, who had been watching out the kitchen window, asked "What are your plans for Tony? It appears he has no family."

Laughlin said, "Yea, I know. He was born in Missouri and then they moved down here. It makes me wonder if his Paw was running from something."

Melissa remarked, "I know one thing, he had a good Maw. She read the bible to him and they sang hymns together."

"Well, to answer your question," responded Laughlin, "I'll let him continue to stay here in the bunkhouse, send him to school with Dusty and we'll see how it works out. He's old enough to have responsibilities, the same as Dusty. We'll see how he responds to discipline or if he's lazy. You know I will monitor him and Dusty. I don't want Dusty influenced by Tony unless it's good. What are your thoughts?"

"Laughlin, in the short time he's been here I've grown very fond of him, and since we can't have more children, wouldn't it be nice if Dusty and Tony grew up together like brothers?" said Melissa.

"Well," thought Laughlin, "come spring roundup I'm gonna make wranglers out of 'em. They both can outride any man on the ranch right now. I want them roping, branding, learning how to herd steers, cut 'em out, rope and de-horn. Wranglers first; I know they want to be Rangers, but wranglers first. They follow Boots around like his shadow, don't guess that's bad. Boots graduated from 'Ole Laughlin's School of Hard Knocks. He's a top notch cowboy and Ranger." Laughlin put his arm around Melissa, pulled her closer, kissed her gently on the lips and said, "Now that we've got all this worked out, why don't you dedicate the remainder of the night to me."

Melissa blushed, looked at Laughlin and said, "Oh Laughlin, I love you so much." They got up from the swing, went inside the house and turned out the lanterns. Dusty was staying in the bunkhouse with Tony.

The next day Dusty and Tony were riding the south pasture checking the fence. With Trailer following close behind, Dusty asked Tony, "Do you ever think about that Indian that killed your Ma' and Pa'?"

Tony answered, "Yea I do, everyday. They call him Three Fingers. I didn't tell Boots and Ryder about me seeing him as they rode off from our cabin."

"You seen him?" asked Dusty.

"Yea," said Tony. "When I was at the river getting water I heard shots and by the time I got back the house and barn were burning; Ma' and Pa' were laying dead in the front yard. I hid in some brush and they rode by me as they left."

"What did he look like?" asked Dusty.

"I saw him good. He was riding a paint horse, brown head with a white star on his forehead, white body with brown spots. He had war paint markings on his neck and haunches. He had a short braided horse tail beard hanging from his reins and decorated with beads. He wasn't a young brave, he was older, had long hair, dark skin and thin face. Was wearing buckskin britches with beads sewn up the side of each leg and was wearing moccasins. He had two feathers in his hair and had a green shirt with a yellow bandana hanging down his back. He was carrying a rifle in his right hand and he had two fingers missing from his hand. My Ma' and Pa's scalps were hanging on his side. I'll never forget him Dusty and someday I'll kill 'im, just like he did my Ma' and Pa'."

Dusty said, "When we're eighteen and Rangers maybe you and I can go hunt him down. We've got to learn to shoot good with a rifle. Pa' says the Indians are afraid of Rangers with long rifles."

Tony said, "Yea, I agree. I'll never forget him riding in front of me with Ma' and Pa's scalp. Someday I'll scalp him, just wait and see."

The boys continued to ride the fence and talk when suddenly Tony said, "Look there on the ground; blood."

They could see something, probably a calf that had been killed and dragged under the fence; leaving a blood trail.

Dusty said, "Look here," and pointed to a large track, "it's a cougar." Then, remembering what Laughlin had told him about cougars, urged, "Come on, let's get out of here, all we have is my 25-20. Let's go back and tell Pa' what we found."

Too late, Trailer smelled the blood and the cougar. He ran under the fence, nose to the ground, following the scent left behind.

"Stop Trailer, come on back, that cougar will kill you!" shouted Dusty.

"What are we gonna do?" asked Tony. "You can't call him off the trail; it's too fresh." Dusty replied, "Pa' always told me to come back if we seen a cougar, but I can't let Trailer get killed, let's follow him."

CHAPTER 21

They dismounted, climbed over the fence and started running in the direction of Trailer; he was barking as he ran. About three hundred yards inside a clump of live oak trees, they could hear Trailer. Dusty new he had the cougar in a tree; he could tell by the way he was barking. The boys ran hard and fast thru the brush hoping to get there before the cougar attacked.

As they ran the barks became closer. Just ahead was a big live oak with Trailer trying to climb the tree; circling and barking. Up in the tree was a huge cougar; it was on a limb and had part of a calf lying on the limb. Apparently, the cougar had been enjoying his meal when along came Trailer.

The big cat could be heard screaming at Trailer and was probably going to jump out of the tree and onto Trailer.

Dusty loaded a cartridge into the chamber of the little 25-20 lever action. He told Tony, "I'll have to get a head shot; let's get closer."

By now the cougar had been alerted and was looking straight at them.

Dusty said, "Tony, walk to my right slowly, he'll watch you; when he turns his head, I'll put one in him." Sure enough the cougar watched Tony as he started to circle the tree and turned his head offering up a perfect shot.

Dusty took careful aim, placed the front sight directly on the cougars' ear and squeezed slowly as he had been taught. BANG, the rifle spoke, the cat went limp and fell to the ground; he was dead. Trailer was on him, biting, growling and pulling on the carcass.

"Great shot," spouted Tony; then he looked at Dusty, who was shaking all over and asked, "How did you hit 'im if you were shaking like that?"

"Didn't start shaking till after I shot," said Dusty. "I gotta sit down; My hearts jumping out of my chest." Then he started taking deep breaths.

After Dusty got over the shakes, they each took a rear leg of the cougar and started dragging it. After about an hour of dragging, they were in sight of the horses.

Suddenly Smokey and Cyclone started stomping the ground, nickering and rearing trying to pull away from the fence where they were tied.

Dusty said, "Go lead them away from the fence then come back and help me drag the cougar under it. Then get Smokey and your rope. We'll drag him back with both of our ropes tied together to keep him away from the horses. They're scared to death of 'im."

Tony held the horses while Dusty tied the ropes to the cougars' leg before walking over to Cyclone and taking the reins from Tony. Once the cat was secured, they mounted up and Tony spurred Smokey to pull. When the cougar moved back, the horses started running. After a short distance both horses tired and slowed to a walk.

The boys rode into the front yard with the cougar as Dusty hollered into the house, "Maw, Maw, come see what Tony and I have!"

Melissa came to the porch with Laughlin behind her. She saw the cougar and Laughlin caught her in his arms as she passed out.

After a light scolding, Laughlin told Dusty and Tony he would prepare the cat and they would take it to Uvalde. Zeke Plummer, the saddle maker and taxidermist, could mount it. The cougar, on a log in the family room, would be a good conversation piece and a good story for Dusty to tell.

The next morning the cat was loaded in the wagon and Laughlin and the boys took it to town. People gathered around to see the cat and hear Dusty's tale.

Oral and Nathan saw the wagon coming and walked over to the saddle shop where Laughlin and the boys were unloading the cat.

"Hello boys," said Laughlin, "see what these two boys brought in. He was killing my calves."

Both men commented on the size of the cat and the good shot Dusty had made with his small caliber rifle.

Oral said, "Laughlin, we just got a telegram from the sheriff in Eagle Pass. Three Fingers is in jail."

"You don't say," said Laughlin. "How did that happen?"

"Rene and his banditos brought him in; wanted the reward," remarked Oral.

Tony overheard the conversation as his complexion turned to red, because of the anger he harbored for Three Fingers. Then he looked at Laughlin and said, "Sir, I want to ride to Eagle Pass. Do I have your permission?"

Laughlin said, "Tony, I know how you feel, but the Circuit Judge is in Laredo now and, in about a week, he'll be in Eagle Pass. I promise you I'll take you there for the hanging. Now promise me you won't run away and do something foolish."

Tony said, "I promise sir, but I've got to be there when they hang him."

After returning to the ranch Laughlin told Melissa, "We've got to keep an eye on Tony. They've got Three Fingers in the jail at Eagle Pass. As much as he hates that Indian he might get a pistol and ride down there and shoot him. I promised him I would take him for the hanging, after all Three Fingers did kill his folks. The boy deserves to see him die."

Laughlin told Boots and Ryder to start their route to Abilene; usual route, spend a day or so in each town on the way and give Cletus some help when they get to Abilene. Laughlin figured Cletus would be glad to see them since he always has a lot of trouble in Abilene.

After several days passed, word was received by Oral that Three Fingers would be hung in seven days.

Laughlin told Melissa he was taking Dusty and Tony to see the hanging. He said it was time for Dusty to see things like this and he wanted him there to support Tony. They were going on horseback; no wagon, he was going to ride Sam.

Laughlin informed Dusty and Tony they were leaving early in the morning. The next day, at daybreak, the horses were saddled up, provisions were put in the saddle bags by Melissa along with ponchos and bedrolls. The boys were already mounted and waiting by the porch.

As Laughlin came out the door he had two 44-40 rifles in his hands. He handed Dusty one and the other to Tony.

He said, "Dusty, leave the 25-20 here. You're ready for this." Then he looked at Tony and said, "This is yours to keep. I've been watching you shoot Dusty's rifle, you're ready for one of your own."

Both the boys smiled and said, "Thank you sir."

Laughlin mounted up as they waved goodbye to Melissa, turned their horses and looked toward Eagle Pass.

The days were pleasant and the nights were chilly, but in southwest Texas things could change overnight. The ride to Eagle Pass was uneventful and Laughlin enjoyed his time with the boys.

The closer they got to Eagle Pass the more the mood and expression on Tony's face began to change.

Laughlin wondered if it had been a good idea to bring him, but once again ruled in favor; he deserved to see Three Fingers die.

When they reached Eagle Pass, they went straight to the jail. It was manned by two deputies; the sheriff had ridden off two weeks ago and hadn't returned; later it was learned he had run off with a rancher's wife.

They entered the jail; the office was separate from the cell room and both deputies, Cal and Lem, were in the office.

Laughlin identified himself and asked, "Who's in the cell room with the prisoner?"

"Nobody," answered Cal. "Hell, he ain't going no where. Only one way out of here and that's thru that front door you just came thru."

Laughlin said, "One of you boys needs to be back there at all times. This man is a killer, a brutal savage killer."

Cal said, "He don't look so mean in that cell, just sits there and looks out the window like he thinks someone's coming to get 'em."

Laughlin barked, "Open the door, me and these two boys are going in. He killed one of 'ems parents."

The door was opened; they stepped inside and looked into Three Fingers cell. He was sitting, as said, looking out the window with his back turned to the group.

Laughlin asked, "Do you speak English?"

Three Fingers never moved; he just continued to look out the window.

Laughlin spoke again, this time in Comanche, "Three Fingers, you killed this boys Ma' and Pa'."

Three Fingers turned from the window, stood up and said in broken English, "Your Pa' good warrior, fight hard."

Tony stared at Three Fingers with cold hard eyes, a look that Laughlin had never seen in a twelve-year old boy before. Tony continued to stare; then said, "I've come to see you hang. I wanted to revenge my folk's death by killing you myself; but now, I'll just have to watch you hang."

Laughlin put his arms on Tony and Dusty's shoulder and said softly, "Come on, let's get out of here," as they left the cell room.

Once outside in the jail office, Laughlin told the deputies to keep Three Fingers under constant guard and he would be there in the morning to help them walk him to the gallows.

That evening Laughlin talked to the boys about Three Fingers and tried to console Tony. It was very upsetting for Tony to see Three Fingers, but Laughlin knew after the hanging, Tony would feel better knowing that justice had been served.

Early the next morning, before sunrise, they were awakened in their hotel room by a loud knock on the door. It was Lem, one of the deputies.

Lem said, "Cal's dead. Throat been cut and Three Fingers is gone."

Laughlin dressed quickly, told the boys to stay in the room and ran to the jail. Once in the jail, he saw Cal lying up against the cell bars: throat cut, cell door open and keys still in the lock.

"How in the hell did this happen?" growled Laughlin.

"I don't know" mumbled Lem, "I went outside to walk around and wake up; next thing I knew I saw the Indian run out the door, jump on my horse and ride away."

"Went outside to get fresh air, hell, you got whiskey all over your breath." Laughlin threw a hard right hand that landed flush on Lem's jaw, knocking him to the ground. "I ought to shoot you, you drunken bastard."

Laughlin went back inside and saw fragments in the floor and a four-inch hole in the ceiling. He figured one of Three Fingers braves got on top of the roof and gouged a hole in it big enough to drop in a knife. Three Fingers lured Cal to the cell, reached thru, pulled him to the cell bars, cut his throat and reached the key ring hanging on his belt. It was easy after that, he ran thru the front door and jumped on Lems horse while Lem was sucking on a hidden whiskey bottle.

Laughlin went back to the room and told the boys what happened. Tony asked, "Are we going after him?"

"No use," said Laughlin, he'll never stop until he reaches his hideout in the mountains over in Mexico. We could never catch up to him."

"Good," said Tony, "I'm glad he got away. Now when I'm old enough I can hunt him down myself."

"Yea," said Dusty, "but I'll be with you. We'll hunt him down together."

Having no further business in town, Laughlin, Dusty and Tony, headed back to Uvalde and the Big Iron.

Meanwhile, Boots and Ryder had gotten off the train in Abilene, gone to the boxcar and unloaded Bad Moon and War Paint.

They cinched down their saddles and rode to Sheriff Meeks's office. As they rode they observed the town; it seemed busy with lots of people in the streets. It was midday and noises were coming from the three saloons in town.

They tied up to the hitching post, in front of the sheriff's office, and entered the jail. Cletus sitting at his desk, smiled when they walked in. He got up and said, "You boys are a welcome sight. I've got more than I can handle."

"What's going on," asked Boots as he poured him and Ryder some left over coffee?

"Well," said Cletus, "we've got our usual drunks, fist fights and whatever; but now there's been some rustling going on and it appears we've got horse thieves in the area. Glen Ray and Fred told me they got some horses missing from the Double J." Then he paused for a sip of his own coffee and continued, "Those boys are sure doing good on that ranch Mr. Fox left 'em. They've got plenty of cattle, selling horses to the Army and raising fine racehorses. Gonna be a big race here in two weeks; you know, Trade Days, street dance, chicken fights and lots of headaches for me."

Boots said, "We'll be around for a while, at least until the big race is over."

"I appreciate that" responded Cletus, "Things always slow down some when folks know the Rangers are in town."

"Ryder" said Boots, "go on over to the hotel and get us a room. I'm going to the newspaper office."

When Jane saw Boots coming towards the newspaper office, she opened the door, ran and threw her arms around him. Boots hugged her and held her; then he gave her a kiss on the cheek as they went inside the office.

Jane was full of questions; her father was there and he welcomed Boots. Just then Jane said, "I worry about you all the time you're gone; I'm so happy you're back. How long will you and Ryder be here?"

"Oh probably three or four weeks," answered Boots.

"Good," said Jane, "you'll be here when the singers are here. Two sisters travel all over the place and entertain. They'll be here in a few days and perform at the Palace Saloon for two weeks. You can take me, it'll be fun."

Boots felt fear rush thru him as he thought to himself 'Boy, am I in a mess. How am I going to handle this? Jeanette and Linda here, me with Jane, oh man. What am I going to do? Please let something happen in Del Rio or somewhere so the Captain can send me on assignment.' Boots left the newspaper office and went to the hotel.

Ryder was in the room stretched out on the bed. He saw Boots and said, "Hey partner, are you alright? You look terrible."

"Ryder," replied Boots, "I'm in trouble, big trouble. Jeanette and Linda will be here in a few days."

Ryder said, "That's great, I can't wait to see Jeanette, but I'm a little jealous. You'll have two girls and I only have one." Ryder burst out laughing; he was enjoying Boots' dilemma.

"Shut up Ryder," said Boots, "it ain't funny. I'm in a mess."

"Ole Don Juan finally got himself in a mess. Why one of those women might just shoot you," smirked Ryder. Then he got a real sullen look on his face as he continued ribbing Boots with, "Then I won't have a partner; maybe I could partner up with Dusty and Tony; they're too young for girls."

Boots hollered, "I told you it ain't funny, this is serious. I'm in a mess."

Ryder would not let up as he continued, "My suggestion is you start riding for Mexico. Get a head start; both them girls are good riders but maybe you can out run 'em." Then Ryder burst out laughing louder than the first time.

Boots just looked at him, shook his head and mumbled, "No help at all, sorry no count partner."

About five thirty, there was a knock on the door, it was Jane. She said, "Papa sent me over to invite y'all to dinner at the restaurant with us tonight. Will y'all come?"

Boots, without letting her in the door said, "Yea, yea thanks. I'll be there but Ryder can't make it, he's taken real sick."

"Oh, I'm so sorry," said Jane, "we'll see you at seven."

When she left Ryder said, "What do you mean? I ain't sick, I'm going." He was grinning ear to ear, not often had he seen Boots in a situation he couldn't handle.

Boots convinced Ryder to remain in the Hotel room while he went to dinner alone. He would give the girls Ryder's apologies; saying he had an upset stomach. Without Ryder present, Boots could make it through the evening meal without any mention of him and Linda. The dinner went off without a hitch.

The next day Boots and Ryder rode out to the Double J ranch to visit Glen Ray and Fred.

The last time Boots had seen Fred was when he helped track JoJo. They rode thru the front gate and into the ranch. Glen Ray and Fred were at the horse pasture where Fred's brother was exercising Three Paws, their champion race horse.

"Hola amigos," said Fred when he saw Boots.

"Hello Fred," said Boots, "this is Ranger Ryder McCoy. Ryder say hello to Fred and Glen Ray, they're ex-Rangers and were damn good ones."

When they dismounted, Fred came over to Boots and said in a low voice, "Amigo, you ok?"

Boots, knowing he was referring to the JoJo incident, answered, "Yea," then paused and said "yea, I'm alright, thanks for asking."

Fred nodded and said, "We're going to cook in a pit tonight just to celebrate our guests, Boots and Senor Ryder."

Glen Ray said to Boots, "Is Laughlin still as fast as he used to be?"

Boots smiled and replied, "Probably faster, age hasn't slowed his hand at all."

Glen Ray shook his head and said, "Fastest gun hand I ever did see."

That evening after enjoying their pit cooked steaks they sat around the open fire and talked.

Boots said, "I hear you say Three Paws can run like the wind. Is he faster than his pa, Whiskey?"

"It'd be awfully close," said Glen Ray, "but I'd bet on Whiskey. They ran together in a race once, but Whiskey picked up a stone and had to drop out. Otherwise, he always refused to let a horse get ahead of him. There was no holding him back, he just wanted to run. Of course, he's getting old now."

How 'bout Sam," asked Glen Ray, "how's he doing?"

Boots said, "Laughlin still rides him to town and back and exercises him daily. Not a day goes by that Laughlin doesn't comb and curry him; a great love affair between them two."

"What are y'all doing in Abilene," asked Fred.

"Laughlin sent us. Cletus has his hands full and with the big event coming up we were sent to help. Y'all having any trouble out here," asked Boots?

"We lose a few cows every now and then, but we're not full fenced, it's not a real problem but I hear there's trouble in town. A fellow named Barney Ray Evans and another one named Toby Bryant are making trouble for Cletus. Cletus thinks they work out of Abilene, rob out of town banks and then return to Abilene. He thinks they held up the bank in Lubbock and later in Amarillo; both men were out of town when the banks were hit. They're both mean and pistol whip wranglers when they're drunk, taking pride in clearing out the saloon. Want all the ladies to themselves."

"Within reason, who cares what they do in the saloon," said Boots, "the banks are our concern. Thanks for the advise, we'll deal with 'em when necessary."

It was getting late so the men said their 'good-evenings' and retired for the night.

The next morning Boots and Ryder rode back to Abilene and went to see Cletus.

"I want to see what this Barney Ray and Toby are made of. Where are they?" asked Boots.

"Over in the Red Dog Saloon," said Cletus. "Barney's sweet on Velma, one of the girls, and Toby stays drunk; but he's always at Barney's side."

Boots gave Cletus an understanding look and uttered, "If you don't mind, stay here in your office; I prefer me and Ryder take care of this."

Cletus said, "You're the boss, whatever you do is fine with me."

Boots said to Ryder, "Stay at my side. Toby is yours, I got Barney."

They shook Cletus's hand and walked down to the Red Dog. It was crowded with drunks, poker players and ruffians; a typical Texas saloon.

When they entered the saloon and were served, Boots said, "Bartender, point out Barney Ray and Toby to me."

The bartender pointed to a poker table and said, "Barney's the one with the girl hanging on him, Toby's sitting to his left; the one drinking whiskey."

Boots asked, "Do they spend a lot of money here?"

"Yea," said the bartender, "they always got money."

Boots, with Ryder at his side, turned and walked to the table where Toby and Barney were sitting, stopping about two feet in front of them.

Barney was short; he wasn't dressed like a wrangler, he was sloppy; more like a cheap card shark. He was overweight with a dark ruddy complexion, long dark hair, protruding dark eyebrows and red whiskey soaked eyes. On the other hand, Toby was skinny and dressed like a drover. He had brown hair and wore a handle bar moustache; he looked exactly like what you would expect a cowhand to look like.

Boots waited for Barney to look up then pulled his vest back, exposing the Ranger star, and said, "My name is Boots, I'm faster than you and I'm meaner than you, make a move and you're dead." Without taking his eyes off of Barney, Boots pointed towards Toby and barked, "Same goes for you or my partner will put a bullet between your eyes."

After a momentary pause, he continued, "I hear you boys like to disrupt things around here, have lots of money and disappear for some time. Now hear me and hear me good. It's time for you boys to move on and stay gone."

When it appeared Barney was going to respond, Boots stuck out an open palm and blurted out, "Don't say a word, just get up slowly and walk out, then ride out. No need to respond and don't dare give me a reason to pull on you; if you do, you're dead."

Barney looked at Toby; then, as they got up slowly, Barney reached for the money lying on the table.

Boots ordered, "Leave it; Velma that's yours for putting up with scum like this."

She grabbed the money while Barney and Toby left the saloon. The Rangers went to the bar and ordered whiskey.

Boots turned up his shot glass, drank the whiskey, sat the empty glass down, looked at Ryder and winked.

Later back in the sheriff's office, Cletus said, "The entire town is talking abut what happened back at the saloon and it's tamed the town down some."

Boots smiled and said, "Call us Rangers or Town Tamers, take your pick."

Cletus was correct, the town cooled off when word got around about the Rangers being in town. Boots thought to himself "Taking care of Barney and Toby was easy, now comes the next crisis, Jeanette and Linda's visit."

Time passed quickly. It was Wednesday, Jeanette and Linda were due in Abilene Thursday and their first performance was scheduled for Friday evening.

Boots told Ryder to be ready. They needed to go back to the Double J ranch to see Glen Ray; Boots didn't want to be in town when the train bringing the girls arrived. When he said they had to go to the Double J for a couple of days, Ryder was upset. He knew Boots was dodging any meeting with the girls; but it was so much fun watching Boots trying to manipulate him, that he didn't complain.

As deviously planned, Boots and Ryder were at the Double J when the train arrived carrying the girls. However, Jane, from the newspaper, was there; she wanted to do a story on them. After identifying herself to Jeanette and Linda, the threesome made a dinner date for the interview. Jane wanted to know how their life in the southwest compared to life back east.

When asked, Jeanette responded, "Oh my goodness, it's so different. It's fun and exciting and the men, well the men are real men. We have been seeing a couple of Texas Rangers, they're rough and rugged, yet handsome and charming."

Jane's eyes opened wide, as she raised her eyebrows and said, "Yes, I know what you're talking about. What are the names of the Rangers you're seeing?"

Jeanette answered, "Linda is seeing Boots Law and I'm seeing the cutest one, Ryder McCoy."

"I do believe," said an excited Linda, "they're here in Abilene or maybe on their way, we're just dying to see them again."

Jane's face color went from shocking white to furious red, as she said, abruptly, "Thank you for the interview, I'll be seeing y'all at the Palace."

As Jane left the restaurant she stopped on the boardwalk and said out loud, "Okay Ranger Boots Law, you'll be wishing you were facing down outlaws instead of me; just wait till I see you."

CHAPTER 22

It was Friday morning; Boots and Ryder were still at the Double J. when Ryder said to Boots, "It's Friday, the first performance is tonight, let's go. I want to see Jeanette."

Boots took a deep breath and said, "Alright lover-boy, let's mount up."

As they were riding in to town Ryder said, "Boots, I've always liked your horse, 'ole War Paint and I like your revolver too; think maybe I could have 'em after one of them girls kill you?"

"Shut up Ryder," said Boots, "I told you this ain't funny."

"What are you gonna do pardner? I can hold one of 'em while you fight with the other one, don't want 'em both on you at the same time."

"I told you to shut up," said Boots, "I'm just gonna go in there and tell the truth, that's all I know to do."

As they rode into town and down Main Street, the newspaper office was on the left side and the hotel was on the right side of the street. As they were headed down the street, Jane came running out onto the front porch of the news office shouting, "Boots, I need to see you; and I mean right now!"

About the same time, a voice was heard from the balcony porch of the hotel, it was Linda. "Hi Boots, hi; It's me Linda, come on over. I've been dying to see you."

Boots, dreading the confrontation, slumped in the saddle, hunkered over and continued to slow walk his horse.

Ryder remarked softly, "You're on your own cowboy." Then he spurred Bad Moon, galloped to the hotel, registered and went up to his room. Ryder had a big smile on his face as he laid down on the bed and waited for the 'fireworks'.

About twenty minutes passed before Boots walked in, pulled off his hat, threw it down carelessly and flopped down in a chair. He was obviously languishing over his dilemma.

Ryder, trying not to laugh, asked, "How'd it go pardner?"

"I'll tell you how it went," said Boots with his head down and cupped in both hands, "Jane dumped me outright; said she was going to see that nice Mr. Stewart Coffee, the attorney. Then Linda told me to get lost; said not to bother trying to see her anymore. Told me to go see my newspaper girl."

Then he paused, kicked at his nearby hat and lamented, "Hell, I ain't got no girl anymore. Tonight, I'll have to go to the show by myself."

"Now, now, don't fret," said a gloating Ryder, "you can go with me."

"Yea, sure" said Boots, "Jeanette probably hates me too, now that I hurt her little sister."

Ryder walked over, put his arm around Boot's shoulder and said, "I don't know what to say 'ole buddy, maybe you could ride up to Ft Davis and join the Army; or high-tail it to Juarez with Sgt Hackett & his wife they'd protect you."

"I told you Ryder," growled Boots, it ain't funny. One more remark and I'm gonna pull on you."

Ryder threw up both hands in a peace offering gesture; he knew when to back off. There was no further conversation that afternoon while Ryder readied himself for the upcoming entertainment.

Evening came and Ryder went to the Palace while Boots stayed in the room. Late that night, when Ryder returned, Boots was still waiting up.

"How'd it go?" queried Boots.

"Oh it went real well," responded Ryder, "Jane was there with Mr. Coffee, the attorney; then Jeanette and Linda came by and sat with me after the show."

Ryder was having fun with Boots' discomfort, so he paused and added, "Oh yeah, that nice young man, Bill Strother, the rich rancher, came over and joined us. Linda seemed to like him a lot."

"Damn it," said Boots as he kicked a chair across the room.

Once again, Ryder knew not to over-do it, so he washed up and went to bed. Not another word was spoken by either of them the remainder of the night.

The next morning they got up and went to the restaurant for breakfast. After eating Ryder said, "Ok now seriously, what are you going to do?"

Boots, was really in turmoil as he mumbled, "I really don't know. I like both of them a lot; but hell, I couldn't choose even if I had to."

"Well," said Ryder, "I suggest you tell both of them what you just told me. To my knowledge you've made no commitment to either of them, they don't own you. Tell 'em you want to continue being a free spirit and hope to see both of 'em. Hell, find yourself another one, have three girl friends." Ryder couldn't help himself as he added, "You're doing so well with these two."

To Ryder's good fortune, Boots, who hadn't caught that last remark, said, "I don't like that attorney seeing Jane and I sure don't want that rich rancher seeing Linda."

"Let me pass along something my old grandpa used to say," offered Ryder, 'Pigs get fat, hogs get slaughtered'. Boots, don't wind up losing both of 'em. Come on, drink your coffee and let's go chase some outlaws."

"You're right," said a relieved Boots, which always happens once he sees the light, "I may as well level with both of 'em; I'm going over to the newspaper office to see Jane....... wish me luck."

Boots entered the office, Mr. Wyatt greeted him and said, "Jane is in her office behind closed doors; but I'll tell her you're here."

"Thanks," said Boots, as he took a chair and waited.

Jane came out, walked to Boots and said, "Yes, what is it, Boots?"

Boots got up, removed his hat and asked, "Can we take a walk and talk?"

"I suppose so," said Jane. Then she added, rather coldly, "Though I can't imagine whatever for. Let me tell father I won't be gone long."

They stepped onto the boardwalk and walked in silence until they reached the churchyard when Boots said, "Jane, I've handled this all wrong. I can face men down but I don't know anything about dealing with a woman. You have always been here for me and I have expressed my thoughts about the Rangers and our future. I have never made any commitments to you."

"Boots," said Jane, "you are exactly right. I'm the one that wanted more out of this relationship, possible marriage and a family. You warned me about a Ranger's life, you never committed to anything. I'm the one that's out of line, not you. It's just that I love you Boots and have decided to take whatever you give me. If it's just a tiny piece of you or all of you, I'll accept it."

Boots, who had been sitting on the church steps, hat in hand and looking at the ground as she spoke, was surprised at the sudden change from her cold reception. He looked up at her and said, "Thank you Jane, let's not rush our relationship. It will either get stronger or go way with time."

After walking Jane back to the newspaper office, Boots went to the hotel where Jeanette and Linda were staying. He found their room and knocked on the door. When Linda opened the door, she was dressed in a baby blue robe, her long golden hair was hanging down her back and she had sleepy sexy eyes trying to focus on Boots.

She said, "Hi cowboy, where you been?"

Without answering, Boots said, "Linda, can we talk, will you meet me in the restaurant?"

"Sure," said Linda, "but you're welcome to come in. Jeanette is here but she's asleep, we can talk here."

Boots said, "Alright," and walked in. She closed the door behind him as he sat down in a high back chair. Boots had his hat in his hands and was nervously fidgeting with it. After a moments pause, He said, "Linda, I didn't come to your show last evening because I was trying to resolve this situation I've gotten myself into."

Linda interrupted and said, "You're talking about you, me and Jane, right?"

Boots looked down at the floor and nodded in the affirmative as Linda remarked, "She's beautiful, you're handsome and exciting, even a blond like me can figure that out. Let me save you from an awkward explanation."

Boots nodded his agreement once again, and his apparent relief, as Linda continued, "I like you a lot, and if you aren't married I'll continue to include you in my life. I must admit though, you make me feel different than any man I've ever known; I'm not sure I like that. However, you and I can continue with our current relationship. I can live with that, no strings attached."

Linda, who had been standing as she spoke, walked to where Boots was sitting, sat down on his lap, looked into his eyes and said, "I hope to see your big 'ole sexy blue eyes looking at me tonight when we perform."

With that, she kissed a surprised, but relieved Boots and led him out the door as she prepared for the nights entertainment.

When Boots returned to the hotel room, Ryder, who had been waiting anxiously, blurted out, "Are you alright, no knife wounds, no bullet holes."

Secretly he was really concerned, but he was still enjoying the situation Boots had gotten himself into.

Boots sat down on the edge of the bed and said, "One loves me, but has turned me loose; the other cares for me, but expects nothing from me."

"Hell!" said Ryder, "that's the best of both worlds, but remember, either one of those girls could have any man she wants."

Boots, who wasn't really listening, said "Ryder, you be careful with Jeanette, you could lose your heart to her real easy. She's beautiful and well educated; a classy girl that demands respect just by the way she looks and acts. All the men in every town they appear in are gonna be after both of them."

Ryder laughed and said, "I hear you 'ole buddy, but just remember, ladies love Rangers just like babies love puppy dogs."

Boots grinned and said, "Ok, just don't come crying and whining to me when Jeanette breaks your heart."

Ryder was laughing on the outside, but on the inside his heart was burning, he was already in love with Jeanette.

It was Saturday night; Boots and Ryder were seated at the Palace waiting on the show to start. The house was full and, for some reason, louder and more unruly than usual. Once again, Jane was with Stewart Coffee, the attorney.

While the girls were performing, one drunk in particular was loud and boisterous; disturbing their songs. He was a big, dirty looking man; wearing his vest over a long sleeve shirt with rolled up sleeves. He had a dark moustache, snuff stained yellow teeth, and a mean reputation that preceded him.

Cletus, who was mingling with the crowd to keep things under control, made him sit down and shut up a couple of times while the girls were singing.

After the performance the girls always went to their dressing room, changed clothes and then joined the Rangers at their table. Linda came out a few minutes ahead of Jeanette, sat down at the table, looked at Ryder and said, "She'll be right out, tonight she wants to be extra pretty for you."

Ryder nodded his understanding and managed a soft, "Thank you."

Jeanette came out of the dressing room and started walking toward the table to join the group. As she walked in front of the stage, the big drunk jumped up from his table, ran to her, threw his arms around her and in his drunken stupor said, "How 'bout it honey, give 'ole Big Dave a kiss," as he tried to kiss Jeanette.

Ryder sprung from the table like a cougar attacking a deer, grabbed the man by the shoulder, pulled him away from Jeanette and, with pistol drawn delivered a blow to the drunk's ear. Blood flew, Dave's ear was split and he was cut up to his hairline. Before Boots and Cletus could get to Ryder, he had given the man a severe pistol whipping. It was all Cletus and Boots could do to pull Ryder away.

Big Dave was on the floor with his face covered in blood and already beginning to swell. He was lying unconscious with blood running from his cuts and forming a pool on the floor.

Cletus pointed to two men and ordered, "Drag 'im over to the doctor, after he's been sewed up I'll put 'im in jail for awhile."

Boots had pushed Ryder over to a corner and was still restraining him; he was like a crazed animal. "Calm down partner," urged Boots, "calm down, you damn near killed that man."

Ryder, still breathing hard, was furious and said, "If he puts his filthy hands on her again, I will kill 'im."

Jeanette and Linda came over to help calm him down.

Ryder looked at Jeanette and asked, "Did he hurt you baby? I should have killed 'im."

Jeanette kissed him and said, "Calm down, every thing's alright, come on, we're going to the hotel room."

As Jeanette led Ryder out of the saloon, Boots rejoined Linda at the table. When he sat down Linda said, "I've never seen anything like that. I pity the man that harms Jeanette when Ryder's around."

Boots remarked, "Ryder's not only my buddy, he's a Ranger and would do the same thing to protect me, you or anyone else that was being wronged."

But in this case, Boots knew without a doubt that Ryder was in love, deeply in love. He also knew he could protect his partner from every thing except getting his heart broken. Hopefully that wouldn't happen.

Having witnessed Ryder's actions, Jane was a little envious when she laid down that night. She wondered if Boots would have done the same if she was the one being molested. Jane's heart was hurting, she wanted Boots and wondered if she had lost him to Linda.

Meanwhile, in Uvalde, Laughlin had been teaching the boys proper use of their big bore rifles. He was showing them how to use the pegs on the rear site for elevation and explaining windage. Surprisingly both boys were learning fast and becoming excellent marksmen. Even though they were best friends, they were also highly competitive.

Behind the barn one evening, while Laughlin was conducting a practice session, Melissa came down to watch and asked, "How are the boys doing?"

Laughlin grinned and said, "They both can out shoot most of the men I know and they've just turned thirteen."

"When will you teach them about the pistol?" inquired Melissa.

"One thing at a time; when they turn sixteen we'll start working with the pistol," answered Laughlin. Then he added, "both of these boys have a big thing on their side, they're not hot heads. I watched Tony when he saw Three Fingers in that jail cell. He hates him and would like to have shot him, but he stayed calm and under control. I'm sure he'll be calm if he ever has to face a man."

Melissa said, "Don't you think they have another thing in their favor?"

Laughlin looked at her in wonder and asked, "What's that?"

"You," said Melissa, "you're the best. Who could teach them better than you?"

Laughlin grinned and said, "Thanks, but have I ever taught you anything?"

Melissa blushed and said, "Plenty, Ranger McFarland, plenty." Then she hollered, "Mighty fine shooting boys. Now don't lose track of the time; I'm going to the house to cook supper, be there when it gets dark."

Laughlin told the boys they were finished for the day, except for cleaning their rifles. He had told them their rifle was like their horse; it required care, their life might someday depend on it.

Dusty and Tony obligingly sat down on the steps of the bunkhouse porch and were cleaning their rifles when Tony said, "Someday, I'll get these sights on Three Fingers and he'll hit the ground just like that cougar did when you head shot 'im. Yes sir," said Tony, "I'll head shoot 'ole Three Fingers; then I'm gonna scalp him."

Dusty chimed in, "You can bet I'll be with you; we'll get him alright."

They continued cleaning their guns as Dusty added, "Pa' says Three Fingers usually has a brave with him named Running Fox; says he's every bit as mean as Three Fingers."

Tony looked at Dusty and said, "You think we can find his trail; much less follow it.?

Dusty thought for a moment and replied, "Pa' says the best tracker he knows is Fred Ramirez over in Abilene. Says he knows the mountains in Mexico, bet he could help us track him."

"Well I'll tell you this," said Tony, "the day we turn eighteen, let's try and get your Pa' to swear us in as Rangers; then we'll go after him."

Dusty nodded in agreement, then asked, "Do you remember seeing Jerry Jack at church, the Preaching Ranger."

"Yea," said Tony, "why do you ask?"

"Well, his folks were also killed by Indians," Dusty replied, "he shot and scalped the Indian that did it and he wasn't much older than us at the time. Now he's a Ranger; don't ride out on chases much any more. He preaches at the church, kinda Reverend Morgan's assistant."

About that time Tony's stomach growled and he said, "It's starting to get dark and I'm getting hungry."

"Me too," said Dusty, "let's put our rifles up and go see if mama's got supper ready."

Back in Abilene, the sun was trying to break thru a thin layer of clouds on an otherwise humid and overcast summer day. It appeared the weather would be good for tomorrow's 4th of July Jamboree. It promised to be a typical celebration; with horse races, chicken fights, cakewalks, street dancing, lots of drunks, and fistfights. Who knows what else? It would certainly be a busy day for Cletus and the Rangers.

The three lawmen had a sunrise breakfast; then left the restaurant and returned to the jail to await the horse races scheduled to start at noon.

The jail was only a few doors down from the bank but on the opposite side of the street. Ryder stood up from the table where they were drinking coffee, walked to the stove and said, "I'll brew us some fresh coffee, it's gonna be a long day." As he was cleaning the coffee pot he looked out the front window toward the bank. He quickly set the pot down and said, "We've got trouble at the bank."

Eight masked men rode up in front of the bank; six went inside while two remained in the street holding the horses.

Boots went to the window, looked out and said, "Get your rifles; Ryder, you and Cletus take a window, I'll be at the door. We'll cut 'em down as they come out of the bank."

Shortly, the six men that went inside came out carrying bags of money. Boots stepped out onto the porch and hollered, "**Texas Rangers, don't move!**" A shot was fired that buzzed as it went by Boots head and struck the jail.

Then all hell broke loose; rapid gunfire was coming from both sides of the street. Boots dropped one of the men holding the horses and another as he tried to mount up. Lead was flying, some of the hold-up men were trying to mount up; two others ran back inside the bank.

Two men made it to their horses and rode off, one wounded; two more ran inside the bank. There were two dead in the street, two escaped with one of them badly wounded and four were holed up inside the bank.

Boots said, "Hold up, don't shoot, we've got people in the bank." Then he shouted, "Give it up, you're trapped, come on out with your hands above your head."

A voice from inside the bank shouted, "We've got four hostages in here, we'll kill 'em if you don't throw out your guns and let us ride off."

Glen Ray and Fred were in the staging area getting Three Paws ready for the horse race when they heard the shooting. The bank robbers had not seen them as they came down the street on the boardwalk. Glen Ray signaled to Boots they were going behind the bank. Boots knew to keep the attention directed toward him to cover Glen Ray and Fred so he started hollering again, "Give it up, you're trapped."

Glen Ray made it behind the bank with Fred at his side. He looked thru the alley window and saw all four men were at the front wall looking out in the direction of the jail. The customers and bank employees were lying on the floor behind the cashier's window.

Glen Ray whispered to Fred, "I'll kick the door in, everything on the left is mine, the other two on the right belong to you."

Fred nodded his approval as Glen Ray kicked the door opened and both men opened fire. Only Rangers could fire as quick as the shots that were heard.

The front door opened, Glen Ray stepped out onto the porch and holstered his pistol. It was over in less than three seconds. Boots, Ryder and Cletus came from across the street and entered the bank. The smell of gunpowder was over whelming, it was as if an early morning fog was brewing in the bank. Groans of a dying man were heard and the smell of blood was mixed in with the pungent odor of death.

The dying man was Barney Ray, Toby Bryant was dead; lying face down next to two more lifeless bodies. The customers and employees were safe, but scared to death and quickly left the bank.

Cletus looked at Glen Ray and Fred as he said, "Thanks, you boys haven't slowed down a bit. With that rapid gun fire, for a moment I thought Laughlin was inside doing the shooting."

Glen Ray smiled and said, "Remember, he taught me and Fred." Then he slapped Cletus on the back and added, "I reckon y'all can handle it from here. Fred and I have a race to run."

Cletus organized a posse to go after the two that got away, but asked Boots and Ryder to watch over the town until he returned.

From inside their hotel room, Jeanette and Linda had heard the gun shots and ran to the balcony just in time to witness the shoot out. When they returned to their rooms and sat down with a cup of coffee, Jeanette looked at Linda and said, "We're fools if we allow ourselves to fall in love with those two. Boots and Ryder could be dead instead of the holdup men. Linda, I know how I feel about Ryder, but how do you feel about Boots?"

Linda replied, "I'm not ready to fall in love and surely not for marriage." She sipped her coffee, then continued, "Boots is handsome, brave, fun loving and the most exciting man I have ever met and I could easily fall in love with him. As a matter of fact I'm fighting now to keep it from happening. He's the man every woman dreams about and he could have any woman he wants, but I'm not sure he'll ever be a one woman man. Right now I'm just playing the cards as they're dealt. How about you? Exactly how do you feel about Ryder?"

"It's the same as you," she responded, "only one exception. Ryder has already said that he loves me. We've talked, we're not going to crowd each other; we're going to take our time and maintain a long distance relationship. But the truth is, Little sister, I'm scared. When he defended me in the saloon I felt something I have never felt before for any man. Like you, I am fighting to keep from falling head over heels in love. Neither one of us have ever known men like these two Rangers."

With the gunfight over, the Rangers had returned to the sheriffs' office. The door opened and in walked Jane.

When she saw the Rangers, she said, "Thank God y'all are alright."

Boots asked her to sit down at the table and then he poured her a cup of jailhouse coffee.

She took a sip, then in her ever professional manner, said, "I'm here to interview y'all about the shootout."

The Rangers sat around the table answering all of Jane's questions. After she had written down all the details, she said, "Thank y'all, I'll be leaving now."

Boots said, "Jane wait. Ryder, give us some privacy."

Ryder rose from the table and walked outside.

Boots reached across the table and put his hand on Jane's; he could feel it trembling.

He said, "Baby, look at me. I'm all right. No holes in me. I'm alive."

"I know you are Boots," said Jane as tears came to her eyes. Then she looked into Boots eyes as only a woman in love can and said, "Boots, I've tried not to fall in love with you, but, it's not possible. I love you; I worry about you. I'm miserable when you're not with me. I know you care for me, but you don't love me. I will wait for you forever; I'll never love anyone but you."

Boots, still holding Jane's hand softly said, "Jane, there's been other women in my life, but none like you. You're what I want when I take off the star and unsaddle War Paint. As I told my brother, Sterling, in Austin, his job is making laws for Texas; my job is taming Texas and making it a great state."

Knowing if he stopped talking he might not be able to continue, he added in rapid succession, "At one time the Rangers were the only law enforcement in the state. I'm proud to be a Ranger and part of the history kids will study about in the years to come. My first love is being a Ranger and I'm married to the State of Texas. It's not fair for me to marry you then ride off on a three-month chase. I could come home shot up and quite possibly not come home at all. I won't put you in that kind of situation. I can't ask you to wait for me, you must live your own life; mine could end today."

Jane said, "Boots, I'm not asking you to change, just want you to know how I feel about you. Our lives are in Gods hands, if he wants us to be together, eventually it will happen."

Boots got up from the table, pulled Jane into his arms and kissed her passionately.

Two and a half years passed, Dusty and Tony had practically grown into young men. Dusty was the image of Laughlin and had the personality of Boots, carefree, laughing and happy.

Tony was a thinker, very smart, quiet and it could be seen in his eyes he wanted revenge from what Three Fingers had done to his Ma' and Pa'. His eyes reflected a hurt that was still inside of him.

Both boys were good wranglers; they could ride, rope, shoot and care properly for the horses or the cattle.

Dusty was probably the best horseman on the ranch, he loved to ride and ride fast. The boys were large for their age and could take care of themselves when necessary. They would be a true test for any man in a fistfight. They were constant companions and it was evident they loved each other.

Tony had been removed from the bunkhouse after his first six months on the ranch. He and Dusty shared a room with bunk beds in the house. When he spoke to Melissa and Laughlin they were Ma' and Pa'.

Tony's hair was blond; he had green eyes and a strong build. He wasn't sure of his birth date so he took the same date as Dusty; they celebrated their birthdays together. Three days earlier, the boys turned sixteen.

One evening they were riding fence together and talking. Dusty said to Tony, "My Pa' told us when we were sixteen he would teach us to shoot a six-gun, remember that?"

"Yea," said Tony, "but I ain't gonna ask him about it."

"I am," said Dusty. He laughed and said, "We gonna be rootin', tootin' gun toting cowboys. Yea," hollered Dusty, "come on let's race," then he spurred Cyclone as Tony spurred Smokey and away they went with Dusty and Cyclone in the lead.

That evening after supper Melissa and Laughlin went to the porch swing as they often did to watch the sun give way to the moon. Dusty and Tony were in their room when Dusty said, "Come on, lets go talk to Pa'."

Tony swallowed hard and said, "Alright, but you do all the talking."

The boys opened the front screen door, walked out on the porch and sat down on the steps.

After a moment Dusty said, "Nice night, ain't it?"

Melissa answered, "It sure is, but I'm kinda wondering why you two young boys are sitting out here watching the moon come up."

Laughlin winked at Melissa; then in a stern voice barked, "You boys got something on your mind?"

Dusty squirmed, looked at his feet and then looked up at Laughlin the way he had been taught when speaking to a person and said, "Pa', remember you said when me and Tony were sixteen you would teach us how to handle a six shooter."

"Yea, I remember," said Laughlin.

"Well, we're both sixteen," said Dusty.

Laughlin smiled and said, "Get up in the morning, get your chores done by noon and then we'll go out behind the barn and get started."

The next morning the boys were up before sunrise getting their work done. Finally it was noon, dinnertime. Melissa hollered to the boys, "Come join me and your father, you've got to eat before you practice."

"Did you hear what she said?" asked Tony.

"Yea," said Dusty, "it's time to eat."

"That's not what I meant," said Tony, "she said come join me and your father. I wish they were my Ma' and Pa'."

Dusty looked at Tony and, seeing his eyes were wet with tears, thought to himself, 'now I've got something else to talk to Ma' and Pa' about.'

After watching the boys gulp down their meal, Laughlin got up from the table and went to the hall closet.

He came back with two special built leather holsters holding two brand new 45's. "Happy sixteenth birthday," said Laughlin as he handed each boy his gift.

Laughlin could see the excitement in the boys eyes as he instructed, "Hold it, don't strap 'em on. Let's go to the barn, y'all got a lot to learn and it starts by listening."

Behind the barn was the practice area Laughlin used several times a week. He told the boys to sit down, make themselves comfortable and be prepared to listen. Laughlin stood in front of the boys and began, "Most guns are worn for protection. Some guns are worn to perform a job; such as I do as a Ranger. It's for protection, but it also invites trouble and trouble surely will come when you're packin'. Your life depends on how accurate and fast you are. Notice I placed accurate ahead of fast. It makes no difference if you're fast but can't hit a hay bale at thirty feet. By being fast and accurate you stay alive."

He paused to make sure the boys were attentive. Seeing that they were, he continued, "Today we'll start with accuracy which starts with concentration. You must have hand eye coordination and that's possible only with subconscious training. For example, when you walk you don't look at your feet, your brain tells them to move. In the beginning, as a baby, before subconscious training, it may be done that way but, after training, it's done subconsciously. That's the way you must learn to shoot accurately."

Once again he paused; this time it was to allow the boys time to absorb what he had said or to ask any questions they may have so far. When he was sure they understood what had been said, and, since they apparently didn't have any questions, he pressed on, "In front of you there are two hay bales, one for each of you. There's a horse shoe wired to each bale. You will concentrate on the open part of the horseshoe; draw your pistols slowly, while subconsciously aiming and dry firing; do that fifty times while I watch."

Both boys were told to strap on their holstered weapons. Laughlin made some minor adjustments and then told them to proceed.

At first the boys were clumsy being unaccustomed to a pistol. After completing the fifty slow draws and dry fires, they looked much smoother. Laughlin said, "Very good, now place one cartridge in your pistol, make a slow draw and fire."

Both the boys did as instructed and, surprisingly to Laughlin, they did quiet well. They were within eighteen inches of the horseshoe.

Laughlin said, "You will fire fifty live rounds just as you dry fired. This will continue until you hit the center successfully. It may take several sessions before this is possible. Once you hit the center, then we will practice a timed quick draw. Remember, you must think and you must practice."

After the first session Laughlin returned the pistols to the closet. The boys were on the front porch waiting for Laughlin to come out of the house and evaluate them.

Dusty said, "Boy it was fun, but I didn't know it would be this hard, Pa' makes it look so easy."

Laughlin overheard the remark and said with a smile, "It'll come son, be patient."

Tony said, "Sir, you're said to be the fastest gun alive. Is that true?"

Laughlin said, "We don't worry about that, we just keep practicing, someday old age will slow me down, and I'll hang it up. Before we're finished, I'll expect you boys to be faster than me; but it'll take a lot of practice and ammunition. Y'all did good today; we'll try it again in a couple of days."

For the past two and half years Ryder and Boots had been ranging over Texas as always, putting down any trouble that was brewing. Basically, just patrolling Texas. Jeanette and Linda had taken their show back east to the larger population and more money. However, they stayed in touch with the Rangers by sending mail to Uvalde. Ryder was heart broken when they left and wondered if he would ever see Jeanette again.

Jeanette and Linda, unbeknownst to Ryder and Boots had gone back to separate themselves from the Rangers. Each of the girls knew they were in love and found it necessary to get away.

Back at the Big Iron, Dusty and Tony were putting their horses away for the night when Dusty saw Laughlin returning from town in the buckboard and coming thru the front gate.

Dusty turned to Tony and said, "If you'll take care of my horse I'll go help Pa' unload the supplies."

"Fine," said Tony, "I like caring for the horses, you go ahead."

When Dusty finished helping Laughlin, he asked, "Pa', can you and I talk?"

Laughlin answered, "Sure, let's go in the study."

They entered the room and sat down as Laughlin said, "This is unusual son, what's on your mind?"

"It's Tony," said Dusty. "I need to talk about Tony."

Laughlin said, "Go ahead, I hope y'all aren't having problems; you seem to get along better than brothers."

"That's what I want to talk about," said Dusty. "I ain't got no brother and neither does Tony. I've heard you and Ma' could adopt him and he can be my brother."

Laughlin asked, "Who told you that?"

"When we were at church Brother Morgan said we acted like brothers and I said I wished he was my brother. Brother Morgan said you and Ma' could adopt him; then legally, he would be my brother."

"That's right," said Laughlin. "That's something me and your mother have talked about, but we would never mention it. We both agreed that if you ever came to us we would discuss it. There are things I'm sure you're not aware of, that need to be explained to you."

Dusty said, "Like what Pa? He doesn't have a family, we're all he's got."

Laughlin said, "Son, if we adopt Tony, when your Ma' and I die, he would be entitled to half the ranch."

Dusty said, "That's alright with me, there's enough here for both of us."

Laughlin grinned and said, "I'll discuss your request with your Ma'." Then Laughlin said, rather sternly, "In the mean time you don't discuss this with anyone, not even Tony. If it's brought up again it will be by me, end of discussion, understand?"

Dusty got up from his chair and said, "Okay Pa', thanks for listening;" then he left the room.

Laughlin continued to sit in his chair thinking. It was a really unselfish thing Dusty was asking and he agreed Tony was growing into a fine man. Yet, he realized, there were a lot of things to be considered. As promised, he would discuss Dusty's request with Melissa, but he wouldn't act hastily.

Three months passed quickly with the boys practicing three to four times per week on their speed and accuracy. Dusty was talented; maybe he had inherited his gun skills from his father and was noticeably faster than Tony, however, they were both very accurate. After a long practice session, Laughlin told the boys to meet him at the bunkhouse for coffee.

Laughlin went to the house, put the guns in the closet as always and joined the boys in the bunkhouse. He sat down at the table, stirred his coffee, took a sip, then said to the boys, "Y'all have done well. I'm proud of your progress. Now it's time to discuss the mental part of shooting. Y'all are aware of the subconscious training in hand eye coordination. Now let's discuss attitude while carrying a pistol. First thing to remember is the pistol is used only for protection. Use it when your life is in danger and don't draw your weapon unless you are going to use it. When you shoot, shoot to kill, many a lawman has died from a wounded man."

As before, Laughlin paused on occasion for emphasis or understanding, then continued, "You must never be out of control, anger causes your timing to break down. Make your draw relaxed and smooth." Then he smiled and said, "Take your time, but hurry. I will keep your pistols locked up as usual and give 'em to you only when you practice. You have your rifles; continue to practice with them. The Indians fear Rangers with rifles and a rifle is used much more than your pistol. Both of you boys have seen what an accurate rifle shot can do, even with a small caliber. Dusty dropped that cougar with a single shot in the head from a 25-20."

The next day Dusty and Tony were rounding up strays. They were riding slow and talking as they rode. Tony asked, "What do you think will happen when we're eighteen and ask if we can join the Rangers?"

Dusty grinned and said, "Ma' will cry for sure, but Pa', I think, wants us to be Rangers; but, of course, he's afraid of the dangers we'll face."

Tony said, "Dusty, you're really lucky having a Ma' and Pa'. Your Pa is a legend; not only do they say he's the fastest gun alive, I've heard he's the bravest of all Rangers."

"Yea," said Dusty with pride, "I'm proud of my Ma' and Pa'. Hey, look up yonder. Do you see that?"

"Yea," said Tony, "it's a Chaparral and he's jumping up in the air."

"Let's go see what he's doing," said Dusty.

The boys rode up to within thirty feet and stopped. There was a five-foot long rattlesnake coiled up and rattling in front of the Chaparral. When the snake struck, the Chaparral would jump straight up and peck the rattlesnake on top of its head. This continued for about ten minutes; then the snake stopped moving, he was dead. The Chaparral had pecked a hole in the top of the snakes' head and into its brain. Dusty and Tony were amazed; they had heard wranglers in the bunkhouse talking about it. Now they knew it was a fact, they had just witnessed it.

They dismounted, cut the snakes' head off and carried it back to the ranch where it would be skinned and dried like jerky. They decided to make hatbands out of the skin. When they returned to the ranch Laughlin rode by them going toward town at full gallop.

Melissa was standing on the porch as they arrived; she was crying. Dusty asked. "What's wrong? Where's Pa going in such a hurry?"

Melissa said, "It's Oral. Nathan sent a rider to tell Laughlin to come fast."

When Laughlin arrived and entered the sheriff's office he saw Oral laying on a bunk bed on his back. Nathan, Doc Mills and Brother Morgan were tending to him. Laughlin walked to the bed, saw Oral's forehead, it was purple; a sure sign of a heart attack.

Nathan turned to Laughlin with tears running down his cheeks and said, "He's gone, Laughlin, he's gone," and then he burst out crying.

Laughlin helped Nathan to the domino table and sat him down. He said, "Take it easy, calm down. What happened?"

Nathan said, "We were playing dominoes and ran out of coffee. I said 'shuffle the dominoes and I'll make a fresh pot.' When I sat back down at the table he looked at me, grabbed my hand and said 'thanks for being my friend, my time has come. I hear the angels singing.' He was clutching the bible that was always on the table in his other hand. I jumped up and grabbed him, keeping him from falling forward. Laughlin, he took his last breath while I was holding him."

Mr. Presswood, at the funeral home, took care of the body; telegraphs were sent notifying friends and relatives. The funeral was delayed due to Herman Fox, Oral's brother, having to travel from San Antonio. The funeral was held in the church and his body was buried in the town cemetery. Laughlin had a marker made with a special inscription.

It read:

Here lies part of Texas history

He gave it his best

Now he's gone to rest

Nathan was visibly shaken by the loss of his friend; he and Oral had been constant companions for several years. They shared the jail and made their rounds together. There would be an election for a new sheriff, but Nathan, even though he was a Ranger, would continue to work out of the sheriffs' office.

Boots and Ryder weren't able to attend Oral's funeral; they had spent several days in Eagle Pass and were patrolling the border on their way to Laredo. Riding with them were two rookie Rangers: Red Simpson and Buster Adams. There had been some cattle-rustling going on and it appeared the cattle were being taken to Mexico.

Red was a tall lanky red-headed, freckled face man and wore his gun on the left side. He had a nervous disposition and talked all the time, some of the tales he told were suspect.

Buster was just the opposite, less than six fee tall, broad, big boned and strong. He had a dark complexion, bushy eyebrows, dark brown hair and brown eyes. Buster was rarely seen without a big chaw of tobacco in his jaw. Before answering any questions or starting a conversation he had to spit tobacco in order to be understood. He was said to be fast with his pistol and wasn't afraid to fight any man; gun or fists.

Just before reaching Laredo they looked across the river and spotted a camp. There were eight standing horses, a campfire and four men mingling about. Ryder stopped his horse, stood up in his stirrups, shaded his eyes with his hat and looked hard across the river; then he relaxed, sat back down in his saddle and said, "That's Rene and his Banditos, I recognize the dapple grey he rides."

"Bet on it," said Boots, "he may be in that camp, but he's got rifle sights on us right now. Ryder, identify your self and see if he responds; lets keep it friendly."

Ryder nodded, rode up about twenty yards and yelled, "Hey Amigo, it's me, Ryder!"

In a barely audible voice, Rene responded, "Amigo, I see eet eez you, bring your horses across and join our fogotta."

Ryder turned towards the Rangers and said, "It's okay, he wants us to come to his campfire."

Boots remained suspicious as they cautiously crossed the river. Once across, four men with rifles appeared from the scrub brush and escorted them into camp.

Rene greeted them with, "Hola, Senor Ryder, eet eez good to see you. Get down, have some caw-fay."

After the Rangers dismounted and seated themselves by the fire, Rene poured the coffee, looked up at Ryder and said, "Senor Ryder, why eez eet you and zee Rangers ride zee reever. You know eet eez my reever and I take care of any problems."

Ryder said, "Rene, someone's running cattle across the river and into Mexico. I hope it ain't you and your vaqueros."

"No, eet eez not I," said Rene.

"Good," said Ryder, "the Rangers do not want to fight you. In Mexico, you are like the Rangers in Texas. We need to remain friends."

"Si," said Rene, "me and my vaqueros we no steal herd; maybe some time we keel one for camp but, we no steal big herd. Mucho work herding cattle; right vaqueros? Then he laughed heartily and added, "Senor Ryder, you and zee Rangers you my friend. Rene know who geets zee cattle. I make sure he no get no more, but you no can have cattle back; comprende?"

Ryder rose to his feet along with the other Rangers and said, "Gracias Rene, we comprende, you've got a deal."

After hand shakes all around, the Rangers mounted up as Ryder said, "Adios Amigo."

"Vaya con Dios hombres," replied Rene.

After they rode off a short distance Boots said, "Ryder, you think they'll ride ahead and ambush us?"

Ryder said, "Nope."

"Why are you so sure," wondered Boots?

"Because," offered Ryder, "we have sort of an unofficial truce; besides, they respect the strength of the Rangers. Hell, if they didn't, by now they'd be riding our horses and carrying our guns."

That seemed to satisfy Boots so they rode on in to Laredo. Immediately upon their arrival, they got a room, took a bath and met Sheriff Starrett for supper. It was a fun supper; Luke was an old seasoned sheriff and when he asked Red about his background, it got very entertaining.

According to Red, he had fought and scalped Indians, knew Wild Bill Hickock, drove cattle to Montana and had been married four times; five actually, but one was to a squaw and, according to Red, that didn't count.

Finally, Boots said, "Gentlemen, it's time to say goodnight. I just hope Red doesn't talk in his sleep." They all laughed and went to their rooms.

Late in the evening of their second day out of Laredo, the four of them were following the stage trail north to San Antonio when they passed thru a tiny town called Fowlerton. Red started talking about the stage road and how it followed the paths of old Indian trails.

Red, forever talking, said, "This creek we're crossing runs into the Frio River and its called Dead Men Walking Creek."

Buster laughed, shook his head and asked, "Red, why is it called Dead Men Walking Creek?"

CHAPTER 23

"Well, let me tell you," said Red. "It musta been purt near 50 years ago when the stage to Beeville was held up by four men. They took the strong box, shot the lock off of it and got all the money. Then they killed the stage driver and guard. Now it seems a young man and his purty young bride, newlyweds they were, had been on their way to Beeville to start a new business. Hold up men killed the husband, raped the girl and then killed her."

"How do know all this?" asked Ryder, while grinning at Boots.

"'Cause my grandpa told me about it and he don't lie. Now, story goes, after the hold up men left; the team, pulling the stage, wandered off down the trail. Somers 'tween here and Beeville a wrangler saw the stage and drove it to Beeville. The sheriff, an old fella named Otto Kruger, sent the bodies to Beeville, formed a posse and rode out to the holdup site".

Red paused for the first time to take a breath when Buster said, "Go on Red, Go on." Then he chuckled a little to cover up his apparent interest in Red's story.

"Okay, Okay," said Red as he continued, "By the time the posse got there and began tracking, they were plenty mad and had been drinking lots of whiskey. Grandpa said it was late in the evening when they saw a campfire and rode in to find four men sitting around the fire. The men in the posse, angry and drunk, tied their hands behind their backs and took 'em down the creek until they found a hanging tree. The four men all said they were innocent, that they had left a cattle-drive and were

332

going to their home over in Sabinal. Otto and the drunken posse didn't listen; they hung all four of 'em on one tree; then they rode off and left 'em hanging for the buzzards to feast on."

By now Buster, who was just a bit superstitious, was beginning to buy into Red's tale. He urged Red to continue then laughed; but it was obvious he was a bit nervous.

Red, who would have gone on with or without Buster's urging, continued, "When they got back to Beeville there was a telegraph at the Sheriffs office for Otto. It was from the sheriff up in Pleasanton, they had captured the outlaws and had a written confession. Well, the posse hadn't told anyone in town that they hung four men; so, when Otto got the telegram, they decided to ride back out the next day, cut 'em down, bury 'em an take an oath never to tell anyone what happened."

At this point, Red reached in his pocket, pulled out a plug of tobacco and took himself a big chaw.

By now Buster was a nervous wreck. He didn't try to hide his excitement any longer as he practically shouted, "For Pete's sake man, what happened then."

Red put the plug back in his pocket and said, "The next day, the same men in the posse and Sheriff Otto, all sober now, rode back to the hanging tree. When they found the tree, the ropes were there, still hanging, but the bodies were gone. Now the story goes that in the years to come, on separate occasions, Sheriff Otto and several of the men in the posse, were found hanged. It's also well known that wranglers and drovers, coming thru this area in the past, and to this day, swear they have been sitting around the campfire when suddenly a cold breeze will blow.....even in the heat of summer; then four ghostly images of men will walk thru the camp, looking at each face around the campfire to see if any of them were in the hanging party."

Ryder looked at Red, laughed and said, "I don't believe nothing you said. You made all that up."

Buster, riding beside Boots, softly asked; "You don't believe any of that; do you Boots?"

Boots grinned and said, "I don't know, but one thing's for sure, we ain't camping here tonight."

When they arrived in San Antonio it was late, the ride had been long and hot. Boots and Ryder said they were going to get a room, take a bath and come out later for supper. Red and Buster decided to go to the saloon for drinks and talk to the ladies. Buster needed the drinks after listening to Red's story.

Boots and Ryder had been to their rooms, had their baths, put on clean clothes and were walking to the restaurant; anxious to enjoy a good meal. When they entered, Buster was sitting at a table enjoying his T-Bone, mashed potatoes, gravy and cornbread. As they joined him, Boots asked, "Where's Red?"

Buster grinned and said, "Y'all ain't gonna believe this. We were in the saloon having a drink and one of the working girls came down from upstairs, Beatrice was her name. She had reddish brown hair; must have weighed two hundred and fifty pounds and she was missing a lower front tooth. Hell, the arms on her were bigger than mine; oh she was a sight to see."

Then he paused and, with some of the tension gone from the "Creek" story, chuckled and said, "Anyway, she saw ole Red, ran over to him, bear hugged him and drug him upstairs; they're still up there. Oh yea, before she got him by the arm and drug him off, he told me she was his third ex-wife."

They all had a good laugh over Beatrice and Red; then they had a few more drinks, engaged in small talk and went to their respective hotel rooms. They figured Red was tied up for the night.

The next morning Boots, Ryder and Buster met at the restaurant. Red was a no show. After finishing breakfast, they left the restaurant, went outside and mounted up. Boots and Ryder were going to Uvalde, while Buster and Red would be heading for Ft Worth.

Once in the saddle, Boots said, "Me and Ryder are leaving for Uvalde, you can wait on Red or ride on alone; I'm not very impressed with him as a Ranger."

Buster readily responded, "Same here. I'm riding on without him."

As they passed the saloon, the upstairs window was raised as Red stuck his head out and shouted, "Hey, you boys go on, I'm giving up the Rangers and going back to Beatrice, my true love."

He paused for a moment, started to go back in, then yelled, "You boys be careful, been nice riding with you." He turned his head back over his shoulder and said, "I'm coming sweet cheeks, old Red's coming back to bed."

Boots shook his head, looked at Ryder and said, "I can't wait to tell Laughlin about Ranger Red and his lady."

Ryder said, "Yea, the Rangers are sure gonna miss ole Red."

They had a big laugh and headed toward Uvalde, as Buster turned his mount towards Ft. Worth.

When Boots and Ryder reached Uvalde it was Saturday. They went out to the ranch and gave their report to Laughlin, including Red's reconciliation with Beatrice. They all had another big laugh at those two as Laughlin remarked, "They sound like a matched set to me."

Since this was the down season on the ranch, most of Laughlin's ranch hands had taken a few days off and headed for the nearest saloon or brothel.

Things were also quiet in the area and, without any pending assignment from Laughlin, Boots and Ryder accepted his invitation to stay in the bunkhouse until his wranglers returned.

The boys, Dusty and Tony, were in need of ammunition, so they rode into town and purchased some from Uncle Bester.

After leaving the gun shop, they rode over to the sheriff's office to play dominoes with Nathan. During the game they were talking about various things when Nathan told Tony that Three Fingers had been raiding and stealing horses west of Eagle Pass.

Nathan said, "The troopers from Ft Clark at Brackettville, are down there looking for him now. Sure hope they catch him."

When Tony heard this he froze for a moment and thought to himself, 'Please God, don't let them catch him. Save 'em for me. I promised Ma' and Pa' that I'd be the one to kill him.'

As they rode back to the ranch, Dusty asked Tony, "Are you alright?"

"Yea," said Tony. Then he looked at Dusty and, in a somewhat indignant manner growled, "Why?"

"Oh, you just look concerned," answered Dusty, "can I help?"

"No, no I'm fine," said Tony. Then, realizing he had been a bit harsh, said, "Sorry I was a little rough a minute ago; but just the mention of Three Fingers, sets me off."

Dusty nodded his head and waved Tony off with an understanding gesture.

When they arrived at the ranch Laughlin helped them practice with their pistols. Once again he said, "You boys are doing really good. You're fast and you're accurate. That's what we've been looking for."

The next day, Sunday, was church day. Dusty went into Tony's room to wake him, but he was gone. His bed had not been slept in.

Dusty told Laughlin; then ran to the barn to see if Smokey was there. When he discovered Tony's horse was gone, he ran back to the ranch house, head down, and said to Laughlin, "Pa', Smokey's gone too, but I know where they went."

Without waiting for any response from Laughlin, Dusty continued, "When we were in town, Nathan told us the troopers were chasing Three Fingers west of Eagle Pass. When Tony heard that, it upset him something terrible. I'm sure he's gone after 'em; he don't want no one getting Three Fingers but him."

Laughlin, without any hesitation, ordered, "Son, go down to the bunkhouse, pick six men and tell 'em to be armed and mounted in ten minutes."

Melissa came in the room all dressed for church and asked, "Laughlin, what's wrong?"

"Tony's missing," he said as he walked toward the hall closet. He opened it, looked at Melissa and said, "His pistols gone, Dusty was right, he's gone after Three Fingers."

"Oh my God," said Melissa, "you've got to go bring him back."

"I am, we're leaving now," replied Laughlin, "Dusty you stay here, take care of your momma."

"No sir," said Dusty, "I can outride and outshoot any man on this ranch. I'm going with you."

Laughlin looked at Dusty, slightly angered at his backtalk, but proud he was quickly becoming a man, and said, "All right young man, let's get mounted."

While Laughlin, Dusty and some ranch hands were starting their pursuit, Tony was going cross-country straight toward the Rio Grande. His plan was to stop at any ranches or cabins and ask about Three Fingers. Even though he knew that, since the troopers were searching for him, that renegade Indian was probably already on the Mexican side of the river.

When Tony reached the Rio Grande, the provisions he had taken, prior to leaving the ranch, were gone. Game was plentiful along the river so he knew food would be no problem. He also figured that Three Fingers was most likely somewhere between Acuna and Juarez; riding the river just like he was.

His meals would be rabbit or venison; he didn't have money to buy any of the makings, but the protein would be enough. It was late in the evening so he set up camp next to the river. The day had been hot and he was exhausted. There was no time to set out a rabbit snare and he wasn't about to chance a gunshot until he knew the whereabouts of Three Fingers. He was hungry but his desire to find Three Fingers overpowered his growling stomach.

During the night he was awakened by what sounded like distant thunder; but the skies were clear. He listened for awhile but heard nothing else. Oddly enough, he rested well for the remainder of the night.

The next morning Tony saddled up, rode to a vantage point and scanned the area. In the far distance he saw a dust cloud and several riders going north. He assumed it was the troopers, heading back to Brackettville after giving up the chase. Evidently they had been camped within five miles of him and were now headed home.

Realizing, with the Troopers headed back to Brackettville, he would now be alone, Tony began to remember; before his pa' died, he had heard him talking with other farmers and town folk about the Indians. It seemed the Dead Horse Mountains had been a hiding place for years. Old timers said the Indians would camp in the basin of the mountains, ride out on raids and return to the basin. Story was no white man ever returned from the basin.

Tony was certain now that the soldiers had chased Three Fingers, and his raiding party, across the river. With this "fact" in mind, he headed down the Mesa in the direction the troopers were coming from. His intentions were to find where the Indians had crossed the river. It would be where the troopers turned back. It should be easy enough to find since there would be the hoof prints of a large number of horses.

After being in the saddle for about four hours he spotted buzzards circling in the sky. He rode ahead carefully until he saw dead horses and bodies lying on the ground.

It was the scene of a bloody battle. It appeared the Indians had been camped when, during the night, the soldiers attacked and killed the entire raiding party. The heavy gunfire was probably what Tony had dismissed as distant thunder the night before.

With pistol in one hand and knife in the other, Tony went from Indian to Indian, scalping and checking their hands. Three Fingers evidently had escaped or this was a different raiding party.

Confused and not having a clue which way to go, Tony rode down stream for about a mile and then set up camp. He knew he couldn't go into the mountains; that would be like committing suicide; so he decided to find a rabbit for supper, bed down, get up early and follow the river to Del Rio.

After setting up camp, Tony decided to stake out Smokey next to the campfire. That would put the horse just a few feet from where he was sleeping. He always thought Smokey could smell an Indian; probably wasn't true, but it wouldn't hurt to believe it anyway.

All the time Tony was preparing camp, he was uneasy; felt like he was being watched. He removed his rifle from the scabbard, laid down and placed it next to his body; in his right hand he was clutching his forty-five revolver. Around midnight, Smokey nickered, raised his ears and started pulling against the stake rope. It was a dark night, no moon; beyond the camp light it was dark, totally dark. The campfire was flickering, creating dancing shadows on the brush.

Suddenly a man's body, with knife in hand, flew thru the air landing on top of Tony. Tony raised his pistol, stuck it in the man's stomach and fired six times. The body went limp and Tony could feel warm blood on his own body. He rolled the man off him; it was an Indian. In his right hand was a knife being held by Three Fingers. Tony removed the knife from the Indian's hand, grabbed his hair, lifted up the head and scalped him with his own knife.

Tony held the scalp up towards the heavens; the blood was dripping down on his face as he looked at it and let out a victorious yell saying, "It's done, Ma', Pa', it's done."

Back in Uvalde, Laughlin had wired the Army at Brackettville before leaving to find Tony. He was told to look south of Eagle Pass; the troopers were searching west of there and, so far, hadn't found anything. Apparently, they hadn't received word regarding the troopers encounter with Three Fingers' raiding party.

After searching south and north of Eagle Pass and finding nothing, Laughlin called off the search and headed back to the Ranch in Uvalde..

Dusty had begged him to keep looking but Laughlin said, "No, he'll show up somewhere and then we'll move again."

Dusty pleaded, "Pa, we've got to keep looking for Tony."

Laughlin said, "Dusty, Tony's almost grown; he can take care of himself. Besides, he knows the way home if he wants to come back."

When the sun rose, Tony drug Three Fingers' body up on a knoll, found a large flat rock and placed the body on it for the buzzards. As he rode away, the scalp of Three Fingers was tied to his belt.

While riding, Tony was reliving the last two days over and over in his head. What he figured was: when the troopers attacked during the night, they killed everyone but Three Fingers who probably fled to the river and hid. Having no horse, he attacked Tony; he was after Smokey.

Tony headed his horse north toward Uvalde, as he rode he wondered how he would be received at the ranch after leaving the way he did. The sun was bearing down so he rode slow. As he rode on, he began to feel like a new person; finally the load on his shoulders had been lifted; he had avenged his Ma' and Pa's death.

About an hour before sunset he saw an unbranded calf, a maverick. For two weeks he had survived on rabbit; tonight he would have beef. Wild burros and mavericks had provided food for the Indians and settlers for years. He smiled and said, "Thank you God for the beef." With one shot from his 44-40, he dropped the calf. He built a fire, cut out the back straps and started cooking the meat over coals from the campfire.

As Tony sat by the fire cooking his meal, three riders came out of the dark and into his camp. The campfire provided light enough for him to see the three wranglers.

One of them asked, in a demanding voice, "Where did you get that steer you're cooking?"

Tony, feeling very uneasy said, "This is no steer, it's an unbranded maverick, and I shot it for food."

The same man spoke again and said, "I'm Leroy Kitchens, me and my two buddies are wranglers on the Kingfisher ranch. You're on his ranch and we say that's his steer you're eating. Been lots of rustling going on, you're probably one of 'em that's stealing cattle and taking 'em to Mexico."

Tony said, "I'm traveling back to Uvalde and needed food. I ain't no rustler."

Leroy said to the other two men, "Boys, get his gun and tie his hands behind his back. We're gonna hang us a rustler, Mr. Kingfisher will pay us a nice reward."

Leroy untied his rope from his saddle and started forming a loop. The two wranglers dismounted and started toward Tony.

Tony said, "Hold it right there, don't come any closer. I'm warning you."

The two men looked at each other, laughed and one of 'em said, "The kids warning us, don't that scare you." With that said, they reached for their guns

Tony was faster and a slug from his forty-five buried deep in the chest of one of them. The other man got off a shot that went by Tony's head and a second shot from Tony's forty-five ended his trail riding days.

Leroy's horse spooked from the gunfire; but once in control, Leroy rode out of camp quickly. Tony checked both men; they were dead. Tony's legs were weak and shaking; he had just had his first gunfight and had killed two men.

The moment of the gunfight had been quick; after regaining his composure he started thinking about what to do. Leroy would surely ride to the Kingfisher ranch and tell Mr. Kingfisher a rustler had killed two of his wranglers. Soon thereafter, riders would be coming after him.

He rounded up the dead men's horses, tied each man over his saddle and ran them out of camp. Tony knew, like all ranch ponies, they would head back to their corral. He removed the meat from the fire, put it in his saddlebags and mounted up. He knew they would never take him in for a trial; the riders would lynch him on site; so, he patted Smokey on his neck and said, "Let's go to Mexico."

As he rode toward the river he thought how his life had changed. A short time ago he was on the ranch with Dusty and waiting to be old enough to join the Rangers. Now, he was running for his life.

He thought about returning to the ranch, telling his story to Laughlin and going to trial; but, he decided not. Leroy would testify that he was a rustler and killed two of his men when they tried to bring him in. Tony felt like he had no chance, even with Laughlin's help.

Laughlin had taught him and taught him well, he knew he was fast. He hadn't drawn his pistol until his life was threatened and then, when he fired, he shot to kill.

As he rode towards the river he said a prayer; asking God to forgive him for taking two lives and then, he asked for guidance. Tony made it into Mexico without detection.

A year passed by quickly; Tony had managed to eek out a meager living as a ranch hand or store clerk whenever and wherever he could find work. He moved a lot to avoid detection; always watching over his shoulder for the law or hands from the Kingfisher Ranch. Somehow, he had managed to avoid discovery by changing his name and keeping on the move.

There was a reward poster for Tony and from time to time it was said he was seen along the border and around Del Rio. Since there wasn't a picture of him on the poster, just a really bad drawing, he managed to escape the law and any would be bounty hunters.

Dusty and Laughlin were back on the Big Iron tending to the ranch and directing Ranger activities while Boots and Ryder were in Uvalde.

One day, when the stage came through, Bill Sims, the postmaster, sent word over to the Sheriff's office; he had mail for Ryder. So Ryder went to the post office, thanked Bill for the letter, stepped outside onto the porch and opened it. The letter was from Jeanette; it read:

Hi Ryder,
I hope you're doing well. I've tried to write this letter several times and couldn't make myself do it. As you know we are now

living in Chicago and entertaining locally. Linda met a wealthy man who owns a foundry and manufacturing shop. He builds track for the railroad and coal cars for the trains. They are engaged and will soon be married. Our relationship is unfair to both of us, it's long range and our lifestyles will never mix. You will always be the daring, handsome Ranger that you are, and I will always be a showgirl. It's become time to end our relationship and move on. It's best that I just remain a memory.

Love, Jeanette

Ryder folded the letter, took a deep breath, put the letter in his wallet and thought how fortunate Boots was to have Jane still waiting on him.

At the Big Iron ranch, it was mid-afternoon; Laughlin was out overseeing new fencing when he looked out across the pasture and saw Dusty riding hard. Dusty reigned up and said, "Pa', Sam's down, you'd better come quick."

Laughlin rode up to the corral and saw Sam, lying on his side. Sam heard Laughlin, tried to raise his head and get up; but, he couldn't.

Dusty, almost screaming, asked, "Pa', what's wrong with him?"

Laughlin, with sadness and love in his eyes said, "It's his kidneys son, they've been failing for a while now." Laughlin walked over to Sam, leaned forward, both knees on the ground. Then he picked up Sam's head and held it to him. He looked down in Sam's eyes and said, "I remember the day Herman Fox gave you to me and how strong and smart you were. Remember that old rattler you saved me from? We had lots of chases together; you never tired and were always sure footed." By now tears were running down Laughlin's face as he continued, "No one has ever ridden you but me. Father time is the biggest outlaw of all, steals the years away from us and we can't stop him. Your time has come and I won't be far behind you."

Laughlin lowered Sam's head to the ground, stood up, pulled his pistol from the holster and said as he wept openly, "You were the best, enjoy the sweet grass on Heaven's ranges. Thanks for all the memories. good bye old pal." Laughlin, with tears streaming down his cheeks, aimed the pistol at Sam's head, said "I can't bear to see you suffer," and pulled the trigger; Sam was gone.

Behind the barn a special corral was built to be used as a cemetery. Sam was buried there with a head stone that read:

Here lies Sam
His memory will
Live forever
Till once again in Heaven
We will
Ride the Ranger Winds

Two weeks went by; then, one night after supper, Laughlin went to the front porch and sat down on the steps. Dusty came out later, sat down beside him and asked, "You alright pa'?"

Laughlin nodded yes and answered, "Thanks for asking son."

Dusty hesitated for a moment or two and then said, "Pa', I'll be eighteen tomorrow. Can we talk about me becoming a Ranger?"

Laughlin turned slowly, looked Dusty in the eyes and said, "Son, we have a lot to talk about. Let's turn in, tomorrow's another day,"

The two men got up and Laughlin put his arm around Dusty; they entered the house just as the sun began to set on the Big Iron.

Somewhere in the vast reaches of the Texas west, Tony was bedding down alone. He too would be eighteen tomorrow and longed to be united with Dusty, Laughlin and Melissa. Sometime during the night, he dreamed of him and Dusty wearing the Texas Star and riding the Ranger Winds. Would his dream ever become a reality?

THE END